For David

Let me not to the marriage of true minds
Admit impediments. Love is not love
Which alters when it alteration finds;
Or bends with the remover to remove:
O, no! it is an ever-fixed mark,
That looks on tempests, and is never shaken...

— FROM SONNET 116, WILLIAM SHAKESPEARE

FIRST DATES

1

By the time Esther reached the turn at the railway bridge into her road, she was quite alone. One of the fast trains shot past, a bomb-burst in the silence, and she jumped like a ninny. The road was narrow and long, hugging the curve of the railway line. Her rented little terraced house was a still a good walk away, down at the far end, part of a run-down row made affordable both by its distance from the convenience of the high street and by its proximity to the concrete flat-blocks, where washing fluttered like bunting in the boxy balconies and neon graffiti lit up the walls.

Esther walked quickly, looking straight ahead, clasping her handbag tightly under her arm, fighting sinking spirits both at how insecure a forty-eight-year-old woman could still feel mid-evening on a city street, and how desperately far she remained from the newly single future she had dared to envisage for herself, leaving Lucas and moving – via a miserable couple of months with her parents – to London two years before. The July night air was muggy. Her feet felt spongy in her high heels, and her mane of hair, long since collapsed out of the shape she had painstakingly created with her tongs, was gluey on the back of her neck. She wanted to take her jacket off, but feared the kerfuffle of stopping in the lamplit dark, looking like the middle-aged woman on her own she was, vulnerable and faffing, easy prey for anyone seeking a target for their own disappointments.

The jacket had been wrong anyway, tight like most of her wardrobe these days, as well as overly formal and trying too hard for a first date in what turned out to be a riotously crowded, riverside, East Sheen pub. She had identified Chris Mews at once, reassuringly similar to his profile credentials, tall and shaven-headed, and looking the opposite way as he waited on the fringe of the mêlée of smokers and drinkers gathered round the pub entrance. Noting his smart-casual style of dress and relaxed demeanour, Esther had felt her jitters ease slightly; crisp, dark-blue jeans, loafers, and a tan T-shirt, loose enough to curtain the gentle swell of stomach underneath, he looked like one of those men appealingly and enviably easy in their own skin. His height meant he carried his extra weight well, Esther had decided, double-checking her jacket was buttoned up across her own tummy bulges, before bracing herself for the camera-click of first impressions as his head turned.

'Hello, Esther. Nice to meet you.' His northern vowels sounded stronger than they had during their two phone conversations, which had covered all sorts of promising ground from parenting challenging teenagers to a mutual enjoyment of crime thrillers. Spotting her, he had stepped forward at once, his right hand outstretched, the piercing dark-brown eyes, which had dominated the online picture, half disappearing among the crinkles of his smile.

'You too.' His grip was warm and firm. Esther smiled back without having to try, glad of her mother's good teeth and Nordic blonde hair that hid the greys so well, and getting a flashback to the contrastingly awful limp, clammy handshake of Jim, the widowed violinist, two weeks before.

'A widower! A musician! Ideal!' Viv had cooed in the half-serious, half-joking way designed to boost the spirits of her oldest friend, while also reinforcing her frequently voiced, professional opinion that no woman – least of all Esther – needed a partner to 'complete' herself. This still-new venture into online dating should just be about enjoying herself, she had counselled, slipping into full psychologist mode – about making the most of this period of freedom while Dylan was on the post-A level visit to his father. Esther had dutifully agreed, managing not to say how easy that was for Viv to say, surrounded by steadfast Brian and their four vibrant, grounded children. She hadn't mentioned either just how hollow her rented little home always felt without her rangy, maddening eighteen-year-old bounding round it; nor how visceral were the stabs of envy at the thought of Dylan loafing with Lucas in Cambridge instead, and having the luxury of Lily, his brainbox elder sister, just down the road, already throwing herself with typical Lily-like energy into life as a postgraduate.

'It's only a few weeks,' Viv had added gently, detecting Esther's misgivings in her uncannily brilliant way. 'See it as a chance to really let your hair down, sweetheart; to start being all the things that husband of yours put a stopper on for twenty years.'

What things? Esther had wanted to ask, in danger these days of forgetting what it was she had lost touch with, what the hell she had been trying to get back to when Lucas's behaviour finally tipped her into throwing in the towel after two decades.

Appearances so *did* matter, Esther had decided, admiring the smooth globe of Chris's head as she followed him across the sticky floor of the pub to the cluster of dining tables at the far end of the bar; as did the basic, oh-so-telling courtesy of being truthful in dating profiles. The violinist, Jim, swung back to mind, along with the mesmerizingly botched and fragile comb-over that had momentarily stopped her in her tracks when he waved hello. In the profile photo there had been a rather cherubic head of light, gingery curls. Widower, she had reminded herself, her heart readying to soften nonetheless at the memory of the wife's lost battle with cancer, referenced in his biog. But Jim's preferred subject had turned out to be himself: his musical credentials, all the famous concert venues he had graced with his presence, in the second line of a row of violins. When Esther had ventured an allusion to her own modest musical abilities, he had told her how much harder the violin was to master than the piano. The mention of her teaching beginners had prompted a look of haughty pity. And yet, out in the street after an interminable hour, he had appeared distraught and astonished when she'd diplomatically rejected the notion of a second meeting.

'But why?' he had asked, flinging out his thin arms. 'You don't know me.'

Esther had shaken her head, gormless and guilty. Not to want to know a person. It felt like a crime. As she had watched him trudge away, the slender frame hunched in defeat, the comb-over raised like a flimsy sail, relief had been accompanied by the unsettling after-taste of her own cruelty. *Life has hurt me too*, she had wanted to call after him, *just in different ways. I am not really strong, only trying to be.*

Chris Mews, with his easy manner and big smile, was immediately so much more promising. By the time they were wedged into their little corner table and had placed their orders, he had teased all sorts of information out of her, including the fact of her imminent late-July birthday the following Saturday.

'Maybe I could take you out to celebrate?' He raised his pint of beer to chink against her wine glass. 'If things go well, of course, and you don't have other plans.' He shot her a mischievous grin. 'I'm not till January, so we'll leave that one on the table.'

'Maybe,' Esther murmured, her hopes bouncing even though she knew it was too soon. 'I mean, that would be nice. If things go well. As you say. No jumping the gun.'

'No gun-jumping allowed.' He grinned, directing a finger-pistol at his temple.

Esther's stomach performed another lurch of anticipation. She had no birthday plans and was starting to dread the fact. Dylan would still be in Cambridge, and Lily was about to head off backpacking with Matteo, her boyfriend since their days of hand-holding in a school lunch queue. It wasn't fair to expect Viv and Brian to fill the blanks in her diary, just because Richmond was a stone's throw from Kingston – nor her parents, for that matter, who lived in Amersham, an hour down the motorway. Proximity to both had been a key factor in Esther's decision to settle in West London, but such dependence, almost two years on, was starting to feel like failure. In desperation, she had that morning emailed Shona, a long-silent friend from uni days, suggesting they fix something up, not just with her birthday in mind, but in the hope of rekindling the friendship generally.

'Sorry,' Chris announced suddenly, 'I need the little boys' room. Would you excuse me?'

'Of course.' *Little boys' room*. You couldn't judge someone on one piece of terminology, Esther scolded herself, seizing the chance to sneak a check on her face in her handbag mirror. No specks between her teeth yet. No smudges on her nose. Hair good. The lack of a social life was why she was here, she reminded herself firmly, scrolling her phone but finding nothing new except a couple of work emails.

Esther steepled her fingers, trying to look composed, instead of like a woman wondering when her blind date would emerge from the toilets. As more minutes passed, she fiddled again with her phone and then pretended to read a junk mail envelope in the bottom of her bag, while continuing to brood on the embarrassing narrowness of her social circle. The falling away of Cambridge friendships had been something she was prepared for – that it had always been so much more Lucas's world than hers had been a consistent thread in their tapestry of difficulties – but the continuing challenge to fill the void remained an unwelcome surprise. It was because she worked mostly from her laptop, Esther brooded, and because Dylan's vast, impersonal, West London sixth-form college meant barely encountering a teacher, let alone other parents. Her five little piano students were dropped off and scooped up like parcels; while her neighbours were exactly what she remembered from her early post-uni days in London, exchanging nods and names, but bent mostly on keeping to themselves. The pair on her left, Dimitri and Sue, both worked nights, he as a taxi driver and she in a care home, and Carmela, the old lady on the other side, emerged only to issue squeaky summonses for the large tabby that used Esther's overgrown back garden as its toilet and hunting ground.

'Sorry, got caught on a call,' Chris explained, looking a little flustered, and arriving back at the table at the same time as their food. 'Hey, I'm going to need your help with these,' he joked, indicating the mountain of chips smothering the rib-eye and a few squirls of salad.

'No, I'm fine...'

'Go on, you know you want to.' He laughed, turning the plate round so the fries were within easier reach.

'Thanks.' Esther took two, dipping them into the dressing that had come with her chicken salad, but which she had asked to have on the side because everyone knew that was where the calories lurked.

He watched the dunking in amusement. 'We could ask for ketchup. Or here... have some of my French mustard.'

'No, this is fine. Fabulous.' The chips were very good and Esther began to relax. She took two more, and then another, relishing suddenly the simple almost forgotten pleasure of being out in the company of a warm, presentable man. Yes, she told Viv inside her head, she was an independent woman who knew her own mind blah blah, but there was being single and being lonely and, boy, had she learnt the difference. Especially when Dylan wasn't around. An exception that would soon be the norm. Esther felt the usual flutter of selfish panic. A level results were almost a month away. Then it would be university. Then he'd be half lost to her, like Lily.

'All right?'

She blinked Chris's crinkly smiling features back into focus. 'Very all right, thanks, Chris.'

'I'm going to get another one of these – the first slipped down so well.' He tapped his glass, waving at a waiter. 'Are you okay with your wine? Would you like another? Or maybe a cocktail?'

'Oh no, I am fine for now, thanks. This is delicious.' Esther sipped her Sauvignon Blanc to prove the point. Aware of her cheeks starting to do the pulsing thing that meant she was too hot, she peeled off her jacket, draping it over her chair, and shuffled closer into the table so as to be sure of keeping her stomach out of sight. Having settled herself, she sensed Chris had been watching her intently.

'I am seriously tempted to jump that bloody gun, Esther,' he murmured, 'just so you know.'

'Are you? Well... that's... nice.' To be so rusty at flirting, it was pitiful – and also weird, like feeling seventeen and seventy simultaneously.

'Leos and Capricorns are a match made in heaven, by the way – it's common knowledge. July and January. They go hand in glove. A perfect fit.'

Esther couldn't help laughing. 'Well, that sounds fortunate, though I'm afraid I'm not exactly an expert on astrology...'

'Nor me.' He let out a roar of a laugh, tipping his head back and displaying flashes of old-fashioned fillings, reassuringly like hers.

He was fifty-two, she remembered, like Lucas. But so not like Lucas. Another species.

'It's all nonsense,' he went on, 'but that's what it's feeling like, right? Between us? Now? You and me, Esther? The stars aligned?'

'It's certainly feeling...'

'Blimey, you must get tired of hearing it, but you are bloody gorgeous. Your hair. Those blue eyes. Seriously, Esther. *Seriously*.' He reached for his pint, keeping his eyes fixed on her over the rim as he swigged.

'Oh... thanks... I... my mother is half Swedish...' Esther faltered, both because compliments were impossible to respond to without sounding like an idiot, and because she was starting to get the unsettling sensation of having boarded a runaway train.

'I'm not mad about wine, to be honest. I much prefer this stuff they make from hops.' He tapped his glass. 'Are you okay with that? You won't tell me off?'

'Tell you off? For liking beer? Why would I ever do that? In fact...' Esther was going to mention some of the wine-snobs she had met round Cambridge dining tables, but Chris appeared to have hit a groove.

'Because being told off... Jesus, have I had enough of that, I can tell you.' The gleam of charm in his eyes darkened for a moment. 'But what I want to hear,' he urged, making a visible effort to compose himself, 'is more about *you*. The stuff you write that you mentioned on the phone, for those business magazines, for instance; how you keep the wolf from the door. Tell me more. I want to know *everything* about you.' He grinned mischievously.

He proceeded to listen, with a touching show of intense interest, while Esther tried to inject as much sparkle as she could into the music degree that had somehow led, via menial editorial jobs, to a patchy career as a writer of business copy and provider of private piano lessons.

'Lucky students, having such a hot teacher, is all I can say.'

Esther laughed uncertainly. 'Thanks... but to be honest, Chris, which I think is important...'

He glanced up quickly, a forkful of food poised in front of his mouth. 'Oh, blimey, yes. Bang on, Esther. Honesty. Every time. In everything.'

'Good, because...' Esther paused, shooing Lucas from her mind '... because actually, my students are far too young to think along such lines. Only two of them are boys anyway, Billy and Craig, nine and thirteen respectively...'

'Hah, well, Billy and Craig will have you in their fantasies, that's for sure.' He took a hearty swig of beer that left two dots of froth at the corners of his mouth. 'Boys start very young. Trust me, Esther. I speak from experience.' He swiped the froth away, his eyes holding hers again in their intense way. 'Mind you, with that teenage son of yours, you presumably know a bit about—'

'Oh yes, I know a bit about boys,' Esther cut in quickly, not wanting the conversation to go anywhere near the ups and downs of Dylan's teenage years, and feeling a surge of protection for dear Billy too, with his pink translucent jug ears and tumbling, stubby, hopeless piano fingers. Chris was just trying to inject some sparkle into her own life for her, she told herself, wishing it were down an avenue she could more readily enjoy. 'So, tell me a little more about your work,' she countered, proceeding to return the compliment of looking riveted while he described falling into IT via a failed start-up, and now being within reach of a top management post.

'Strategic thinking rather than *doing* – that's the dream in my book, Esther. Actually, I love my job,' he blurted with sudden bitterness, starting an assault on the remains of his steak as if it were an animal still requiring slaughter. 'It's having to give away most of my earnings to a heartless bitch that I'm not so keen on. That was her on the phone. Before. Why I took so long.'

'Sylvie?' Esther prompted feebly, recalling the name from the brief sharing of relationship histories during the phone call that had preceded the agreement to meet. 'Oh, splitting up is awful, isn't it?' she ventured, truly wanting to offer comfort, but wishing the dreadful sawing of the ragged slab of meat on his plate would stop. 'However it gets dressed up...' She faltered, Lucas's fury at having to sell their end-of-terrace Cambridge house coming back to her: the rants about stepping off the property ladder, the loss of *guaranteed* future *worth*. He had spat the words, more distressed, it had seemed to Esther, at the loss of this financial potential than at the decimation of their love and their marriage. 'At least you have your lovely daughter... Kelly, wasn't it? Fifteen, going on thirty-five, I think you said.'

Chris dropped his steak knife with a clatter that made her jump. 'I don't *have* Kelly,' he growled. 'In fact, I have no access.' He swigged angrily from his beer glass, slamming it down on the table. 'I was with lawyers today. That bitch of a mother has poisoned her against me.' Esther flinched as a catalogue of grievances began to spew out. Sylvie had fleeced him and frittered away what she took. She had slagged him off, not just to their daughter, but to every friend and member of their respective families. One unscheduled ring of the doorbell now of what had once been *his* home, and it was calls to the police and having the locks changed.

Esther, chewing her bits of chicken and rocket leaves far more than they required, was aware of shrinking into herself. Here was a different, more extreme sort of emotional calamity than hers and she wanted no part of it, not because she was mean-spirited, but because it demanded an energy of which she simply did not feel capable. First world problems maybe, but it was all she could do to carry her own current load.

People, no matter what they looked like, weren't what you wanted them to be, that was the lesson. Behind the scenes, everyone – including her – was messed up, damaged, and full of potholes. It was all a complete minefield, and she just wanted to go home.

'I've been going on. Forgive me, Esther,' he groaned suddenly, parking his elbows on either side of his plate and dropping his head into his hands.

'It's okay, but actually...' Something inside her had quietly snapped. The hubbub around them was deafening, the air so hot and thick it was hard to breathe. 'I have to be getting back.'

'Now? But you haven't finished. What about another drink?' He gestured helplessly at the salad remnants on her plate and the half-full wine glass.

'I have to get back because... my son...'

'Dylan, you mean?'

Esther found suddenly that she did not like hearing Dylan's name fall from this stranger's lips. Chris didn't know Dylan. Or her. Or anything about her misfiring life. And she didn't want him to. In fact, in that instant, she would have taken back every single sorry personal detail she had divulged if she could – from the little potted history in their first phone conversation about her and Lucas, falling in love and out again, to the existence of little Billy and Craig. 'Yes. I... Dylan and I... we have an early start tomorrow...'

'But I thought you said he was in Cambridge? With his dad?'

'Yes, I did say that... because he is.' Esther folded her napkin into a messy square and straightened her cutlery over her uneaten food. 'But tomorrow we are heading off to check out one of the universities he has applied to. The University of the West of England – the one that's Bristol but not Bristol,' she blagged, deciding untruthfulness with strangers maybe didn't matter quite so much after all, especially when it was only a half-lie anyway, since they *had* visited UWE, and the nice people there had offered Dylan some very reasonable grades. 'I should have mentioned that I can't be late,' she added lamely, forcing her hot arms back into the jacket and placing two precious twenty-pound notes on the table, 'but please do stay and finish your drink.' She stood up so abruptly she barged the person behind with her chair and had to apologise.

'No, no, no, no...' Chris was on his feet, plucking notes out of a wad with a silver clip that he had pulled from his back pocket. 'I'm coming too.' He paused to drain his glass, firing a what-are-you-looking-at glare at one of their many close neighbours ogling the scene. 'I shall see you safely back to Kingston,' he declared grandly, partly for their audience, it seemed to Esther.

'There really is no need, thanks,' she murmured, setting off back through the bustle round the bar, regretting even that he knew the area in which she lived.

'Come on, it's the least I can do,' he called, loping after her.

Outside, Esther kept up her stride in the direction of the station, cursing the state of penury that meant there was no question of escaping into a cab. Not that there were any in sight. Chris jogged until he was parallel. 'Please, Esther, this is no way to end the evening. I talked too much about myself. I know. Surely that—'

'Sorry, Chris, but I'm just going to head home and would prefer to walk alone. If you don't mind. Thank you.' Esther's voice sounded firm and icy, even to her.

'Let me call you an Uber, then.'

'No. Thanks. I'll take the train.'

'Okay,' he said, wan all of a sudden and letting her walk on. 'Goodbye, then.'

'Bye,' she fired back, not looking round as she went even faster, nose in the air and fighting the now familiar sensation of behaving like a total cow. The hopeless mishmash of humans trying to find soulmates struck her with sudden, depressing force – it was always the wrong people wanting the wrong people, looking for a magic she herself had once believed in, but now knew didn't exist.

On the train she had composed a text, pressing send the moment she got a signal.

Chris, thank you for the evening. Sorry to have ended it so abruptly. I have realised I am just not in the right mind-set for dating at the moment. I wish you all the best. Esther

The street lamp nearest her house was doing its usual on-off flicker, creating an air of menace rather than security. Esther glanced furtively around as she crossed the road. Her throat was swollen with the dumb urge to cry. She had lied to Chris. She didn't prefer to walk alone. She *preferred* to walk *with* someone. For one, unguarded moment, Lucas shimmered as something to miss rather than resent. They had begun so well – thanks to chance rather than dating algorithms.

At her front door, Esther swayed. Her fingers were numb round her keys because of gripping them so hard, supposedly in readiness to ward off an assailant. A good stab at the eyeballs was the advice. Yeah, right, like she would ever manage that. She'd go quiet with terror, more like, become one of those victims who had juries shaking their heads. The key was gritty in the lock and hard to turn, one of the trillion things in the house that didn't work smoothly: annoying, but too trivial to make a fuss about.

The lock turned at last and the door gave way. In the same instant, a muffled thud from the street made Esther swing round, her heart pounding. But it was only Chico, her neighbour's tank of a tabby, jumping onto the bonnet of a car, from where it crouched, watching her, its yellow eyes lasers in the dark.

2

Esther leant up against one of the book stacks at the rear of the shop for a breather, keeping an eye on the proceedings through a gap in the shelf. Her heels were high and her lower back stiff from charging around in them all day. Professor Tobin, whose catchily titled tome, *Philosophy Maketh Man*, was the reason for the event, was still in full flow to the fifty or so attendees. In his late sixties, with a long, straggly beard that Esther wondered his wife didn't chop off with some garden shears, the professor was attired in a mustard-coloured, corduroy suit and a gold bow tie, which, like his half-moon spectacles, glinted under the ceiling lights of the bookshop. He twirled the stem of his wine glass as he talked – one of the batch Esther had been mandated to collect, along with drinks and snacks, from a nearby off-licence that afternoon.

Just behind his left shoulder, leading the audience with head-nods of appreciation and glass-raising, was Stephen Goddard, Esther's lover as well as her boss, and senior editor in the academic wing of the small London publishing house that had employed her for over a year as its Girl Friday. Charismatic and flatteringly besotted, Stephen also happened to be married; but only until the right moment to extricate himself arrived, as he had spent the last nine months earnestly and repeatedly reassuring her. A literary event out of London would provide a rare and perfect pretext for them to be together properly for an entire night, he had pointed out excitedly, when appointing her to help with the organising; a real treat after all the sporadic, snatched hours at her place, grabbed at if her flatmates were out and his wife was working late. Stephen had booked a hotel in celebration and had been making excited eyes at her through the glass walls of his office all week.

'A spy in the camp?' came a whisper from the end of the book stack.

'Oh... no...' Esther jerked round. 'I just...'

The tall, lithe young man who had issued the challenge, and whom Esther had seen hanging around earlier on, pressed a finger to his grinning mouth by way of a reminder that it wouldn't do to divert attention from the proceedings beyond their hidden corner. 'Have no fear. Your secret is safe with me.' He spoke under his breath, mouthing the words with comedic exaggeration. 'Is it a good view?'

Stepping closer, he peered over the top of Esther's head, allowing her to note the faint stain on the green jumper underneath his shapeless suit jacket. She noticed, too, the density of his dark unruly hair, and how the jumper accentuated the extraordinary flecks of luminous green in his eyes. The eyes had escaped her notice before. She had been too busy rushing around helping arrange books and drinks, and finding a pen for Stephen, who had wanted to lend one to the professor and had forgotten his. All she had observed of this particular guest was that he didn't obviously fit the same mould as the others, being scruffier and younger, and appearing always to hover on the edge of each little conversational group, almost as if he shared her own sense of uncertainty and social unease for not being at the heart of things.

'Me Lucas,' he whispered, mock-punching his chest. 'You?'

'Esther,' she mouthed.

'Star.'

'What?' She bent her head nearer, thinking she had misheard.

'Your name. It means star. Nice dress, by the way.' He stuck both thumbs in the air and Esther found herself giggling.

'Are you an editor?' he mouthed next, miming opening a book and a scowling appraisal of its contents.

Esther shook her head, putting her hand over her mouth to stifle more laughter. She performed a return charade of shrugging her shoulders – as in, who knew what the hell she was? – and then an add-on demonstration of singing and playing the piano.

'A musician?' He feigned clapping, while Esther wagged her finger to indicate that this was a gross exaggeration of her status.

Stephen's appearance round the end of the shelving unit – proof that in the absence of their attention the speeches had ended – caught them both by surprise. 'Esther. There you are.' He glanced between their faces, his smile taut. 'You are needed.'

'I'm coming. Sorry, I was just...'

'Looking after me,' her new acquaintance interjected easily, reaching to shake Stephen's hand. 'Dr Lucas Shaw. New in town – part-time lecturer in medieval English – very much *not* a philosopher – but hoovering up everything I can. Brilliant talk. Brilliant event. I do apologise for keeping Esther from her duties.' He threw them a quick smile and strolled off.

'Do you know him?' Stephen asked with studied casualness as they headed back into the fray.

'No. He just introduced himself.' Esther tweaked the creases in her dress, which was sky blue and close-fitting and had left an indefensible hole in her meagre finances. She was the thinnest she had ever been, from the conflicting excitement and stress of loving Stephen, and rather hoping that the extravagance of the dress purchase might bolster her resolve to stay that way, as well as giving pleasure to the man who she believed would one day be her husband.

'It will soon be just you and me,' Stephen murmured, the back of his hand brushing hers as they made their way across the shop, giving Esther one of the electric shivers that reminded her why they were where they were: love. It took sacrifice and pain. Patience. It certainly bore no resemblance to the two six-month relationships that had featured and fizzled out during her time at Exeter. Kevin and Ian, bass guitarist and football nut respectively; they seemed inept, unsophisticated toddlers in comparison with Stephen. This was the real thing. 'I've rung the hotel and asked for champagne,' Stephen whispered, 'to be ready for when we arrive. And one day, it will always be that way, Esther. Okay?' For one long, heart-tugging instant, his deep-set, blue eyes, handsomely offset by his wavy, fair hair, found and held hers, before he asked if she could top up glasses and dived back into the throng.

It was three days later that a postcard, sealed in an envelope, arrived in the communal post box of the dingy Shepherds Bush basement flat Esther shared with Shona and two girls who had advertised in *The Lady* about having a couple of spare rooms. Snatching the envelope out of the pile of bills and junk mail, Esther had somehow known at once to whom the exuberant handwriting belonged.

Dear Esther,

I have taken liberties and elicited your address from your employers through underhand means. This is because I would like the opportunity to take you out to dinner. Cambridge is not so far from London and the train service (I have checked) is good. Name your day (except Thursdays when I have to deliver a late-ish lecture) and preferred time, and I shall be there. Or phone, if you want to say no and need persuading. I have put my college number and extension at the top of this note.

Until soon, I sincerely hope.

Lucas

The image on the other side of the postcard was of a knight on bended knee before an imperious-looking princess, the tresses of her golden hair and long blue gown flowing. The knight's head was raised, his eyes fixed on the princess's face as he pressed her small white hand to his lips. It took Esther a few moments to notice the tiny speech bubble, etched on the dark background in biro beside the knight's mouth, and containing a single word: *Spellbound.*

She had put the card into her bedside table drawer, and then taken it out again to use as a bookmark later that night for the thriller she was reading, a twisting tale of revenge and murder set on a trawler in the Norwegian fjords. A global bestseller featuring a yearning relationship between the married captain and his secret lover, the book had been a gift from Stephen that Esther had been consuming avidly, thrills of recognition flaring at every mention of the captain's forbidden passion. That night, however, her thoughts kept drifting to her new bookmark, to the sort of man who would choose to devote his life to the study of things like knights and damsels and courtly love; and to the word spellbound.

'I am with someone,' she blurted out to Lucas three weeks later, persuaded to meet in a small Italian place near her flat, after two more postcards and a phone call to the Cambridge number originally undertaken with the intention of achieving the opposite outcome. The new cards had been themed similarly to the first, both arriving in envelopes, on consecutive Fridays, one depicting a knight trying to pull an arrow from his heart, with a speech bubble saying, *Aaagh,* the other emblazoned with the words, 'Nothing is sweeter than love', apparently said by some medieval cleric called Thomas à Kempis.

'We have been together almost a year now, and it really is serious,' she went on solemnly, having seen no option but to explain the Stephen situation fully. 'I'm sorry, but just meeting you tonight feels a bit... wrong... which I hope you can understand because...' Esther dried up, in a fresh confusion about having agreed to the date instead of sticking to her guns on the phone, and because ever since picking her up from her doorstep, Lucas, for all the implications in his correspondence, had been notably amiable rather than ardent. It had even occurred to her that this second encounter – with the reality of her, as opposed to some overblown memory of a brief conversation behind some bookshelves – had caused his feelings to retreat.

'Friendship with another person can't be wrong, surely?' he replied coolly, twirling spaghetti round his fork before raising it to his mouth. 'Or does Stephen not allow that?' The fork disappeared cleanly between his even teeth and he chewed slowly, watching her with fixed, inscrutable eyes.

'No... of course not... I mean, Stephen and I both have lots of friends,' Esther floundered, thinking of Shona, and Viv, her best friend since kindergarten, whom she saw rarely now because of her still being at a Scottish university studying to be a psychologist. She and Stephen would make their own friends – their own life together – just as soon as they could; it was something they talked about often. Trying to imagine her companion as part of that mix was hard, even if he was clearly regretting the grand gesture of catching a train to London to take her out for dinner. The spellbinding thing had definitely worn off. Which was good, Esther told herself, aware even so of a small, absurd – utterly unjustifiable – flutter of disappointment. Despite that, she started to feel somewhat off the hook and, when Lucas started asking questions about her life, began to talk more freely: about the blow while studying at Exeter of facing up to not being good *enough* to pursue a career in music – as a pianist or anything else; about her hopes that the mundane role at the publishers might prove a stepping stone to better things; about longing for Stephen to get a move on with the ordeal of speaking to his wife.

'It seems to me that being in our twenties is all about seeking that elusive balance between ambition and happiness,' Lucas offered, kindly, when she had finished. 'And to my mind, in the end, what one *is* should always matter far more than what one *does*, or who one is *with*, for that matter.'

'Oh yes, that's so true...' They were interrupted by the arrival of the bowl of mango and chocolate ice cream they had elected to share for dessert. The waiter set it down with a flourish between them, together with two long spoons. Esther picked hers up and then hesitated, not wanting to be the first to start.

'I felt totally lost for most of my first three years at Manchester,' Lucas confessed cheerfully, plunging his own spoon into the dessert with no sign of the same compunction. 'Between lectures I spent a lot of time hanging out and drinking myself stupid with people I didn't like much.'

'No girlfriend?' Esther asked breezily, keeping her own focus now on tackling the mounds of ice cream, which was delicious, and melting fast.

'Not really. Recently there was someone called Caroline, but she didn't think much of me heading south.' He pulled a face. 'All I'm attached to these days is my passion for early English texts.' He laughed easily, sitting back. 'A passion that began when I bumped into Sir Gawain and his green knight, a good while ago now. But one thing led to another. As things do.'

It was an observation that was to echo at the back of Esther's mind several hours later, as they lay, still fully clothed, but breathing hard, side by side on her bed, their mouths raw from kissing and her head spinning with a combination of remorse and arousal.

She had dropped her guard, that was the trouble, feeling sufficiently chatty and well disposed after the meal to invite him back to hers for a quick coffee before his train. That she had made her position clear had been her logic, and – as Lucas himself had so deftly pointed out – there was no crime whatsoever in making a new friend. When they were tucked into opposite ends of the flat's big sagging sofa a little later, blowing the steam off their respective mugs of coffee, Esther had found herself sufficiently at ease to volunteer several personal details, including the annoying nature of Rick, her younger, sporty charmer of a brother, and their parents' – at least their mother's – most favoured child, and the mind-numbingly blinkered, middle-class existence of her parents, fussing between bridge evenings and rounds at the local golf club.

'The stultifying suburban dullness of my upbringing is actually the biggest embarrassment of my life,' she announced gleefully, expecting him to laugh.

But Lucas's eyes dropped to his coffee. 'I would trade my childhood for dullness any day, suburban or otherwise.'

'Really? Oh, I see... I mean, I'm sorry...' Esther held her breath, feeling glib and inadequate; torn between wanting him to go on and knowing she had no right to want any such thing.

'No siblings.' He set the mug down on the little table by the sofa and leant back, folding his arms across his slim chest, to belt himself in, it looked like. 'A father who prefers whisky to milk on his cornflakes. Despite the fact that the preference cost him his career.' He stared straight ahead, puffing his cheeks and blowing air out of his mouth, as if continuing to speak required physical effort. 'A mother who looks the other way. The three of us tucked into a cottage in the wilds of Shropshire. It wasn't what you would call a recipe for fun.'

'No, it doesn't sound it. I am so sorry.'

'No need to be. It is done with. I left and never look – or go – back. At least, only very occasionally. Because of my mother. She could leave. She *could*... but she never will,' he said bitterly, unlacing his arms and giving them a shake.

'Your father...' Esther ventured. 'So what did he do, if you don't mind my asking?'

Lucas snorted. 'Good question. No, I don't mind, but only because it is you doing the asking and *I* brought the subject up – rare for me, I can assure you. The reason I did so was because I wanted...' He scowled. 'I wanted it known. By you.' He blinked as he looked at her, his expression for a moment so guarded, so boyish, that Esther had a sudden vivid glimpse of the timid, bright-eyed child he must once have been. 'My dear father is – was – a doctor. A GP. Trusted by the local community.' His voice was sharp with scorn. 'That thing about not being able to choose your families, it's so true. But it doesn't mean you have to hang out with them, right?' He swivelled so that he was facing her properly, a sheepish grin suffusing his face like light. 'Sob-story done with. Okay?'

'Okay,' Esther murmured, still embarrassed at the pettiness of her own complaints, but touched at having been confided in. She found herself marvelling, too, that, for all the obviousness of the good looks of the man sitting beside her, she had been dead right about the underlying uncertainty in his demeanour. A smart talker, for sure, but with a kernel of shyness inside. It was endearing. It also made it tricky to know how to *be*, how to react...

'I really like you,' he blurted, plucking suddenly – with badly chewed nails she hadn't noticed before – at a thread in the upholstery along the back of the sofa. He crossed one long leg over the other and then swung it awkwardly back to the ground. The thread grew and he snapped it off. 'In fact, it is probably only fair to tell you, *Esther*...' he seemed to hover on her name, rolling the word softly round his mouth '...that I have found it hard to stop thinking about you for... let me see now...' He made a big show of tugging up the sleeve of the starchy, new-looking, dark-blue shirt – worn, possibly even purchased, in her honour, Esther realised – to consult the cheap, clunky, chain-linked watch on his wrist. 'Four weeks, one day, three hours and twenty-one minutes. Hence the postcards.'

'Hence the postcards,' she echoed stupidly, adding, before she could stop herself, 'though I have been wondering if you had changed your mind.'

'Really? What a reckless and erroneous thing to wonder.' A lilt had crept into his voice, a merriment. He had got his legs sorted and was edging closer.

'I am *with* someone, remember?' Esther groaned. 'And *not* wanting to betray them... I am not like that, you see, Lucas. I am loyal. I am...'

He had stopped his edging and was staring at her, frowning in puzzlement. 'Loyalty? To this Stephen Goddard? But surely you can see that the man betrays you. Every day. With his wife.'

The clang of the gate at the top of the wrought iron stairs outside made them both start. Loud footsteps followed – Shona's, Esther guessed, from the familiar clack of heavy heels on metal. 'Quick,' she whispered, leaping to her feet and beckoning Lucas to come with her, an impulse based purely on the impossible notion of having to switch to awkward introductions and small talk.

By the time the front door thudded shut, Esther and Lucas had parked themselves on Esther's narrow bed – there being nowhere else to sit – and were propped side by side against the pillows and head-

board like an old married couple. Along the passageway came the
sound of the toilet flush, running taps, a loud thump, and voluble cursing, before the slam of another door.

'Now, where were we?' Lucas picked up Esther's hand and turned it
over, examining the palm.

'Nowhere,' Esther said faintly.

Lucas traced the tip of his index finger along all the fortune-teller
lines, so lightly that it tickled. 'The map of you,' he said softly. 'And I
think it shows many things, including a great capacity for love.'

Esther had been half holding her breath, when he used the hand to
pull her nearer, closing his eyes in preparation to kiss. She saw his
eyelids flutter, the intensity of the intent, before she closed her own.

'Ditch him,' Lucas said later, when the kissing was done with and
they were saying goodbye on the pavement, Esther having led the
tiptoeing navigation through the flat and up the stairwell. 'Not neces-
sarily to be with me.' He spoke gravely, keeping his distance now,
standing so far away that Esther found it almost upsetting. Their
clothes had remained in place, but just five minutes before they had
been entwined, tasting each other, holding each other, Lucas
displaying a tenderness that had felt at once tentative and alluringly
assured.

'But because, in my twenty-seven years of experience,' he went on
grimly, 'learnt in part, I am sorry to say, at my dear father's knee –
married men are often happy to take lovers. It is the enthusiasm for
owning up to the deceit which they are less good at, not to mention
keeping promises to leave their wives. Walk away from Stephen,
Esther.' There was pleading in his tone now. 'Not for anyone else, but
for *you*. We each have a duty to guard our own backs in this world.
Trust me, no one else can do it so well; not even a smitten mug who
would like the chance to make you fall for him instead.'

MANY HAPPY RETURNS

3

'Just checking whether Dylan crashed at yours last night?'

'Why would he do that when he's with you, Lucas? In *Cambridge*.' Esther had sat up so quickly the room was spinning. The clumsy lunge for her mobile had knocked over her bedside glass of water and for a moment she was too sleep-befuddled to think what to do about it. That it was her birthday, that the caller might be Lily, or Viv, had been the only half-lucid thoughts to enter her head, even as she registered that it was in fact her ex-husband's face on the screen. 'Why would he be with me?' she repeated stupidly, already swinging her legs out of bed, tugging her nightshirt down, rubbing the sleep from the corners of her eyes and righting the glass. The water was pooling round Viv's birthday gift, a leather-bound journal emblazoned with the unnerving command, 'Write Your Life!', which had arrived the day before in an Amazon box Esther had opened without thinking. Inside, there had been a card, containing apologies for not being able to drop by, because of the kerfuffle of cramming in consultations and trying to get the family off on holiday to France that weekend.

'Because there was a party,' Lucas said levelly. 'In London. An eighteenth. He's got keys. It's obvious he'll have decided to stay at yours. You know what he's like. Last-minute merchant.'

'Yes, thank you, Lucas, I do know what my own son is like. And no, it is not remotely obvious Dylan is upstairs.' Esther was trying to be cool, but could hear the catch of panic in her voice. Anger, too, was stirring. The arrogance of Lucas, the insult of always being told things rather than listened to – two years apart and a decree absolute had changed nothing. 'I would have heard him.' She snatched the journal from the flood as she talked, throwing it onto the bed, aware of a fleeting, guilty certainty that she would never meet the book's challenge anyway. Viv always meant well and was big on the therapeutic importance of writing things down. In the early days after the split, when Esther had been stuck in the miserable, unnerving time-warp of camping with Dylan at her parents', her old friend had got her scrawling her darkest invectives on pieces of paper, stamping them underfoot and then ripping the whole lot to shreds. 'How could it help?' Esther had wailed, only to find a surprising release in the sheer expenditure of energy, not to mention the faint notion of stamping on Lucas himself, and his catalogue of marital crimes.

'Whose party anyway? Do you even know?' It was satisfying to see him flinch. He never owned up to his feelings. He never owned up to anything. Esther yanked open her bedroom door as she talked, straining her ears for sounds upstairs. Motherly anxiety was jetting through her bloodstream now and she wanted Lucas to share it, to *admit* to it. 'But hey, let's look on the bright side and hope it doesn't involve ambulances this time, shall we?'

'Don't be dramatic, Esther, that was years ago.'

'Three years, Lucas. Three measly years.' Esther strode out onto the landing as she talked, managing in the process to catch her little toe on the door frame, which caused a stab of pain so blinding that she half collapsed onto the floor, clasping her foot and dropping the phone.

'What on earth are you doing?'

'I am going up to Dylan's room, Lucas,' she hissed, picking up the mobile, teeth clenched against the after-waves of pain. 'What else would I be doing?' She gave the screen a glare as she hobbled on towards the steep little staircase leading up to her tiny top floor. Behind

Lucas's head she could see the geometrically neat bookshelves of his treasured medieval texts, bright in the shafts of light falling through the tall windows of his Cambridge rooms. He looked spruce from his shower and morning stroll to college. Before that, Esther had no doubt, he would have done his usual dawn jog along the Cam, as yet oblivious to the emptiness of the smaller of his airy flat's two spare bedrooms, the larger allocated for Lily who, living now with Matteo, barely used it. Lucas liked to lay it on thick about having their twenty-two-year old daughter, still studying at a college across town, under his care, just as Dylan for two years now had been primarily under Esther's; but as they both knew, Lily was a breeze compared to her younger brother, always more independent, and so brimming with drive and self-sufficiency that it could hurt.

'Panic over,' Esther gasped, as much from relief as from the discomfort of managing the stairs with her injury. 'Look.' She held the phone up so Lucas could share her view of the roughly torn piece of paper fixed to Dylan's bedroom door with a blob of chewed gum.

HEY MUM, SURPRISE!
PHONE DEAD, DIDNT WANT TO WAKE YA
HAPPY BIRTHDAY !!!!!
D XX

'I knew it...' Lucas crowed.

Esther was too thankful to mind his smugness. She raised a finger to command silence instead and gently opened the door a crack, needing badly to see Dylan with her own eyes. Her heart settled still further at the sight of a foot poking out from under the mountain of the duvet, so Neanderthal in shape and hairiness that for a moment a wave of incredulity overtook her at the memory of the white-ringleted, blue-eyed tot who, not so many years before, had regularly caused strangers to coo over the buggy in parks and supermarkets. Both children had her Scandi colouring – Lily with the extra blessing of the fine-boned petiteness of Esther's mother, Astrid – but Dylan as a baby had definitely been the cutest. He had also been the more difficult, agonisingly reluctant to be born, taking twenty-three hours compared to Lily's two and a half – 'a child on a mission,' the midwife had joked of her daughter. A similar resistance to the business of finding content-ment had dominated Dylan's babyhood. Sleeping, feeding, being held, not being held – all the things a swaddled Lily had taken to with ease, her son had fought from the get-go like a raging mini sumo wrestler. The only thing guaranteed to make him chortle were the antics of his toddler sibling. Lily predictably had caught on to this power quickly, so often using the trick of springing out of hiding places shouting 'boo' that it was the first word ever to blow from Dylan's lips, as well as the name he still used for her sometimes, when they were horsing around.

Esther had been engrossed by the sibling closeness that unfolded, the secret sign language, the sheer self-containment, the private hilari-ties. Only Lucas's insistence that Lily's atomic brain-power warranted moving her to a different school had seen its easing. Left behind, Dylan's softer, more drifty nature had begun to emerge in earnest, manifesting itself in markedly poorer grades than his sister's and in dreamy insouciance. He was more like her, Esther would jokily and protectively point out – knowing what Lucas was thinking and not saying – with a good heart but tendencies towards chaos and great intentions that didn't always come off.

Esther softly closed Dylan's door, experiencing a faint shudder of a memory of the ambulance incident with which she had taunted Lucas. An accident and a one-off, Dylan had promised breezily, sitting up in the A & E cubicle bed afterwards, as if losing consciousness forty-five minutes after swallowing a small white tablet 'gifted' by a stranger at a party could happen to any fifteen-year-old. Luckily, the doctor on duty, a square-set rugby-playing sort and straight talker, had stepped in with a chilling catalogue of the range of potentially fatal reactions to MDMA: hypertension, hyperthermia, overheating, overhydration. 'Basically, you could die, mate, and that's the bottom line.'

Parked beside the bed, gripping one of Dylan's arms just to be holding onto a piece of him, Esther had gratefully noted her son's eyeblinks of shock, his thin, pallid face growing pastier as the list went on. She had glanced across at Lucas – standing a little apart, back against the white plastic curtain – in the hope of sharing the moment. But he had remained aloof in his anger, his eyes fixed only on their idiot son. Esther had experienced a rush of despair. That there could be no pulling together in such a crisis had felt intolerable. How could she still be with a man who remained so closed against her when he chose? It was the opposite of what she had imagined. It could not go on. But even as the thought had formed, Lucas's eyes had travelled to hers, ablaze with all that she'd needed to see: relief, affection, fatherly forgiveness, hope. There were reasons Lucas was as he was, Esther had reminded herself, as she always did; reasons no one understood like her. The fight to love and be loved, that was every marriage; it just took different forms.

'How was Lily?' Esther ventured now, gripping the flimsy banister pole as she went back down. It wobbled under her grasp, and for a moment the steps below her heaved. One slip and she would go head-long. An image flashed across her brain, of her crumpled body on the landing, neck and limbs splayed awkwardly. Dylan having the grisly job of finding her. *And on her birthday too, of all days...*

'Lily is in Rome.'

'I know Lily is in Rome, Lucas. But you were seeing her before she went, weren't you?'

'Oh yes, she dropped by with Matteo. They both seemed fine.'

The usual somersault of envy flipped in her gut. It had made perfect sense for Lily to stay in Cambridge, because of her studies, not to mention the blessing that was Matteo; but it also meant that Esther's hunger to see her daughter was never quite appeased. Lucas sensed that hunger, Esther was certain. Lily was like his trump card, and he played it ruthlessly.

'Many happy returns, by the way.'

'Yeah, right.'

'I hope you have something nice planned.'

'Yup. Lots, thanks.' Esther spoke tartly, silently thanking Shona for having come through with an offer of dinner, even though it turned out that tricksy Carole, fellow barrister and life-partner for the last ten years, wanted to come too. Apart from that, the highlight of her day was to be the usual lesson with Billy. Though at least there would be a smidge of Dylan now too, she reminded herself, thinking about silver linings.

Arriving safely on the landing, she raised the phone to study her erstwhile husband properly. Lately, Lucas was big on *being friends*. The reason, as Esther well knew, was because someone called Heidi had been brought out of the shadows, a thirty-three-year-old postdoc from Heidelberg University – an acquaintance of some six months, Lucas maintained, though Esther had her doubts. This intellectual and physical bombshell of a woman (googled by Esther many times) had met both children now. 'Oh yeah, Heidi's nice,' they had both insisted, facial expressions snapping shut like clams.

Heidi from Heidelberg! When Esther had told Viv they had laughed hysterically, and kept laughing, while inwardly Esther waged war with the illogical push-pull of not wanting something, but minding that someone else did.

Lucas's luminous green eyes met hers steadily from the phone screen. They were intimidatingly alert, the skin around them still remarkably unlined for a fifty-two-year-old. Esther searched for some glint of all the early, lovable self-doubt, despite knowing it was long gone. Lucas was an eminent professor now. His books of literary criticism were on university reading lists across the country. He was a frequent speaker at international academic conferences. Milan. Prague. Frankfurt. He was quite the jet-setter. He even had his own YouTube channel, where he posted his lectures, and two thousand followers on Twitter. He had been on the telly once – a guest on a history series – as well as on a couple of artsy radio programmes, talking engagingly about things like modern takes on courtly love and the feminist themes to be found in his beloved Gawain. Even his dark hair looked sure of itself these days, Esther marvelled, closely cropped and barely peppered, springing from its roots with all the ebullience that had been in evidence when they first met twenty-five years before.

'A birthday dinner of some kind, then?' Lucas asked in his new jolly voice.

'Yes, Lucas, a birthday dinner of some kind,' Esther conceded tightly, finding the conversation no easier for the fact that Lucas had once been good at birthdays, before broken nights and infants hollering for bottles and breakfast cramped his style. He would *pretend* to forget and then wake her with a bed-tray of coffee, fresh berries, mounds of sunny scrambled eggs, and a garden flower-head lolling out of an egg cup. A parcel would be scrabbled for from under the bed, perfectly wrapped with inner layers of tissue paper and outer flourishes of trailing ribbon. Nestling inside would be something quirky or exquisite: a piece of porcelain, a first edition of poems by someone she hadn't heard of, a kimono. Most of these gifts had long since been bagged up and taken to charity shops. Viv had supported the wisdom of this, but also told Esther not to be afraid when memories surged. They had their own validity, she said, and should be allowed to play themselves out; though sometimes Esther thought a lobotomy would be more effective.

'How about you? All good with Heidi?' she countered with a briskness designed to ram home the hateful impossibility of such pleasantries. Lucas was not, and never could be, a *friend*. He was the person with whom she had once shared, not just merry birthday breakfasts, but moments (for Esther anyway) of sublime, unparalleled physical ecstasy; the person whose tears had merged with hers over the miracle of two new-borns; whose hand she had grasped when, just pregnant with Lily and not knowing it, they had stood side by side at the graveside after his poor mother's suicide. The grasp had been holding Lucas upright it felt like, while John, his father, swayed, dry-eyed and chisel-faced with drink across the grave. It was from that day that the full father-son estrangement had begun, and Esther had shared the pain of that too, saying she understood even when Lucas's hardening refusal ever to refer to the situation – let alone explain it properly to their own children – had started to drive her mad.

'Yes, all good with Heidi, thank you Esther,' Lucas replied dryly.

'You should have kept track of him, Lucas,' she burst out. 'It is your *job*, for eight measly weeks, to know where Dylan is.'

'He's an official adult – and I knew exactly where he would be.'

'You *guessed*.'

'Correctly, as it turns out. Look, when he surfaces, tell him to call, would you? And say I shall expect him back this afternoon.'

'No. *You* can tell him, using this invention called a *phone*, for which I am *still* paying because of your refusal to factor it into his allowance. And before you say it, no, Dylan is not lazy, he's desperate to earn some money – he told me, he's been applying for bar work...'

'Don't start, Esther, for Christ's sake.'

'I am not starting, and for the record, he swotted pretty hard for those bloody exams in the end. It would be great if you could at least tell him you know that.'

'I might wait until the results in three weeks' time, if it's all the same to you.'

Esther moaned softly, stifling retorts as Lucas continued to expand on his theme. Exams – academic success – were how he judged everything; taking him on about it was like wrestling concrete. She sought refuge instead in the view of her long, narrow, brambled garden through the landing window, where something was moving through the thickets, making them bounce. A fox probably, but Esther thought instead of a predatory fish nosing its way through a thick green sea, and then of Chris Mews. Hunter or suitor? And was there even a difference? Despite the firmness of her farewell follow-up message after their date, he had texted several times now, saying absurd things like he 'missed' her, and wanted to 'try again'. Esther had responded with silence. How could you miss someone you didn't know? Or have another go at something that hadn't started?

There was an ugly wasteland beyond her fence, the rail track running through its middle like a spine. The trains had kept her awake at first but now she barely noticed them. And maybe that was the secret to contentment, Esther chided herself: going with the flow instead of trying always to take everything head-on.

Lucas had moved on to the happier subject of Lily's *congregation*, as he annoyingly liked to refer to the graduation ceremony taking place on the Saturday immediately after Dylan's results.

'I've booked Wilsons for lunch – weekends are busy, but they can squeeze us in outside. And I've made sure Dylan knows, so he's not gallivanting about somewhere celebrating. I assume I was right to include Patrick and Astrid?'

'Yes. Thanks. Mum and Dad have said they are planning to make a weekend of it.'

'And we'll go halves on the bill, okay?'

'Okay.' Esther bit her lip. This was perfectly fair. Apart from Lucas's pension, their divorce settlement had been fifty-fifty. Lucas was the last person with whom she could share concerns about how the 'savings' account she had set up after the settlement continued to shrink instead of grow, chiselling away at her dream of one day buying a garden flat, ideally with at least two bedrooms and in a slightly less shabby street.

'With Matteo, that means we'll be seven in total.'

'Okay. I see. Good.' No question of Heidi then, thank God.

Having got herself downstairs, Esther made a cup of tea and perched on her back doorstep, pulling her nightie over her knees. It was only eight o clock, but a low canopy of grey cloud and a heaviness in the air suggested the start of another muggy day. Over the wonky boundary fence to her left, Carmela's clusters of electric-yellow roses drooped like tired revellers, their petals blowsy. On her other side, through the patched-up jigsaw of slats and wire, she could just make out Dimitri and Sue's sun loungers and a couple of scattered cans and bottles from the previous day's alfresco fun.

Her injured toe had swollen into a ghoulish, purple cocktail sausage, too sore to touch, let alone waggle. Proper shoes of any kind were going to be out of the question for a while, which meant flip-flops with whatever she decided to wear that evening. Shona, tall and naturally slim, would look glamorous because she always did, Esther reflected gloomily, happy to be diverted by her phone, buzzing into life with a string of birthday messages. Viv, her parents, Lily, even Rick had remembered, from whatever highly paid job he was currently doing on Norwegian oil rigs.

Many happies. Gift on next visit. Honest! Rx

Esther smiled to herself, long since accepting of how much better she and her brother were at liking each other from a distance. She opened Lily's last, releasing a little whoop at the sight of a link to a spa day gift for two in September.

Girls together! Happy Birthday Mum xx (Date moveable)

She scrolled to the most recent picture to arrive from Italy, of Lily and Matteo sitting cheek to cheek on Rome's famous Spanish Steps, both in brightly coloured shorts and T-shirts and wearing matching sunglasses. Above their heads, a superimposed neon arrow pointed at a building under the caption: 'RIP John Keats'. The familiar ache for her daughter swelled inside along with a sort of fear. The two of them were still so young. Still in the thick of it. Love. They had no idea it could go wrong.

The sensation of being watched was so sharp and unexpected that Esther's neck clicked as she glanced up. She stared into the chest-high garden wilderness advancing on the little crumbling patio, seeing nothing. The landlord had once promised to provide some garden tools, but she had given up chasing. Foxes, she told herself again, flinging a last mouthful of tea at the brambles before limping back inside to shower.

4

Lucas placed his phone face down on his desk, out of temptation's way, and stood up to stretch, reaching diagonally across the top of his head with first one arm, and then the other. He then closed his eyes, inhaling and exhaling deeply, trying the thing of keeping his tongue on the roof of his mouth, as Heidi had demonstrated.

'You will achieve instant relaxation, but the out-breath must last for five seconds longer than the in-breath, and the exercise completed at least a total of four times to be effective.' There was a commanding matter-of-factness to his girlfriend which Lucas loved almost more than anything. No passive aggression, no leading with emotions, no sea-changes of mood.

On the laptop on his desk, his new paper on symbolism was still not progressing as he had hoped. He had been longing for the end of term – the real chance to work that every university vacation provided – but three weeks in, and it was starting to feel as if he was going round in circles. So many good ideas, all refusing to be marshalled. Tension was the problem. Tension and Dylan. Lucas snatched up the phone and tried his son, as he had been doing at regular intervals since the discovery of the empty bed. The ringing tone played out, as it had done every time, to the automated option to leave a message.

'It's Dad. Again. I know you are at Mum's, having solved the mystery of your absence for myself. Call me.' Once upon a time a ringing phone was always answered, Lucas reflected darkly, dropping the mobile back on his desk and despairing at the capacity of a person he loved so deeply to be such a frequent cause of aggravation. If Dylan fell into line, life would be perfect. Well, nearly. Lucas tugged open the top left drawer of his desk, just far enough to enjoy the buzz of seeing the small, black, leather box nestling behind a pile of envelopes. No rush, he told himself, but soon.

Heidi was part of the distraction. Wanting her was exhausting. Lucas slammed the drawer shut and crossed to the window, allowing his lover's manifold physical assets to come to mind, as they always wanted to: long, shining, mahogany hair, piercing, hazel eyes, small, even teeth inside a soft, full-lipped mouth, all set on top of a statuesque, toned body worthy of an athlete. Lucas adored how Heidi looked, but sometimes when they were out together, he had even caught himself half wishing he could turn the vividness of her assets down a notch or two, like a dimmer switch. It was flattering that people looked at her – at them. Yet, the sense of scrutiny, the lurking fear of being regarded as some sort of cliché, could still be unsettling and unpleasant. On the last day of the summer term, when Heidi had joined him for a post-lunch coffee in the senior common room, an upstart Physics lecturer had joked afterwards – with Heidi barely out of the room – 'Well, you're punching there, Professor – congrats.' *Punching*? By the time Lucas had figured out what the bloody man meant, he had slapped his shoulder and moved on, chuckling.

Lucas hadn't mentioned the incident to Heidi. It was too demeaning to both of them. He certainly had no wish to remind her of the nineteen years separating their birth dates, but only because of its genuine irrelevance. Never in his life had he felt fitter, more alive. While Heidi had laughingly admitted very early on that it was men way beyond her own age bracket to whom she was always most attracted.

'Maturity is very important for me, you see, Lucas. In fact, most of my partners have been many years older.' They had been sitting at opposite ends of her futon at the time, sipping fruit tea from spotty mugs after a companionable afternoon stroll along the backs. It was Lucas's first visit to her flat. The domestic intimacy was intoxicating. When she followed these remarks by reaching across the space between them to trace her fingers down his cheek, the sensation was as electrifying as the burst of certainty that he had no wish to be part of a mere procession of 'mature men' passing through this woman's life. He wanted more. He wanted to be centre-stage. Ideally forever. 'That feels good,' he began huskily, falling silent, mesmerised, as Heidi withdrew the hand and slid off the sofa onto the floor.

'A man who knows who he is,' she continued in her calm, matter-of-fact way, positioning herself on her knees directly in front of him, placing one hand lightly on the top of each of his legs. 'A man who is good at what he does.' She gently pushed his legs apart, edged herself into the space this created and then tipped her face up for a kiss, pulling back after they had barely got going. 'A man with a big brain.' Instead of more kissing, which was what Lucas, heart pounding, eyes half closed, had been anticipating – aching for – she got to her feet.

'I would like you to come with me,' she declared, taking hold of his hand. Lucas allowed himself to be led. They entered an adjoining room containing a compact double bed, and she began at once to undress, continuing to talk in her disarmingly precise way. 'I hope you know, Lucas, that the brain is the most powerful sex organ in the human body. For a woman anyway. What we imagine is what turns us on. And I must tell you that you have made my imagination work very much.'

'And you mine.' He laughed, exultant, reaching for his own shirt buttons, only to find her slim fingers closing round his to stop him. 'Could you stay dressed for me please, Lucas? I would find that arousing. To be naked, with you clothed. For a while. Would you mind?'

No, he wouldn't mind. Dear God, a celibate saint wouldn't have minded.

Lucas had savoured every second of the undressing and all that followed, thanking whatever hidden force had inspired the organisers of the faculty dinner the month before to seat them side by side. Still in the thick of settling divorce terms, he had been feeling so low he'd almost not attended, mentally composing an email of apology-for-absence while grimly knotting his bow tie and having to redo it several times because it had been one of Esther's skills and he never got it quite right. Only some stubborn shred of a refusal to admit defeat had got him out of the door, arriving too late for the drinks but in time to make it to the dinner. Even then, the first sight of Heidi, rivetingly gorgeous in high heels, standing composed beside him while the Latin grace was read out to the hall, her muscled shoulders swelling out of an off-the-shoulder, black velvet mini-dress, hair piled high, Lucas's initial reaction had been a sort of weariness at the demands such a dinner companion might make on his energies, seeking all the things he felt least equipped to give: charm, wit, interest. The elderly woman in a dog collar on his other side had looked a much easier bet.

As soon as the first course was delivered however, five pale prawns on a bed of lettuce, Heidi started throwing out parallels between Orwell and Dostoevsky, displaying a knowledge of Russian and European literature that greatly exceeded his own. The prawns took a lot of chewing, which saw him through a round of dutiful exchanges with the guest on his other side, who turned out not to be easy at all, although this undoubtably had some connection to Lucas's eagerness to return his attention to Heidi. When at last he did so, there she was, her open face split into a smile, waiting for him, it felt like; and on they went, leaping from subject to subject like old friends playing catch-up. It transpired that her family ran a clothing company and lived in Bonn; that she had been a junior national gymnast, spoke several languages fluently, and was in Cambridge working on her 'habilitation', as European academics called the second doctorate before becoming a professor. Over mouthfuls of dry chicken breast, softened by excellent wine, they moved back to literature, Lucas professing his admiration of the feisty women in courtly tales, and Heidi drawing enjoyable parallels between medievalists and romantics. By the time dessert arrived, succulent slices of something involving blackcurrant and chocolate (they could have been chewing leather, for all Lucas cared), she had mentioned the end of a recent relationship in Germany and the desire for a fresh start, to which he had responded with a pencil-sketch summary of his defunct marriage to Esther. Thimbles of port and cups of coffee saw them exchange email addresses and phone numbers, both by then oblivious to the eighty or so other guests.

Afterwards, Lucas had half danced back through the cobbled streets along which he had trudged a mere four hours before. Dodging carousing students, waving at a few he recognised, he reached his still echoingly empty new flat in what felt like seconds, and bounded up the steps.

Nice to meet you

He texted the moment he was inside, throwing himself lengthways onto his sofa, but then deleted it, only to re-compose it, but not pressing send until he was between his sheets, grey and crumpled, he saw suddenly, and shamefully in need of a change. No immediate answer came, but Lucas told himself not to mind. She liked him. He knew she liked him. Too pumped to sleep, he lay on his back watching the wreaths of cloud drift across a half-moon, on full view thanks to his still curtainless bedroom window. Just the desire – the willingness – to fall in love again felt exhilarating, proof that he wasn't dead inside after all, that with Esther gone, the weight of failure and blame she had always been so quick to bestow on his shoulders could begin to recede properly at last, making way for a future more rejuvenating than he could ever have dreamed of.

* * *

Lucas dropped his forehead onto the window with a sigh, Esther's castigating tone on the phone still rankling. How naïve to have imagined that the quickest, cleanest divorce money could buy, for all his reluctance and its grimness, would mark an equally clean end. Esther was still *there*, still with this power to affect his mood.

It would be better when Dylan – always a battleground – was more off their hands, Lucas consoled himself, and when he could finally kick the habit of driving past the house he had been forced to sell, punishing himself with the sight of the Cheshams' silver Audi parked up by the front door steps. Antonia and Giles. Head teacher and a Maths fellow respectively, with three small, earnest children and family money, to judge from the rapidity of their cash offer. As they had cottoned on to the reasons behind his desire for a quick sale, their smiles had seemed to widen with an insufferable combination of compassion and prurient interest. It wasn't the future he had planned either, Lucas had wanted to shout at them, and so could they perhaps look to their own laurels instead of speculating about his?

Down in the courtyard the domestic bursar emerged through a side arch, clutching a laptop and talking intently to a tall man in a dark suit whom Lucas didn't recognise. Lucas kept his forehead pressed to the glass, tracking their progress across the central path of the quadrangle. Were they illicitly entangled? he wondered idly. And if so, then good luck to them.

Sensing his gaze, the bursar looked up to wave, some bangles round her wrist catching the light of the high morning sun. Lucas raised a hand in response. American, ex-City, formidable, and forensically good with numbers, she rubbed some people up the wrong way, but Lucas liked her a lot. The pair continued briskly through the portico into the next courtyard. Definitely *not* sleeping together, Lucas decided, turning away from the window.

He was lost, at long last, in concentration at his desk when there was a faint rap on his door. Shouting an absent 'come in', expecting it to be Lauren, the staircase bedder, on a bin-emptying mission, he was surprised to glance up and see the wide, pale face of one of his first years peering round the door.

'Hello there, Moira, shouldn't you be at home, or backpacking, or on a beach or something?'

The girl's look of pinched anxiety melted into a timid smile. 'Yes, I mean... sorry to disturb you, Professor Shaw...'

'No, not at all. Come in, come in.' Lucas left his chair to greet her properly, pulling the door wider so she could enter the room. Even so, she continued to dawdle in the doorway, clearly still shy, despite his and his colleagues' best efforts all year. There had been an encouraging make-over of sorts since the end of the summer term though, Lucas observed, noting the blood-red lipstick jazzing up the slightly top-heavy, pouting mouth and the way the once pitiful straggle of a fringe had been chopped almost back to her hair-line, revealing a broad, alabaster forehead, dark eyebrows, and a proper view of the girl's disconcertingly sombre, grey eyes. Her clothes suggested an increase in self-confidence too, the usual baggy, grungy leisurewear on display all year having been replaced by a crisp, white T-shirt and denim shorts; while shiny Doc Martens gripped her feet and ankles like manacles, accentuating the paleness of her long, thin legs.

'Enjoying the summer, I hope? Up on a visit, then? Or gainfully employed maybe? How can I help? You have the reading list for next term, don't you?' Lucas gestured at the sofa during the course of this welcome, experiencing a small stab of pity at the way she darted past at last, head ducked as if running the gauntlet. It made him think how right Heidi had been in one of her recent beefs about female students still – for all the strides made and the naturals like Lily – being more prone to reticence and self-doubt. Boys, generally, were still so much better at bravado, he had agreed, prepared to fling out half-baked ideas, to blag if necessary – anything for the fun of hogging the debate and the limelight. It might be a matter worth raising with the Master, Lucas reflected now, resolving to keep a special eye on Moira during the next term when his courses took centre-stage. There were several glib and cocky members of her year group, and she would need encouragement if they weren't to overwhelm her.

Yet, as the girl perched on the lip of his small sofa, hugging her canvas bag as if it were the only thing keeping her afloat, Lucas also found himself seeing – and half admiring – the fierce solitariness in her, the refusal to relax. He could recall, just, that push-pull feeling from his own early student days in Manchester: the fight to keep this new, intimidating world at bay versus a deep gnawing hunger to find a place in it. Moira Giddings was from a North London secondary school without any established pattern of Oxbridge entrance, he reminded himself, going over her credentials in his head, with passion and abilities that had made her selection a no-brainer. The mother and father swam into focus too, larger-than-life sorts, beaming and proud at the termly parent dinners.

'Sorry, Professor Shaw...'

'Just Lucas is fine, remember?' he interjected cheerily, aware that Dr Reece, the Shakespeare fellow who had been in charge of the bulk of the year's supervisions, would almost certainly have instructed otherwise. 'So, what can I help with, Moira? I know the list looks daunting, but it's for dipping into. This is supposed to be a holiday too, don't forget.'

She tugged at the shorts, which appeared to be cutting uncomfortably into her thighs now that she was seated. 'Oh, no. I mean, thank you, I was worried about that.'

'No need to be worried.' Lucas smiled, hoping suddenly that the visit was not going to end up dragging on. He remained on his feet, leaning against the side of his desk, arms crossed. Five minutes, he decided, and then he would fire a pointed look at his wall clock.

'Sorry.' She coughed into her hand, displaying what had to be false long fingernails, intricately patterned and studded with glitter. 'I know you must be busy.'

'Well... yes...' Don't show impatience, Lucas warned himself, saying gallantly to compensate, 'Though being interrupted in my labours can also be a welcome break.' She laughed at this, infusing Lucas with one of the rushes of satisfaction that had nothing to do with being a good supervisor and everything to do with being liked. 'Okay, Moira, let's have it...' He caved in, shooting a pointed look at the clock. 'Tell me what you're after and I'll do what I can.'

The elaborate talons fluttered to her fringe, perhaps missing its previous incarnation. 'Oh God. Embarrassed now.' She glanced towards the window and then down at her bare knees. 'Okay.' Her chest rose and fell as she took a deep, wheezy breath. 'So, I've been working on something...' she scrabbled to open the buckle on the canvas bag as she talked, sliding out a slim purple folder '...and I'd be, like, so grateful, if you'd take a look at it.'

'What sort of something?' Lucas asked, ready to be impressed by any attempt to get a foothold on the following term's topics.

'It's just a few pages... I... I'm going to be a writer, you see. It's a novel... well, the start of one...'

'Whoa there.' He held up his hands, laughing as kindly as he knew how. 'Moira, that is tremendously exciting of course – I mean, wow, congratulations. But I'm afraid...' He went to perch on the arm of the sofa next to her in a bid to establish as friendly a rapport as possible during the course of delivering the response she had no wish to hear.

'I felt I had to ask such a favour in person—'

'And I am honoured, Moira, truly, but—'

'I'm not in a hurry or anything,' she countered breathlessly, 'but I've written and rewritten it and just need someone to tell me whether it's any good or not, someone who knows...'

'But, Moira...' Lucas spoke very gently '...I am not a novelist. Nor do I know any novelists, come to that,' he added, somewhat hastily, since he was acquainted with several, none of whom he would ever want to bother with such a request. 'However, there must be all sorts of writing groups, online, or on Facebook...'

'*Please*, Professor Shaw, it's like, twenty pages, and all I want is like a straight *literary* opinion. I mean, it would just give me... oh, do you know, it doesn't matter...' It was as if a plug had been pulled inside her. The bony shoulders dropped. The folder was rammed back into the bag. She stood up, a little unsteadily, revealing the red indents made by her shorts, criss-crossing her upper legs like evidence of self-harm. 'It was dumb of me to ask. Stupid.' She flung the word with a thick voice. Her grey eyes, catching Lucas's, were wide and watery.

'Stupid? Not at all, Moira. That is the very last thing you should feel. You have to remember, sweetheart,' Lucas added in a jokey American accent – anything to divert the girl from what looked like the imminent possibility of tears – 'I'm a medievalist! My sole speciality is picking apart what people wrote eight or nine hundred years ago – dragons, knights, damsels, mystics, the codes of courtly love – for that, I'm your man.'

Moira seemed frozen in some sort of agony of defeat. She dropped her moist-eyed gaze to the carpet, as if a solution might lie in its faded swirls. 'Come on, now,' Lucas chivvied kindly, while Esther niggled at the back of his mind again. *Stupid* had been one of her favourite weaponised words, slung out during the course of complaints that were supposedly about Cambridge, but which always ended up being about him and how he made her feel. Lucas had no idea, she would accuse bitterly, what it felt like to be looked down on, day in, day out, for having no stellar academic credentials, and no career to speak of, other than lowbrow freelance editing jobs cobbled together round motherhood. Lucas would assure her that she was clever – and mad – because he had never encountered anyone, himself included, who did not recognise and appreciate her intelligence. But telling Esther was never enough. Nothing for Esther had ever been enough.

'Okay, Moira, leave it with me, and I'll take a quick look—'

'Ohmygod, Professor Shaw, thank you so much.'

'I've no idea when...' The purple folder was already being pressed into his hands. 'And only because you asked so nicely,' Lucas went on, already wishing he could retract the offer. 'So, no spreading of the word, you hear? I can't have the thousands of would-be Ben Lerners and Sally Rooneys imagining they can knock on my door for literary guidance which I am in no position to offer...' The regret was thickening. She hadn't cried. She had been almost out of the door. He could already hear Heidi gasp, calling him a soft touch. 'But promise me you'll find a writing group to join, okay?'

'Yep. Sure. Thanks, Professor. And I won't say anything.'

'You better not,' Lucas quipped, a little wearily, dropping the purple folder onto his to-do pile. He would do it soon, he vowed, as the thump of footsteps receded down the staircase; maybe even that afternoon. Twenty minutes max, and then the folder could be slid into her pigeon-hole with a couple of lines of encouragement. The trick, as with all chores, was not to make a meal of it.

Back behind his desk, he put on the Brandenburgs, which worked their soothing magic as always. The symbolism paper began to flow a little. So much so that after an hour he succumbed to the reward of calling his girlfriend.

Heidi's beautiful face filled the screen, smiling, but with an index finger raised to indicate that she was still on her morning stint in the library and couldn't speak. Lucas mouthed *I love you* and she mouthed the same in return, blowing a kiss before vanishing.

The emptiness inside him afterwards made Lucas pull the desk drawer open again. At Heidi's sensible insistence, they never saw quite as much of each other during a Dylan visit, and he had been missing her badly. 'Your children must not think I am taking their father away,' she had said in her practical way after their love-making the previous evening, Lucas having grabbed at the chance of Dylan's London party to invite her to the flat. 'Then they will like me. And soon, Liebchen, your Dylan will be at university and we shall have the rest of our lives, if we want.'

The rest of their lives. It was the sort of comment that she had started lobbing out from time to time, in a gloriously understated manner that gave him goosebumps, and hope. Dreamily, Lucas reached into the back of the drawer and took out the small leather box. The sprung lid opened with a little creak, revealing the most expensive item of jewellery he had ever touched, let alone purchased. The deep-blue sapphire circled by tiny diamonds glittered in its blue velvet bed, so bright he had to blink. Little wonder jewelled rings made it into the plots of countless fantastical texts, ancient and otherwise, Lucas mused, feeling the sharp edges of the stone as he pressed it gently to his lips. He wasn't going to put a foot wrong this time around. Not a single one.

5

Esther sat on the chair beside the piano stool, watching Chris Mews' birthday roses, glorious in her best blue vase, shake in protest at Billy's clunking hit-and-miss attack on the piano keys. There had been a card with the bouquet:

Thinking of you on your Special Day, Chris xxx

which was now in her bin. To dispose of the twelve stems of brilliant-crimson flowers too, had seemed both unnecessary and something of a crime.

'Well done, Billy. Let's try that again, but more slowly, okay? And this time I'll tap my foot to help you keep the rhythm.' Esther demonstrated, slapping the sole of her good foot on the floor and then nodding her head and humming the first few bars of the piece, a simple march, to get him going. This worked for a few seconds, but then he began to strain against the beat she was keeping, like a pony on a leash, wanting its head. Billy was a big fan of speed, Esther reminded herself with despairing fondness, as she had learnt from all their scattered conversations about the mini league football team whose multiple victories, according to Billy, were invariably based on his ability to outrun anybody on the pitch.

She watched the back of her young pupil's bobbing head, the jug-ears reddening with concentration and exertion, pondering how teaching – like learning – was about so much more than the subject matter, and precisely why she liked it. In Cambridge it would never have occurred to her to give piano lessons. Her piano, an early gift from a godmother and shipped from Amersham soon after she and Lucas got married, had never fitted easily into any of their various homes, ending up always in hallways or behind doors. Even in their final, rela-tively spacious house, it had lived wedged up against the wall alongside the table in the dining room, which also happened to be directly under Lucas's study. No matter how pleasant the 'noise' drifting up through the floorboards, he explained, after Esther had treated herself one child-free afternoon to a session of rusty playing, it still – regrettably – interfered badly with his concentration. Could she wait until he went out? If she didn't mind? Not that he wanted to be unsupportive.

Viv had voiced an early theory with regard to her and Brian, that every marriage, no matter how blissful, reached a pivotal moment, when the last vestiges of its original innocence fell away, revealing two very different people glaring at each other, both badly in need of rolling up their sleeves to start the real work required to achieve harmonious, lifelong cohabitation. With them, she said, it was trig-gered by Brian's defence of a decision to prioritise finishing an emer-gency root canal treatment over ensuring getting to the hospital in time for the arrival of their second-born. He had got there just after the birth, not even in time to cut the cord. That it was the *wrong* call was what mattered, Viv had seethed, making her truly wonder who – *what* – she had married. He should have downed tools. There had been a perfectly capable colleague on hand. He should have put her, and their child, first.

Between her and Lucas however, it had always felt to Esther as if the very opposite pattern was in play. Their own, hideous, irrevocable tipping point – reached a few weeks before the actual split and still hard to look back on – had been preceded by a million tiny destructive moments, each as imperceptibly corrosive as the drip-drip of water hollowing out rock. It meant that when the crisis came there was nothing for them to fall back on, no resources left on which to draw.

'I've finished, Mrs Shaw.' Billy was peering at her with a combination of satisfaction and uncertainty, his stout little arms folded across a pale blue school sweatshirt stained with evidence of the day's meals and activities.

'Yes you have, and well done. What about a biscuit to celebrate? Would you mind fetching the tin? I've got this silly sore foot, you see... it's on the kitchen table...' Esther called as he bolted off, swerving nimbly round the edges of her closely packed furniture. 'We'll end with a couple of our duets,' she went on cosily when he was back and they were both dipping into the tin, Billy picking out anything with chocolate on as usual, while she stuck to custard creams, three in total because it was her birthday and the hope of a slap-up brunch with Dylan had proved short-lived.

* * *

'Hey, Mum,' her son had greeted her sleepily, appearing mid-morning in the kitchen doorway in torn jeans and a T-shirt, pushing his fair, tousled hair off the dark ridge of his eyebrows, his voice croaky from his late night.

Still examining Chris's roses, which had just been delivered, along with a spindly lilac orchid in a pot from her parents, Esther had spun round happily, arms wide to accept his bear hug. 'Bad child, for not saying you were staying over.' She breathed in his earthy scent, not minding the evidence of partying mingled into it. Alcohol, but no trace of tobacco; no one smoked any more – they couldn't afford to, Dylan had explained dryly when she once asked about the habit among his new sixth-form college friends. 'Dad rang and made me check you were upstairs... he is *not* pleased.' Esther pulled a face, too happy at having him there to sustain any effort to be cross.

'So, you saw my note, right? And yeah, sorry, it was kind of last minute. I'll call Dad... but happy birthday, anyway.' He kissed her cheek and pulled away, drifting to the fridge, tugging open the door, and scanning its contents. 'Got any juice?'

'Sorry, only milk. And not from the carton, please,' Esther cried, forgetting her toe and grimacing with pain as she leapt to grab a glass from the drainer which she thrust into his hands.

'So, what's wrong with your leg?' he asked at once, throwing her a frown of concern before filling and then emptying the glass in a series of swift gulps.

'Oh, nothing. I stubbed my toe.' Esther cast a mournful look at her feet, clad since her shower in her only pair of flip-flops.

'Bad luck.' Dylan absently swiped the milk moustache off his upper lip and took the glass to the sink to fill with water instead, which he sipped before setting the glass down. 'I've got you a present.' He turned to lean against the sink, looking pleased with himself.

'You *have*? Not as good as last year's, surely,' Esther teased, remembering the mouth-wateringly delicious lemon drizzle cake, which had been conjured from a recipe off the Internet to make up for the absence of an actual gift.

'I'll get it in a sec, but first I need to tell...'

His gaze had locked on something over Esther's shoulder. She turned to see a willowy Asian girl, stepping into the kitchen, barefoot and wearing a long cotton T-shirt and boxers.

'Mum, Mei Lin. Mei Lin, Mum,' Dylan mumbled in a rush that managed to sound both sheepish and defiant.

'Mei Lin. How nice to meet you.' Esther offered her hand with a warm smile, hiding her shock so as not to add to Dylan's discomfort, while inwardly absorbing the fact that the mountain of bedding, gazed on with such sentimental motherly relief and adoration a couple of hours before, had contained not one occupant but two. A one-night stand or something more? It was impossible to tell and even more impossible to ask. The girl, in contrast to the pair of them, was exuding genuine serenity, and in possession of the kind of beauty that made you want to stare: slim, shapely limbs, piercing, black eyes and long, inky hair, brutally shaved above one temple, but otherwise falling in silky swathes over her high pale cheekbones.

'Good morning, Mrs Shaw.' She withdrew her fingers the instant their palms made contact. 'And many happy returns.' Her voice was sweet and breathy and accented with the brand of cut-glass English produced by expensive private schooling. Eighteen or nineteen, Esther guessed, though the classically stunning features made it hard to tell.

'Thank you, and please call me Esther...' The T-shirt and boxers belonged to Dylan, Esther realised suddenly, a notion so ludicrous – that anyone should find appeal in her son's underpants – that for one moment she almost burst out laughing.

'I believe this is for you,' Mei Lin went on, pressing a large envelope that she had been holding behind her back into Esther's hands. 'You left it upstairs, doofus.' She pulled a face at Dylan, the mask of adult calm dissolving for a moment as she giggled.

'How very exciting. Thank you.' Esther made a jokey to-do of shaking the card, pretending to listen out for what it might contain. Inwardly, she was still computing the new situation. Among the groups who had passed through the house, there had to have been girls who weren't just friends, but nothing had ever been made clear. A milestone moment, then, however one looked at it, despite being handled in typical Dylan-clumsy fashion. 'First, shall I fix us all some brunch? I don't know about you, but I'm—'

'We'll just grab some cereal and head off, if that's okay, Mum,' Dylan chipped in quickly. 'I'm sure you've got stuff planned, anyway.'

'Oh yes, I'm seeing a friend later.' Esther busied herself with the kettle, making a cup of tea and keeping half an eye as the two of them settled side by side, passing sugar, milk, and cereal as if they did it every day of their lives.

'So, are you at college too, Mei Lin?' she ventured brightly, dropping into a chair with her mug and picking up the birthday envelope. 'Hanging on for the dreaded A level results, like Dylan – under three weeks and counting...'

'*Mum...*' Dylan rolled his eyes.

'I'm only asking.'

'Actually, I don't go to college. I am an artist.' Mei Lin pushed aside her barely touched cornflakes and reached for the one banana sitting inside Esther's small fruit bowl.

'An artist? How wonderful,' Esther cried, unable to suppress a wish that the banana had been asked for. 'What sort, exactly?'

'I work mainly with space and shadows.' Mei Lin peeled back the panels of mottled yellow skin, taking one small, dainty bite and then setting the banana down, for good it looked like. 'Charcoal, sketching, photographs – I am interested in the reflections of us that we don't even know are there and over which we have no control.'

'Wow.' The girl's confidence was jaw-dropping, and admirable, but it caused Esther a pang or two of protective affection for Dylan, squirming beside this powerhouse, looking half-goofy and half-proud. 'That sounds fascinating, Mei Lin. Maybe I can get to see some of your work one day.'

'Oh sure, you'd be most welcome, Mrs Shaw.'

Esther returned her attention to the envelope. 'Now, what do we have here?'

'You'll never guess,' Dylan declared gleefully. 'And by the way, has *Italy* come through yet?' he scoffed, in the affectionately competitive tone he reserved for his uber-capable and conscientious sister.

'Yes, a lovely spa thing... but look at this...' Esther went on hastily, not wanting to take the spotlight from whatever was about to be unveiled, and then hooting with laughter as she pulled out a home-made card featuring a photo-shopped picture of herself as Wonder Woman.

'You might just need super-powers for the present, is the idea,' Dylan explained, as Esther unfolded the A4 piece of paper inside the card: an invitation to choose from a list of thrill-seeking experiences, not one of which – she could see at a heart-sinking glance – she would ever volunteer to undertake, except perhaps to save one of her children.

'You'll do the bungee jump, I'm guessing,' Dylan yelped, clearly deeply entertained by the wild improbability of his gift. 'You've got a whole twelve months to decide, and actually, not all of them are *that* scary.'

'Dylan, it's a brilliant present. Inspired. But no, I don't think I shall be hurling myself into a ravine on the end of an elastic rope.'

'There isn't a ravine, actually.' He pushed his own empty bowl aside and reached for the abandoned banana, demolishing it in three big bites. 'Apparently, it's just a place off the M4 with a big crane. A friend of Mei's did it.' He nudged his companion, busy now on her phone. 'Right, Mei?'

'Oh yeah,' she murmured, looking up at last, 'it's totally cool.'

'You said how you wanted new challenges, Mum, remember?'

'Did I? Are you sure that wasn't some other mother?' Esther laughed. 'I'll let you know what I go for. Wonder Woman! *C'est moi!*' She did a silly pose, fists on her hips, which produced a gratifying groan from Dylan, and a glance of total bafflement from his girlfriend.

They had left soon afterwards and Esther had seized Chris's bouquet, taken it to the pedal bin, but then wavered. The notion had hit her with a thud that even Dylan now *had* someone. As did Lily. As did Lucas. Their broken little unit was reconfiguring. It was just her, the one who had insisted that the breakage between her and Lucas was too deep, too vast, to fix, who was still in limbo, still alone.

Esther lowered her face into the flowers, letting the velvet-soft petals tickle her nose. That Chris had found out her address was disconcerting, but presumably easy enough to do. He was keen on her and that wasn't a crime either. For all the slight weirdness of the date, she had found him physically quite attractive. Was having *someone* better than having no one? That was the bigger question. Esther had dithered and then dropped the card and kept the roses. *Thinking of her* on her *special day*. Words could mean everything or absolutely nothing. Only actions counted – another Lucas life lesson.

* * *

'Esther, breathe.'

'Carole was sick and Shona loves Carole,' Esther wailed. 'She had every right to cancel... that is how loving couples behave.' She hadn't meant to cry, only to call Viv to wish her and Brian a happy holiday. It was gone ten o' clock, and instead the litany of the day's swerves had poured out of her in embarrassing, self-pitying depth, all the discombobulations and the final disappointment that had led to exactly the introspective, empty evening she had feared and tried so hard to prevent. 'It's only a daft birthday. It's late and you're trying to pack... I am an idiot.'

Viv was sitting on the edge of her and Brian's bed, laptop open on her knees, a half-empty suitcase behind her. Her soft, sandy hair, clearly treated to a recent cut and colour, neatly cupped the line of her strong, angular jaw, matching the freckles that always came to the fore in the summer, giving her a wide-awake cuteness that Esther could never imagine fading.

'Birthdays matter,' she said in her steady way. 'You need to ice that toe and you're quite right to be cautious about the flower man, and as for Dylan—'

'And your lovely present, I haven't even said a thank-you,' Esther cut in, glad Viv couldn't see the stained and page-swollen state of the journal since its morning dousing, nor the sneering 'happy bloody birthday to me', now scrawled in smudgy biro across its opening page. 'I am an ungrateful cow. Fact number two.'

'Esther, stop this.'

'I didn't want to see Carole anyway,' Esther went on, despite having made the point already and despite Viv barely knowing Shona, let alone her partner. 'I don't like her much, and I don't think she likes me. I just thought Shona and I... you know...' She pressed her soggy tissue to her nose, feeling again the stab of disappointment when the call had come through; standing in the kitchen in her for-best, blue, linen dress, good-to-go two hours ahead of schedule, toes painted to distract from the scruffy flip-flops, her face done up as well as she knew how.

'Oh no, poor Carole,' she had said as soon as Shona had described the temperature and raging sore throat. 'Summer flu maybe?' She had shifted to the kitchen window and fiddled absently with the miniature Wedgwood pot that lived on the sill, an early gift from Lucas, too dear to have qualified for a charity-shop run.

'Flu. Exactly.' Shona had sounded as if she were directing a jury. 'I could be a carrier. With viruses you just can't be too careful, can you?'

'No, you can't,' Esther had echoed, feeling flattened, and finding the pot somehow falling through her fingers in the same instant. It had exploded with a dull thwack on the stone tiled floor. Esther had counted the scattered shards as Shona had talked out her apologies, and then crawled around picking up each fragment, making a little pile of them on the windowsill.

'Have you eaten anything, sweetie?' Viv coaxed.

'Biscuits, mainly. And ice cream. And some vinegary old Pinot Grigio.' Esther smiled ruefully, sniffing now and all cried out. Back in the day, it had been Viv who was more prone to a messy life, she remembered suddenly – boys, pregnancy scares, divorcing parents – until she went north and found psychology and Brian. 'Sorry, Viv.' She rubbed under eyes where she knew her heavy evening make-up would be in smudges. 'Thank you for letting me rant. I'm totally fine and must let you go.' As she spoke, Brian, who had made a speedy exit once Esther's distressed state became apparent, put his sunny, handsomely rugged face round the bedroom door.

'Sorry to interrupt, ladies, I just need to get... ah, there it is.' He snatched up a short, thick black cable from the floor, pausing to add, 'Hey, Vivvie, if Esther's feeling blue, she could join us in France for a few days, couldn't she? We've got five weeks, after all.'

The pair exchanged a look, too fleeting to read, but Esther was already saying no.

'Brian is right,' Viv said levelly, once Brian had pulled the door to. 'I should have thought of it myself. We've got heaps of time – I'll have to do the odd online consult, but Brian had so many unused days, it seemed silly not to take them. And of course, it would be lovely to have you, Es, you know that.'

'Viv, you showed me pictures. There aren't enough bedrooms.'

'Nonsense. The elder two can double up for a few nights.'

'Viv, no.'

'Think about it. You could come after Lily's graduation. There are still cheapish flights to Nice if you shop around. The place is an hour from the airport. We're hiring a car, but the bumf says there's a bus to a nearby town that we could scoop you up from. I'll forward all the details. Call it an extra birthday present, if it makes you feel better. Even if it is just a few days, the break will do you good. Now get some sleep.' She did a mock glare and blew a kiss before disappearing from the screen.

Esther fell back among the sea of sofa cushions where she had spent the evening. She pictured the dry, sultry heat of southern France – fields of sunflowers and lavender; the world at bay for a little instead of snapping at her heels.

Her eyes were half closed when something flitted across the window. She jolted upright, hugging a cushion. A large bat? An owl? Peering out, she saw nothing but a full yellowy-orange moon casting a gentle glow over the garden. She pressed at her temples, aware of a headache starting.

'Bed, Esther,' she growled to herself, straightening the cushions and doing a limping trudge up the stairs.

She was under her duvet when her phone flared with another message.

Hope u got my flowers and had a lovely day. Chris X

Truly not a quitter and all of a sudden it was freaking her out.

I don't know how you got my address. Please don't contact me again.

A reply came back at once, and though Esther's heart cantered for a second, there was no need.

Okay. Sorry. Over and out.

For a moment, Esther liked Chris Mews better than she ever had and it left her with a small bubble of emptiness. It was a relief to turn the light off and feel the weight of the day lift at last. A birthday on one's own brought pressure, and it was done.

CONGREGATION

6

Esther rang her bike bell to shift the pedestrians ambling across the wide paved road. Mid-June, and, as so often in Cambridge, some sort of ceremony had been taking place in Senate House, shining regally in the gated quadrangle on the opposite side of the street. Tourists were pressed up against the tangle of bicycles along the railings, fighting for sight-lines as a multicoloured crocodile of dignitaries processed down the steps from the portico entrance, their fancy hats, hoods, and gowns rippling in the light breeze.

Good, bad, or bonkers? Eighteen years in, and still Esther could never quite decide about the university pomp and paraphernalia of her adopted home town. In her buoyant mood that morning it seemed endearing and took her straight back to the flock of haughty, speed-walking flamingos that had made her and Lucas giggle during their TV dinner the night before, plates of shepherd's pie, peas, and carrots balanced on their laps. Both children had just set off on trips abroad – Lily to New York with Matteo, and Dylan to a family in Salamanca to improve his Spanish before the sixth form.

If anything, it was trepidation that Esther had felt during the afternoon drive back from Luton airport, having done the Dylan send-off alone because Lucas, typically, had some last end-of-term meeting that couldn't be missed. Two weeks without either child buzzing around was unprecedented, and it had occurred to her that Dylan especially, even when he was being problematic, provided a distraction from the niggling white noise of her and Lucas's separateness. They had become like spinning plates, Esther decided desperately, swinging into the supermarket because she had forgotten to get anything out of the freezer for supper; connecting through the children rather than each other, avoiding all the well-trodden areas of conflict, precisely because they were so well trodden. The drawbacks of Cambridge, how Lucas was, how she was, how Dylan was... with just the two of them, there would be nowhere to hide.

She had got as far as boiling and draining the potatoes for the pie when Lucas, sporting a smile that was almost shy, sauntered into the kitchen.

'Could I crush a garlic clove or something? Or chop an onion? Save you reaching for the Kleenex? And tomorrow night I'm going to cook.' He turned his back on Esther's double take to set about scything the large red onion that she had placed on the chopping board, converting it into the meticulous, gossamer-thin slices which, once upon a time, during early days of shared meal preparation, had provided easy fodder for ribbing. 'Grilled prawns, or something simple. I could go to the fish market. Here, let me do that. This is ready for the frying pan.' He pushed the board towards Esther and seized the masher she had just removed from its hook, along with the saucepan of potatoes, embarking on a pulverising so energetic that flecks of mash flew across the hob and up the wall tiles.

Esther had to suppress a prickle of irritation. He was trying. It certainly made a welcome change from working in his study until being summoned, and then taking so long to arrive the meal was half cold. She directed her energies to the carrots instead, swiping the peeler deep into their skins and mentioning the David Attenborough as a possible source of evening entertainment, tentatively, because Lucas was big on fighting the temptation to watch telly while eating.

That Lucas was making a serious effort only really dawned on her after the flamingos had finished strutting, when he took their plates and went to wash up without being asked. He returned with mugs of tea, saying he'd like the telly off if Esther didn't mind, and what music would she like to listen to instead? Esther, disarmed, even a little suspicious, said Debussy, and reached for her Kindle, only to find Lucas joining her on the sofa and quizzing her about the new museum catalogue job, saying it sounded a serious step up the ladder and who knew where it might lead?

'I know I work too much and I am sorry, Esther,' he went on, once the subject of her working life and career hopes had received an unprecedentedly exhaustive analysis. He turned the music off and left his armchair to sit next to her on the sofa. 'I am not supportive enough of you. It will get better, I promise.'

'Lucas...' She gave him a despairing, affectionate smile. Such promises had been made before, though not for a while. 'Thank you. I would like that. Very much.' She returned her concentration to the page of Mick Herron on her screen, thinking the moment was too lovely to risk ruining by saying anything else.

Lucas had picked up a paper to read, but tossed it back onto the coffee table. 'Sometimes, Esther, I feel like Sisyphus, hauling his boulder; the need to prove something – to myself, to the world – over and over again. It's exhausting.'

He turned to her with an expression of such bleakness in his eyes that she felt fear as well as hope. He wanted to talk. Properly. Such moments were gold dust.

'The Viv brigade would probably say it was because of my mother,' he went on, laughing harshly and averting his gaze from the flash of astonishment that escaped Esther before she could stopper it.

'Because?' she asked gently.

Lucas shook his head. 'Oh, you know. The son who wasn't enough to stop his own parent deciding to sling a noose of bed-sheets round the branch of an apple tree, then having to spend the rest of his existence proving his worth. That sort of thing.'

'Lucas, that's not—'

'Don't worry, I know it's all hocus pocus.' He was smiling suddenly, unnervingly. 'I only blame one person, who, I am happy to confirm, rarely crosses my mind. But all of it does seem to have left me with this relentless hamster wheel of a need to justify my presence on the planet. And you, my dear sweet Esther, bear the brunt.' He took the Kindle off her lap, and then laced his hand with hers.

They intertwined fingers, Esther acutely aware of the hard ridges of her marriage rings against his skin. 'It is all right, Lucas,' she murmured, feeling that it truly was, and glimpsing the entirety of them suddenly – how they had begun and all that they had weathered as part of an inseparable whole.

Upstairs, in the dark of the bedroom and the new quiet of the house, they had reached for each other again and differently, with what had almost felt like the tenderness of strangers. Afterwards, with Lucas asleep on his back, his arm up against Esther's, she had lain awake, heart still pounding from pleasure, and reflected on the invisible, yawning chasm between having sex and making love; a difference that Lucas had never found easy to acknowledge. The stuttering of her libido during the exhaustion of early motherhood had, unquestionably, been integral to the start of their difficulties, Lucas insisting on taking it personally, despite her repeated reassurances. Even when more regular relations were restored, those times – Lucas's hurt and umbrage every night she put sleep before sex – had left a sour note that had never quite dissipated.

But not last night, Esther reflected, unable to resist smiling to herself as she hopped off her bicycle outside the entrance to Lucas's college. Last night had been of a new order. Like before but better. More honest. More loving. Respectful to the point of reverence. And the talking properly too. Communicating. It felt like a new phase. It lent the tinge of something like a second honeymoon to the two children-less weeks stretching ahead.

'Good morning, Mrs Shaw. Long time no see.'

'How are you, Arthur? And how's Smudge?' Esther laughed as the college cat hopped up onto the counter, headbutting the man's square chin.

'We're both very well, thank you. And yourself?'

'Great, thanks. Both children away – yippee.' Esther pulled a comical face and then waited for the electronic security gate to take its usual age to open. 'See you,' she called, enjoying the flap of her summer skirt against her bare legs as she pushed the bike across the courtyard, keeping to the path between the grass that was not for walking on and the pristine borders of yellow and purple pansies.

Parking the bike out of sight under the arch of Lucas's staircase, she took the flight up to the first floor two steps at a time, humming to herself. His door was slightly ajar, so she went straight in.

'Surprise...' she began, breaking off at the realisation that the room was empty; although not for long, to judge from the open door. Esther went to peer out of the window, down at the bright, geometric beauty of the empty courtyard, absorbing the pleasing hush of the place without the students. Lucas had said something about seeing Ralph Conway, his closest friend as well as the college's Senior Tutor, to discuss admissions.

Esther strolled to his desk, where his laptop was flashing its screen-saver of the Grand Canyon. Printer paper, she remembered suddenly, thinking of her own laptop, now containing a finished summary of Barbara Hepworth's life, which she had been unable to print off because of running out at home. Esther opened the desk's side panel of large drawers in search of stationery. The bottom, final one contained paper, but only a thinnish wad, so she knelt down to separate out ten or so pages to keep her going. As she slid the remainder back in, her eye was caught by a small, grey phone, lying along the back of the drawer. She fished it out, seeing that it was a mobile, a very small old-fashioned one, not dissimilar to the first model they had bought Lily. Esther turned it over in her hands. Lily's had been blue. This one was stone grey. A Samsung. Heavy footsteps and men's voices sounded on the stairs, and a moment later Lucas bounded into the room, followed by Ralph, his crinkled light brown hair in the wild mop that always made her think of candy floss.

'Esther,' Lucas exclaimed in surprise.

'Yes, I thought I'd drop in.'

'Hello there, Esther,' Ralph said, in his warm Glaswegian rumble, waving over Lucas's shoulder and grinning. 'How lovely to see you. Are you well? You look well.'

'I am, thank you, Ralph.' Esther had got to her feet, still clutching the paper and the phone. 'I decided to come by and then remembered I needed some printer paper.' She flapped her pages. 'The Hepworth retrospective, I've been doing a bit of the catalogue.'

'Splendid. Catherine and I saw her stuff in St Ives a few years ago. Mind-blowing.' He turned to Lucas. 'I'll leave you both to it. Take that coffee another time. Lovely to see you, Esther.' He flashed his big bearded smile and shot off, slamming the door behind him before thumping back down the stairs.

'I needed some printer paper,' Esther repeated, aware that Lucas had a slightly fixed look on his face. 'And I found this.' She twiddled the phone.

'Ah, thank you.' He smacked his forehead in a demonstration of his own gormlessness. 'A student left it. I'd completely forgotten. I'll drop it at the lodge.' He stepped towards her, holding out his hand.

'Oh, I see.' Esther looked again at the phone. 'A bit retro for a student.' Something odd had happened to the air around them; a stillness. Lucas was grinning extravagantly, his palm stretched in front of her. Like a Master asking a pupil to hand something over, Esther found herself thinking; something she shouldn't have. 'Which student?'

He laughed loudly. 'Ah, well, that I don't know, I'm afraid. I found it. Down the back of the sofa...'

'We could try and find out, surely.' She carefully placed her thin sheaf of paper on the desk and started to examine the phone more closely.

'It was a while back, and who knows how long it had been there? It's probably dead.'

It had a button saying 'OK', which came to life when Esther pressed it.

'Here, let me see.' Lucas tried to swipe the device from her hands, but Esther, acting on sheer reflex, whipped it behind her back.

'Don't be silly.' Lucas tried a laugh, but was clearly annoyed. 'Come on, Esther, give it to me and I'll take it to the lodge.' He rolled his eyes like a parent with an impatient child.

But the atmosphere had grown stranger still. The air between them seemed to be vibrating, to the point where Esther could almost hear the thrum of it. A sense of a choice – a crossroads – was unfolding at the same time. She could hand the phone over and it – along with Lucas's annoyance, the very last thing she wanted to invoke on this day of all days – would go away. Instead, she clenched the little mobile to her chest and moved round the desk so that it could sit between them, a bulwark. Keeping half an eye on Lucas, standing rigid, his expression darkening, she pressed the menu button. The phone was so simple, it did not have a passcode. Calls received. Messages received. But the sent messages box was empty. Wiped clean. Aware of Lucas advancing round the desk, Esther edged the other way, selecting a text at random.

'Come on, Esther, for God's sake. It's not nice to snoop on someone else's stuff.'

Fyi I still WANT you, Lucas. Now. NOW...

Lucas made his move, lunging round the desk, and she flew, hurdling his briefcase, wrenching the door open, and on up the stairs to the top-floor toilet. She heard his thunderous feet behind her on the old wooden stairwell. The crash of shutting the toilet door and the snap of managing to slide the lock across was followed by the slam of his fist on the other side, so hard the hinges rattled.

'Esther, come out. Please. I beg you. Come out.'

Keeping her eye fixed on the door, Esther shuffled backwards, reaching behind her to lower the toilet seat before sitting down. She leant back against the cistern, holding the mobile delicately now, like the bomb it was, containing their end.

7

_____

The August sun was so blinding that Esther left the door open and ran
back for her sunglasses. Feeling the protest in her little toe –
compressed inside smart shoes for the first time in three weeks – she
raced upstairs to grab her flip-flops for driving, putting her car keys
down on her bed and then having to go back for them too.

'Morning, Esther.'

'Sue!' Esther exclaimed, startled, hastily finished locking the door
and doing her shoe-swap, juggling her smart handbag and mac. Her
neighbour was crouched on her doorstep with a trowel, bedding a tray
of fragile green tendrils into a flower tub. 'Nice to see you. I'm in a bit
of a—'

'We took a parcel for you.' Sue glanced lazily up, smiling at Esther
through her fringe.

'Oh, goodness, thank you...'

'Came yesterday morning. Dimmy took it, actually. I was out for the
count.' She patted a patch of the soil round a new sprig with the back
of the trowel and scooped out another from the tray.

'That was kind of him. I was at a client meeting and now I'm afraid
I've got to...' Esther paused to yank at her dress, a dusty pink stalwart
that she always forgot bunched round her midriff, emphasising

exactly the section of her she was most keen to mask. 'Could I possibly collect it later, do you think, Sue? Only, I am in a bit of a hurry.'

'Well, you must be going somewhere nice is all I can say. You look gorgeous.' Sue got to her feet as she spoke, dusting dirt crumbs off her palms.

'My daughter's graduation,' Esther admitted with a smile, her heart sinking uncharitably as Dimitri emerged to join the doorstep chat, his broad grin baring the big gap between his two front teeth.

'Doesn't she look gorgeous, Dimmy?'

'She surely does. All right, Esther?' He draped his arms over Sue's shoulders, his dark eyes twinkling in a way that drew attention away from the dark under-pouches of fatigue.

Driving people home all night. Esther couldn't imagine it. 'Yes, thank you, Dimitri... I...'

'Go get her that package, Dimmy, there's a love. She's in a hurry.'

'Okay, babe. Won't be a tick. Hold your horses, Esther.'

'Then it's done, right?' Sue said sweetly

'Yes.' Esther smiled, surrendering to the waves of determined kindness.

'Daughter's graduation, now that is *nice*,' said Sue, 'and with your lovely Dylan too – you must be one proud Mum.'

'Oh, yes...'

'Something I'm hoping to know about one day. We're trying madly.' She had lowered her voice and was holding up crossed fingers. 'Dimmy hates me telling anyone. He's starting to worry about his sperm count.'

'Oh goodness, best of luck,' Esther murmured, a little distractedly, because Dimitri was taking his time and Sue mentioning Dylan had given her one of the heart-lurches that had being going on since Thursday morning.

'Not *one* C, but *three*,' Lucas had roared down the phone. 'That means the child hasn't just failed to get the *mediocre* grades kindly demanded by the good people at UWE, he has *ploughed the whole fucking lot*. Quite how you managed, all these months, to dupe yourself, and me, into believing he was doing *any work at all,* remains a complete, bloody mystery.'

'Blaming me solves nothing,' Esther had countered furiously, her own upset compounded by the possibility of Dylan overhearing his father's crushing words, and with the imminent celebration of his sister's academic triumph somehow making everything worse. 'Getting angry won't help either,' she had added miserably, having a horrible sense of being sucked back into the marital quagmire she had sought to escape. Lucas bossing everything. Rowing about Dylan. Her the good cop, him the bad. 'I have no idea what happened either – I need to speak to Dylan. But there are re-sits, right?'

'He will have to work his bloody socks off, padlocked to his laptop if necessary. I've already told him. A day off for Lily and then revision starts.'

When Esther had finally got Dylan himself on screen, hunched and wan-faced, her son's shrugs and dejected dunnos had shredded her heart. He had done his best. He didn't know what had gone wrong. He would do what his father said. He didn't want to come back to London anyway. He had just started a job in a pub, which he hoped he'd be allowed to carry on with. When she'd ventured a question about Mei Lin, hoping to cheer him up, he had retorted that she was just a friend and what did that have to do with anything? A response that bore out Lily's brusque claim to be unaware of any girlfriend. He had felt unreachable, and one of Esther's aims for the graduation day was to find a way back to him.

When Dimitri finally bounded out of the house with a small, thin, cardboard box, Esther unceremoniously jammed it into her handbag, calling thank yous as she ran to the car.

'Better late than late,' he shouted cheerily.

After a morning in the sun, the inside of her little Ford was a furnace. Esther dumped all that she was carrying onto the passenger seat, wound down the windows and had just turned the engine on when Sue's face popped up beside her.

'Meant to say. We're having a bit of a do tonight. Barbecuing. Nothing fancy. Do come.'

'Thanks, Sue, though I doubt I'll be back in time.' Esther rammed the car into gear.

'And Dylan too, if he's around.' Sue peered into the back of the car, as if Dylan might be lurking there.

'Right. Bye, Sue.' Esther lurched out of her space, stopping only just in time as a motorcycle whined past. It cut in front of her, swinging up to the front door of her other neighbour. The rider gave Esther a hard stare as he pulled off his helmet, shaking out a mane of dark, corkscrew curls.

Esther ignored it, using the moment to check a route on her phone and finding that she would still make it in time. She messaged Lily to field her parents, who would be absurdly early because they always were, and then set off more gingerly, Dimitri's merry 'better to be late' ringing in her head. It was going to be a good day. Lily's day. Lucas had all the tickets, and would no doubt stroll up to the Senate House in his casual way with five minutes to go, because that was what *he* always did. And tomorrow she would be packing for France, because Viv had insisted, and resisting Viv was always useless. *Go with the flow, woman*, Esther warned herself, putting on the radio and settling back into her seat.

8

Lucas gave the bedroom door one sharp rap before going in, deliberately not allowing time for an answer. The state of the place said it all, he reflected grimly, surveying the clothes in drifts between half-flattened boxes from various deliveries, coat hangers, grubby trainers and several charger wires zigzagging through the chaos. The wall of bookshelves, still gleaming from the costly refurb he'd had done before moving in, now contained all manner of things apart from books.

'Dylan, move it, for goodness' sake.' Lucas hadn't meant to begin this day, of all days, combatively but, really, it was impossible. He strode round the end of the bed to open a window. The room smelt, a horrible mix of sweat and something that was sweet and off at the same time. The window gave way in a rush, delivering a lovely gulp of fresh air and the clear view of a fat, half-smoked spliff on the outside sill.

Lucas spun round and jerked a corner of the duvet, far enough to reveal a fuller picture of his son, spreadeagled on his front. 'Tell me, Dylan, how does smoking weed fit in with your professed desire to *save* money? Quite apart from damaging your brain – which, I would humbly suggest, needs all the help it can get right now; not to mention the minor detail of breaking the bloody law. Jesus, Dylan, I am not naïve but I had dared, given past experiences, to expect better from you.' The bedding, bed, and its occupant remained quite still. So still indeed that, for one heart-stopping beat, it even occurred to Lucas to wonder if he could be glaring at a corpse. This momentary terror, when his son deigned to stir at last, shifting so that he was sitting upright, insolently, or so it seemed to his father, see-sawed into an anger so intense that Lucas had to clench his fists to contain it.

'A friend gave it to me,' Dylan mumbled, shoving at the flop of his hair.

'Oh, well, that's absolutely *fine*, then. Hooray. No problemo.' Lucas unfurled his hands, running them over his face in a bid to compose himself. It didn't help that his own day had begun so exquisitely, waking in the misty dawn light to the tickle of Heidi's long hair on his face. Spending the night at hers had never been the plan. But when Dylan, sullen with his exam catastrophe, had retreated into his room for the evening, Lucas had not been able to resist the chance to see his lover, stealing out of the flat like a thief.

'I know it's breaking all our rules,' he had admitted, the moment Heidi opened the door, summoned by his pleading text from the street, 'but I need you. *Need*. Do you understand? There are things I have to say, things you must hear.' Instead of the scolding, pragmatic response he had half feared, she had stepped into his arms. 'Liebchen,' she had whispered, her breath warm in his ear, 'I need you too.'

'Look, I don't want to make a big deal of it, okay?' Lucas told Dylan more gently, removing the spliff from the window ledge and holding it behind his back. 'It's gone nine, time to get your act together. You must look smart. It is an important day for your sister.'

'Well, thank you for the reminder, Father.'

Lucas bristled, but reined himself in. 'What do you have to wear anyway? Anything?' He picked his way through the mess to the wardrobe, widening the already half-open door. An old baseball cap dangled from a hook at the back. On the rail, a crumpled, collarless shirt hung half off a hanger. Next to it a pair of tracksuit bottoms dangled from their waist-tie. 'You'll have to borrow something of mine.'

'Get out of my grill, Dad.'

Lucas swung round. 'No, Dylan, I shall not get out of your *grill*.' He spoke calmly, aiming for a tone that was comedic rather than critical. 'Your mother may have seen fit to spoil you into idiocy, but I think we can now all agree that it is not a strategy that has produced positive results.'

Dylan opened his mouth to speak and then snapped it shut. His light-blue eyes narrowed into fierce glints. 'All you and Mum want is for me to be like Lily,' he muttered. 'Well, I am not her.'

'No, you are not. Nor do I want you to be. But at least your sister has never had to be reminded – time after time after time – of the incalculable value of hard work—'

'I *did* work—'

Lucas snorted, a part of him glad that they were at last having the conversation crying out to be had. For two days, ever since the hideousness of Thursday morning, he had tried to go easy, to give Dylan the chance to speak – as Heidi, and Esther for that matter, had advised – but that had got them nowhere. 'Forgive me, Dylan,' he sneered, 'but your grades would suggest otherwise.'

His son's face twisted, his gaze finding the wall to his left, then his right. 'I couldn't... I didn't finish... all the questions.'

Lucas went very still. 'And why...?' He had to pause to breathe. 'Why was that?'

'Dunno. Brain-freeze.' Dylan shrugged, seeming to relax, as if this confession was momentous enough to explain everything. As if, Lucas decided with mounting exasperation and an infuriated sense of his own helplessness, his son regarded life as something that happened *to* him, instead of being a matter over which each human being had control.

'Well.' He had to push each word through his teeth to prevent himself raising his voice. 'The big news, Dylan, which you need to grasp – right here, right now and forever more – is that our brains in fact *belong* to us and that we are each therefore solely responsible for how we deploy them. We can, indeed, *unfreeze* them. If we have the willpower – and the guts – to do so. Which is why, once today is over, you are going to devote yourself to the task of preparing to re-sit every single exam. You will not go to parties. You will not throw your money and health away on drugs or alcohol. You will not work in a pub or anywhere else. Because the other big news is that you are in possession of a fantastic brain, if you would only use it. It costs nothing, you know. At least, not if you have the added blessing, which you do, of supportive parents...' Lucas stopped, willing Dylan to recognise the magnitude of this, but he had gone rigid again, his gaze still blank and glued to the wall. 'Because your mother is properly on board about working harder,' he concluded fiercely, frustration engulfing him again, 'make no mistake about that.'

Lucas was aware of a tremble in his knees as he strode towards the door. The sight of Dylan, so pathetic, surrounded by his shambolic life, was worse than anything. 'I'll find a suit – or smart trousers – for you.' He spoke gruffly.

'Like you're such a fucking saint.'

'I beg your pardon?' Lucas turned slowly. Dylan was studying his hands, head hanging, like one readying for the guillotine.

'Nothing.'

'No, please. Repeat what you said.'

'Cheating on Mum,' he growled, swinging his head up to confront his father's stony expression, 'then dumping her so you could get with... *Heidi*.' His voice was thick with disgust.

Lucas's heart was banging inside his chest. 'That was not... *not*... what took place.' Dylan and Lily knew the gist of what had gone on, what he had done – Esther had made sure of that – but not the root cause. Lucas faltered. This was his son. He could not tell Dylan, of all people, what it had felt like to lose your wife to your children; how, with the arrival of mothering, Esther had seemed to cease thinking of him, or caring for him, or *wanting* him as she once had. 'Heidi had nothing to do with Mum and me,' he said stiffly, experiencing a small lift just from uttering his girlfriend's name. 'We only met last year.'

'Yeah, right.' Dylan pulled his mouth into an ugly line.

'Show some respect!' The words flew out of Lucas's throat before he could stop them, blocking the image of his beleaguered child, now frantically swiping at tears, and replacing it with his own father four decades before, towering over him, thundering the same impossible command. To demand respect meant you hadn't earned it. Lucas had known that even at twelve, just as he had known that his father, gripping his battered medical bag, his thick hair pitifully askew, late for work and the school drop-off as usual, knew it too. 'Look, Dylan...' Lucas stammered. His body was prickling all over suddenly, like the pins and needles after numbness. It felt like fear. To lose control, it wasn't how he behaved. Ever. 'I'm sorry, I shouldn't have shouted. The fact is, things went wrong between Mum and me for all sorts of reasons...'

The flat's entrance door slammed.

'Only me,' came Lily's clear soprano from the hall. 'Anybody home?'

'In here,' Lucas called back, stepping towards the door to shield Dylan, hastily drying his face on the duvet. 'Encouraging your brother to get his act together.'

'Ah. A reveille. I see. Well, I am honoured. At least, I think I am...' Lily peered round Lucas as she leant against the door jamb, crossing her arms. There was an atmosphere, but Lily was an old hand at that and alert enough to guess that Dylan's dire exam results would have been at the heart of it. Attired in the formal dark clothes and scholarly gown required for the graduation ceremony, with dabs of colour – blue eye shadow, spots of blusher, pinkish lips – highlighting her neat features, she resembled an exotic flower. Her skin still glowed from the recent sojourn in Italy, and her hair, bleached silvery-white, was pinned into a tight ball on the top of her head, ringed by a piece of black velvet ribbon that matched the one round her neck.

'I was thinking breakfast *en famille* might be nice. I've even brought muffins and my own soya milk for coffee. Mum has texted to say she is running a bit late, so can we get there early to field Gran and Grandad. Matteo's going to meet us there too.'

'All sounds good to me,' Lucas said briskly, 'and you look very smart, sweetheart.' He hugged her, careful not to mess up the bun. 'Coffee coming right up. After I've found your brother a decent *something*.' He flashed a mollified expression at Dylan before heading off to the kitchen, wondering what it would take to make the boy see that all the fatherly raging came from love and the sheer despair of witnessing the squandering of so much potential.

* * *

'Okay, Dyl?'

'Sure, Boo. You?'

Lily eyed her brother steadily from the doorway, perfectly aware that, for reasons neither of them would go into that minute, things were very far from being okay. 'It will all work out, you know, in the end. Nil desperandum.'

'Whatever the fuck that means,' Dylan muttered, getting out of bed and slinging a towel, plucked from the floor, over his shoulder.

'Hey, just be nice today, okay?' Lily wagged a jokey finger, and her brother's expression softened.

'It's all shite, but yeah. Of course. Dad's extra wound up because I smoked some weed.'

'Not smart.'

'That's me.' He widened his eyes, flicking the towel at her before disappearing into the shower adjoining his bedroom. 'Hey, don't eat all the muffins,' he shouted, before his voice was drowned by the sound of pounding water.

9

Looking round the lunch table, dappled by the chinks of sunlight finding a way through the restaurant's fleet of vast canvas umbrellas, Esther had to pinch herself. Lucas was talking wine with her father; Lily was nobly explaining synthetic biology, the subject of her thesis, to her goggle-eyed grandmother; while Matteo and Dylan were engrossed in one of their exchanges of music must-listens. Dessert plates had been scraped clean and empty wine glasses pushed aside to make room for coffee cups, apart from Matteo and Lily, who had opted to share a pot of ginger tea. They looked like any old family on a day out, Esther marvelled. They *were* a family on a day out, riven and scarred, but reassembled and performing as their best selves in honour of Lily. To the outside world – the waiters, the other diners – the cracks were invisible, and this felt integral to what she recognised as a burgeoning sense of triumph.

'But, Dad, we had loads of picnics when we were kids!' Lily yelped, in response to a dry, teasing remark from Lucas about what a pleasant meal it had proved despite his personal dislike of eating outdoors. 'And what about all those camping trips you made us go on, Exmoor, Northumberland...?'

'Ah yes, well, a father has to make sacrifices for his offspring.' Lucas smiled, while Esther, who had borne the brunt of ensuring the success of such wholesome holidays, sweating over tiny cooking pots and holding small hands for treks into woods and communal lavatories in the small hours, found that she had no inclination to contradict. Family stories morphed into legends with retelling, and who cared? The world, with its spiky realities, could wait. All the stress of her late start out of London felt a million miles away. Catching Dylan's eye, she beamed, wanting him to know how proud she was of the way he had supported his sister, cheering so raucously when it was Lily's turn to kneel before the Vice-Chancellor that she had seriously wondered if they might be asked to leave. Outside afterwards, he had led the way with the photo-taking, getting them all to pose on the steps of Senate House. Lucas had used the moment to report, in a lowered voice, the good news of a real 'man-to-man' conversation between him and Dylan that morning. Redoing the exams was going to take some micro-managing, he had added, but it felt like a turning point.

'And there was Ireland too, by that river,' Lily persisted, clearly enjoying the repartee with her father, 'with all those monster-wasps, when Dyl trod on the nest...'

'Exactly. Multifarious natural hazards. I rest my case.' Lucas laughed. 'How many stings was it, Dylan?' He looked across the table, as they all did, for Dylan to pick up the story.

'Like, twenty thousand... oh yeah, what a fun day out that was.' Dylan smiled, but tightly, as if the puff had gone out of him.

'I don't think I've heard about these monster Irish wasps,' offered Matteo, ever helpful, smoothing over the moment. He adjusted the aviators perched in his thick curly black hair and draped an arm along the back of Lily's chair.

'You so *have*,' she scolded playfully, dropping her head onto his shoulder. 'After Dyl trod on the nest he jumped in the river and a fisherman thought he was drowning and pulled him out.'

'Oh yeah, maybe I have.' He grinned and the pair exchanged a look. They were both still glowing from their holiday but Matteo was much darker, his skin tanned into a rich teak brown, thanks to the Brazilian father, who now lived in New York with a second wife and twin baby daughters. His mother had recently moved back to Devon, picking up with both an abandoned career as a folk singer and a holiday-lettings manager whom she had apparently dated decades earlier – 'her first love,' as Lily had dreamily described the man, prompting Esther to perform a quick hopeful riffle through her own early romantic history, but not able to come up with anything other than Lucas.

A waiter, arriving with their bill and a card machine, surveyed the landscape of the table to try and assess where to place it. Esther dived into her bag for her debit card, while her father, too, turned to fumble in the inner pocket of his jacket for his wallet.

'No. Thanks, both, but this is on me,' Lucas said, signalling to the waiter that he would take charge.

'But, Lucas, we agreed,' Esther protested, as surprised as she was pleased, while also noting how far Lucas held the bill from his eyes in order to scan it. A tenderness rippled through her. He was getting long-sighted. Time knew no mercy, not even for her driven, self-centred, impossible ex-husband.

'Come on, now, Lucas,' Patrick chipped in gruffly, starting to count out twenty-pound notes in his meticulous way, fresh from the cash machine by the look of them.

'Patrick, no.' Lucas's voice was stern and affectionate. 'Please. I insist.'

There were murmurings of appreciation from everyone. Astrid seized the moment to flick Esther one of her looks, bringing her back down to earth. Here is your super husband being super, it said, the one you threw away instead of forgiving and bringing to heel. Esther flared her eyes in response, remembering more vividly than she ever wanted to one of the many reasons why the two post-Cambridge Amersham months had been so grim. Her mother's unsympathetic temperament was something she was long used to, but there had been a daily dose of old-fashioned asides to contend with too, along the lines of a wife's duty being to stick by her man – crushing for their lack of empathy, but also suggesting the possibility of some hiccough in her parents' relationship of which she longed only to remain in ignorance. Offspring, even middle-aged ones, were not designed to be curious about the sex lives or misdemeanours of their parents. Having to ignore that fact, in order to explain to Dylan and Lily the reasons behind the separation, had been horrible. With his grey-faced, stumbling apologies, Lucas's mortification had been palpable, while both children went from stunned silences to weeping, hurling recriminations to which he had no answers. Lucas had deserved every moment, and all that followed, but the pain of being the one to shatter Lily and Dylan's protected version of the world had, for Esther, been harder to leave behind.

The bigger truth with her mother, Esther reminded herself wryly, was that she adored Lucas. Just that morning she had flushed like a bashful teenager at his compliment on the chicness of her outfit, eyes sparkling, telling him he was talking nonsense. Except it wasn't nonsense. Her mother did look tremendous for her seventy years, Esther mused, affectionate admiration flooding her as she waited for Astrid to look her way again so she could smile to make the peace. It wasn't a day for battles.

As they all stood up to go, Esther's father nudged her elbow. 'You're off on holiday, Mum said. That's nice.'

'Yes, thanks, Dad. Tomorrow evening. I can't wait.' Out of the corner of her eye she was aware of Lucas pausing before leading the way out of the restaurant.

'Give our love to Viv, won't you?' Patrick went on fondly. 'It seems like only yesterday that you two were doing your homework together.'

'Doesn't it, just?'

He held out his arm and Esther looped hers through it. He had been typically quiet and sweet all day, waiting his turn to congratulate Lily, and seeking Dylan out for a few grandfatherly words on the walk to the lunch. The day was starting to take its toll though, Esther could tell, noting the post-lunch heaviness of his eyelids and guessing that as soon as their taxi had dropped them back at their Cambridge hotel he would be flat out having his afternoon snooze.

'What holiday?' said Lucas the moment they were all regrouping in the street.

'Just a few days in France.'

'Who with?'

Esther hesitated. He obviously hadn't heard the full exchange with her father. For a moment she was half tempted to hint at something more glamorous than falling back on the charity of her oldest friend. But the day had gone so well. 'I'm joining Viv and Brian for a few days. They've rented a place near Nice.'

'Well, I'll hold the fort with Dylan in that case.'

'Yes, you do that.' Esther almost laughed at the hint of self-sacrifice in his tone when Dylan was in his care anyway. It was a small reminder of how little he had changed, and, after the charm offensive of the day, she was grateful for it. Lucas cared about Lucas. End of.

Lily and Matteo were clearly eager to be gone. They had a party to get to – one to which they had invited Dylan – but all goodbyes stalled because of there being no sign of Astrid and Patrick's Uber despite its claim to have arrived. A glorious August Saturday afternoon, and the high street was a hive of shoppers, cyclists, and flocks of tourists following guides. Buffeted by one especially boisterous group, Lucas herded them all nearer the pavement edge as the hunt for the taxi continued. In the same instant, a woman, the last in a string of passing cyclists, hopped off a sleek silver bike and onto the pavement, hoicking the bike with her.

'Hey, Lucas. Hello, everyone. Congratulations, Lily.' The woman swung herself back astride the saddle as she talked, balancing easily on long, muscled legs, shown off to excellent effect in very short cut-off jeans. She folded her arms loosely across a tight vest under which there appeared to be nothing so dull as a bra. A helmet perched on top of the long, gleaming, dark-brown hair, slowing the dawning realisation that this racehorse of a creature, hitherto only ever glimpsed in a photo, was Heidi.

It was Lily's day, Esther reminded herself weakly, suppressing a wave of visceral dismay. With the pavement so crowded, there was no easy escape. Lucas, meanwhile, ramrod straight, like the awkward host at an awkward party, stepped forward to deposit a kiss on Heidi's cheek before using a sweep of his arm to introduce her to them all, galloping through Esther's and her parents' names and saying jokily that of course she knew the other three.

Astrid and Patrick quickly returned their attention to Patrick's phone and the quest for their driver, while Heidi issued a volley of questions about the ceremony and the meal, addressing Lily, who answered sweetly but with sufficient brevity to suggest that she had no desire to prolong the encounter. Esther could have hugged her. Throughout the interrogation Lily hung on Matteo's arm while Dylan stood a little behind, both hands rammed deep in the pockets of the loaned, too-baggy trousers. Only Lucas stayed close to the bicycle and its chattering owner, but with a look of such studied casualness that Esther was tempted to reach out and poke him in the ribs – anything to make the façade collapse.

'There he is!' Astrid cried, jabbing a finger across the road, saving them all. 'The silver one behind the bus, Patrick, do you see?'

'I do indeed. He'll get a ticket there if he's not careful.'

'Well, it is time for me to go,' Heidi announced with the ebullience of a chat-show host. 'Nice to meet you, everybody.' Her eyes moved over their faces, hovering briefly on Esther's before dropping point-edly to the hand gripping the handlebar, her left hand, on the ring finger of which sat a sapphire the size of a gobstopper, circled by diamonds.

There was no time to consider who else had noticed. With the taxi located, they were a tableau coming to life: Heidi pushing off back onto the street, Matteo, Lily, and Dylan hugging hasty thank yous and good-byes, Esther then escorting Patrick and Astrid over the road.

By the time she returned, only Lucas remained on the kerb, hands plugged into his pockets in a stance so strikingly reminiscent of Dylan's that the clever quip she had planned flew from her mind. 'Congratula-tions to you and Heidi are clearly in order.'

'Esther, I was going to tell you...'

'Why? It's your life, Lucas. I can assure you I don't give a damn how you choose to live it.'

'Frankly, my dear, I don't give a damn...' he muttered.

'Precisely. The children are the only thing I care about. Hence being here today. And I will be at Dylan's graduation *when* he gets that far. And at their weddings, and christenings of future grandchildren. Apart from that, I am done.'

'Yes, Esther.' He spoke tiredly. 'I believe that remains true for both of us.'

'So, do the children know? About you and Heidi getting...?' Esther found she could not quite utter the word.

'Not yet... unless they noticed.' He cleared his throat. 'It's rather recent, you see.'

'You must tell them.'

'Please be good enough, Esther, to refrain from telling me what to do. Of course I am going to tell them.'

'Straight away.'

'They've got a graduation party, for God's sake. I'll tell them tomorrow.'

'Or I could tell them.'

'Please don't do that.'

He was clenching his fists inside his pockets, Esther noticed, containing his irritation, and it made her wonder how he was with his *fiancée*, whether Heidi was good at extracting the treasures of trust and warmth that she had believed in herself once upon a time; whether the two of them were truly happy. No doubt their sex life was. Fireworks between the sheets. Lucas was good at those, as many could testify. Esther swallowed. She was so beyond all this, picking at the wound of hurt; but somehow, the thought of someone else making Lucas *happy* – of keeping him faithful – was surprisingly hard. 'How many were there, really?' she asked quietly.

'How many what?'

'You know what, Lucas.' It sickened her to be asking the old question again. But with the sapphire on Heidi's finger, it suddenly felt as if a portcullis were coming down.

Lucas groaned, as one bored of a familiar complaint. 'Really, Esther...'

'*Three*, you said. Around conferences, you said. Long since done with, and just for *sex*, you said, because of my patchy interest.' Her tone was snappy, but inside she was trembling, back in the thick of it. Emerging dazed from the college toilet that fateful day, believing Lucas to have retreated to hunker in his room on the floor below, she had found the mobile being snatched out of her hands. He wanted to explain, Lucas had pleaded, plunging the device into his pocket and launching into garbled explanations about periodically having lost his way, but now having truly found it again.

Esther was never allowed to set eyes on the mobile again, and in a way it hadn't mattered. She had seen enough. Half an hour of scrolling, hunched and weeping on the toilet seat, had drained any inclination or capacity to 'forgive' right out of her. Lucas had never been an easy husband; that he had been an unfaithful one too, took her to a place from where there was no retreat. The messages had been puerile, and often graphic, many wreathed in kisses, and relating to dates that went back several years; not one contained anything so incriminating as a name. The most recent – the one about missing him – was just a week old. But never replied to, Lucas had assured her during the course of his gabbling, still labouring under the delusion that any shred of 'proof' that his infidelities were behind him would ensure their eventual pardon. Having identified three numbers, Esther had tried calling each, but the phone battery had given out. With the dead gadget pressed against her ear, she had begun to feel numb. Their entire marriage was a lie. Almost worse was that Lucas's deceit hadn't made him nicer or more supportive as a husband – that for so many years he hadn't cared enough even to put on a *show* of trying.

'Come on, Lucas.' Esther could feel the sun, hot on the back of her head, building a pressure inside. 'Your last chance to tell me the truth. I mean, it hardly matters now, does it?'

'Esther, you are better than this.'

'*Me,* better?' The words came out as a screech and he took a step towards her, glancing anxiously at the people milling around them. There was such alarm in his expression that a sour laugh escaped her. Lucas hated a scene, almost as much as he hated talking about his childhood or his feelings, or anything else that truly mattered.

'Yes, I messed up,' he hissed. 'Big time. I admitted it often enough. Just as I tried to explain why.' For a moment he looked as if he might be on the verge of seizing her shoulders and giving her a good shake. 'I didn't want to give up, Esther. You did. What's more...' He took a breath. 'You have never acknowledged the part you played, how you made me feel...'

'How I *made* you feel?' Esther was laughing again, scornfully, shaking her head in disbelief.

'Yes, Esther. You stopped caring for me. You stopped wanting me. You used the children as a shield. I was desperate. The other women – and there *were* only three – they meant nothing—'

'Nothing? Really? All three? Poor them.' Esther felt buoyant. She had him pinned, she realised. He could have walked away, but he was still here, still glaring at her. It felt like a new shift in power, towards her. 'You were true to one thing, anyway, Lucas, I'll give you that.'

'Oh, yes?' For an instant his brilliant green eyes had the look of a hopeful, guilty schoolboy.

'The fact that married men prefer not to leave their wives for their lovers.' Genuine bafflement altered his expression and the buoyancy left her. Their very first date – all that wise counsel of his about Stephen Goddard – and he didn't even remember. 'It's always been one rule for you, Lucas, and another for the rest of the world.' She spun on her heel to stalk away, but then spun back again. 'But thanks for today. Lunch. That was generous. I promise I am done with questions. I wish you and Heidi well. Truly.'

Dramatic exit in tatters, Esther traipsed off in the direction of the NCP where she had left the car, trying not to limp in case Lucas was watching.

In the car, she sat for a few moments, kicking off her shoes and letting her heart settle, contemplating the notion that she had spent two decades trying to look after three children, not two. A proper partner in life was what she needed. What she deserved. Lucas was the only planet in his own private universe, and Heidi was welcome to him. Absently, she reached for the slim, cardboard package that she had tossed onto the passenger seat. It had an easy pull-tab for opening. Inside there was no accompanying note, just a small box of ten hand-made dark chocolates, containing – so the blurb boasted – a variety of nut and marzipan fillings.

Esther did not like dark chocolate, or nuts in chocolate, or marzi-pan; and the chocolates had melted and resolidified into misshapen versions of their original glory. Even so, she put one in her mouth before turning the engine on, feeling the fizz of the sugar on her tongue. Sitting in the clogged one-way system a few minutes later, she reached for another. Before long, her own system was humming and ten little paper wrappers were scattered on the passenger seat. The lack of message meant Chris Mews had to be the guilty sender, but so what? An attractive man liked her, and that was not nothing. Even if she had chosen not to like him back.

10

Lucas watched Esther merging into the crowd, tracking her pink dress until it was a speck, before turning for the walk back to his flat. It felt like a new, much-needed finality. Yet, as ever, she had managed to leave him feeling bad. Esther always did, Lucas reflected gloomily. Self-righteously and forensically picking over his failings, that was Esther's way, while somehow never factoring in her own. He kicked at an empty plastic bottle rolling across the pavement, throwing an embarrassed smile at the elderly woman who promptly picked it up and put it in a nearby bin.

Yes, he had messed up big time, but there had been *reasons*. But even after those long, endless months and months of sleepless nights were finally behind them, Esther had often carried on falling asleep on the sofa-bed in the children's room, laying claim to the moral high ground by citing exhaustion from whatever domestic challenges had been going on during the day. Lucas's own fatigue, meanwhile, brought on by working his socks off to keep food on the table and the bills paid, had never seemed to count for anything or to elicit sympathy; not even during the early, hardest baby years, when he sleepwalked through his lectures half the time, spouting his notes like an automaton. In fact, Esther had *weaponised* motherhood, Lucas concluded viciously, rather pleased with the thought and how it justified the consolation he had eventually taken to seeking – discreetly and sporadically – albeit over a period of time the length of which was rather less justifiable. Yet, no deceiver could have been more careful or more *considerate* either, finding equally discreet partners for his liaisons, none of them based in his home town, and each as keen as he was for excitement and distraction rather than any sort of full-on relationship. That Lucas had got so good at spotting such partners was one of the reasons it had proved a hard habit to break; but never once had he wanted to leave Esther, or end the marriage. Indeed, to have been found out when he'd believed all of it really was well and truly behind him remained a twist of bad luck so darkly ironic that Lucas still found it hard to contemplate without pain. The bloody mobile. He had briefly charged it for one last look before destroying the SIM, and then not quite got around to it.

Caught in a crowd waiting for a pedestrian light to go green, Lucas swayed a little as an echo of the old despair stirred: watching Esther drive away, the tops of her and Dylan's fair heads just visible over the luggage. Only the presence of his chalk-faced daughter, standing stiffly in the doorway behind him, had stopped him falling to the ground and howling like a dog.

But now he had Heidi. His fiancée. Happiness pumped through his veins. The night before, returning from the bathroom to find him on bended knee with the ring box open on his palm, she had cried, 'Yes please, Lucas!' before he had even got the words out. 'Yes, yes, yes, yes,' she had repeated, between hauling him to his feet and kissing his face and gazing, transfixed, at the glittering blue jewel that slid easily onto her finger, so big it looked like a bauble on the hand of a little girl.

Recalling Heidi's handling of the recent encounter outside Wilsons, the sheer chutzpah of the woman, Lucas chuckled to himself. Maybe she had engineered the whole thing, he mused as he moved with the swarm across the road. That his fiancée had balls was one of the many things he loved about her. But Esther was right: the children needed to be talked to properly about the situation, maybe over brunch at his the following morning, Lucas decided, swerving left for the Tesco Express near his flat. Once they had slept off their partying. He composed a shopping list in his head as he walked: sausages, some of them veggie for Lily, eggs, bacon for Dylan, wholemeal bread, milk, an organic juice.

Waiting in the queue with his basket of groceries, Lucas messaged Heidi with exclamation marks and a string of heart emojis, telling her to have a lovely time with the girlfriends she was seeing that night, and then wrote to Dylan and Lily about the brunch plan. His phone buzzed a few moments later, but it was only Claire Moore, the College Chaplain, asking if he could stop by first thing on Monday morning. Surprised, wondering if his take-no-prisoners girlfriend could already be pursuing the idea of using the college chapel for their nuptials, Lucas replied at once to say yes. The chapel was famously ancient and exquisite, and Heidi, lying in his arms after they had made love the previous evening, had expressed a strong interest in its feasibility as a venue. She could marry him wherever she wanted, Lucas had declared joyfully.

'Having a good day?' asked the girl at the checkout as Lucas set his basket down.

'I am indeed, thank you.'

'There's a bar of chocolate if you buy one of these.' She tapped a stack of newspapers.

'No, thanks, I have all I need.'

And I really do, Lucas mused, whistling under his breath as he stepped back out into the August sunshine, swinging his bag as he strode back towards his flat.

11

It was nearly seven o'clock by the time Esther turned into her street. The heat of the day had built into the evening, and for the stop-start sluggish London traffic she had wound down both front windows, ensuring early warning of the fact that Dimitri and Sue's party was already in full swing. No wonder she'd received an invitation. By the sound of things, they'd have been wise to invite the entire road.

More immediately distracting was the sight of an ambulance, blue light flashing, parked in the slot outside her house. Esther quickly pulled into a space opposite and hopped out of the car. In the same instant, Carmela's door flew open and two paramedics emerged carrying a stretcher bearing someone who was clearly her elderly neighbour, despite the blanket pulled up to her neck and oxygen mask covering her face. The motorcyclist with whom she had almost collided that morning was at their heels, tugging anxiously on his beard as he talked animatedly into his phone.

Esther paused halfway down her path, wanting to express concern, but awkward at the realisation of how little she knew of a woman who had lived just a few yards from her for almost two years. That Carmela had to be in her seventies, owned an intimidating cat, and liked to shove her wheelie bin into Esther's corner of their shared allocated space seemed suddenly a pitiful sum total of knowledge. She ventured a glance of sympathy at the biker, who promptly hurdled the little rusty wire fence separating the properties and strode towards her. He was in black jeans, ripped above one knee in a way that didn't look quite intended, and a shapeless white T-shirt. He was clearly panic-stricken, his dark eyes darting.

'Whatever has happened, I'm so sorry...' Esther began, faltering as he shook his head grimly.

'Stroke *and* a heart attack, they reckon. It's taken them an hour to stabilise her. I'm just glad I was on a visit. My work takes me away, so I can't come often. She's my aunt.' He spoke at speed, throwing a dazed look at the ambulance, now having its rear doors opened. 'One minute she was perfectly fine – I was just going to the corner shop for some groceries – next thing I know... could I ask a favour, do you think?'

'Of course. Anything.'

'The cat. Would you mind keeping an eye out for it? I'm not sure exactly when I'll be back, and she was worried because apparently it didn't show up for breakfast. There's a flap, so he comes and goes as he pleases. I've left food down. What he loves best of all is milk, but she'd run out and—'

'Cat. Milk. No problem.'

'Amazing.' The ambulance doors were slamming. 'You'll need these. They're spares.' He tossed a set of keys at her. 'I'm Marcus, by the way.'

'Esther. But I'm going away,' Esther cried, only just remembering her holiday. 'Not until tomorrow evening though,' she added quickly, as his eyes flared with dismay. 'Don't worry, I'll get Dimitri and Sue to help out. They're on the other side.' She shook the keys in the direction of her partying neighbours, where the musical soundtrack had thank-fully receded to a muffled thump. 'They're really nice.'

'Yep, we've met a couple of times. I was going to ask them, till you showed up.' The paramedics were clambering into the front seats.

'Go,' she commanded, 'and don't worry about Chico, we'll all keep a lookout.'

Marcus leapt back over the fence and within seconds was shooting after the vehicle on his motorbike.

In the quiet of her hallway, Esther leant back against the door and took a few deep breaths. It had been a long day. To be in her own home suddenly felt like the height of luxury; as did being alive, for that matter, given what her poor neighbour had to be going through. Milk duty could wait just a little, she decided, starting the fight with her back zip as she headed upstairs. She shook the dress off as she entered her bedroom, kicking it into a pink puddle in the middle of the carpet and pulling on jeans and a T-shirt instead. Through her bedroom window, the sunshine had receded to a milky evening light, lending a glamorous silver tinge to the jungled green chaos of her garden. After France she would get to grips with it, Esther vowed, craning her neck for a better view of the quietened festivities taking place next door, and making out the tail end of a line of people, including several exuberant children, clutching plates and queueing from the direction of the patio. Whatever was being served up smelt very good, she had to admit, despairing at her appetite, surging again despite her gorging on Chris's sickly chocolates.

Five Minutes' Peace. The name of an early favourite bedtime story of the children's drifted to mind as she sank into her armchair a few minutes later, taking her phone and a mug of tea with her, boosted liberally with sugar as well as milk because self-denial had its limits. The story's bright witty pictures of the elephant mummy sinking into a bath with a piece of cake, leaving the mayhem of her family life to its own devices, had made her toddling Dylan and Lily giggle every time.

Esther sighed a little wistfully and checked her mobile, finding nothing significant except a very welcome payment notification from her healthcare company client, and a thank-you note for the day from her parents. Not a murmur from Chris Mews, she noted with relief. Esther set her empty mug on the floor and closed her eyes as she tipped her head back against the soft velveteen cover, letting the biggest news of the day swim back into focus. Lucas remarrying. It was only right that he should deal with telling the children, and impossible to guess how they would feel. If there was any fallout, she would know soon enough. An image of the young German woman formed; a Queen Bee perched on her high-tech bicycle, toned and triumphant, calling the shots. Heidi from Heidelberg. Esther snorted, pushing herself out of the chair to see about the milk and the cat. Lucas and the woman were welcome to each other. All she had to do was rise high above it. Very high. And stay there.

Carmela's porch light flicked on helpfully the moment she neared the door. Feeling like a trespasser, Esther gingerly turned the key in the lock and stepped inside. A faintly acrid, fishy smell greeted her, along with a décor that momentarily took her back to visits to her maternal grandparents as a little girl: faded, busy carpeting, tobacco-coloured walls, cumbersome square furniture, draped with crocheted blankets and stained antimacassars. As she ventured from room to room, however, the comparison quickly dissolved under the barrage of religious prints and trinkets arraigned across every wall and shelf of Carmela's ground floor: bleeding Christs, tacky crucifixes, mournful Madonna figurines cradling rosaries seemed to track Esther's every move, weighing down her heart on her neighbour's behalf. The house was so dark, so heavy. There was no joy. Apart from the beloved pet, of course. The realisation flooded her with a fresh sense of urgency about the mission. Spotting a mixing bowl in the drainer, she filled it almost to the brim from the carton she had brought and set it down right next to the cat flap. Unable to locate a key for the back door, she then put the milk carton on the counter and dropped onto all fours, poking her head as far as she could through the flap and frantically emitting her best renditions of the cat-summoning squeaks she had heard so often through the wild tumbles of yellow roses.

Defeated, she checked upstairs, finding the same heavy furniture and furnishings, though the rooms were less cluttered and more peaceful. What tore at her heart, however, was the upright chair parked by every window, as if the world had become something to sit and watch rather than feel a part of. She carried on chirruping, checking inside wardrobes and under beds, and at one point warily lifting a counterpane to examine a lump that turned out to be a folded paisley dressing gown.

Re-crossing the landing to head back downstairs, she heard the strains of a guitar and singing float in from outside. Esther paused to check through the porthole window identical to her own, contorting her neck to ascertain that the party had entered a new, mellower phase, involving an encampment of outdoor lamps and figures sprawled on blankets. She began to hum along softly, recognising the tune, only to find her throat swelling and the encampment blurring. The loneliness of Carmela. It was unspeakable suddenly. Unforgivable. Thank God for the visiting nephew. If her neighbour made it out of hospital, she would try harder, she vowed; she would *care*. Offer to do the occasional grocery shopping, stop by for a chat – how hard could that be? She would certainly hope for no less if a similar state of solitude were to afflict her own old age.

Esther stared out at the clouds gathering in the sky beyond the railway track, bruised by the setting sun. It was actually impossible to believe such a fate awaited her, but then, she realised with a start, it almost certainly wasn't what Carmela had planned either. Life could shove you in all sorts of unexpected directions, some terrible, some good. As at the extraordinary family lunch that day: Lucas and her conversing like companionable relatives; Lily radiant; dear Dylan bravely rising out of his doldrums; her parents at their most endearing.

Until it had all gone awry in the street afterwards. Esther put her hands on either side of the window, leaning into the wall and breathing hard. What an idiot, imagining Lucas would ever admit to anything. She pushed off from the wall and then stepped forwards as a glimpse of movement through the window caught her eye, in her own garden this time – a flitting tall shadow on the patio, disappearing immediately under the lee of Carmela's window ledge.

On trembling legs, she flew back down the staircase and out of the house, forgetting her milk carton, only just remembering to double-lock the door. Adrenalin pumped so hard that her chest hurt, until she found herself charging through her own house, switching on lights, and shouting, 'Who goes there?' like some madwoman in an ancient play. Only as she flung open her back door, confronting the darkness of the garden, did she come to a halt, eyes and ears straining, the hairs on her arms and neck risen and rigid. Next door the party was rumbling on. If attacked, she would scream, Esther consoled herself wildly; Dimitri and Sue would hear her and all would be well. The garden sat, a hunched hulk in the dark. The patio was empty. Next door, the guitarist had started on 'You've Got a Friend.'

'Oh, my goodness sweetheart, well of course I'll ask,' exclaimed Sue in her easy way, a few minutes later, ushering Esther, still in full breathless flow about the reason for presenting herself on the doorstep, into the house. 'Right this minute. Come on through. I hope we haven't been making too much noise. What about a drink? You look all shook up.'

'No, thanks, Sue, I'm okay.' Esther followed her neighbour through to the room at the back of the house, where open sliding doors led onto a handsome square of crazy paving. On its left under a rampant tangle of honeysuckle was a large barbecue, its rack greasy and blackened, the embers beneath it smoking gently. Opposite, leaving a wide corridor for access to the garden, were two trestle tables, loaded with used plates, bottles, glasses, and dishes of half-eaten food. 'I just thought it worth asking before I decide whether to call the police,' Esther muttered, embarrassment overcoming her as Sue marched past the tables and clapped her hands, causing the occupants of the picnic blankets to turn their way.

'Of course, pet, of course,' Sue said mildly, clapping again to stop the final threads of conversation. 'This is Esther, who lives next door.' She spoke clearly, but in a slightly lowered tone, mouthing the words in an exaggerated way. 'She thinks someone might have been in her garden...' she paused, to point in the relevant direction '...and was wondering if anyone had noticed anything.'

There were murmurs. A couple of people trotted over to spy through the gaps in the fence; but then a lanky youth scrambled to his feet, looking anguished and uncertain. 'Actually, I kicked a ball over,' he confessed in a sheepish staccato voice clearly still in search of its adult register. 'I used the fence post to climb in and get it. Sorry, Sue.'

'Sorry *Esther*, more like it, Justin, love.' Sue had at some point taken hold of Esther's hand, and was continuing to hold it in a way that should have felt odd, but which was actually rather comforting. 'And that happened just now, did it? Because Esther here has had the fright of her life and needs to know whether to call the police.'

'Yeah, like, maybe ten minutes.' The boy was cringing more visibly thanks to jokey boos and hisses now emanating from his audience. 'That's right, isn't it, Ewan?' he croaked, directing the appeal at a smaller teenager who was sitting nearby, cross-legged and head bowed, busy plucking at bits of grass.

'Yep... I guess...' The younger boy broke off to swipe back at a girl who had poked him in the ribs.

'Okay, thank you, boys,' trilled Sue. 'Mystery solved. As you were, everybody. And Justin and Ewan, a big sorry to Esther please, for scaring her out of her wits.'

The two boys mumbled meek apologies.

'It's fine, really. Thanks.' Esther smiled at the sea of faces. She felt faintly stupid, as well as deeply tired.

'Dim will go to yours and have a proper look-see all the same, won't you, Dim?' Sue insisted briskly as the party hubbub restarted, and Dimitri, who had been one of the ones to look through the fence, came hopping towards them, pulling on his trainers. 'What a horrible scare after your special day, eh?' She rubbed the arm of the hand she was still holding. 'Esther looked like she'd seen a ghost, Dimmy. Was it lovely though, Esther, the graduation?' she went on, once Dimitri had loped on ahead of them through the house, to fetch a torch, he said.

'Oh yes, it was, but...' Esther reclaimed her hand and explained about poor Carmela.

'Oh, the poor love,' Sue said softly, 'that's terrible. He's a good man, Marcus, *when* he comes. And of course, we'll do our bit with the cat while you're away. There was a husband once, apparently, years ago.'

'Poor Carmela,' Esther whispered, feeling again the shame of her own ignorance and a rush of fondness for Sue, always so open-hearted despite going through who knew what with the baby quest she had mentioned on the doorstep.

'All set, ladies,' announced Dimitri, bounding down the stairs and brandishing a hefty black torch. 'No time to lose.'

'You give him your keys and stay here,' Sue instructed at once, opening the front door for him and talking over Esther's efforts at protest. 'Hurry now, love, and *no* heroics,' she called as he raced off. 'He'll be able to get out the back, will he?' she asked Esther.

'Oh yes... in fact, I think I may even have left the door open,' Esther admitted feebly.

Sue laughed. 'What you need, Esther love, is a small brandy and a cup of tea.'

12

Staying at Jakes. D

Lucas examined his son's message through a swirling exhalation of smoke, trying not to mind about the lack of apostrophe. Three drags and an enjoyable floating sensation was filling his head. It had been over thirty years, and he had never been a regular partaker – alcohol having been his preferred student drug of choice – but the spliff contained decent stuff. Lucas summoned an image of Jake to mind before tapping out his reply, recalling an earnest, likeable boy from Dylan's secondary days, who had got top grades and been a fearless, if not always effective, goalkeeper.

Ok. But 9 o clock sharp tomorrow morning. As AGREED. Dad

Lucas began to type *I love you* but deleted it, fearing the urge to gush was the weed talking. Of course, he loved Dylan. He had said as much that very morning during the course of the brunch, which had gone even more smoothly than he had dared hope, thanks in part to Dylan doing his new thing of taking over the cooking and making an excellent job of it, crisping the bacon to perfection and finding mushrooms and tomatoes to add to the feast. Yes, both his children had admitted shyly, exchanging conspiratorial looks across his small dining room table, they had spotted Heidi's laden ring finger. But no, they weren't surprised, only pleased for him, and totally cool about the whole thing. Lucas had lost a little fluency in delivering assurances that Esther would always be their mother, but his drift was quickly acknowledged and the awkwardness left behind. Lucas had said how much he loved them both and they had said it right back. There had been goodbye hugs at the door, along with the concession that Dylan could remain off the revision hook until the following morning. All in all, it had been perfect, as Lucas had relished reporting to Esther before deciding to have this small, private celebration of his own.

He drew again on the reefer, more carefully now because he was in danger of scalding his lips. He wished he could capitalise on Dylan's overnight absence by seeing Heidi, but the evening with girlfriends had been arranged long before. There would be other chances to be together now, thousands of them, Lucas reminded himself. *Fiancée.* He said the word softly under his breath, and then more loudly, proclaiming it to the room.

Getting Dylan over the line with the re-sits was the only hurdle on the horizon and Heidi, thankfully, was totally on board with that. The importance of academic endeavour was the last thing that needed explaining to his fiancée. And maybe his son would share that understanding too. Soon. The stub of the spliff fizzed as Lucas ran it under the tap before dropping it into the bin. Maybe Dylan would even thank him, one day. In the meantime, he would astonish him with his patience, Lucas vowed. He would not lose his rag. He would be encouraging and positive, just as he was, so effortlessly, with his actual students. It would be a new leaf for both of them.

ABROAD

13

The fish sparkled on their beds of ice across the market stalls, silver, pink, grey, their gills and tails still twitching. Some of them were veritable monsters of the deep, and with bemused expressions on their faces as if, Esther decided, her heart going out to them, their minds were still half on whatever business they had been about when the fishermen's nets snatched them from the water. Beside her, in a floppy straw hat and faded gingham shorts, her black bikini top visible through her white linen T-shirt, Viv showed no sign of such sentimentality, bargaining with the vendor standing guard over a vast barrel of mussels in her enviably fluent French.

They were to have the mussels for a late lunch, in white wine and herbs, along with hunks of the wholemeal sourdough bread Brian had made that morning, baking rather than *cooking* being a new passion, as he'd explained when Esther had bent close to admire the loaf. 'I like to do things well if I can,' he'd admitted simply. 'It's good to have you out here, Esther,' he had added warmly, giving her a quick half-hug with one arm. 'We should have done it long ago.'

Esther followed Viv as she moved along towards the meat stalls, aware of walking in the relative cool of her shadow and also of a dreamy state of relaxation of which she had forgotten herself capable.

just the manner of finding out that was somewhat galling, on that day of all days. The children are apparently fine about it, though, and that is all that matters.'

'And you being all right, that matters too.'

'I *am* all right,' Esther insisted, slightly riled again because Viv was doing her staring thing, peering over the top of her sunglasses.

'I think you still miss him.'

'I do not miss Lucas, and you saying so is unhelpful.'

'Ice cream?' Viv had stopped by a youth who was sitting next to a makeshift board of prices, propped up against a large ice box. 'He's got Magnums.'

'Yes, please. Thanks.'

'You are so ready to meet someone, Esther,' she went on mildly as they dropped their wrappers into a bin and drifted on.

'I thought I didn't need someone to *complete* me?'

'You don't. But then again, I know how tough you've been finding it... and this business of imagining seeing people when there's no one there,' she went on, quickly switching to a much lighter tone, 'a classic sign of subconscious companionship-seeking surely...'

'There *was* someone – a boy collecting his football,' Esther protested, laughing in spite of herself.

'But there were those other times, you said, in the garden.'

'A couple of weird moments... Viv, what is this? I feel like I'm being told off. And I *have* been trying to meet someone, as you well know.'

'You have. Violinists and gift-senders. Sorry, Es.' She smiled apologetically. 'It's only because I know how lonely you get, sweetie, not to mention how life-enhancing the right partner in life can be, how supportive...' She stopped, clearly not wanting to brag about Brian. They had arrived at the little clifftop car park where the taxi that had brought them was to pick them up. There was a perimeter wall facing the valley. Viv leant against it, twiddling her Magnum stick and still looking pensive. 'But maybe it's time to throw a bit more money at the cause? There are some good sites, but they cost.'

'Not a lot of money to throw at anything at the moment, Vivvie, but

Day three of not having to be in control. Not having to make decisions. It was bliss. They had also been tasked with the purchase of chicken and sausages for that evening's barbecue, a subject discussed with vigour during the course of a hearty breakfast of pastries, sliced straw-berries, kiwi, and platefuls of scrambled eggs. The family's easy collec-tive capacity to eat ravenously while discussing future meals had reinforced Esther's appreciation of what a coherent unit it was. As the house guest – the outsider – she had felt some awkwardness about joining in, dropping her gaze to her plate and dabbing at the croissant flakes with a fingertip while fighting off an unedifying ripple of envy.

It was the force of Viv herself that made everything work, Esther had decided, leaving the table to see to the washing-up. Brian might bake bread and be devising a grand kayaking trip for the morning, but it was Viv who quietly inserted the provisos about beds being made first and Finn and Amber sitting out the treat this time in order to make inroads into their respective holiday work assignments. She had emerged with a cool bag of drinks to join the final moments of the send-off in the drive, looking strikingly petite beside her children – all lanky, like their father – and praising Brian's expert strapping of three bright yellow kayaks to the roof-rack of the hire car, between issuing reminders to the younger two about not taking their phones and remembering to reapply sun-cream.

'I know you don't want to talk about it,' Viv said now, placing a fat parcel of meat on top of the fish bundles as they left the market.

'That's not true. I *have* talked about it,' Esther cried, knowing immediately to what she was referring, 'just as I have all the other scin-tillating things that have been going on in my life.' She directed her gaze to the breathtaking view as the tic of annoyance passed. A medieval village on a hilltop. She had given up taking photos to try and do justice to it. Having a therapist for a best friend had its drawbacks as well as its benefits, she reminded herself, tracking the metallic glints of the river, which – somewhere – contained three yellow kayaks, as it wound its way along the lush foliage of the valley bed. 'I've told you – I am happy for Lucas *and* Heidi. Truly. Good luck to them both. It was thank you for caring. I'll think about it, okay?' Esther managed to catch the last blob of her own ice cream, inwardly still bristling, partly because of the earlier comment about Lucas, and partly because of the increasingly unwelcome sense that she was being told what to do. She couldn't work out whether Viv was being particularly pushy or whether it was just her being touchy and defensive. 'And anyway, I really do feel supported,' she quipped, thinking of the recent interactions with her neighbours. There had been a warm text from Sue that morning, telling her to have a happy holiday and reporting that, while there was no sign of the cat, Carmela was apparently holding her own in hospital.

'Ah, yes, Sue and Dimitri,' said Viv, with her customary quickness, 'they do sound special.'

'They are. And so are you – inviting me here. All of this.' Esther gestured at the sloping fields of maize and sunflowers, shimmering in the late morning sun, and the Pyrenees, a ghostly, snow-capped necklace on the horizon beyond. 'Letting me gate-crash your gorgeous family holiday. You lot sort of make me jealous, actually, but in a good way.'

'Jealousy is never good,' Viv murmured, getting up and waving at the taxi that had swung into the square. 'And by the way, on the dating business, be wary of quick judgements. I thought Brian was the opposite of what I wanted until we kissed, remember? One snog and I was a goner.'

'I'll bear that in mind.' Esther laughed as they clambered into the taxi.

They travelled in a companionable silence back down the narrow, zigzagging roads, the faint smell of the sea rising from Viv's basket.

14

The Master, perched behind her broad desk, her elegant, white bob and big, red-framed glasses making Lucas think of a small, outlandish bird. Behind the lenses she had the quick eyes of a bird too, strong and blue, but never settling. She got to her feet the moment he entered, smoothing the crumples out of her trouser suit and indicating for him to take a seat in one of the high-backed armchairs set at angles round the stone hearth, where two porcelain dogs guarded a set of fire irons and a wood basket that he had never once seen used. Above them, a gold-framed oil painting of the college founder, dressed in full academic regalia, stared imperiously towards the mullioned windows that overlooked the garden.

'You are well, I hope, Lucas?'

'Yes, Master, extremely, thank you.' Despite her short stature, she had a commanding manner. 'The long break is such a good opportunity to get some real work done,' Lucas added energetically, doing his best to fill the large and not very comfortable chair in the manner of one without a care in the world, crossing his legs and folding his arms across his beating heart.

'The Chaplain is running a few minutes late. Tea? Coffee?'

'Neither, thanks.' Lucas unfolded his arms. The inside of his mouth felt curiously sticky. 'Actually, a glass of water would be good,' he said, spotting a full jug sitting inside a circle of glasses on a tray, lemon slithers floating on its surface.

'Certainly.' The Master crossed the room, looking, Lucas couldn't help thinking, as if she was glad to have something to do other than not-talk about what they were going to have to talk about once Reverend Moore arrived. 'I hope you know, Master, that when Claire told me on Monday, I was stunned and appalled,' he burst out as the glass was handed to him; 'it is all total nonsense.'

He was thrown a brief, regretful smile. 'That is not a word we can, at this stage, consider using. *Nonsense.* But I do have every hope that we might clear things up quickly... ah, here she is,' she cried, with evident relief, as a knock on the door heralded the arrival of the College Chaplain.

'Claire, thank you for coming. Take a pew... if you'll pardon the expression.' They both laughed, and Lucas envied them. 'Tea?'

'No, Master, I'm fine, thanks. Lucas, hello.'

'Hello, Claire.' Lucas experienced a moment of longing for the conversation he had once imagined about using the chapel for his and Heidi's wedding. As it was, the spring in his step as he had bounded up the Chaplain's staircase two days before was like glimpsing a lost innocence. He drank deeply from his glass even though the water was showing no signs of easing the stickiness in his mouth. That the two women were clearly very much at ease with each other did nothing to lessen his discomfort. Indeed, it introduced the faint, unpleasant sensation of being outnumbered. *Women.* Everywhere. Changing things. Twisting things. With Edward Sinclair, the previous Master, at the helm, the entire sorry business would never have been allowed to proceed with such unwarranted formality, Lucas was sure. 'I need hardly say that all of this is absurd,' he reiterated bitterly. 'Utterly unnecessary. The girl clearly needs help...'

'And we are going to clear the matter up as soon as we can, Lucas,' the Master repeated evenly. 'However, I am sure you will also appreciate the need to take any accusation of this nature very seriously.

Crucially, and encouragingly...' she smiled at the Chaplain '... Moira has spoken only to Claire. We both remain hopeful, therefore, of sorting everything out without an official and more public complaint...'

'Good God... surely not.' Lucas fired a pleading look at the reverend, who did not respond, keeping an inscrutable expression fixed on the Master.

'As you are both aware, we have a college code for such matters,' the Master went on steadily, 'first pursuing a route through mediation, with the Senior Tutor—'

'The senior... you mean, getting Ralph involved? Surely that won't be necessary?' Lucas could not keep the thickening sneer from his voice. 'And as for *mediation*...' He sat forward, elbows on his knees cradling his glass, plumbing every remaining ounce of his patience to speak in a more measured tone. 'Look. Could we please just invite Moira in here to talk it through?'

'Moira has made it clear that she does not want to be in the same space as you,' remarked the Chaplain mildly, as if commenting on the weather rather than landing a blow so akin to a kick in his nether regions that Lucas gasped aloud.

'She... what? But this is farcical.' He threw himself back into the chair. 'She turned up at my rooms that day without any warning, asking for my opinion on some creative writing – which I very much did *not* want to give – only succumbing...' he immediately regretted the word, but pressed on '...because she was insistent and actually seemed to get pretty distressed when I tried to turn the idea down. I was doing *her* a favour,' he cried, breaking off abruptly at the realisation of having picked a poor phrase there too. The intense gazes of the women seated on either side of him felt like crossfire. 'Honestly, all I did was to try and help her.'

'Okay, Lucas, thank you. Meanwhile, I believe Moira has written a statement. Claire, could you perhaps read it out?'

Lucas released a small groan as the Chaplain extracted a folded piece of paper from the folds of her gown and started to read aloud. It began with Moira stating her full name and the date on which the encounter took place.

> '"...I knocked on Professor Shaw's door to make a quick enquiry but he insisted I come in and made me sit on the sofa. He said how happy he was to be interrupted by my visit and asked me to call him by his first name. It all felt kind of weirdly intense..."'

'I did not *make* her sit anywhere, and I tell all students to call me by my Christian name. As I said, this is ludicrous...'

The master held up her hand, her striking eyes now on fire with warning. 'We must hear what Moira Giddings has to say. Only then can we come to a view as to how to proceed. I understand completely that this is painful for you, Lucas. Trust me, nothing is at stake here except getting at the truth—'

'Nothing at stake?' Lucas thundered, with more volume than he had intended. 'And as for the truth, here it is: Moira Giddings barged her way into my rooms, pleaded with me to look at some pretty dire attempt at an opening chapter of a novel, to which I agreed with great reluctance and against my better judgement – purely because she seemed so upset when I refused. I kept my word, had a quick look, made some comments in the margins, and put the damn thing back in her pigeonhole the next day. End of story. I haven't heard a word from – or about – her since that day, not until Claire's summons on Monday. Perhaps,' he rushed on, ignoring the tight expressions on the faces of his audience, his brain galloping, 'it was my comments on her creative efforts that have set this in motion.' He dabbed a finger at a trickle of sweat running down his temple. 'Yep, I bet that's what this is all about. I was encouraging, naturally, but also pointed out a couple of pitfalls to watch out for... look, the girl has a delicate temperament. We all know that about Moira, right?' He sat forward, getting into his stride. 'That she was one of the really shy, struggling first years? In fact, Master, I had it in mind to talk to you about that very subject,' Lucas rushed on, seizing on the memory of this intention, 'how girls can still get swamped more easily than boys, how they need drawing out of themselves, and what we could do about it.' He slumped back in his chair, out of steam. There would be no response. They were merely waiting for him to finish. 'Sorry. As you say, this is not easy for me. Please, do go on.'

More beads of sweat were sliding down his temples, and he dug for his handkerchief to wipe them away properly. He had to keep his cool. He thought with horror of Heidi, probably already on her way to the tea house where they had agreed to meet prior to enjoying a walk along the river in the sunshine. A cloudy morning had cleared into an exquisite August day. They were going to find a lovely spot and have a video call with her family to discuss their big news. They were going to talk dates and venues.

'I, too, am truly sorry about this situation, Lucas,' the Master said, raising a hand to keep Claire from launching straight back into the statement. 'You will of course be invited to make your own statement. To put your side.' She sighed with what sounded like genuine compassion. 'The point, it seems to me, is that there is no way *round* this situation, only a way *through*, which we shall find, I promise you.'

'You're right about Moira struggling,' put in the Chaplain helpfully. 'One of those with a fear of falling short.'

'Exactly,' Lucas agreed glumly, 'but she seemed fine that afternoon.'

'I thought you said she was upset.'

'Well, she *got* upset...' He faltered, remembering Moira's striking, and uncharacteristic, choice of clothes that day, but quickly judging it to be too much of a potentially explosive observation to share. This was a minefield, and he was going to need all his wits to navigate it. 'That was why I agreed to look at her writing.'

'Shall we continue hearing her statement?' said the Master smoothly.

Lucas hunkered down deeper into his chair, wanting only to plug his ears as the words continued to fall from the reverend's mouth, each sentence more dreadful than the last. How he had told Moira he was *her man*. How he had called her his *sweetheart*. How when he sat on the sofa arm, he had brushed against her chest. 'I did none of these things,' he blurted, unable to bear the litany a moment longer. 'I did not say one inappropriate word or lay so much as a finger on her.' Lucas delivered the sentence as a solemn declaration, while inwardly suppressing a new panic that maybe – maybe – Moira had dressed to be taken notice of by him that day. Maybe he had been a lamb intended for this slaughter. The Chaplain, with a nod from the master, resumed her reading.

'"He swore me to secrecy, about the visit, about his help…"'

'Well, yes, I did,' Lucas interjected helplessly. 'Purely because I didn't want all my students thinking I was open to giving a literary leg-up. Is that so unreasonable?' Neither woman spoke. And after a moment or two, Claire continued reading.

* * *

'Lucas!' Heidi stood up to wave from the back corner of the tea room. 'I wanted outside, but there were no free tables,' she explained, pulling a mock sad face as he arrived at her side. 'I have an apple juice, but you would like tea?'

'I love you,' he murmured, kissing her cheek before sitting down, having to squeeze into the chair because of a buggy parked by the neighbouring table. The occupant of the buggy, ruddy-cheeked, hair in ringlets, was using both hands to press a chocolate muffin against her mouth, sucking rather than eating it.

'Isn't she cute?' Heidi fluttered her fingers at the baby. 'But how has your day been, Liebchen? Your home-schooling A level student, is he – how did you say it? – *buckling down*?' Her beautiful eyes danced. She was a lighthouse of happiness, on full beam. Only a fool would want to interrupt it.

'He is, thank you.' Lucas managed a smile, picturing Dylan as he had left him, seated at the dining-room table with his laptop and a revision timetable sketched out on a piece of paper beside him. It already sported a couple of ticks, even if they were being overrun by the webs of intricate doodling that drove Lucas mad. If there were a uni course in daydreaming, that would be the dream ticket, he had teased, earning a long-suffering scowl from his son. 'I'll make a scholar of him yet,' he told Heidi, glad to latch onto something real and important beyond the other subject burning a hole in his head. 'And what about you? How was the PhD student from Canada? Sofia Cofie, wasn't it?' He smiled harder, glad his state of preoccupation hadn't prevented him from summoning the right name.

'Yes, and, Lucas, I think she will be super fun to supervise. Really smart.' Heidi talked on, between sips of her apple juice.

All would be fine, of course. In the end. The Master had communicated as much in the firm grip of her parting handshake, holding on for an extra second of what had felt like a display of trust in him. He was to write up his version of events, and Moira would be talked to again by the Chaplain, about all the options, including the possibility of further discussions rather than actual mediation. This was the outcome Lucas longed for. The prospect of Ralph Conway, whom he counted as a close friend – or any other fellow – getting involved was intolerable.

So much for his efforts to be kind to the girl, Lucas brooded as Heidi left him to join the queue for the café's toilet. If he erred on the side of informality with students, it was only because it made interactions on both sides more free-flowing and rewarding. Never once, in two decades, had such an approach rebounded. Indeed, every single student under his tutelage to date, on finding themselves in Moira's position that day, would have simply skipped off feeling fortunate and enthused.

But then each life was a self-written narrative these days, Lucas reminded himself bitterly, with possessive pronouns attaching to notions of 'truth' and everybody busily curating versions of themselves, tinderboxes all for taking offence – chanting about rights to be 'heard' and 'seen', when all that was really being chased was a chunk of the limelight...

Lucas blinked the bustling café back into focus. Even to think so condemningly felt like a crime. The baby smothered in chocolate was staring at him hard, as if she saw into the heart of his iniquity. Lucas widened his eyes in return, making his thick eyebrows dance and pulling a funny face till she giggled. The father noticed and smiled gratefully. Lucas smiled back, feeling calmer. The world, for all its trip-wires and failings, was still, mostly, a friendly place. Only Moira Giddings didn't like him. Only Moira Giddings, for some reason, wanted to see him torn to shreds.

Ten minutes later, they were settled on a park bench, Heidi in the crook of his arm with her laptop balanced on her knees, conversing with a gallery of four smiling faces, and occasionally a fifth, when Heidi's much younger eighteen-year-old brother, Stefan, bobbed into view. Lucas had met her parents, Klaus and Erica, a couple of times in the past, and had always found them very welcoming. Engaged and energetic, running what was clearly a very successful leisurewear company, they exuded the same warm and business-like air as their daughter. The family already knew of the engagement, Heidi having – at her own request – broken the news to her parents over the weekend. Everyone was thrilled, she had assured Lucas. Even so it was a relief to see their beaming faces for himself and to enjoy the gratifying oohs and aahs when Heidi waggled her show-stopping ring.

'You know what you are taking on with Heidi, yes?' joked Klaus, in his brittle, excellent English. 'She has the iron will.'

'Yes, she does indeed, Klaus, and that is one of the many reasons I want – and am honoured – to become her husband. The biggest mystery to all of us is why she accepted me.' Both his future parents-in-law burst into laughter, after which the joke needed to be translated for Heidi's grandparents, Elsa and Heinrich, whose slightly bemused, healthily weathered faces, topped with shocks of thick white hair and side by side on the screen, resembled portraits of sibling twins. They were keen hikers, Heidi had reported fondly, describing how they regularly walked their two German shepherds up the famous mini-mountain called the Drachenfels near their Bad Godesberg home. One of the dogs appeared now, putting paws the size of spades on the lap of Heinrich, who seized one, waggling it in salutation at Heidi and Lucas. A volley of quickfire conversation in German ensued, giving Lucas the chance to check on the time, and for his stomach to heave at the prospect of the conversation that would follow the end of the call. He wouldn't be able to dither either, since it was almost one o' clock and he had promised Dylan he would pick up something interesting for lunch. He did his best to maintain an expression of engagement while the on-screen exchanges continued, reminding him of the full extent of the language barrier, a fact from which Heidi's and her parents' fluency had always afforded protection.

He would learn German, he decided, nodding and smiling without comprehension when they all laughed. Dylan still had his GCSE books. He could use those and get Dylan to help him. It would make a refreshing change to flip the teacher-pupil, father-son relationships on their head – to demonstrate how learning never ended and should be a part of life and not something driven at solely for the purpose of passing exams. Even Esther would struggle to pick holes in such a plan.

Heidi snapped her laptop shut and stood up the moment the family farewells were done. 'Now for me it is the library,' she said, looping her arm through his as they walked the few yards back to the park gates. 'And you don't have to accompany me,' she laughed when Lucas kept hold of her arm, turning left with her instead of right, towards his flat. 'I know you must get home for Dylan. For these weeks he is the priority, right? We have agreed.'

'Yes – Heidi darling – we have, and thank you, but...' Lucas was aware of his palms turning damp and his heart sprinting. He didn't *need* to tell her, did he? But they had sworn honesty, and he was innocent. 'Actually, Liebchen, there is something I need to talk to you about...' A frog in his throat refused to clear and he had to cough several times. 'An unpleasant something, that just needs...'

'Oh, yes? Is it that you want lawyers to do for us a pre-nup?' She had begun walking very quickly, throwing him glances, which slowed Lucas's realisation both that she was joking, and that it was her own, serious assets that she had in mind. Her well-groomed parents, the retail outlets across Germany, the energetic, handsomely aging grandparents – it all contributed to a picture of a level of affluence that he hadn't quite taken on board before. 'All I want is you, Heidi, and nothing more.' He could hear the bleakness in his voice as dread pulsed again. He needn't mention the Moira business. Keeping things to himself – compartmentalising – had served him well in the past. Until it hadn't. 'I would be totally happy to keep our finances separate,' he said after a pause, 'if that was what you wanted.'

Heidi slowed her pace to throw him a faintly puzzled, affectionate look. 'But that is not what our vows will say, Lucas. After marriage we shall be bound as one, in all things.' She reached to clasp his hand, as deeply solemn as he had ever seen her. 'Trust, Liebchen, and sharing.'

'Trust and sharing,' he echoed hoarsely.

She had come to a halt so that they were facing each other. 'You are worried about something, Lucas, I can tell. Is it Esther? I have already told you, I will never try to play mother to Dylan and Lily...'

'No, no, it's nothing like that... but, thank you for saying so. No, it's just a stupid thing that has arisen at college,' he said as they turned again to walk on. 'It is going to take a little sorting out.'

'What stupid thing?'

'To do with that student, Moira Giddings.'

'That girl who persuaded you to give an opinion on her creative writing?' Heidi snorted, shaking her head, and Lucas felt a little better.

'That's the one.' He let out some breath and launched, grimly and doggedly, into all that had now transpired, including the conclusions of the morning meeting and a summary of his efforts to point out the ludicrousness of the accusation.

Heidi stopped again, so abruptly that he had to retrace a couple of steps. 'But this is bad, Lucas. Terrible. A nightmare.' Her beautiful hazel eyes were huge with dismay.

'Yes, it is.' He tried to hug her, but she pushed him back.

'Moira Giddings has made this accusation? To you?' She gave a sudden punch to his shoulder, quite hard, filling him with confusion as to whether it was a gesture of solidarity or attack.

'Yes, she has, but—'

'*Inappropriate* behaviour? She has said this?'

'Yes, but it is all nonsense, Heidi – you know that, surely. I did nothing. *Nothing*. Except help the damn girl, for Christ's sake.'

Heidi was swearing too, by the sound of it, in German. She plucked a hair clip from her back pocket as she cursed, performing the usual deft, mesmerising twists with sections of her long hair, before expertly stapling it all into place as a topknot. 'You did not touch her?'

'Heidi, for God's sake—'

'Even a little bit. In a friendly way? That could have been misinterpreted?' Her eyes were hooded and wary. 'This is so... Lucas, I need to know the truth.'

'I have told you the truth,' he retorted, at such volume that a passing couple tried to catch his eye. A lovers' tiff, their faces said – we've all been there.

'No physical contact, Lucas? No words that could be misinterpreted?'

'No,' he cut in savagely, 'and frankly, even to have to bear this interrogation – this doubt – from you of all people – is... Jesus Christ.' He ran his hands over his face, groaning with relief when he felt her cool fingers arrive on top of them.

'I am sorry. I am in shock. It is such a bad thing to happen.'

'I should never have helped her,' he moaned. 'I should have held firm, told her to leave. I should—'

'Maybe she has an obsession with you,' Heidi murmured, but without conviction. 'Young girls, they can be dumb like that.'

'Or maybe she did not like my comments on her work. Not that I was harsh...'

'Yes, that could be it. I suppose.' She sighed heavily.

'It will blow over, sweetheart,' Lucas consoled her hastily, 'for the simple reason that I did nothing wrong, and everyone – everyone, including and especially the Master – wants it sorted.'

'I hope so. But... but... I hate that such a thing should happen.'

'Me too.' They had reached the junction near her library and dejection was swamping him again. Soon they would part, with nothing between them feeling as it normally did. 'Please try not to worry. I'll call you later, okay? I'd better get home now.'

'Sure.'

'And let's go away for a few days before term starts,' Lucas urged, desperate to ignite a flicker of the buoyancy he knew and loved. 'Paris, Prague, Portugal – anywhere beginning with P, basically.' It was a poor joke and her expression remained distracted and stern. 'To celebrate our engagement?' he prompted. 'When Esther is back from France and can share the Dylan load, I'll have more time.'

'Or maybe we could visit my family in Bonn.' Her expression remained sombre, but he could hear the relenting in her voice. 'Today, talking to them all, it made me a little... homesick, you know?'

'Of course, it did. What a brilliant idea. Heidi...' Lucas took her arm and steered her under the lee of a shopfront. 'You do believe me, don't you? *Nothing* happened. The girl is a fantasist.'

She plucked at a button on his shirt. 'Yes, I believe you.' Her gaze found his properly at last, with some of the glints of love that he had been aching to see. 'And you will make it all right, won't you?' She sounded like a forlorn little girl, a version of her he had never seen before.

'Yes, darling, I will.' He cupped her face in his palms and they rubbed noses. 'You are my sweetheart and my life.'

'*Du für mich auch, Liebchen.*' Their lips brushed and they went their separate ways.

* * *

On the opposite side of the street, Dylan ducked into a card shop, so abruptly that his rucksack, stuffed to bursting, bashed into the shoulder of a man standing near the entrance checking his phone.

'Easy, mate.'

'Sorry, mate… sorry.' Dylan hardly dared glance back. His father had said he had a meeting in college, a good mile away. There had been no mention of meeting Heidi. Not that there ever would have been. His father did what he wanted, while making up rules for everyone else. Dylan didn't want to have to hear about his father's personal life anyway. It grossed him out even to think of it. He wished it could just stay private, like stuff in his own life. The brunch for a big talk about the engagement had been cringey. Whatever Heidi and his dad were planning, he didn't want to know and he didn't care. His dad was a tool.

Dylan squinted through the window of the shop, struggling because of the dirty glass and the distance. It was them right enough though, going in opposite directions now, the creepy public snogging done with.

Dylan stayed by the carousels of cards for a bit longer, just to be safe. He checked his phone for his ticket, even though he knew it was there, and then live departures. It was dead on time, which meant he had to hurry. He was still careful as he left the shop, checking both ways for signs of either of them coming back. The man he had bumped into hadn't moved from his stance by the window.

'Keeping to my space this time,' Dylan quipped, holding his arms up.

'No worries, mate. Have a good day.'

'You too.' Dylan's heart hopped. It *was* going to be a good day. How could freedom not be good? He merged with the flow of people heading in the direction of the station, hooking his thumbs under the rucksack's straps to ease the pressure on his shoulders. It hadn't seemed so bad when he set off. But everything got heavy if you carried it long enough.

15

The poolside, with its shield of poplars, was cast in evening shade. Behind it, the setting sun fired the sky with streaks of crimson and orange. Up on the terrace, Finn and Amber, tasked with the evening barbecue, were already running very late. Brian, spruce in light-brown chinos and a white shirt after his evening shower, was adopting a supervisory role from his sun lounger, working his way through a book of crosswords between refreshing Esther's and Viv's wine glasses and his own tumbler of gin and tonic. Arty and Bess, after groans about their rumbling stomachs, were playing ping-pong in the barn, from where howls of victory and frustration punctured the faint tap-tapping of the ball.

Esther lazily peered round her Kindle. Viv was a couple of feet away, curled into a wicker chair on the terrace, reading a novel in her fervent way, eyes wide, turning the pages as if her life depended on it. Esther's own book was proving less adept at holding her attention. She set it aside and watched a beam of the fading sunlight fall across the white, cotton dress she was wearing instead. Her skin was starting to glow. She always tanned well, like Dylan. Lily was the paler one, taking after Lucas. Three days in and three still to go. Three precious days.

Her phone had been silent since Sue's update, and that felt good too. As if she really was off the hook for a while.

Her mind drifted to earlier that afternoon, when the kayaking party had failed to appear at the agreed time. Phone messages had been left, until Viv had insisted that lunch should be embarked on by the four of them anyway, since the contents of the pan could easily be reheated for a second sitting when required. Clearing up afterwards, Esther had been aware of Viv humming under her breath as she moved around the kitchen, wrapping up the sourdough, parking the lid back on the saucepan of mussels.

'How worried are you really, Viv?' Esther had found herself exclaiming. 'I mean, is there a riverboat patrol service or something you can call?'

'I'm sure they are fine.' She had patted Esther's shoulder, as if she was the one in need of greater reassurance. 'Brian is the most sensible and resourceful man I have ever met. That's why I married him.' She had smiled, reached for a tea towel, and begun drying the plates Esther had left in the drainer. Twenty minutes later the unmistakeable thrum of a car engine had sounded from the end of the dusty lane leading to the villa. The three kayakers had exploded out of the vehicle, hair clinging round their faces, eyes shining, talking all at once about the derring-do of exploring a wild part of the river where there had been no signal and how the return to the car had coincided with the discovery that Brian's phone battery had died – perfect proof, the children had protested, that they should be allowed to take their own phones next time. Esther had stood a little apart from the reunion, enjoying the rush of family joy while recognising she could not share a place at the heart of it. Life did not have to be a series of lurching disasters, was her foremost thought, and one she vowed to hang onto. Far more things went right than wrong. You just didn't notice them so much.

* * *

Brian trotted off for a conference with the barbecue chefs before returning to top up her and Viv's glasses of white wine. 'Dinner will be ten minutes, *mesdames,* my team assure me.'

'I think your team are wonderful, and I don't care how long dinner takes,' Esther said dreamily, floating a little from drinking on an empty stomach, and from the wonderful, almost forgotten sensation of being looked after.

'Which is why you are the most perfect house guest.' Brian chuckled, doing something resembling a salsa jig to the music now blaring out of a portable speaker.

An hour later, Amber and Finn were grinning with satisfaction at the praise of their culinary efforts, while their younger siblings leapt to the task of clearing empty plates in order to fetch the dessert – fresh blueberries, flapjacks, and scoops of vanilla ice cream – all demolished in minutes despite everyone saying they had no room. There was talk of a game – cards or charades – during which Finn was despatched to the kitchen to fill the water jug. 'There's a phone going mad in here,' he called, waving through the kitchen window.

'Whose phone?' Viv shouted back.

'Esther's,' Finn replied, putting his head round the terrace door. 'Can I open more wine, Dad?'

'More wine, indeed,' Brian cried, ignoring a look from his wife. 'Open away. The stuff with the blue label, not the black.'

'And bring Esther's phone, there's a good boy,' Viv instructed, leaning across to press Esther back into her seat. Esther was more than happy to obey. The floaty feeling had evolved into a sense of deep well-being. She grinned her gratitude at Finn, who delivered her phone with a flourish a couple of minutes later, before handing the bottle of wine to his father and going back inside for the water jug.

At the sight of her screen, Esther was aware of the hubbub around her receding. There were rows of notifications: missed call after missed call from Lucas and Lily, as well as countless messages. The most recent was a text from Dylan, which Esther, heart crashing against her ribcage, read first.

Hey mum whatever dad says dont worry. I just couldnt do it. am travelling. got money and will get jobs. never wanted uni anyway. pls dont message or call. Dx

* * *

'Esther, I am not telling you what to do.'

'Oh, really, Viv? Are you sure about that? Because all I want – all I *need* – is to get home as *soon as I possibly can*. And you're making me feel bad about it.'

'That is the last thing I am trying to do. All I meant to say was that getting some sleep and catching a plane tomorrow morning makes more sense than ordering a taxi and rushing to the airport right now. It has gone midnight. You are in a state of shock, and little wonder. But Dylan, wherever he is, has communicated with you. Which means he is clearly – albeit in a dramatic way – seeking space, as teenagers do. Look, Esther, I'm sure that deep down he is okay—'

'You have *no* idea how Dylan is.' Esther gasped, staring across the candle now guttering on the table between them. She would have been packing her suitcase, had Viv not insisted they talk. The children had long since sloped off to their rooms, their hunched shoulders and quiet voices communicating their awareness both of Esther's home drama and of the row that seemed to have broken out with their mother. Brian, visible through the big kitchen window, was washing up as if his life depended on it. 'Dylan might need me. He could be home now. I should get myself there just in case—'

'Esther, he has a key. He might like it that you are *not* there. He's just rebelling...'

Esther glanced up sharply. She had dared to relax, she realised wretchedly; she had dared to think the world could be kind, when all along it had been plotting this new mauling. She longed to picture Dylan at home, lounging on the sofa with his phone and the telly, waiting for her; but all she could see was him disappearing into a plane, heading for some unimaginable, far-flung place, a small, lone figure being swallowed up by the world.

'He wants some space,' Viv said again. 'I know that doesn't make any of this remotely easy for you, but it is worth trying to maintain a bit of perspective. Yes, go home tomorrow, Esther, but don't panic is what I mean. Teenagers wouldn't be teenagers unless they—'

'Oh yes, like you would know with your four angels...'

Viv jerked back as if she had been slapped. Her lips tightened into a closed thin line. She swigged from the glass of water she had poured. She had done one for Esther too, but it remained untouched. 'Esther, you're upset.'

'Bloody right, I am upset. And I intend to get myself on the very next flight home, whenever it is and whatever it costs. *If* you don't mind.' She began to push her chair back, but Viv's hand arrived on her arm.

Viv paused, inhaling and exhaling in such an exaggerated display of mustering patience that Esther felt suddenly as if insult was being heaped on injury; as if she weren't a friend in need, but an annoying, unreasonable patient, being managed. *Tolerated.* 'Look, Esther.' Viv released the words wearily. 'Book any flight, and I'll drive you to the airport.'

'I would hate to be an inconvenience. I'll sort a taxi.'

'Esther, for heaven's sake—'

'No, Viv. I am finding this pretty hard: to be around you, always dishing out advice for things you've never had to face yourself.'

This time Viv opened her mouth to speak and then clammed it shut so tightly it looked as if her face might explode. She snatched her water glass and stalked back into the house. Esther stayed in her chair, hearing murmurings from inside – Viv's voice uncharacteristically fast and shrill, Brian's a slower rumble. In her own glass, a small flying insect was doing a frantic breaststroke between efforts to abseil up the sides.

'I hope she'll forgive me,' Esther muttered, aware of Brian having arrived at her side and starting to not quite believe all the things she had just said.

'Forgiveness? Oh, don't you worry, she's good at that. Very good.' Brian reached across to the spitting candle stump, squeezing its flame between his thumb and forefinger. 'How else do you think we've managed to stay together so long?' he added with a wry laugh.

'But she makes it look so easy. All of it. You, the kids, being here. Life.' Esther flung an arm at the house. The arm felt heavy, and she realised how far she still was from being sober. 'And I know everything she said makes sense, about sleep and waiting until the morning, but it's just so...'

'I tell you what, I'll make you a cup of tea to take up to bed. Won't be a tick.'

Esther obeyed, slumping her head into her hands and letting the three-way FaceTime call with Lucas and Lily come back to her: Lucas, disconcertingly robbed of his usual maddening unflappability, his face a death mask, his voice high with emotion, as if it were about to splinter, as he veered between worry and curses at their son's idiocy and selfishness. Lily too, pallid with shock, had been graver than Esther had ever seen her, allowing anger to burst through her expressions of concern. Dylan excelled at making everything about him, she hissed, close to tears. He didn't care enough about the effect he had on others.

'But just to leave... he must have been so desperate,' Esther had cried.

'Calm down, Esther...'

'No, Lucas, I will not calm down. And you should have told me *at once.*'

'I thought he might... I only waited a bit... and then you didn't pick up anyway,' he had countered miserably, waving the crumpled, paltry note that had been left on his dining room table:

Need time-out. Gone travelling. Sorry.

'His head is so in the clouds,' Lucas went on, making a visible effort to collect himself. 'He'll soon run out of steam and money and come home...'

'*Will* he, though? I mean, how do we *know* that?' Esther shouted. Lily flinched, tears now streaming down her face. 'Lily, sweetheart...' Esther took a deep breath, digging for sobriety and calm, 'do you have *any* idea where he might have gone first?'

Lily swallowed and gave a pitiful shake of her head. 'But he has messaged you, right, Mum?' she said, in a tiny voice. 'So, my hunch is that he is sort of okay, and, like Dad says, will come home soon enough.'

Esther returned her focus to Lucas, her head spinning again. 'You told me you had it all in hand. You said he was okay. You said that the two of you had had a good talk, that everything was all right. That *he* – Dylan, our darling child – was *all right*. You, Lucas, said that. You.'

'I thought he was,' he whispered.

A silence followed. A silence in which Esther had a dizzying sense of the widening distance between the four of them. When she and Lucas had been together, there had at least been cohesion of sorts. Something for Lily and Dylan to believe in and hang onto.

'I am going to see about flights,' she had said hoarsely. 'Try to get some sleep, Lily, darling. We'll talk tomorrow.' She hadn't even been able to look at Lucas as they all signed off.

'Fresh mint tea, and I've done a quick google of flights.' Brian set a large steaming mug on the table in front of her. 'There's one that leaves at eleven-thirty with plenty of seats. I've sent you the link. And by the way, nothing is always easy, for Viv or anyone else.' He was gripping the back of the chair next to Esther's. 'Dylan will come through this and be absolutely fine, you know that, don't you?' he went on in a rush. 'Didn't Lucas do a similar runner at a similar stage?'

Esther looked up sharply. It was easy to forget that the men had once known each other quite well, though the friendship had always been about her and Viv, rather than any merging of their two families. 'That was very different, Brian,' she murmured, knowing he was only trying to be kind. She reached into the glass and gently fished out the limp, twitching insect with the tip of her finger. 'You mean Lucas leaving home the moment he got his place at Manchester, because things there were so bad...?'

'Yes, because of his father's problems and—'

'Lucas getting away wasn't about *space*,' Esther interjected, bridling again at Viv's glib verdict on Dylan, 'so much as survival. His mother wasn't as brave, or as lucky. John was an incubus, Lucas used to say, sucking the life and hope out of everything.'

Brian nodded sadly. 'His mother. The suicide. I remember. A bad business.'

'Yes,' Esther muttered, momentarily lost to the recollection of the handful of occasions on which she had met her father-in-law; the kid-glove politeness she had shown, while quailing inwardly because of what she had been allowed to know about the benders and the rages, and the enforced conspiracy of silence that had enabled him to continue practising medicine until some brave local whistle-blowers had put a stop to it. He had had the unmistakeable, dead eyes of a drunk. The memory of Lucas's mother, Linda, was even harder; a small careworn woman, who had never been more than a foot or two from John's side, like a beaten dog currying favour. Intermittent, early efforts by herself and Lucas to persuade her of other life-options – with their support – had been ignored. She had not known she had her own breaking point, it seemed to Esther, until it arrived.

'Dylan has gone in search of himself, I expect,' Brian persisted, still hanging onto the chair, and managing to deliver the platitude with a gaucheness that somehow made it comforting. 'As young people do. No doubt he'll come back when he is adventure-weary or broke, or both. The prodigal son. Far sooner than you fear, I bet. Then he'll turn into one of those whizz kids with starry careers because they were gutsy enough to jump off the gravy train. Look – at least he's been in touch, right? The way I see it, serious rebels don't write messages to their mums, do they?' He threw her his immaculate smile and picked up both her water glass and her mug of tea. 'I shall take these upstairs for you now, and Viv's got a client in the morning, so I'll be the one to pop you to the airport. If you go for the eleven-thirty, we'll need to hit the road by eight. If that sounds okay.'

'It does, Brian. More than okay. Thank you. I'll book it now. You have been very kind,' Esther murmured, suddenly deeply tired. 'I am really sorry to be ending my lovely stay with all this palaver. I have had the most wonderful time. You and Viv... I can't think where I would be without you both.' She wiped a rogue tear from her cheek before getting up to follow him inside, noting – with a little lift – that the half-drowned insect was nobly staggering to its spindly feet.

'Glad to help.' He smiled, waiting for her to go first so he could turn off the terrace lights.

GARDENING

16

Strapped into her window seat, the heat haze shimmering on the runway, Esther kept her phone on till the last possible moment, reading and re-reading Dylan's message. True to his word, all her subsequent efforts to make contact had been stonewalled. His phone sounded dead, without even the option to leave voicemail. Every one of her laboriously composed WhatsApp messages, begging for him to come home, to communicate, packed with assurances about no recriminations and a way forward being found, still sported the single grey tick indicating they hadn't even been delivered. Efforts to cling to the comforts offered by both Viv and Brian kept ricocheting round her head through a fog of clammy panic. Yes, Dylan was eighteen; but to call a child 'adult' just because of a birthday struck her as more and more absurd. Dylan's main strengths were wild hopes and bucket-loads of kindness. To think of this beloved, vulnerable soul pitting himself against the world made Esther tremble. As did her fury at Lucas, for bringing the catastrophe into being, no doubt thanks to his usual brute tactics – ready always with the stick and forgetting the bloody carrot – and then compounding everything by keeping the news to himself for half a day. Worse than anything, however, was thinking of what Dylan was going through, fighting down his doubts and sadness, the sheer *terror* of failure that had to have driven him away.

The young man with tattooed arms in the seat next to her was giving her looks. She had been saying Dylan's name under her breath, Esther realised, hurriedly putting the phone in her bag and closing her eyes. She kept them closed as the plane accelerated, pressing her back into her seat. Her eyes felt gritty, but there was no question of sleep. She had managed only fitful dozes through the night, eventually clambering into bed after one o' clock, once she had bought her new ticket and packed her bags. The sun had brought her fully awake at six. After showering and dressing, she had torn a page out of the 'Write Your Life!' journal – brought out of consideration for Viv, and still containing nothing beyond the original scornful birthday greeting to herself and a to-pack list for the holiday – in order to write a proper apology for their awful argument.

She had got as far as

Dearest Viv, I was an ungrateful cow and you are amazing...

when a rap on the door produced Viv herself, dressed in running gear.

'Look, Viv—'

'No, you look. It's all done with. I didn't mean to upset you.'

Esther flapped her piece of paper, close to tears suddenly. 'No, Vivvie, you were trying to help and I reacted unforgivably. I'm writing to tell you so...' she shoved the diary back in the bag, not wanting Viv to see the desecration of a gift designed for much higher purposes '...as well as to thank you so very much for having me...'

'Really, Esther, it's fine.'

'I was just in a state because—'

'Of Dylan. Of course you were. And you're on the eleven-thirty, Brian says, so that's great. Getting home – I know I would want exactly the same. I can't imagine the worry. I hope he gets in touch again soon. He will, I'm sure. Because he loves you.' She walked a little on the spot as she talked, rolling her weight through each foot in a manner that contributed to the impression – for all her comforting words – of keeping herself at a distance. 'Keep us posted, won't you?'

'Viv, please, last night, the things I said... they were inexcusable...'

'No. Not at all. Really, Esther, it's fine and I'd better head off now or I won't be back in time.'

'For your client.'

'Exactly. And to see you off too.'

'Great. Thanks. Okay.' Esther folded her message in two. It didn't feel okay. 'And I am so grateful to Brian for...' Esther had to put her head round the door as Viv was already several steps away, her electric-blue trainers squeaking faintly on the tiled floor.

'Viv. Seriously. Thank you. For everything.'

'No problem. See you later.' She waved once before disappearing down the stairs.

Their farewell hug by the car an hour later was only marginally more satisfactory, Viv allowing Esther to hold her, it felt like, before rushing off to get to her client notes.

The drive to the airport, however, had been an unexpected pleasure, flying through the gold and green curves of the countryside with the windows down and Brian belting shouty accompaniments to Frank Sinatra songs. Just being in motion had been consoling, an in-between moment, to gather strength for whatever lay ahead. Esther felt a welcome echo of something similar now, as the plane levelled out in the expanse of blue above the cloud-line. The engine noise had calmed to a thrum. Distant chinks and clinks signified the preparation of a snacks trolley. For two hours, no one could do anything.

Reality didn't start to weigh heavily until she emerged from the train station into the light of the late London afternoon. Maybe Dylan was home. She almost ran the whole way, dodging people, with her small pull-along suitcase making a racket over the cracks in the pavements. But somehow, at the first glimpse of her little house, as still as Carmela's, junk mail sticking out of the letter flap, Esther knew in her heart that it was empty. So great was the let-down that it took a moment to register that there was something on the doorstep; a large something, basking in a shaft of late afternoon sun. Bloody Chico. Esther stopped, picking up her case so as not to alarm the animal as she approached. Maybe it was an omen. Creatures that went missing could turn up again.

Esther opened the gate slowly. A car shot past, but the animal didn't so much as glance sideways. She put the case down before venturing up the path. Clocking her approach, the cat tensed slightly, before continuing to lick a front paw. Esther took one step at a time, while the cat played the game of ignoring her. He looked well fed, the black tiger markings in his dark grey fur gleaming chevrons in the sun. She got her house keys ready. An open door, a shove, and the job would be done.

17

Libraries had something of the church about them, Lucas decided, his eyes travelling round the high ceilings and the walls of books, planted between the big tables like mighty buttresses. There was the same air of reverence; the same dimness of light, despite the sunbeams slanting through the high latticed windows, dust motes thick as midges dancing in their rays. He stole a glance at Heidi in the seat opposite, envying her engrossment in her labours, and the earnestness with which she tackled every challenge, inspired, it seemed to him now, by a certainty that he could recall possessing himself once upon a time – that life could and would get better; that a steady trajectory towards the stars required only the drive of a determined ambition to bring it into being.

Under the shield of the table, Lucas had a go at flexing his left foot, feeling again the twinge of the calf muscle he had somehow overexerted on the towpath that morning. Heidi, sensing the movement, or his gaze, looked up from her books. For a moment, their eyes locked across the broad oak table, hers asking brightly how he was getting on, and his making a sterling effort to lie that all was going swimmingly.

She was off to Bonn the following day, for a ten day visit to her family, which he recognised she needed and which, for reasons all too plain – and about which she had been stoically sympathetic – she would now undertake alone. They would holiday together, they had agreed, just as soon as Dylan had seen sense, and the Moira situation was resolved. A week on from the horror of being grilled by the Master and then returning to a Dylan-less flat, Lucas was aware of something like shame pushing through his outrage and upset. For two key elements of his life to swerve so violently off course smacked of failure. A failure that did not sit well with how he loved Heidi, which was as much about proving himself a worthy and strong protector as all the other obvious ingredients of mutual intellectual respect and physical attraction. It did not help that, although he hated discussing Moira with her, she brought the subject up all the time – to understand properly, she said, and because she was surely more of an expert on women's feelings than he was. She had even wanted to help edit his statement about the alleged incident, backing down with reluctance when he'd insisted that he had it in hand. In truth, it was further humiliation – in Heidi's eyes – that Lucas sought to avoid. This was his own, demeaning, battle, and he would fight it alone. Lucas had summoned the courage to confess as much that morning, while lying on her bed and watching her start to pack, admiring the orderly way in which she steadily filled the suitcase, everything fitting just so.

'You are not to waste a moment of worry on me, is what I am trying to say. Just concentrate on having a wonderful holiday. Everything will get sorted, I promise.'

She had stopped at once, and looked at him, her eyes soft and solemn. 'I know that is what you want, Lucas. But it is hard, no, just to forget what is going on? Though of course I shall do my best.' She smiled properly, and he was so glad to have dared to speak out. But then, as if the moment had released some much-needed pressure inside her too, she suddenly launched into a diatribe about Dylan, how she hoped Lucas didn't mind her saying so, but his son was selfish as well as crazy. 'You were trying so hard, Lucas, like you always do with him, and this is how he repays you. I would never do that to my own parents, and neither would Stefan... but we know it is because Esther has spoiled him,' she had ended quickly, perhaps reading the tension in his expression and reaching for a conclusion they could both agree on.

She had resumed her packing, leaving Lucas to grapple with a peculiar blend of reassurance and discomfort. That the conversation hadn't triggered one of the forensic what had – and hadn't – happened between him and Moira interrogations felt like a step forward; and yet the outburst about Dylan had been hard to hear. His fiancée had every right to voice opinions on anything she chose, Lucas had reminded himself – their lives were shared territory now. And yet such remarks also made him feel very distant from her, coming as they did from a person, no matter how loved, without any comprehension of the complicating animal anxiety of loving a child, even one that behaved liked an irredeemable pillock.

The stint in the library that morning had been Heidi's idea, to kick-start his faltering progress on the symbolism paper, she had declared in her bold way. His work should not be allowed to stop, she had counselled gravely; it mattered too much. While she was in Germany, he was to throw himself back into it. Lucas had eagerly agreed and set out his laptop and notes on his section of the big table with high hopes and real purpose. This particular library was a favourite of his, and Heidi knew that too, it being the work-space where the first draft of his Gawain book had poured into being. Yet that morning, within minutes, he had sensed that no such magic would be within reach. Re-reading his notes and opening paragraphs, he could see only lines of writing and not their meaning. His once formidable powers of concentration – Esther used to complain at the efficiency with which he shut out the world, and her – felt like a memory of someone else. Instead, his brain flip-flopped, spending nanoseconds on each of myriad subjects, none of them productive. At one point he even caught himself starting a Dylan doodle in the margin of his notebook until a flicker of attention from across the table had him flinging his fingers back to the keys.

What is a symbol?

Lucas typed as the hopelessness continued to spread, a palpable weight in his limbs. Writing something was better than writing nothing. Something could be improved on. Nothing was a blank screen. Lucas stared at the words, telling himself to get a grip. There were no longer any excuses for being so hamstrung. Heidi was proving a stalwart about every damn thing, and the previous afternoon he had finally sent his statement to the Master, a lucid, concise, unambiguous account of Moira's visit to his rooms of which he was proud. Not 'his' truth but 'the' truth, Lucas had mused darkly during the days of working on it, crafting and recrafting the testimony into a shape that could brook no misinterpretation. The next step now, if Moira played ball, would be a further meeting, and he felt hopeful about that too. Time had passed. Dust had settled. The new academic year was just a few weeks away. Resolution was in everybody's interests.

And on the Dylan front too, the last twenty-four hours had presented a promising development, in the form of two postcards, both of the Eiffel Tower, one for Esther and one for Lily. Esther's had contained some typewritten daft sentence about how good the crêpes were, and Lily's a small capital D initial beside a kiss. They had shown them off on a FaceTime call the previous afternoon, and Lucas, between reiterating frustration and anger at the situation, had shared the rejoicing at this proof that Dylan still lived and breathed.

Lucas switched tabs to check his email. There was nothing from the Master or the Chaplain, only various administrative matters he couldn't face, along with a note from Ralph saying he and the family were back from Rhodes and what about a pint before the imminent mayhem of pre-term preparations?

I'm actually up against it at the moment.

Lucas typed back feebly, his innards convulsing at the memory of the Master saying the Senior Tutor would have to be involved if the mediation route was pursued. Mediation. Good God.

Give me a week and I'll get back to you.

He finished, quickly pressing send and hating the oddness of not wanting to meet with someone whose company he usually enjoyed. A few moments later a text notification popped up on his phone.

If you're up against it you def need a pint. What about tonight? R.

Heidi is off to Germany tomorrow so no can do – sorry.

Lucas composed the text slowly, picturing Ralph's jovial rotund face and quick, brown eyes, the energy and intelligence flying like sparks. A decade younger than him, and a historian who had traded in his academic path for the more practical one of helping to run the college, he managed a complicated, thankless job with boundless efficiency and warmth, as well as a healthy irreverence for nonsense. He was exactly the friend he needed, Lucas reflected bleakly, if only the circumstances were different.

Saturday then? The Swan at 6? Catherine has a concert so it will be a quickie.

Okay. Thanks. Btw Heidi and I are engaged.

Hurrah! And huge congrats. Pints on me in that case. R

Noticing that Heidi was also on her phone, Lucas messaged her too, watching across the table as it landed.

Think I'll head off.

Ok. Because of lunch with Lily?

That's tomorrow. Just need a break.

Ok. I have yoga, and then drinks with Etienne and Iris. You coming?

No, if that's ok.

Super-ok. I won't be late.

I love you.

Und ich dich, Liebchen.

Back home twenty minutes later, Lucas rummaged in his iced-up bottom freezer drawer for some frozen peas to hold against his throbbing calf, pitched into some new gear of distress by the walk home. Strapping the bag in place with his dressing gown cord resulted in scores of peas shooting across the kitchen floor. In no mood to mess around with a dustpan and brush, Lucas steered them into a rough pile with the inside of his foot and hobbled along the passage towards the sitting room.

On the way, he stopped for a glance into Dylan's room. It was echoingly empty; his son, such a master of mess, having left nothing except the ring stains on the bedside table and the pitiful note, which Lucas had thrown in the bin in a fit of rage and then retrieved to show Esther and Lily.

Need time-out. Gone travelling. Sorry.

The 'sorry' was something, Lucas conceded now. Before closing the door, he sniffed the air, noting with a twist that even the off-smell had gone. Back in his sitting room, he fell into an armchair, lifting the foot of his injured leg onto a low, spindly-legged coffee table, which Esther had rescued from a skip and then never liked much.

To miss his son's slovenly habits made no sense. Indeed, it felt like a cruel trick, Lucas brooded, recalling his eagerness to reach the moment when Dylan would be properly off his hands. Now that day had presented itself, and all he could feel was anguish. Dylan was such a dolt, that was the trouble. A misguided, optimistic, rebellious dolt. Picturing how he was going to manage navigating a uni curriculum and campus had been a big stretch, let alone this new, imbecilic, underfunded attempt to explore the entire bloody world.

When his phone vibrated, Lucas swooped on it with relief. 'Lily!' She was clearly calling from her and Matteo's kitchen, perched on the little stool they kept parked by the back door. Her shining blue eyes, lighter and bigger than Esther's, seemed to fill the screen.

'Hey, Dad, how's it going?'

'Not too bad. Has Dylan been in touch again?'

'Nope. Has anything arrived for you?'

'Not yet.' Lucas found he had to force a smile. To be left out shouldn't matter. 'I don't need a postcard,' he went on quickly. 'I just want him to come to his senses and get himself home.'

'Same here... er... look, Dad, I'm sorry but I won't be able to make our lunch tomorrow.'

Lucas dug inside himself to smile again. When had life got so damned hard? he wondered as another wave of hopelessness washed through him, arriving from nowhere as they all seemed to; tides with their own rhythms. 'Oh, that's a shame, but... never mind. Next time, eh?' Back in the day, during her early undergrad phase, they had lunched every week, at a veggie place Lily liked. Such easy, happy times, they seemed now, for all the difficulties behind the scenes.

'Cool, Dad, thanks. Sorry – a lot on – and yeah, we'll fix something soon.' Lily leant closer to the screen suddenly, squinting. 'Are you in bed or something? You look sort of... are you okay, Dad?'

'Yes. I'm super-fine, I...' Lucas broke off, aware he had used one of Heidi's superlatives. 'Just putting my feet up a bit. Literally.' He waggled his phone to show his foot resting on the spindly table. 'I managed to tweak a muscle this morning and I'm icing it. Nothing serious. Just bloody annoying. I was going to drive Heidi to the airport tomorrow – she's off on a visit home – but I'm not sure I shall manage it.'

'Poor you.'

'Oh, it's nothing.' Lily's eyes were darting upwards, to a message from another quarter, Lucas guessed. 'I'll let you go, sweetheart, but could I just ask... I mean, did Dylan mind about the whole Heidi thing? Do you?'

Lily's gaze froze for an instant, her saucer eyes growing wider still. 'No, Dad, we are both cool with it.'

'Because we talked it through over brunch that day, didn't we?' Lucas continued doggedly. 'We talked it through and you both were fine.'

'Yes, Dad, we talked it through and it's fine. All we want is...' she paused, releasing the rest of the sentence on a rush of air '...is for you – and Mum – to be happy.'

'And you are sure your brother would echo those sentiments?' Lucas knew he was pressing Lily too hard, and probably unfairly, but he couldn't shake the new suspicion that had taken root in his mind. Was Dylan punishing him? Was it that simple?

'Look, Dad, I really can't speak for Dylan, can I?' Lily was sounding faintly exasperated. As she spoke the door behind her burst open and Matteo appeared.

'Hey, Lucas, how's it going?'

'Great, thanks, Matteo. And how's the world of chemical engineering?'

'Busy. Glad Dylan is on the radar.'

'Yes, that is tremendous news. We're all very relieved.'

'Matteo's auditioning for a second singer,' Lily pitched in eagerly, play-wrestling Matteo out of the way. 'Loads have applied. It's mad. Including a couple of girls from school. Katya the goth, remember her? And Jane Jessop. They were both in the choir. We've got the first *ten* coming to try out this afternoon.'

'That sounds fun. Let me know the next gig date. Maybe I'll come.'

'Really?'

'Sure,' Lucas lied, his mind flying back to the days when Esther had played groupie, while he'd marvelled at her commitment to a cause that really didn't warrant it. If Lily had been in the band, yes, but not

Matteo, bellowing into a mic fizzing with static while he and two mates raked at guitars, and another clashed around with some drums.

After the call, Lucas sank back into his chair. His eyelids wanted to close. He fought it. Defeated old men slept during the day, and he wasn't one of those.

18

The garden centre, driven past so many times, proved a revelation. There was a spacious car park, an airy café, its tables spilling out onto an attractive patio in the hanging-plant section, and wide concrete aisles that made the manoeuvring of her trolley a breeze.

That morning, she had resolved to clean Dylan's room, but then hovered at the door, unable to go in. He was okay – or at least, he had been, at the moment of sending the card of Paris's most famous landmark, with the printed handwritten message that managed to seem distant and close all at the same time. But since then who knew? Esther had frozen with her fingers clasping the door handle. To embark on the task of changing the rumpled bedding, to plunge her hands into the piles of paper and gadgets ranged around the shelves, had grown impossible in the same instant. It was too close to an admission that Dylan would not be home any time soon; that they were all still at the beginning of what had to be gone through.

Trembling a little, she had quietly retreated downstairs, latching onto the idea of tackling the garden instead as she'd caught a glimpse of it through the landing window. Equipment would be required, and even that had been a pleasing distraction. She had made a list, using a page in Viv's now thoroughly violated journal, always to hand on the kitchen table, and then, typically, forgotten to take the list with her. Nonetheless, ten minutes in, and Esther was in danger of finding the shopping enjoyable. Her trolley had grown so laden it was getting difficult to push and contained several major items that had not made it onto the list, including a giant pair of shears, gloves the size of gauntlets, a small wheelbarrow, and an electric lawnmower, neatly packaged in a big green box. That she hadn't held back was partly thanks to an unexpected proposal from her healthcare company's HR department in her inbox that morning, offering a monthly retainer on top of the big rebranding project she was already signed up for. The luxury of having a little money was not having to expend as much energy *thinking* about it, Esther decided, recklessly tossing a hefty pair of secateurs onto her pile.

Nine days on, and with September looming, the brief sojourn in France felt a world away, but Brian and Viv had only got back the night before. Having deliberately been leaving them in peace, apart from updates about Dylan, Esther had seized the chance to phone that morning in order to reiterate her thanks and apologies.

'Esther.'

'Viv, so you're back? Did you get my messages?'

'Yes, and yes. Thanks. Lots to get on top of here, as you can imagine...'

'Of course. Just checking you are all okay and wanting to say another massive thank-you for—'

'No need, Esther – honestly. And great news about Dylan being in touch. He'll come home soon enough, walking taller, maybe even fluent in French.'

'Oh, thank you, Viv – that's just what Brian said when—'

'Did he? Oh good. And Paris is pretty close, isn't it? Which sort of helps. I should imagine.' The old warm readiness to offer advice still wasn't quite there, and she was a fool for phoning at such an inopportune time, Esther scolded herself. The first morning back after a long holiday – who had time to chat then? She switched quickly instead to suggesting a date when she might express her thanks by having them both over to dinner. Her own diary was virtually empty, apart from her September spa treat with Lily, but it took until the last Saturday in October – Halloween – before Viv conceded that this was a date that might work.

'But, Vivvie, that's ages away...'

'I know, I'm sorry, Esther. But the autumn is already mad-busy workwise for both of us – not to mention four new terms starting at four different educational institutions to get on top of. The weekends have all been gobbled up.'

'Yes, of course.'

'And by the way, how's that sick neighbour of yours?' she added, sounding a bit more like the old Viv.

'No word as yet. The bloody cat appeared and then vanished again.'

'Annoying. But remember, it was a favour asked of you, and nothing you should beat yourself up about.'

'I shall. Thanks, Viv. Sorry to have disturbed your morning, and see you soon.'

Feeling slightly abandoned, Esther had been left recalling her homecoming and the thwarted hopes of herding Carmela's pet in through her front door. At the final moment, intuiting her intentions, the animal had scrambled sideways, hurdling the low fence into Dimitri and Sue's front garden and then disappearing through the tangle of gnarled and sprawling rhododendrons separating them from the next house along.

'Well, at least we know he is around,' Sue had declared cheerfully, knocking on Esther's door a little later, having been alerted to the situation by text. 'Which is something good to report to Marcus – *when* he gets in touch. There's not been a peep all week. But how was your holiday?' she had urged. 'I must have got it wrong, because I thought you weren't back till the weekend.'

Esther had said she hadn't got it wrong and did she have time for a cup of tea? The Dylan trauma had started tumbling out of her before the kettle boiled. Apart from getting up to fetch Esther's kitchen roll, placing it near Esther when she sat down at the table with their mugs,

Sue had stayed quietly in her chair. Sipping her tea, she'd let Esther talk herself out, offering no attempt at comforting sound-bites except, 'He's your boy and he loves you,' which she'd said several times over, between tearing off sheets of the kitchen paper to blow her own nose.

* * *

Would weedkiller reduce her workload? Esther wondered, eyeing up some huge, ready-to-spray dispensers, complete with shoulder straps for easy deployment, and picturing herself, Ghostbuster style, blitzing every bramble in the garden. The display was out of reach, giving her the idea of balancing on a lower shelf for a closer look. It was in this position that her attention was caught by a man who looked uncannily like Chris Mews, standing at the far end of the next aisle. Hopping off the shelf, Esther gingerly ventured nearer, using a handy cluster of yucca plants as cover.

'Excuse me, madam, is this your trolley?' She swivelled round, rustling the jungle of dry leaves as she stepped clear. The young man addressing her was shaven-headed and wearing overalls in the store's trademark colours of neon-orange and yellow. He had made a point of shifting her trolley out of the middle of the gangway where it had somehow drifted during her spying mission. 'Were you looking for something in particular?' He threw a worried glance at the yuccas, tugging at the lurid jacket, which was emblazoned with two lopsidedly pinned badges, one saying 'Darren', and the other 'HERE TO HELP!'

'No, thanks, that is...' Esther cast a look up at the array of weed-killers, but finding it hard to concentrate now she feared Chris might come sauntering round the corner at any moment.

The young man was suddenly grinning. 'It's Dylan's mum, isn't it?'

'Darren,' Esther cried, the smile and the boy's higgledy-piggledy teeth aligning with memories of the teenagers occasionally to be found lounging round her house on a weekend morning. 'How are you?'

'Yeah, not too bad, thanks. Going to Newcastle. Media and Politics.'

'Wow. Well done. How lovely.' Esther beamed at the boy, wishing she could be the mother of a son going off to Newcastle to do media and politics.

'Dylan all right, then?'

'Yes... well, he's doing some travelling...' Esther faltered, a rising hope of information falling flat.

'Is he? Awesome.'

'So, you're not in touch?' Esther ventured, it dawning on her properly how little she had known about Dylan's London college life compared to the goldfish bowl of the early Cambridge school years that had preceded it.

'He kind of dropped out of our group a while back, to be honest.'

'Did he?'

'Better get on now.' Darren had started shooting glances up and down the aisle. 'Say hi to him for me, yeah?' He waved as he started to walk away.

'There was a girl, Mei Lin – did you know her?' Esther called, trotting in a bid to catch up with him, which was a challenge with her trolley.

Darren turned round to answer, continuing walking backwards and swinging his head. 'Nope, sorry.'

'Okay... but if there was anyone you could ask?' The boy had reached the end of their aisle and Esther had to raise her voice. 'I could give you my phone number, or...' But with a cheery head-nod, he was gone.

'Giving out phone numbers to young men now?'

'Oh, my goodness... Chris... I...'

Chris Mews laughed heartily at his own joke, hoicking the large bag of ericaceous compost he was carrying higher onto one hip. Seen close up, he looked different from their dinner date, Esther observed: fresher faced, his brown eyes full of sparkle behind the dark-rimmed glasses. His clothes looked smarter too: a short-sleeved blue and yellow check shirt tucked into crisp, navy jeans.

'Good to see you, Esther. Sorry I've been silent for a while.'

'But... I mean, there is no need to be sorry, because...' Esther laughed uncertainly, thrown by this airbrushing of the broken agreement to desist from further communications. 'Because...' she tightened her grip on the trolley handle '...because... like I said... I mean, you shouldn't have sent me any...'

'I behaved like a complete knob on that date of ours,' he interjected, shaking his head. 'I wasn't, as they say, in a *good place*. So, sending you a couple of goodies was the least I could do. I hope you enjoyed them.'

'Well, yes, but...' Esther faltered, picturing the red roses lighting up her piano top and the chocolates. 'We had agreed not to be in touch any more though, hadn't we? And to be honest, Chris, I was kind of... put out... that you had somehow got hold of my address. I mean, I re—'

He groaned, rolling his eyes in the manner of one acknowledging a misstep. 'Oh God, Esther, forgive me for that. I am a thoughtless jerk. I was just so eager to make amends. I never meant to make you feel uncomfortable.'

'But how did you find it out?' Esther cried, curiosity getting the better of her and feeling more at ease because of how nice he was trying to be.

'Oh God...' He groaned again. 'You are going to think me a total nutter but, when we met that time, there was an envelope with your address on, sticking out of your bag... I have a bit of a photographic memory, you see,' he confessed sheepishly, 'but *please* don't hold it against me – I would take it back if I could. Erase it from my hard disk.' He was swinging his head in self-castigation. 'It was presumptuous and inexcusable, Esther. *Mea culpa*. The only defence I can offer is liking you and wanting to make up for having made a mess of things.'

'Okay. Well, thanks. But now...' She gestured at his full arms and her heaped trolley. 'I'd better be on my way, and you too, by the look of things.'

'Can I give you a hand with that? It looks heavy.'

'No, I'm absolutely fine, thanks.' Esther set off quickly, not looking back.

He accompanied her to the checkouts anyway, picking the next queue along to pay for his compost and then waiting for her. 'I could at least help you get this stuff into your car. Then I promise to leave you alone. I'm a decent person, Esther,' he added, with sudden, endearing urgency, as the swishing automatic doors released them both into the car park. 'I'd hate to think you don't realise that.'

'Oh, but I do,' Esther began, breaking off as her trolley almost took off down the slope towards the cars and Chris lunged in to offer assistance. 'Thanks, that's kind.' She dug for her car keys while he took over, balancing his purchase on top of the lawnmower box and steering as she led the way towards her car.

'You look great, by the way,' he called.

'Do I? Thanks.' Esther threw a bemused glance down at her white top, the faint stain of pollen on the sleeve that had been there for years, and her old jeggings, doing their usual miraculous job of keeping her tummy under control and showing the best of her legs. At the car, she opened the boot and then failed in a wrestle with the clip that allowed the back seats to flatten. 'Bloody thing.' She gave it a slap. 'It won't budge.'

'Let me have a go.'

Esther manoeuvred out of the way so Chris could take a turn, having to laugh when the clip cooperated with one easy tug. She then stood to one side, amused and helpless, as he insisted on loading everything from her trolley into the boot. Watching, Esther found it impossible not to relish the ancient, half-forgotten pleasure of sharing life with someone physically stronger, someone who, she couldn't help noticing, was endowed with a pleasingly broad back and arm muscles, bulging under the confines of the checked shirt.

'Will you be all right the other end?' He slammed the boot shut and dusted his palms.

'*Yes*, thank you. I don't need rescuing, you know.' Esther shot him a wry grin, remembering suddenly all the things Viv had said, about the first snog with Brian and not being too quick to judge.

'I know, and it is very refreshing.' He was grinning back, delight lighting up his face. 'So many on that bloody website do. I've given it up, actually. Hard to go on when you've found what you were looking for.' He threw her a rueful look as he bent down to resume command of his bag of soil, and Esther found their first easy, open phone conversation coming back to her, the one that had made her agree to a date.

Her instincts were so rusty, she reflected despairingly. She was all over the place. 'Look, Chris, many thanks again, but I've a lot to be getting on with.' She jangled her keys.

'Yes, indeedy. Me too.' He gave the bag of soil a fond pat. 'Esther, could we try meeting again, do you think?' he blurted. 'Would you at least consider it? If I were to message you in a day or two?' He took a step backwards, as if to show he had no intention of crowding her. 'And I promise to respect however you reply. Okay?'

'Okay,' Esther said quickly. Deciding to get to know someone was like gambling, she consoled herself, turning out of the car park a couple of minutes later, and seeing Chris Mews still framed in her rear-view mirror, waving. You piled your chips high, knowing each time that you could win or lose the lot.

* * *

Sitting on the lawnmower box half an hour later, absorbing the fact that it would be several weeks – possibly months – before the wall of brambles in front of her required its services, Esther found herself wondering how things were going with the daughter. Kelly. Fifteen, and being 'poisoned' against Chris by the wife, Sylvie. Esther shuddered, grateful that, despite all the distress and discord, she and Lucas had never sunk to such levels. Viv's claim, that she missed Lucas, still rankled every time she thought about it; but that didn't stop her recognising that her ex-husband – for all his selfishness and weaknesses – was, at heart, a decent person. It was one of the main reasons it had taken her so long to lose faith in him.

The gauntlet gloves were immediately useful, as were the long-handled shears. Esther began to feel powerful as she hacked and slashed, creating bouncy piles of clippings, which she ferried with her new barrow to create as tidy a mountain as she could manage along the fence. The nagging anxiety about Dylan began to recede properly for the first time in days. Just to be *doing* something felt fantastic. When the clippings had dried and shrunk, she would have a bonfire, Esther decided. It would be less hassle than trying to book in at the dump; Carmela, bless her, wasn't around to moan, and she couldn't imagine Sue and Dimitri kicking up a fuss.

By the time the afternoon was turning to dusk, the enormity of the task Esther had set herself had begun to dawn. Three solid hours of toil, and she had chopped into barely a quarter of the narrow thirty yards or so of garden. Digging up the roots once the clearing was complete was going to take even longer. Every so often she hit an easier patch, thanks to a few feet of a tunnel, burrowed by foxes, she assumed, but for the most part it was like macheteing her way through a rainforest. Sunday too, then, and for several weekends yet, Esther realised, sighing as she downed tools at last, pausing to admire her handiwork, as well as the setting sun, streaking the sky with red behind the trees beyond the railway line.

19

Lucas doubled his scarf round his neck as he set off for his Saturday evening drink with Ralph. Almost overnight, high summer seemed to have lurched into a fierce early autumn, eye-watering winds and temperatures low enough to make your bones ache. Despite two days of total rest, his calf muscle was tighter than ever, and he had a hint of a raw throat too, which he badly wanted to see off before Heidi's return the following weekend. He would have cancelled Ralph were it not for the Master's grenade of an email, landing in his inbox that morning, explaining that Moira, despite the best efforts of the Chaplain to persuade her into a conversation between all parties, still 'did not feel comfortable being in the same space' as him. Official mediation had therefore been agreed as the 'way forward', which meant Ralph getting sucked into the vortex. The Senior Tutor had already been apprised of the situation, the Master had added in her final paragraph, and next steps would be settled on shortly.

Lucas ploughed up the heaps of wet leaves as he walked, trying not to limp because doing so seemed to be causing an ache in the hip on the same side as his poorly calf. One pain seemed to lead to another, he brooded, feeling as if he had become like some kind of sinking ship. But maybe Ralph had some good ideas, he consoled himself, stooping under the low lintel of the entrance to The Swan. Like all senior tutors, the man wielded considerable power within the student and fellowship communities of the college. He was universally liked and had a cool head. Most importantly, he knew and respected Lucas.

It immediately transpired, however, that Ralph, too, had almost cancelled their drink. Not because of a sore throat, but because of his new knowledge about the Moira allegation and the Master's plans for resolving it. 'I'm just not sure we should be talking about it,' he admitted bleakly, when they were still leaning on the bar, having just taken receipt of their pints. 'Sorry, Lucas, it must be hellish for you, but there is the question of impartiality and so forth.'

'Impartiality? I am being accused of a heinous crime, Ralph, which I did *not* commit.' Lucas, took a long swig of his beer and set the glass down firmly. 'You've seen my statement. That bloody child presented herself that day, wheedling for my attention and help on something I had no desire or qualification to give—'

'Don't say that at the mediation session, for Christ's sake,' Ralph growled, leading the way to an empty corner table. 'At least, don't say *wheedling*. The power of language...'

'I can assure you, I am perfectly aware of the power of language, Ralph,' Lucas retorted. 'It is, after all, my trade.' He folded himself into the chair that had its back to the room, drinking steadily for a few seconds and exhaling deeply after he had swallowed. 'Apologies. I am out of sorts, to put it mildly.'

'I can imagine.'

'Can you?' Lucas offered a pained smile across their small table. Though the man sitting opposite was probably his closest friend, they had never been confidants. Lucas hadn't gone in for those, at least not since Esther.

'And hey, congratulations again to you and Heidi. What tremendous news.' Ralph raised his glass and Lucas lifted his in response, both men aware of not managing quite the display of joy such news deserved. For a few minutes Ralph nobly quizzed him on how the engagement had come about and the time-scale of their plans, before offering up a self-deprecating account of Catherine taking three times of asking before settling on a yes. 'Sometimes it's sheer grit that sees you through,' he continued kindly, 'and I am sure we can get this awful business sorted out. I mean, it's in everyone's interests, right? So, chin up. How's the rest of the family, anyway?'

'All good,' Lucas muttered, finding that he wasn't up to sharing the fact of Dylan gallivanting off to Europe instead of working for his re-sits. There was only so much pity a man could take.

'My fear,' he blurted, when Ralph returned with a second pint for Lucas and a half for himself, 'is that the girl wants some sort of moment in the sun. You know the kind, Ralph. She can't quite get the attention she wants, so she tries other ways.'

Ralph was eyeing him warily. The main focus of his role as Senior Tutor was student welfare, which meant an acquaintance with the foibles of every student. 'Yes, she struggled to settle,' he said levelly, 'seemed to hold herself a little apart, but...' He paused, leaning closer and lowering his voice. 'Asking her not to tell anyone, Lucas, now that was unfortunate, as was your choice of *vocabulary*. Not to mention the Post-it note with the manuscript. What the devil were you thinking?'

Lucas felt his stomach heave. Somehow, he had forgotten the scribbled 'shhhh' on the sticker he had attached to the folder before posting it into Moira's pigeonhole. 'For God's sake, Ralph, the whole business was about trying to be *kind*, while not triggering a deluge of similar requests. She begged for my help, I tell you, virtually in tears. I thought she would be grateful. Trust me, I won't be such an idiot again.'

Ralph tugged up his jumper sleeve to check his watch, a slick black smartphone band Lucas hadn't seen before, and then got to his feet with a sigh. 'Look, Lucas, speaking as your friend, and quickly, because I really should *not* be discussing it, and if I don't go soon, I shall be hung, drawn *and* quartered...' He drained the last inch of his half-pint. 'I think I understand where you are coming from, and your statement is excellent, but to show some true sympathy and understanding for Moira is going to be not just welcome, but *vital*. Who knows what she inferred from your exchanges that day?'

Lucas sat still, belting his arms across his chest while a sudden, despicable urge to punch Ralph's kindly face swelled inside. Ralph with his picture-perfect life – the easy-going Catherine, and their three peas-in-a-pod children – the only thing hanging over his head was wifely castigation for staying too long in a pub. 'There was nothing to *infer*...'

'Maybe, but that isn't the point,' Ralph countered, with a terseness that hurt. 'You have to respect how she – Moira – was feeling. How your actions *allowed* her to feel.' He tucked in a loose flap of shirt. 'You cannot discount other people's emotions in this world any more, Lucas, and, though it can get messy, it is for the best reasons. We all need Moira to feel understood if we are to move forwards on this. We need her – and indeed all our students – to feel *safe*, right?'

Lucas nodded because he did not trust himself to speak. He felt like a student himself, a dim one, being lectured. '*Et tu, Brute,*' he muttered as Ralph walked away. Once the saloon door had swung shut, he went to the bar to order another pint and a double chaser, which he drank steadily and swiftly, back in the chair that faced the wall and not the room.

Paying a call to the toilets before leaving, he leaned towards the basin mirror as he washed his hands. He looked fine. Surprisingly okay, in fact. No one would know the turmoil inside.

Out in the street he was aware of both his throat and his leg hurting a little less and his spirits trying to lift. He would push for the mediation to happen as soon as possible. Get it over with. Innocence cut through bollocks – it always did. He was worrying too much, anticipating worst-case scenarios. Dylan doing a runner had made him feel fragile, that was the trouble. His skin was thinner, less equipped to deal with anything. In the meantime, Ralph was right: he just needed to retain the courage of his own convictions, power on through, stay strong. He would start by going into college for the first time in days; maybe even do a spot of work, he decided, with the wild optimism of one who has downed three pints and a double Johnnie Walker on an empty stomach.

Ewan, on duty in the porter's lodge, gave him a cheery wave as he passed by, calling out how cold it had turned.

'Freezing,' Lucas agreed, hurrying across the courtyard to his staircase and wondering, as the hollowness inside his stomach increased, whether there might be any biscuits left in the tin he kept for students. As it turned out, there weren't, and the air in his room had the stale coldness of an empty fridge. He turned up the radiator, which gurgled discouragingly, and wrapped his scarf more tightly round his neck before sitting down at his desk. The idea of settling to any work had already crumbled. Instead, he spent some time composing a message of thanks to Ralph, apologising if he had seemed negative and assuring him that he recognised the welfare of Moira as being paramount. Ralph was key now. He needed to keep him onside.

When his phone lit up with a video call from Heidi, Lucas threw himself onto the sofa to take it, propping a cushion behind his head. 'Liebchen, what a lovely surprise, I thought we agreed tomorrow. I've just had a drink with Ralph – it's looking like mediation, which is a pain, but he will navigate us through, I am sure of it... Heidi? Are you okay...?'

'No, Lucas, I am not *okay*. I am terrible. I...'

The cushion tumbled to the floor as Lucas sat up, properly taking in his fiancée's ashen face and the red rims of her eyes. 'Are you sick?' A cold dread was already squeezing his heart. A dread that caused him to talk on, like a madman, about whether she was unwell, and, if so, all she needed were rest and analgesics. His brain whirred as he jabbered, while Heidi shook her head and tried to get on top of her tears. Lucas became aware of the big central window, just a couple of feet from the end of the sofa. He could fling himself out of it in seconds. Two storeys up – a thirty-foot drop onto the old stone slabs below – it would do the job. The image, so visually clear, brought a small point of calm deep inside the fear.

When Heidi, in a halting, wretched voice, mastered her emotions sufficiently to confess that she had managed to lose her precious engagement ring, Lucas could have wept with relief.

'On a walk... with my grandparents... I threw a stick for the dogs, and somehow it flew off. We looked and we looked...'

'It's only a ring. We can get another,' Lucas cried joyfully, even as he remembered that the ring hadn't been insured. It had cost three thousand, seven hundred pounds. But who cared, he decided wildly, if the heart of its erstwhile owner was still his?

'We looked and looked,' Heidi repeated. 'Everywhere. Then it started to rain.' She paused, raising her eyes, gluey still from weeping, to look properly into his. 'So much bad luck, Lucas. It is like the universe is against us.'

'The *universe*?'

She turned her head at the sound of something Lucas couldn't hear. 'And now Mutti is calling, so I must go. Lucas, I am so sorry for the ring... so sorry.'

'Heidi, wait—'

'I have to go. We are eating now. I am sorry, Lucas.'

'Can we talk tomorrow, then?'

'Yes. Tomorrow.' She had gone calm and flat. Her mouth looked swollen, and he found himself wondering how crying could do that.

'The ring, it doesn't matter,' he said softly. 'Okay?'

She nodded. 'Okay. Thank you, Lucas.'

After the call, Lucas stayed on the sofa. Despite the chill in the room, he felt hot and drained. His throat pulsed. Fatigue was pulling him down, a drug, promising oblivion and respite. He swivelled and lay on his side on the sofa, drawing his knees up, using his palms as a pillow for his cheek. The universe. Against them. He kicked the thought away and closed his eyes. Sleep came fast, bringing not rest, but a labyrinth of dead ends, blocking hopeless quests for lost rings, lost children, and answers to questions he couldn't understand.

Esther woke early on Sunday morning, full of resolve to throw herself straight back into her manual labours, only to be blind-sided by a second postcard from Dylan, falling out from between a pile of junk-mail catalogues as she was dropping them into her recycling bin.

'I almost threw it away,' she confessed, her voice trembling slightly, once she had succeeded in getting both Lucas and Lily on a FaceTime call. 'Then we wouldn't even have known...'

'That he's in Barcelona supposedly en route to Buenos Aires?' chipped in Lily scathingly. She was tousled and still in her pyjamas, clearly tetchy at having been prised from her bed. 'It doesn't exactly *change* anything, does it?'

'But how the hell can he afford to go there?' Lucas grunted. 'By magic carpet?'

'He must have savings from his bar work, and be getting jobs as he goes,' Esther said feebly. 'I mean, that is what he said he was going to do. Lily, I don't suppose you have heard...'

'No,' she snapped, 'I have not. And I still think he is an idiot.'

'Let's see it again,' Lucas said, in a voice so croaky that Esther realised he had to be fighting off some bug. His skin was doing that thing it did, of looking colourless as opposed to pale, and there were scaly bits on his lips that made her long to reach for her lip balm.

'So, he's into churches, is he?' remarked Lily archly, as Esther obligingly held up the postcard of Gaudi's famous cathedral. Esther guessed that the absence of a second communication for his sister was a factor in this sour mood. Lucas still hadn't received so much as one, but they all knew better than to draw attention to that.

'The Sagrada Familia is a bit more than a church,' he muttered.

'The Casa Batlló was my favourite,' Esther murmured, her pulse quickening as the usual image of Dylan surfaced, a speck swallowed up by hordes, lost and unprotectable. '"All well. Don't worry,"' she read out again. 'So that's something.' A silence followed, and Esther found herself wishing Dylan could see the three of them at their phone screens, hanging on his every bland, printed syllable, desperate to understand and get him safely home.

'I bet he's enjoying putting everyone in a lather, as per,' Lily declared, sounding affectionate now as well as exasperated, before signing herself off with a mumble about another busy day of band auditions.

'I mean, at least he's still alive,' said Esther, after she had gone.

'Yes, that continues to be a matter for great celebration.'

'Are you *taking* anything, Lucas? You really don't look...'

'I'm fine, thanks. A lot on, that's all. Work-wise. You look well. Are you well?'

'Not so bad. Coping.'

'Good. Coping. Yes, that rather sums it up.'

* * *

It was good to have the garden to get on with. Esther had put on old tracksuit bottoms and a fleece, not minding the turn in the weather, colder still since yesterday, but dry. She cut and chopped and piled, too lost in a trance of determination to bother with lunch. Her shoulders ached and her hands hurt, despite the mighty gloves; but the sense of progress was moreish, even as it dawned on her that, with her slow pace, it would certainly be many months before the ugly lumps of cleared ground, riddled with roots and stones, could begin to resemble the pristine lawn of which she dreamed.

By five o'clock, with her head thrumming, a hunger headache hovering, Esther was ready to stop. She had progressed to within ten feet or so of the buried potting shed – the ridge of its roof was tantalisingly close, like an upturned rowing boat sticking out of the high dense sea of thorny foliage. One last cut, she decided, forcing her aching arms up to perform the task, picking out a huge, thick mini-trunk of a branch. It slid gracefully from its moorings revealing, just as she was about to turn her back on it, the start of another fox-run, much bigger than any of the earlier ones. Big enough even for her to crawl along, Esther calculated in surprise, hauling the cut branch out of the way and dropping onto her hands and knees to investigate.

It actually felt nice being on all fours, relief for her aching back and arms. So much so that she spent a few moments arching and bending her spine, before starting to shimmy forwards, commando style, wary of thorns and of coming nose to nose with a fox, but also quite enjoying herself. A few feet in, the tunnel curved round a particularly gnarled and knotted section of undergrowth, and then opened quite suddenly onto a space wide and high enough to sit in. She scrambled inside, incredulous. It was a green cave. Like something out of a fairy tale, except clearly beaten out of the undergrowth by real hands. Opposite her was an entrance to another tunnel, going deeper into the garden.

Esther sat back on her heels, allowing these observations to sink in. Somewhere in the air outside, a bird chirruped, thickening the silence that followed. Her hair, fixed for convenience into a ponytail, had flopped annoyingly out of hold. Esther took a few moments to retie it, scraping every strand back into the toggle as tightly as it would go, fighting the strong temptation to retreat the way she had come. But this was *her* garden, she reminded herself fiercely, feeling for the hard comforting rectangle of her phone in her fleece pocket before crawling forwards to the next tunnel.

When, after a few feet, it widened suddenly, into another cleared section, she froze. For this was not a cave so much as a shoulder-high space, beaten back this time to accommodate access to the front of the potting shed. The upturned boat revealed itself to be a solid roof, melded into the knitted canopy of ivied brambles surrounding it. The latched door, its handle gone, was pushed to, but ajar. Set into its top half was a small square dusty window. The stillness now was absolute. Even the birds had fallen quiet. Esther crept towards the door to peer inside, hearing only the pumping of her heart in her ears. The pane was dirty, but she could make out a large trug basket beside a pile of old black plastic sheeting and blankets. Near it, on the ground, was an upturned plastic lid containing what looked like the crusty remains of food. Propped against the wall behind was an assortment of ancient implements, including a rusted hand scythe, a broken tennis racket, a fishing rod, and a croquet mallet. The entire ceiling was ragged with cobwebs, thick as knitting. Glinting in the dim light on a narrow shelf above the sports equipment were several candle stumps and some tins; one of which, Esther noticed, was cat food. Right by the door, under her nose, a stack of bricks served as a fourth leg for a broken chair; beside that, on top of an upturned white metal bucket, was a small flowerpot stuffed with cigarette stubs.

When the blankets moved, Esther let out a sound she did not recognise as her own. Turning to sprint, she forgot to duck. Her hair snagged on something in the barbed lattice overhead. She cried out again, in terror and then pain as she tore her hair free to plunge towards the mouth of the brambled tunnel by which she had arrived. Somewhere in the distance she was aware of the faint, piercing ring of an electric doorbell that could have been hers. Once. Twice. Then something seemed to grab her leg. She tried to scream again, but the need to breathe prevented her, as did the realisation that the thing against her leg wasn't grabbing but rubbing, while emitting a purr like a rumbly engine.

'Jesus, Chico, Jesus.' Esther placed a trembling hand on the animal's broad back, close to tears as her shock played out. She threw a glance back at the shed, its door still a few inches ajar, just as she had first seen it. Someone had been using the space inside, sitting, smoking, feeding the cat, but they were gone.

EXCURSIONS

21

Lucas had made a point of booking a seat in the quiet carriage. So he could work, he told himself, while aware that what he really wanted was to avoid the risk of proximity to other people, talking and laughing into each other's faces and phones; leading a mostly carefree existence, which had been his privilege too, not so long ago.

As it turned out, the train was mercifully empty for a Monday morning. As he settled with his laptop on his tray table, sipping from the latte he had bought at the station, the autumnal browns and auburns of the landscape streaming past the window, an echo of his old self hummed. He was still on paracetamol and his calf ropey, but his throat was definitely less sore; and to be doing something at last, instead of sitting like a doomed man waiting for execution, also felt pretty bloody good. He had told Moira's father as much in their email exchange, reiterating how grateful he was for the invitation to talk man to man, father to father, about the entire *misunderstanding* that had arisen with his daughter. Ever since, how this chance of a proper conversation might go had been playing with mounting clarity and hope in Lucas's head: the opportunity to explain and reassure, the parallels that could be drawn and shared as parents, maybe even confiding some of his own current agonies and difficulties with regard to Dylan.

Lucas scrolled through to the opening page of his symbolism paper, so familiar now. Two months in, and he had edged up to a measly nine hundred words – shameful and dispiriting for an academic supposedly at the top of his game. Stress made you indecisive, Lucas brooded wearily, recalling the number of shirts he had pulled on and off hangers that morning. In the end he had opted for a moss-green one of brushed cotton, so old it was starting to fray at the collar and cuffs, but soft as a friend against his skin. It had been one of the first gifts Esther had given him, early proof that she was good on colours. Good on a lot of things actually, which, if he was honest, Lucas could now see habituation had led him to take for granted. A full fridge; regular, healthy meals; organising the children's lives – clubs, homework, play-dates, doctors, dentists, holidays – he had been off the hook for most of it. That young husbands nowadays didn't get nearly such an easy ride was plain; Ralph being a case in point, always haring off the moment college commitments permitted so as to pull his weight with something going on at home. But then he and Esther had been different creatures from a different generation, Lucas hastily reassured himself; and Esther, unlike Catherine with her supersonic vocal talent, had always been happy to recognise that her more piecemeal career fitted better than his with managing the family. Or at least she had seemed to be happy. At first.

How strange to remember love, but not to *feel* it, he pondered, deliberately summoning Heidi to mind instead; a bulwark against the past. They had talked again on Sunday and she had been rueful but much more composed about the loss of the ring. A new, more urgent focus for concern had presented itself in the form of one of her grandparents' beloved dogs falling sick, with a suspected tumour, along with a dilemma about whether to accept an out-of-the-blue invitation to go on a five day trek in the Black Forest with some Heidelberg friends the following weekend until Wednesday. It would mean extending her stay, and Lucas had told her to do so without qualms, telling her, truthfully, both that she deserved it and how grateful he was that it would give him more time to clear up the Moira mess before she returned. The thought that such a clear-up could now be hours away was beyond exciting.

Lucas shut down his work tabs and for the rest of the journey into and across London found his mind wandering beyond the usual lurches of consternation about Dylan, to parenthood instead. It was never a breeze, and Heidi, with her fierce feminism, would put him through his paces, for sure. She was in no hurry, she had said, but the day would come. And he would step up to the mark, Lucas vowed, resolving to tell her as much next time they spoke. He would prove his love and his worth. He would be a better husband, a better man.

As he stepped down onto the platform at Twickenham another image rocketed inside his head before he could stop it: of Esther, a pink scarf flying round her neck, white jeans tight round her shapely legs, tottering on too-high heels after she had somehow slid through ticket barriers to meet him on a London visit. 'I couldn't wait,' she said, planting breathy kisses across his ears and nose and cheeks, 'not one more single second.'

Lucas fumbled for his ticket and hurried out onto the street, pausing to check his phone for the postcode Charlie Giddings had given him. It was a local park, a place where, as he had put it, they could 'walk and talk'. With the mediation session now scheduled for the following Monday, still six days away, the timing was excellent in terms of giving everyone the chance to regroup. The ridiculous parameters outlined for the session still filled Lucas with outrage every time he thought of them: two adjoining college rooms, so that Moira could have her wish of not having to 'share her space' with him. He was to be kept in the second room, caged like some sort of rapacious beast. Persuading Moira that such extreme precaution was both absurd and unnecessary – that they could conduct their discussion face to face – was one of his key hopes for meeting her father. If her own parent could see reason on this, then it could prove a stepping stone to defusing everything.

Later, Lucas would wonder at what precise moment it dawned on him that the entire mission was a mistake. He'd had misgivings, of course, given the delicacy of the situation, but had taken heart from the fact that Charlie Giddings had been the one to reach out to him. Their mutual promise of complete discretion had been reassuring too.

The enormity of the encounter certainly didn't come into proper focus until Lucas turned into the cul-de-sac that housed their agreed meeting spot. Lucas spotted Moira's father at once, parked with the rigidity of a statue by the gated entrance, arms folded across his burly chest, such a far cry from the jolly, avuncular man Lucas had in his mind that he stopped in his tracks. By then Charlie had noticed him, and there was no option but to plough on. It had started to drizzle too, giving the day the look of an old film.

'Professor.' The word was full of sneer and fired, an opening salvo, before Lucas had drawn near. He opened the gate and walked through it, leaving Lucas to follow.

'Mr Giddings, I...' Lucas felt his calf twang as he hurried to catch up. His throat was full of croak and he fumbled in his coat pocket for his pastilles, popping one in his mouth. 'Thank you for this... all I want is to assure you that absolutely nothing—'

'Now, you listen to me.' Charlie Giddings spun round, jabbing his forefinger at the bridge of Lucas's nose. He was so like her, Lucas saw suddenly, with the eyes strikingly wide set and the mouth with the upper lip protruding very slightly over the lower one. 'Are you calling my daughter a liar?' The eyes were the same shape too, and grey as slate.

'I am certainly not trying to... deny... her truth...' Lucas faltered, latching onto exactly the vocabulary he despised in a bid to try to rescue the conversation. 'How I made Moira feel... I cannot...'

'Do you have even the remotest idea...' a speck of saliva landed on Lucas's cheek '...of the courage it took that girl of mine to even go to that place of yours? How out of her depth she felt? How scared? Every night Julie and I had her on the phone, saying she wanted to come home—'

'I am extremely saddened to hear that, but, Mr Giddings...'

'We *trusted* you. We trusted you with her, our precious child. Make no mistake, if I can get you struck off, I will.'

A screeching crow burst out of a nearby tree, filling Lucas with foreboding as it flew away.

22

Esther stood at her bedroom window, staring through the bars of rain at her half-shorn garden. In the steely mid-morning light it resembled a battlefield; the cleared ground a pockmarked no man's land, the shed a hump under the thatch of camouflage beyond. She had managed a couple of productive hours at her desk, despite a fitful night, snatches of which had been spent scribbling garbled thoughts about her garden dramas in Viv's journal, while the rain drummed on the patio. That her neglected wilderness had been harbouring another person was not only unnerving, it also made her feel supremely stupid. To *not* know. To *not* see what was under her own nose. It made her wonder about other things that might have passed her by. It had also brought Viv and her uncharacteristically wild theory about loneliness to mind. Someone *had* been watching her. Viv had been wrong.

By the time Esther had made it back through the brambled tunnels to her abandoned gardening gear, the rain had been falling in earnest. To her surprise, the cat had followed, darting inside as soon as she opened the back door, where it had embarked on a cautious tour of the kitchen, before lapping noisily at a saucer of milk she'd put down. One nimble leap, and it had then settled on the kitchen table, licking its paws and rubbing them over its whiskers between casting disdainful glances at Esther, trundling in and out with her bits of garden equipment, which she'd stacked into as tidy a pile as she could in a corner.

The incentive to reclaiming the potting shed thus greatly increased, but fearing the return of her squatter, Esther had found a drawing pin, and a biro, and torn a page out of Viv's book.

TO WHOM IT MAY CONCERN: THIS IS PRIVATE PROPERTY. PLEASE RING FRONT DOOR BELL IF YOU NEED HELP.

It had nonetheless taken all her resolve to pull on her cagoule and wellies and plunge back through the tangled maze to the shed, ears and eyes straining to discern anything untoward through the clamour of the downpour. Her heart had hammered with relief to see the shed door at exactly the angle she had left it. Even so, she had completed her task at a run, pushing the door to, and stabbing the note into place with the drawing pin, before diving back for home.

In the kitchen, she had peeled off her wet outer clothes and cobbled together a kitty litter with newspaper and an old baking tray. Trembling from something more than being cold, she had sought calm via alternating sips of tea and wine, messaging Sue about what had happened – asking her to pass on the news about the cat to Marcus – and then quickly put the phone down to prevent herself calling Viv. To be in the thick of aftershock – when nothing bad had happened – was daft anyway. She didn't *need* Viv. And Viv, with the new acerbity that had been slightly in evidence even before their horrible argument, certainly didn't need her. And yet how nonsensical after all their years of friendship, Ether had chided herself, seizing the mobile and calling anyway, only to find herself going straight to voicemail.

'Hey, Vivvie, I hope you are okay...' Esther had hesitated, not really wanting to leave some glib summary of the latest myriad shenanigans in her life, but then doing exactly that, Sunday evenings were prime family time, she'd reasoned, when she had got to the end without Viv interrupting, aware that finding justifications for Viv's reluctance to communicate was becoming something of a habit. A longing for Dylan had surfaced unhelpfully into the bleakness that had followed, a visceral ache, simply to feel her son's rangy teenager body in her arms. Thirteen days and it was Buenos Aires now. The Falklands, the tango, lots of beef – Esther's knowledge of Argentina was pitiful, making it utterly beyond the wit of her imagination to picture Dylan there. He didn't speak Spanish. How on earth was he managing? Or maybe he wasn't managing at all. Maybe he, too, was sheltering in some dilapidated garden building, trembling and hungry, too scared to ask for help.

When she had crawled between her sheets a little later, her phone, beeping with a message from the charger by her bed, had felt like rescue. Viv, she thought, almost tumbling off the edge of the mattress in her eagerness to read her words.

Hi Esther, Chris here. It was very nice to bump into you. I am now writing to ask if you would consider having dinner with me? I know I do not deserve a second chance, but I am hoping (fingers crossed!) you are kind enough to give me one. I was in a bad place when we met before. That is over. To meet, even just as friends, would make me a very happy – and grateful – man. I attach a link to a restaurant in Richmond. I am hoping next Tuesday evening might work? It will be on me. The least I can do. Best wishes, Chris.

That he had waited almost two days was good, Esther decided, reading the lines over several times and resisting the urge to answer with a 'yes' straight away. The restaurant looked fabulous. An invitation to dinner with an admirer. It was the perfect tonic for a person who had been in danger of feeling a bit wobbly and alone.

* * *

Esther turned her back on the rainy morning view and headed downstairs to press on with her work. A brochure launching health insurance services tailored entirely for women was not only a worthy cause; it was earning her good money. On her way down, her phone

buzzed with two new notifications: one from Chris confirming receipt
of her acceptance of his invitation with a link to the dinner booking for
the following Tuesday, and one from Sue, comprising a string of startled face emojis and a promise to be round within the hour.

'It's because I don't trust you,' Esther told Chico, finding the animal
crouched and looking tragic by the front door. She went to try and
stroke the cat's head, but it hissed and scuttled off to the kitchen.
'Thanks for the gratitude,' she muttered, noticing in the same instant a
corner of paper sticking through the jaws of her letter flap. She tugged
it free gingerly, her thoughts flying to the torn-off piece of paper now
pinned to her shed door. But it was a scrawled note from Carmela's
nephew, which, as she realised at once, had to have been there all
night.

*Rang the bell a couple of times. I am afraid my aunt passed away in
hospital yesterday. Might try and catch you before I leave tomorrow.
Thx for trying re Chico, she would have been v grateful. As am I.
Marcus.*

23

As he'd returned to the station, head bent against the soaking, squally wind, Lucas's sole desire had been to put as much distance as possible between himself and Charlie Giddings, as well as his own shattered intentions. It didn't even matter how long it took to get home. There was no one expecting him at his flat or in college, no question of being able to concentrate on any work; and not even the de-stressing possibility of taking exercise, since his calf had tightened worse than ever.

He was in limbo, Lucas realised, a little afraid of his own dejection, as, instead of moving through the station, he stood contemplating the spaghetti junction of the train map. The edges of the lines kept blurring, like his brain. The day already felt endless, but it was still only eleven o' clock. As soon as he was back in Cambridge – or maybe even on the train – he knew he would now have to start composing a letter to explain the misguided acceptance of the invitation to meet with Moira's father. It would need care and precision and humility. The motives – which had been entirely well-intentioned – needed to be emphasised, along with the plea for it not to prejudice his innocence during the looming ghastliness of mediation.

Instead, Lucas's scrutiny of the map of train lines became a calculation of how many stops Twickenham was from Esther's patch of West

London. He knew the Kingston address well enough, the chore of forwarding mail being an intermittent cause for irritation, although a reason to actually to visit his ex-wife's house had never presented itself.

The journey proved straightforward and the street easy to find. Lucas walked along it as quickly as he could manage, battling against the wind with his umbrella.

The grime of London was always a shock. The blackened bricks of the houses and the eyesore of the railway embankment, shadowing the long, thin curve of the road, gave him a shiver of gratitude that he was a visitor and not a resident. The trains alone would drive him spare, Lucas thought, as one thundered past.

It was in a state of mind marginally fortified by a reminder of his own good fortune, therefore, that Lucas stopped to appraise the small house that now accommodated his ex-wife. It sat in a string of squat terraced houses, workers' cottages by the look of them, their once sandy brickwork weathered to a charcoal grey, the paintwork scruffy. It had been Esther's decision to leave, Lucas reminded himself, suppressing another twinge of something akin to sympathy, aware suddenly of the degree of his ignorance about any aspect of her life without him. She wrote copy for business publications. She gave piano lessons. Presumably, she went on the odd date. If she had met 'someone', however, that would have surely become obvious to him – and the children – by now.

Having reached the little front gate, Lucas retreated to the other side of the street to gather himself. It was dawning on him that he should have thought to phone or message first. His mind, the part of his make-up he had always trusted the most, was like jelly. Because of bloody Moira and her unspeakable father. Because of *stress*, a term he had scornfully believed to be universally over-used, until now. Lucas hid behind the umbrella as he pondered, fishing in his pocket for his mobile. He would say he'd had a meeting in West London, he decided – the best lies always being the ones closest to the truth – and that he wanted to touch base about Dylan. His phone screen was so moist it wouldn't recognise his face. Lucas's fingers, stiff and cold, resisted cooperation as he put in his code. A cup of coffee wouldn't go amiss either, he thought – his spirits lifting a little – and maybe even a biscuit. Esther was usually kind, that was one of the things about her.

He was about to press the call button when a well-built woman in bright-green dungarees with electric-red hair, flew out of the house next to Esther's. Ducking her head and cradling herself against the rain, she hopped over the rusting loops of a fence dividing their front gardens and rang Esther's bell. The door opened almost at once and the woman disappeared inside. It was probably just a neighbourly visit to borrow something, Lucas told himself, slipping the phone back into his pocket, resolving to wait it out. A couple of minutes later, a car with a taxi sign on its roof swung into view from the other end of the street, reversing expertly into a tight space a few yards beyond the house. The driver, a swarthy-looking man in a yellow sweatshirt, a peaked cap flattening a thick mop of dark hair, leapt out and strode up the path to ring Esther's bell. Lucas peered round the edge of his brolly, feeling wrong-footed and feeble. Could she be going on another holiday? She hadn't mentioned a new trip to him, but then of course why should she? He peeked again from under the lip of his umbrella, curiosity turning to bafflement as the cabbie, too, was ushered inside.

The hand gripping the brolly was growing numb and rain was starting to trickle down inside the collar of his jacket. Lucas could feel his shirt sticking unpleasantly to his back. He ran a hand over his damp face, remembering with a shudder the flecks of Charlie Giddings' spittle, flying out with all his schoolboy invectives and threats. Moira was his little girl, and he would die protecting her. If Lucas thought he could hide behind his grand job, he could think again. In the end Lucas had stopped trying to object, letting it play out, before delivering one heartfelt denial of all wrongdoing and turning on his heel.

Lucas swapped hands, putting the cold one into the warmth of his pocket and closing his fingers round his phone. As he chewed the options over, debating what to do, a tall, bearded man with a mane of curly, brown hair and an athletic body, wearing dark jeans and a faded denim jacket, emerged from the house on the other side of Esther's, carrying a bulging plastic bag. He lifted a tarpaulin covering a small motorbike parked by the front door, apparently just to check on it, before hopping over the rather higher picket fencing on his side in order to follow in the steps of the troupe who had already presented themselves at Esther's door. As it swung open, Lucas caught a proper snapshot of Esther, wearing a blue shirt, her fair hair looking long and wild, before this guest was also ushered in. A coffee morning, then? A neighbourhood watch meeting? Or a bloody orgy for all he knew. He knew zilch about her, Lucas realised, a strange dismay washing through him.

He turned and headed slowly back towards the railway bridge, closing up the brolly because it was such a fight and he no longer cared. He felt slightly stunned by the morning's events. The miscalculation of the meeting, then spying on Esther like some sad voyeur. Of course she had carved out a new life. For two years he had known that and believed himself indifferent to it. Yet to know something and to see it in action were two very different things.

Lucas dropped the useless umbrella into a bin before entering the station. Less easy to throw away was the shadow of envy, a new and unwelcome distraction as he embarked on a draft of the dreaded letter, his fingers tapping at his laptop while the rain streaked the train window. Esther, for all the concern about Dylan, had looked quite the hostess. Indeed, she looked as if she *belonged*, even in that grungy little street. The word took a moment to arrive. It seemed to encapsulate everything now slipping from Lucas's grasp. It occurred to him in the same instant that he had always felt stronger than Esther, more fortunate. For all the difficulties in adjusting to the divorce, deep down, he had, until that moment, believed her loss to be greater than his.

SPA DAY

24

Lily dropped her head back, glad of the mask of her sunglasses, justified by the mid-afternoon September sun now streaming through the glass-walls along the section of the indoor pool. On the other side of the glass, a stone balcony terrace overlooked broad lawns, high hedges, pathways, and ebullient flowerbeds. A worthy setting for a TV drama, Lily had thought, arriving first at the hotel that morning, relieved to discover that the place lived up to its classy online images and somewhat hefty price tag. That she should be finding herself, five hours later, watching the slow crawl of the clock hands on the dial above the pool entrance, had not been her intention. This was her mother's birthday treat, purchased and arranged with love, she reminded herself; she had no business not enjoying it, let alone struggling, more and more, to conceal the fact.

That her mum was clearly in determinedly buoyant form, full of affection and energy, should have helped, but also didn't. From the welcome glass of prosecco, through their joint mini-pedicures, side by side in big leather chairs, and then over lunch, sitting on stools in the health bar with delicious bowls of salad and freshly squeezed juices, she had bombarded Lily with conversation. Probing for answers on all the obvious subjects – Heidi and her father especially – that Lily felt most disinclined to discuss; and then, when sensing reticence, providing ebullient reports on all the things that had been going on in London. Lots of things, by the sound of it. Things that made Lily in danger of feeling she was listening to a stranger. The dead neighbour. The dead neighbour's cat. The nephew. The garden shed that looked as if someone had used it, but which now, thanks to her mother's efforts, sat proud and exposed and up to storing a range of new garden tools. The nice neighbours, who had a friend, busy that very minute installing front and back CCTV to cover both properties, for peace of mind – though they didn't want payment. And, between every subject, every lively report, the subject of her brother popped up, a recurring pulse. Dylan, Dylan, Dylan. Whether he was all right. When he might come home. Whether he was happy. Whether he was sad. All of it proving, as if Lily needed it, her younger sibling's unfailing capacity to dominate the family agenda, no matter whether he was messing up away from home or under their noses.

Lily wasn't accustomed to feeling mean. She loved her little brother and his hopelessness, but it had been easier during the days when he would listen to her. Days long gone. But in current circumstances, even trying to explain that to her mother was impossible. As impossible as trying to find a way of saying that she didn't mind about Heidi – as a person or a prospective new life-partner for her father. Every subject seemed to lead towards potential explosions, making them all off-limits. So much so that, during the manicures that followed their lunch, Lily had resorted to talking in depth about her thesis instead. She could see her mum doing her best to follow, a slight glaze in her eyes, but at least it was a safe topic. Work – her brain – was the one thing that had never let her down. It was always *there* – a world she could escape into, which provided the opportunity to make things add up, to find *right* answers – instead of grappling with the increasing muddle of real life, soothed her as nothing else. Realising, at some point during her mid-teens, that her dad clearly found a similar sort of solace in his own field of study had been both a revelation and a bond – one that she had once imagined was unbreakable.

Lily flipped over on the sun lounger, so her back was to Esther. It was four o' clock, and they had until six. Two more hours.

'Are you okay, darling?'

'I think I might be coming on, but otherwise all good, thanks,' Lily murmured, picking the one lie that could never be challenged or found out.

'Oh, but, sweetheart, why didn't you say? No wonder you didn't want to swim. I've got some paracetamol in here somewhere...'

Lily could hear her rummaging in her handbag. 'It's fine, Mum. I don't need anything. My first day is always bad, isn't it?'

'Yes, it is.'

Lily heard the motherly softness in her tone; and when a hand arrived on her shoulder, giving a tender squeeze, her entire body flushed with shame.

'I have loved every second of today, Lily, sweetheart. Both you and Dylan truly spoiled me this year, though goodness knows when I shall get around to his.'

Dylan again. It had been at least five minutes.

'Maybe when he's back.' Her mother was sounding bleak, lost inside her own head again. 'I can't think what buying that list of adventures cost him.'

Lily tensed, while the hateful, unsayable observation – that her spa treat for two would outvalue Dylan's thrill-seekers gift any day – stomped across her mind. 'Do you know what, Mum?' she said instead, as brightly as she could. 'I think I'll head back to the changing rooms, if you don't mind. I'm actually getting a bit chilly.'

'Of course, I don't mind, darling.'

'And I know I said we'd do the Jacuzzi, but...' Lily faltered, guilt swamping her again.

'That will be the *last* thing you're in the mood for,' her mother said stoutly. 'Why don't we just have a cup of tea instead? I'll sort that, while you have a lovely warming shower.'

'Great. Thanks, Mum.' Lily, gathering her things, made a show of looking at her watch. 'Actually, though, I might head off soon. Matteo needs the car tonight, and you know what the traffic will be like. But *please* stay, Mum, won't you? Our time isn't up until six.' Lily hurried off towards the pool exit as fast as her complimentary towelling slip-ons would allow, managing to avoid protest, but fully aware of the gaze of puzzlement and concern boring into her back.

In the shower cubicle she took her time, leaning at an angle with her palms against the smooth jade tiled walls so that the fierce jets of hot water could pummel her head. To have raised any maternal alarm bells was the last thing she had intended. She *was* fine. It was just a question of staying strong, finding a moment to talk to Matteo, riding it out. To burden her mother wouldn't be fair. Unlike many of her girl-friends, the pair of them had never had one of those emotionally clingy types of relationships anyway. They were more separate, which didn't mean less loving, and Lily had always thought that cool.

Lily tipped her face up to the wheel of the shower head, forcing herself to keep her eyes open as the tears streamed. It stung like fuck, but the pain was at least something else to focus on.

As she passed through Reception ten minutes later her heart sank ungratefully at the sight of her mother, already seated at one of the elegant round tables on the fringes of the entrance café, overseeing the receipt of a pot of tea, two cups, and a plate of biscuits. She must have changed with lightning speed and looked striking and bright-eyed in her lovely blue silk shirt – one that Lily hadn't seen before and had already complimented her on.

Lily quickly shoved on her sunglasses as she approached, not wanting to provoke any comments on the bloodshot state of her eyes. 'Wow, Mum, thanks, but, like I said, I've really—'

'Lily, darling, please just sit down. A cup of tea. A biscuit.'

'Thanks, Mum, but – and please don't take this wrong – tea would make me need to pee on the drive and I am afraid I literally do not have time for...' Lily gestured helplessly at the table, weighing up her own heartlessness as her gaze travelled over, not only all the tea things, but her mother's iPhone, parked by the little pot and lit up with the exuberant message:

EXCITED FOR OUR TUESDAY DINNER DATE! C XXX

'I've told Matt I'm on my way – he's already cooking supper,' she went on quickly, pressing one hand on her mother's shoulder to keep her seated as she bent to kiss her cheek. 'So, please, just enjoy your tea, Mum. I'm really glad we had today and we'll talk soon.'

Her mother stood up to pull her close. 'Such a lovely birthday present, darling, thank you.'

'Great, Mum. For me too. Forgive me for shooting off, okay?'

'Of course.'

Lily squeezed hard as they embraced, aware of gripping something tightly deep inside herself. She took a gulp of her mum's familiar scent, and then a second, before pulling free and striding towards the big foyer doors.

25

'It's a small tear. See here?' The doctor swivelled his laptop towards Lucas, pointing at an unreadable blur on the screen. 'Quite significant, but not acute. The sort of incidents which, I fear, grow more likely as our bodies age. Rest, elevation, painkillers, ice...'

'I did ice it,' Lucas reminded him plaintively, bending down to retie his shoelace.

'Yes, the old frozen peas technique.' The doctor, who was a lean, energetic youth, with gangly limbs and a slouching manner, grinned approvingly. 'And if you had rested it too, that might have done the trick. But I think, from what you have described, with all the walking on your trip to London last Monday, and then the run yesterday, it really has—'

'It was just a jog.' Lucas grimaced, deeply regretting the desperate logic that a 'stiffened' muscle might benefit from being 'loosened'. He had pulled up with a howl of pain just as a women's rowing eight swept by. Watching the boat speed on, his calf on fire, had heightened Lucas's torment at his own decrepitude. The fact that only a couple of weeks now remained until the start of the new university year rushed at him with fresh force. To be a hobbling wreck, with so much to do – let alone the shadow of Moira to contend with – he didn't know how he would manage.

'So, my opinion,' the doctor was saying, talking as his fingers flew over his keypad, 'is that these recent exertions turned what was a small tear into a larger one. Hence the swelling.'

'How long till it gets better?'

'A month... possibly six weeks. To be honest, that's partly in your hands. The more you can rest it, the faster it will heal. A support bandage might help, but I'm afraid there are no shortcuts. Otherwise, paracetamol.' He pulled an apologetic face and leapt off his chair to tug back the curtain.

'Thank you,' Lucas muttered, unable to contain a wince as he stood up. 'I guess I shouldn't really have bothered A&E, but the way it blew up today...'

'No probs, Professor Shaw. We are here to serve, and it's pretty quiet at the moment, as you can see,' he added kindly, standing out of the way as Lucas shuffled past. 'Take it easy now, okay. Rest, ice, analgesics. If it all flares up again, see your GP.'

Take it easy. Yeah, right. Lucas hobbled back out to the street where the empty taxi rank and small queue of other hopefuls was a reminder that, for all the quietness of the emergency department, the weekend was still rush hour for some. The streets swarmed with people and cars – full of life, that thing he once thought he had the hang of.

It was Saturday afternoon. The mediation meeting, fixed for Monday, hung over the following week like a mighty black cloud, blocking any clear view of what would come after. Forty hours to go. Resting a torn muscle might be possible, but Lucas knew already that no amount of lying on his back would produce any sleep. Calling Heidi in search of support was out of the question. Not just because the Black Forest trekking was apparently meant to be device-free and she wasn't due back in Bonn until Wednesday evening, but because he was too low to face her anyway. They had spoken the previous morning, before she set off, and he had been only too aware of the tightness in his voice – and hers – when it got to updating her on progress with regard to

Moira. She was pleased the mediation was arranged at last, she had said, in her most business-like way, though they both knew that being 'pleased' did not come into it. A proud and vehement champion of women's rights was engaged to a man who had been accused of crossing the most basic of red lines with a *student*. Even if Heidi believed in his innocence – which sometimes, in his darkest moments, Lucas caught himself doubting – it was hardly a situation to rejoice in.

He had quickly moved on to promises to check availability of the chapel for dates the following summer instead, and then made tender enquiries about the poorly dog, Wolfgang, apparently sicker and declining faster than anyone had predicted. Asked, just before signing off, about what else he had got up to during the week, Lucas had been careful to airbrush London from his reply. Charlie Giddings. Esther. The mortification was with him still, as hard to bear as the realisation that some things had to be kept secret after all, even from Heidi; that no slate could stay completely clean.

In the taxi he settled into a corner, carefully stretching his sore leg out on the seat, but making sure to keep his shoe clear of the upholstery.

The driver glared through his rear-view mirror. 'I don't think so, mate, if you don't mind.'

'Sorry, it's just... okay, hang on.' Lucas gingerly lowered the leg back onto the floor of the cab, using both hands.

Negotiating the stairs up to his flat fifteen minutes later, clutching that day's junk mail from his post box, proved another ordeal. After some experimentation, Lucas managed it step by step, moving his good leg first and then quickly bringing the sore one to join it, while clinging for dear life to the banister. Maybe his injured state would evoke compassion from the Monday panel, he mused gloomily and without conviction, fetching painkillers from his bathroom cupboard as soon as he had made it into the flat and swallowing three down with a beer while riffling through the post. Pizza delivery, Indian takeaway, an estate agent and... a postcard. Of the Iguazu Falls.

Lucas held the card by its edges, like a photograph he was afraid of smearing with clumsy fingers. It was a print of a photograph, showing the epic scale of the famously mighty cascades of water, streaked with the red of the South American earth as they poured from the outcrops fringing the three countries they straddled. Argentina, Brazil, Paraguay. What a place. Lucas scrutinised every detail, his heart thudding. Deemed worthy of contact at last. The joy was like heat, until laced suddenly with a chill of terror at the notion of Dylan, hapless, devil-may-care eejit extraordinaire, standing anywhere near such gargantuan torrents. He'd find a ledge, go for a selfie and slip. Or drop his phone and fall in trying to fish it out.

Lucas slowly turned the card over to read the message, fearful of what he might find.

Hey Dad, amazing or what. D.

More heat coursed through him. No question mark, but who cared? 'Bloody boy,' he shouted at the ceiling, taking a celebratory swig of beer and then heaving himself up from the sofa, looking round for a good place to put the card. He chose the middle of the mantelpiece in the end, propped up against a slim, blue vase that had always lived there, but which he never got around to filling with flowers.

26

As she drove, Esther made calculations – the time Lily set off, the time *she* had set off, the likely, law-abiding progress of her daughter versus her own reckless breakneck speed. Except that Esther felt as though she had never in her life driven with greater care. Between overtaking lumbering farm vehicles, speed-camera signs and the occasional roundabout, she flew smoothly onwards, gripping the steering wheel with ferocious intent, focussed solely on catching up with Matteo's little blue Fiat. Something had gone wrong, and she wasn't sure what. All she knew was that it had to be her fault, rabbiting on probably, grilling instead of enquiring, making Lily feel shut out, or pissed off; blowing the chance to which she had been so looking forward, of having her daughter to herself for once. Lily was so socially adept, that was the trouble – so good at appearing interested and asking the right questions. What Esther had overlooked – what not seeing enough of her had allowed her to forget – was how Lily did not volunteer things; how it took the greatest care and gentleness to tease them out.

Precious time had been lost settling the bill for the tea that Lily hadn't wanted. The nice young man at Reception had got confused, trying to add the bill to the one already pre-paid, affording Esther a glimpse of the ridiculously huge amount the birthday treat had cost.

Motherhood was a lot like telepathy, she reflected darkly, rocketing past scrubby harvested fields, fresh still from the recent heavy rain and gleaming gold in the early evening September sun. Especially with a child who had always relished her own self-sufficiency, who did not ask for help.

Esther swerved to dodge a pheasant pecking at something on the grass verge, her concentration leapfrogging back into a state of panic. So, what was wrong now? Lily's ham-fisted, contradicting lies – that Matteo needed the car and then that he was cooking dinner – had been the trigger for the decision to give chase. It wasn't like Lily to be so clumsy.

The familiar longing to talk to Viv pulsed. But not even Esther's voice message on the night after her garden traumas had prompted a call back. Instead, a brief text arrived the following morning, offering sympathy and a startled face emoji, but then pulling out of the 31 October dinner on the grounds that Brian had booked a surprise city-break to Prague. A wedding anniversary treat, so she was sure Esther would understand. Esther did understand, but that hadn't stopped her feeling hurt. Clinging to the notion that it was a good date for some sort of attempt at sociability, she had tried Shona and Carole, but they couldn't make it either. That left Sue and Dimitri, her new stalwarts, who had sweetly said yes, a kindness that still hadn't entirely dispelled the disturbing sense that leaving Lucas had somehow morphed into losing her oldest friends.

Esther's head buzzed. She rounded a bend at speed, the T-junction arriving out of nowhere. The car bucked when she braked, the tyres shrieking as she skidded across the centre of the road, coming to a halt at the foot of a sign on the opposite verge. Blurred traffic shot past, just feet from her front bumper. But none were turning into her road and the way behind her remained clear. Shaking, checking her mirrors over and over, Esther reversed and manoeuvred back into the correct lane. In the same instant a van appeared in her side mirror, approaching at speed, forcing her to get on with the turn. Esther took it slowly, swinging into a break in the traffic streaming towards Cambridge, and squeezing the steering wheel now simply to still the tremble in her arms. It didn't matter and would pass, she soothed herself. She was okay. She would drive all the way to Lily and Matteo's little block of flats if necessary. There was nothing to get back for. Nothing that mattered more than reaching Lily.

The Fiat floated into view a few minutes later. Esther caught up until she was as close as she dared, flashing her lights and her hazards, and tooting her horn. She saw her daughter's first angry glance in the rear-view mirror, and then the gradual gawping recognition that it wasn't a road-rage nut who was tailgating her, but her own mother.

* * *

'So, you're worried about your brother.'

Lily grimaced. 'Well, of course. I mean, we all are. Look, Mum, this was sweet of you – and totally insane. I thought I was being arrested or something.'

'I'm worried about you, Lily,' Esther said flatly. 'Something is up. I know it is.'

Lily sighed, folding her arms and shaking her head. They had pulled into a layby and were leaning side by side against her car. 'Mum, I already told you. My period...' She screwed up her face, in order, Esther sensed, not to look her in the eye.

'Apart from that you're *fine*, you mean?' she countered dryly. 'And meanwhile, Matteo both needs the car and needs you home because he is cooking?'

Lily squinted at something through the trees screening a field of blue-plastic-covered hay bales. 'Actually, the truth is, it has been a bit... hectic... between us recently... with him massively into the band and... me pretty stressed about my thesis.'

'You're too good at worrying about others, that's your trouble,' Esther said gently, having waited for more that wasn't forthcoming. She reached down and picked up Lily's slim hand, planting a kiss on the knuckles. 'Between you and Matteo, darling, is it bad?'

'Oh, no. Truly not. It's just... like... we are both a bit preoccupied with other stuff at the moment.'

'And as for the thesis,' Esther continued, having waited in vain again for elaboration, 'you should obviously talk to your supervisor.'

'Yes. Exactly. I'm going to. This week. I have a time fixed, actually.'

'Good. And as for your father,' Esther ploughed on, feeling like a bloodhound still seeking the right trail, 'and Heidi—'

'I've told you, Mum, I've got no problem with Dad remarrying,' Lily cried, 'and neither has Dylan that I am aware...' She drew in a quick breath, visibly steadying herself. 'Look, Dad did an okay job of talking to us about it, that's all. And I like Heidi. Sorry, Mum, but I do. She's all right. And anyway, the thing about Dad,' she muttered, dropping her gaze and fiddling with one of her newly painted nails, 'is that it's so obvious he needs *someone*. He's just, like, no *good* on his own. Unlike you...'

'Me?'

'Yeah, you, Mum. You just get on with things. You make a decision and go ahead. Like... I don't know... clearing your garden, writing help-notes to homeless trespassers, making all these new pals in London. You're just pretty fearless, I guess.' She pushed off the car, smiling almost normally for the first time, and dusting the back of her jeans in what was clearly a preparation to be on her way.

'Well, in that case I am *fearlessly* going to come and take you out next week.' Esther crossed her arms, blocking the driver's door. 'For dinner. Just the two of us. Before term starts. Name your day. As early or late in the evening as you like.'

'The only day I could do next week is Tuesday,' Lily said at once, a curiously challenging look in her eye. 'So, if that doesn't work then later in the term maybe?'

'Tuesday works,' Esther said stoutly, knowing Chris would understand, managing daughters being something they had in common. 'If

Matteo is out, I can bring stuff to cook. Or we can go somewhere. Whatever you prefer. Just let me know. And now you may leave,' she joked, hugging her and then stepping aside so Lily could get back into the car.

27

Chico trotted into the hall the moment she opened the front door, perhaps in the hope of food, more likely in the hope of escape. Esther quickly slammed it shut, just in case. The cat dawdled, as if he couldn't decide either, rubbing himself so enthusiastically against the thin legs of her little hall table that its drawer rattled.

'Good day?' Esther murmured, kicking off her shoes, enjoying the quiet pad-pad of the animal's hefty paws as he followed her into the kitchen.

She quickly messaged Chris about having to shift their Tuesday dinner, and then delved into the bag of tinned cat food Marcus had delivered the morning after Carmela's death, Sue having kindly passed on the news about finding the cat. With Dimitri and Sue already there, and all of them keen to offer their commiserations, Esther had invited him to stay for coffee, but he had rushed off, looking understandably distracted and promising to be in touch again soon about a new home for his aunt's pet.

'Which is why I am spoiling you, with *rabbit deluxe*,' Esther told Chico as he purred round her legs. She had just finished dolloping the contents into a fresh saucer when her phone lit up with a call from Chris.

'Sorry to muck you around,' Esther said at once, 'but hopefully we can—'

'Playing hard to get, is it?'

'Not at all.' Esther laughed uncertainly, dropping into a chair, one eye on the cat. 'It turns out I need to be with my daughter that night, but let's arrange another date now.' She reached for Viv's diary journal, flicking past a list begun for the spa day, which hadn't progressed beyond 'swimming costume'.

'Ah, I see. Righty ho. I shall try not to mind, in that case. And talking of your daughter, how was today's *girls'* treat, then?' He laughed, as if he had cracked a great joke.

'It was very nice, thanks.' Esther found she was speaking more and more quietly.

'Did you have *treatments*?'

'Oh yes, a manicure, and also a massage which was —'

'Ah, so you're rubbed and oiled all over, like the slippery fish you are...'

Esther held the phone at arm's length, giving it a stare of despairing disbelief. When she put it back to her ear Chris was still talking, his voice softer and looser, chuntering almost to himself, by the sound of it. 'Maybe your *masseur* was a young girl – a *masseuse* – with small firm hands and...' hearing his breathing thicken, Esther was tempted to laugh '...and maybe she rubbed all those parts of you that others have not been allowed to reach. Parts I very much want to reach... parts I like to think about... like right now, Esther... and I mean, *right now*... Christ, talk about keeping a guy waiting, but I tell you what, my gorgeous, things waited for taste all the fucking sweeter. And when I say taste, I mean *taste*...'

'Hey, Chris... I'm really not...'

'Not what?'

'Not in the mood... for this... I mean...' Esther stuttered. *Just hang up*, she told herself, *just hang up*.

'Oh, I get it.' He laughed again. 'The lady is going to hold out on me, is she? The knight is going to have to put away his charger and his lance and—'

'I'm not against knights,' Esther said crisply – a part of her brain swerving unhelpfully to Lucas, and aware of sounding like the prude she wasn't, 'or lances for that matter. I'm just not that keen on people who talk crap when, by the sound of it, they're off their heads.'

'Is that so? Hark at the damsel. Tell me how much you want it. I know you want it—'

Esther cut him off and dropped the phone onto the table as if it were something infected. When it rang again, displaying Chris's number, she put it on silent. Still on vibrate mode, it jiggled on the kitchen table like a child's wind-up toy, to the great interest of Chico, who tried to jab it with his paws.

As the calls kept arriving Esther felt both a little afraid and silly for feeling so. Chris, as he had worked hard to convince her, wasn't all bad, he was just a mess. But no one had to take on a mess if they didn't want to, she reminded herself firmly. She snatched up the mobile and texted:

Sorry, Chris, but we really are done. Two very different people. Please do NOT contact me again. Ever.

The phone immediately fell silent. She stared at it in relief, exchanging a look with the cat, who seemed disappointed. After some thought, she took the precaution of blocking his number anyway.

When her phone buzzed with a message half an hour later, she still jumped. But it was only Marcus.

Sorry to disturb. Saw you were back. Could I drop something off in 5? Leaving v early tomorrow and it can't really keep. Cheers, M.

Esther groaned. By then half watching TV and picking at a plate of leftovers for her supper, still somewhat rattled by Chris's call, she couldn't have been less in the mood for a visit of any kind.

Sure.

She texted back with a sigh, aware she must look a sight, with her skin visibly oily from the massage – having skipped the chance of a shower to get tea sorted. She put on an old favourite wool cardigan that was lying on the back of the sofa, but couldn't summon the energy to check her face or find a hairbrush.

Five minutes later exactly, she opened the door to a sprawling bunch of yellow roses, half a bush's worth by the look of it.

'Sorry, they're only from the garden... not exactly elegant.' He lowered the flowers to offer a smile of apology. 'They're just to say a proper thank you for finding and fostering—'

'You've had a haircut,' Esther exclaimed, unable to hide her astonishment at the transformation.

'Ah, yes.' He touched his head as if he too needed a reminder of the reduction of the thick raggedy tresses to a glossy half-inch, revealing in the process a high broad forehead and a much clearer view of his dark-lashed, wide-set brown eyes. The beard had gone too, making him look considerably younger, Esther noted, more like mid-thirties than the forty-something she had assumed. 'Yeah, the Samson look has gone and I can't say I miss it, despite – of course – the potential loss of super-powers.' He grinned, shoving the flowers at her. 'Anyhoo. These are for you. They're prickly as hell – be warned – but a sincere token of my appreciation nonetheless. And I know my aunt would agree.'

'How lovely, and how completely unnecessary. Thank you very much.' Esther carefully took charge of the thorny stems. 'Your poor aunt. I am very sorry again for your loss.'

'Thanks. Though it was the only likely outcome, I'm afraid. And now it's turning into a bit of a logistical nightmare, to be honest. The family want her buried back in Portugal – Milfontes, where she grew up. I was thinking a cremation here first, but they're having none of it.' Without his gift, he seemed uncertain as to what to do with his hands. 'Sorry, but there's been no joy yet from the cat rehoming place, they've got a backlog apparently—'

'Please don't worry. Just let me know. You must have so much to sort out.'

'I do, rather. Being the only UK citizen in the family. Thanks.' He hovered on the doorstep. 'All good with you?'

'All fine. I've just had a lovely day with my daughter.'

'Super. And all still quiet out the back? No sign of the squatter?'

'All still quiet, thanks.'

A gust of chilly air blew up the drive. Esther pulled her cardigan more tightly around her and turned to retreat inside.

'That's good to hear. I'll be off, then. And I'll keep you posted about the cat.'

'The cat,' Esther cried, realising the door had been wide open for a good two minutes. In spite of his mighty frame, the animal was lithe and wily. 'He couldn't have scooted out, could he? He's always trying. Do you mind having a quick look out there while I check inside?' She raced back along the hall to the kitchen, the flowers springing in her arms, only to laugh at the sight of Chico, stretched across Viv's journal, all four paws hanging over the edges in the manner of one making do with an undersized mattress.

* * *

'So, is there to be no service in the UK at all?'

The roses had been left to take over the sink and they were in the sitting room, where Esther had been subjected to a dry-humoured elaboration on the logistical challenges related to transporting the remains of deceased non-UK-passport holders to southern Europe. Marcus had accepted the offer of a beer and Esther had made herself a peppermint tea, curling up with her mug in a corner of the sofa while he sat in the bigger of her two armchairs, his long legs stretched out under the table. The small celebration of establishing the whereabouts of the pet had seemed to warrant *something*, and Esther had also sensed a reluctance on Marcus's part to trudge straight back to his late aunt's empty house.

'She didn't know many people here. And the family just want her home.'

'Of course,' she murmured, in truth mulling over the unsettling realisation that when you found someone attractive, you just did. Regardless of age appropriateness, reciprocity, one's own troubles, or whether the person in question happened to be mourning dead aunts. In fact, it was all very simple and threw a fresh perspective on the recent Chris Mews hoo-ha that made her head spin. Talk about a bullet dodged. 'So, what do you do, Marcus? If you don't mind my asking.'

He absently tweaked a clump of the trimmed hair, pulling a face that suggested he did mind, but was prepared to consider making an exception. 'I act. Visigoth-for-the-summer.' He laughed – clearly at himself – before going on. 'Mostly in the Lake District, but now preparing to be a dodgy property magnate – operating out of Amsterdam, which should also be fun. I love Amsterdam. And before you ask, no...' he held up a warning hand despite Esther having made no effort to speak '...you won't have heard of me because I am invariably forty-third soldier on the left. Nor will you have seen my films. I mean, no offence *at all*—' he threw her an impish smile '—but I tend to get work aimed at a very young audience – mostly low-budget failed attempts at blockbusters that go straight to streaming. For the record, it actually says Mar*cos* Gerado on my birth certificate. English mother, Portuguese father. But there was another one of those at my Lisbon drama school, so I switched to Mar*cus* instead, and actually prefer it now. It's handy being bilingual though.' He paused to take a sip from his beer bottle, having rejected the offer of a glass. 'And I love Lisbon, but moved over here because...' He groaned. 'Sorry. You really don't want all this.'

'But I do,' Esther protested, tucking her legs more tightly under her and hugging her mug, starting to enjoy this unlooked-for coda to what had turned into quite a day. To be talked to was relaxing. 'Go on.'

'Really?'

'Really.'

He held her gaze for a moment, as if still expecting a change of heart. 'Well, okay. The edited version, then – and nothing to do with my aunt, who came here decades ago. No, the move to the UK was for a girl. As you do.' He threw her a sheepish smile. 'A fellow actor.' He picked at the label on his beer bottle, his expression clouding. 'Izzie Bernard? She was in that biggie, *Mars*. It won all sorts of awards, here and across the pond.'

'I think I've heard of the film, but not her. Mind you, I have been somewhat off-grid for the last couple of years, getting divorced and moving to London, among other things...' Esther stopped, not wanting to get into any nitty-gritty confessions.

'Oh dear. Right. You have my sympathies. I mean, I know how shit that stuff is.' He picked harder at the label, getting nowhere with his big fingers and short nails. 'Izzie is with Gustav Lindquist now. The director?' He shook his head in bemusement when Esther again looked blank. 'They met on her last film. One of the hazards of the job. On set, it can get very... intense. Great when it goes your way though.' He laughed dryly and flopped back in the chair, holding the beer bottle against his chest. 'On the plus side, we've got Lola – who's five.'

His entire face had melted, and the dark-brown eyes were flooded with pride and love. Esther found she had to look away. At least Lily and Dylan had got most of their growing up done by the time she and Lucas split. 'I have two children, nearly twenty-three and eighteen, so pretty much grown-up now – not that you worry less.' She pulled a face. 'Lily is doing a postgrad, and Dylan has recently seen fit to take himself off and explore the world in preference to re-sitting his A levels. Which of course has driven my stress levels off the scale. Parenting never ends, you know, it just, sort of... alters.'

'Now, that is precisely what I did *not* want to hear. Thanks, Esther.' He grinned ruefully. 'Your two, they sound bold and great, though. Wow. I'll be relieved when Lola makes it to six, let alone eighteen. But as for travelling the world... that will be *out of the question*.' He blew air through his lips. 'Blimey, yes, I don't envy you that. I'm very lucky though. Izzie is flexible, and I get to see a fair bit of Lola – between doing things like legging it to the Lake District in order to slaughter fellow marauding hordes, that is. Not *exactly* the dream I had in mind when I entered the Lisbon Theatre and Film School fifteen years ago, but hey, it pays the bills. And keeps me fit. And I'm pretty good on horseback, even when carrying an axe. Sometimes – mostly – like I say, it's a load of fun, but...' He faltered for the first time. 'Obviously not so much recently, what with... everything.'

'Weren't the Visigoths an offshoot from Ostrogoths?' Esther ventured, noting the flinch of upset and wanting to give him time to compose himself. 'Around the fourth century, I think. They attacked the Romans a lot and set up kingdoms in Europe... Spain and Gaul...' She dried up, running out of knowledge.

'You put me to shame,' he declared, brightening at once. 'I mean, I'm the Visigoth around here, right?' He beat his chest, and then flung himself back into the chair, dangling the beer over the arm between his fingers. 'Hey, this is nice, Esther. Really nice. Just what I needed. Thank you very much.' He looked round her little room, crammed as tidily as she could manage with all her bits, and gestured with his beer bottle towards the piano, parked along the wall beside the front window. 'You'll be telling me you're a concert pianist next. I heard you one time, through the wall.'

'Did you? Oh, God, that must have been annoying – sorry. No, all I do is teach – a few beginners, frogmarched here by ambitious parents. They're how I pay *my* bills, along with applying my magical skills to gobbledygook business copy. Whipping bullet points into something readable is my specialist subject, most recently on the scintillating theme of healthcare insurance benefits for women. Not the future I dreamt of either, but then that's rather the nature of futures, isn't it? They never quite come in the packages one imagined.'

He was nodding and smiling. 'Esther, that is *so* true. Which means, surely, that you can add worldly wisdom to that skill-set list of yours?'

Esther laughed, caught off guard by the compliment. 'Actually, Marcos, I think the truth is my real talent lies in being extremely medi-ocre at a few things – useless pieces of general knowledge and piano-playing included – and not truly good at anything...' She had meant to sound self-deprecating and funny, but somehow a tinge of regret had crept into her tone.

'Well, being okay at lots of things sounds good to me.' He eyed her carefully. 'Not that I'm sure I altogether believe you. I mean, for a start, you're clearly a hotshot on Goths.'

Esther smiled, bringing him and the conversation properly back into focus, and sneaking a look at her watch.

'I must go,' he said tactfully, 'but could I put two questions to you first?'

'Sure.' She placed her empty mug on the table and sat more upright, making a jokey show of attempting to concentrate. 'Ask away.'

'Would you play something?' He gestured again at the piano. 'Anything. One minute's worth. A page.'

Esther readjusted the position of the mug. 'Really?'

'Really.'

'I get stupidly nervous playing to other people – it's one of the *many* reasons I abandoned plans for a career in music.'

'Pretend I'm not here, in that case.' He settled deeper into the chair, draping his arms over the sides and closing his eyes. 'Something classical-ish would be nice. I'm rubbish at knowing composers, though, so don't expect any suggestions.'

Esther did not want to play the piano. But Marcus was just sitting there, very still, his closed eyelids fluttering. Waiting. She wiped her hands, slightly sticky from the spa oil in her hair, and nervousness now too. Crossing to the piano, she plucked out Bach's easy-peasy 'Prelude in C' from the pile on the carpet, a short but moving piece currently being tackled by a thirteen-year-old pupil called Alice, who had lately progressed to Grade 5. Esther played the piece with all the tenderness it warranted, humming Gounod's 'Ave Maria' – which had been composed as an accompaniment a hundred or so years later – over the main tune. Afterwards, she swivelled round on the stool, self-consciously tucking her slippers out of view, aware of feeling wide awake again, and soothed.

Marcus took a while to open his eyes; and when he did so she could discern, much to her amazement, the unmistakeable glassiness of tears.

'Thank you, Esther.' He sighed as he spoke. 'That was exquisite. I mean, really.'

'It's a piece that has had several incarnations, and is actually very easy to play. It's always popping up in film scores, though perhaps not ones for *younger* audiences,' she teased, in a bid to lighten the atmosphere, suddenly weighted with something she could not quite put her finger on. 'And by the way, if your second request is for more playing, the answer is not on your nelly.'

'No. That is not my second request.' He shifted to the edge of his chair, set his empty bottle beside her mug, and stood up. His expression had grown more solemn than ever. It had to be something connected to poor Carmela, Esther guessed, inwardly bracing herself.

'Of course, your answer can be no,' he continued gravely. 'It is an impudence.'

'An impudence?' Esther smiled doubtfully, her bafflement growing.

'Yes. Because my second question, Esther...' he was speaking with exaggerated formality now '...is whether you might consider allowing me to kiss you before I leave?'

'Kiss me?' Esther clung to the piano stool, a reaction partly to the sensation of her body temperature shooting up by several degrees. Her cheeks especially, warm from the tea, were literally pulsing with heat.

'It's a bold and shocking request, I know.'

'Truly bold. Truly shocking.' Esther matched his faux-serious tone, while her heart continued to perform acrobatics.

'And, as I say, one issued with no pressure whatsoever. A straight yes or no is fine.'

Was he in fact mocking her? Esther straightened herself on the stool, staring him out, trying not to think how attractive he looked in his cool-as-you-please pose by the armchair, in no hurry to move, commanding the room. Commanding her. He was an actor, she reminded herself, capable of pinging into any mode he wanted. She should keep herself on red alert; defences sky-high. He had praised her wisdom, and she only wished she deserved it. A forty-eight-year-old divorcee, it was high time, surely, to be equipped to take on the world. Yet, she was also, in that moment, extremely taken with the idea of allowing herself to try the treat of kissing, and being kissed by, Marcus. Her lips were actually tingling. It was almost alarming. 'It's only fair to warn you, I'm rusty,' she said, dimly wishing it hadn't been quite so long since her post-breakfast use of her toothbrush.

'Is that so?' He had started to pick his way across the room, stepping over her handbag, and the small coffee table that was always in the way instead of being serviceable. 'I find that hard to believe, Esther, if you don't mind my saying so. Isn't it a bit like riding a bicycle? Once mastered, never forgotten. Either way, I'm prepared to give it a whirl, if you are.'

'And I am oily,' Esther blurted. 'Just so you know. From an aromatherapy massage, today at the spa, with my daughter... so my hair is a bit...' She stood up. He had arrived in front of her. A faint tremor had started in the backs of her knees. Two years was a long time. Except it was more than two years, because proper kissing had been an early casualty of her marriage. Lucas hadn't thought it mattered. She had.

'That might explain why you smell sensational. The scent of you, I've been drinking it in ever since you opened the door.'

'You have? It's probably the roses, then.'

'The roses? Let me see, now.' He bent closer, putting his nose near, but not quite touching, her neck. 'Nope.' His eyes were full of merriment. Seen close-to, flecks of gold gleamed in the brown irises. 'Definitely not the roses,' he said, his voice deadpan. As he straightened, he reached out and picked a swatch of hair off her neck and laid it over her shoulder. 'Do I have an answer yet?'

'Still thinking.' Esther shivered. The shifting of her hair had caused a rush of goosebumps.

From nowhere, Chico appeared, taking a flying leap onto the piano stool, making them both jump. 'Now we have company.' Marcus laughed, reaching down to stroke the cat, who arched his back with pleasure. 'A gooseberry who wants a ringside seat, and you apparently do not like an audience. Houston, we have a problem.'

'Whereas you *love* an audience,' Esther murmured, unable to stop herself reaching out to trace a finger along the firm line of jaw where a shadow of stubble was darkening.

'It is true, an audience brings me to life.' He seemed to shudder slightly at her touch. 'To kiss, or not to kiss.' His voice had turned slightly hoarse. 'That is the question. I am going to have to hurry you for an answer, Esther.'

'Are you?' She moved her fingers up into the short thick hair. 'I am still weighing up the pros and cons, but on balance...' The sentence found no completion because Marcus chose the moment to place his mouth over hers. There was such gentleness in the contact, but also an intense sense of energy being contained, of holding back. He is an actor, and this could be a film, Esther thought, trying to contain some of her own eagerness, and then giving up.

FRIENDS & LOVERS

28

The crumble was made with home-grown rhubarb, Catherine explained, licking her fingers as she spooned the glistening soft, pink filling and thick chunks of golden-brown topping into the six bowls stacked in front of her. Ralph performed exaggerated sniffs and croons of pleasure at the sight, making his three children, their small round faces speckled with the tail-end of the chicken pox responsible for keeping them off school, erupt into giggles. Handed his portion first, Lucas allowed the sweet aroma of the dessert to drift across his face, smelling nothing. He sipped his water, wishing it were wine. On the mat behind it sat two sturdy jugs, one of cream and one of custard, surrounded by various spillages from the previous course – a lamb stew, served with fat broccoli spears, carrots and mashed sweet potato, whisked into peaks. Lucas had eaten steadily, mechanically, tasting nothing, issuing repeated stock phrases of thanks.

'Come to mine for some lunch,' Ralph had said as they emerged from the mediation, lightly placing a hand on Lucas's slumped shoulders. Lucas, too stunned to make decisions beyond the placing of one foot in front of the other, and having to do that carefully, because of his poorly leg, had growled a thank you. 'Good news that you are up to cycling. We can travel in convoy,' Ralph had added, shortening his stride to match Lucas's as they progressed towards the college bike stands.

Launched along the street, it had helped having Ralph's back wheel to follow. Light changes, crossing pedestrians, parked cars, where and when to make a turn, Lucas had imitated each move, leaving the fog in his head alone. A Monday lunch at Ralph's. He had pictured an empty house, slices of bread, some cheese, perhaps a drink. Instead, entering the house had been like stepping onto a whirling carousel: bouncing children, the bright, steamy kitchen; Catherine, drying her hands on a tea towel and shaking her long fringe out of her dusky green eyes before greeting him, her pale face cool as it brushed against his hot cheek.

'Help yourself, Lucas,' she said now, nudging the jugs nearer. 'And yes, Zac, before you ask, do fetch the ice cream, but it will be one scoop not three, all of you, so be warned,' she called as the ten-year-old scrambled out of his chair and disappeared through the door.

'Only Daddy can have two scoops,' Ralph declared in a mock bellowing voice, making his wild eyebrows dance and patting his belly, 'because Daddy is a monster with a monster appetite.'

The two younger children shrieked delighted retorts and tellings-off, while Catherine threw him a look of despairing affection.

'Is Daddy's friend a monster too?' piped up Phoebe, the smallest, slamming her hand against her mouth to contain gasps at her own audacity.

'Of course,' Ralph cried, rescuing Lucas from what felt like the impossible necessity of producing an apt response. Was he a monster? Moira thought so. Moira, so tortured and timid, who had nonetheless somehow managed to detonate a bomb under the foundations of his life. 'That's why Lucas is Daddy's friend,' Ralph riffed on. 'Us monsters stick together.'

'Ralph, really, they need calming down not stirring up,' Catherine scolded mildly, offering Lucas an apologetic smile and then taking charge of the ice cream as Zac skidded back into the dining room wielding the tub between both hands as if preparing to drop-kick a rugby ball.

In the toilet after the meal, Lucas studied the framed collages of family photos arranged round the walls. Ralph and Catherine maypole dancing; toothless babies beaming in the arms of grandparents; Ralph on his knees playing horse for two toddlers; Catherine idly reading a book while being buried in sand by a skinnier version of her skinny son. It was not a family life Lucas recognised, either from his own childhood, or as a father. He had never been wired for playing the fool like Ralph, despite Esther's best efforts to eke such stuff out of him. But he *had* tried to be a good parent. *Hadn't* he? The images in the frames blurred. His lower leg was pounding inside the stretchy bandage that the chemist had assured him would offer protective support.

'*Courage, mon brave,*' Ralph said, with a jarring effort at cheerfulness once Lucas, reaching the end of his limits, had refused coffee and they were on the front doorstep. 'It could have been so much worse.'

Lucas, holding his bike by its handlebars in preparation to navigate his way back to his flat, slowly raised his head to look his friend in the face. In his mind, the fog thinned sufficiently to replay the unspeakable image of Moira – the debasing, shuttling negotiations completed – being hustled to 'safety' along a corridor, her parents on either side of her, throwing jerky looks over their shoulders in case Lucas, poised in the doorway of his allocated room, was already tempted to break the now formalised agreement never – knowingly – to breathe the same air as their daughter. She was to be allowed to finish her degree. To enable this, Lucas, from that day forwards, would be on two years' 'leave'. Two. Years. 'How so, Ralph?'

'Try to think of it as a sabbatical...' Ralph began, before even his determined joviality deserted him. 'Believe me, I am not trying to make light...' He floundered again, perhaps under the glittering misery in Lucas's eyes. 'It was the price for drawing a line.' He sighed. 'A price worth paying, surely. A signed agreement. No official complaint. No courtroom dramas – dear God, Lucas, it really *could* have gone down that road. I think the Master was right to take the offer of a way of steering us out of it. Which isn't to say for a single moment that I do not acknowledge how hard this must be for you. I am just trying to point out the positives. A temporary lecturer will be found to cover. Your post isn't going anywhere. Maybe even regard it as time out from the hurly-burly, eh? Time for your work, and for Heidi. She's back at the weekend, right?' Ralph patted Lucas's arm. 'And you mentioned that that globe-trotting son of yours had at last been in touch? That's good. All this will pass, mate. Just keep your head down.'

A group of students in sports kit, joshing and talking, were approaching down the street. As they passed the front fence, Lucas recognised a third year and quickly turned his face to the house. To have to say hello was beyond him. The city was really starting to come alive now. It was a familiar rhythm, the build-up to the start of each new term, and normally one that Lucas relished. Everything was the same, he realised, close to choking suddenly on a surge of despair, and yet – for him – it was all irrevocably altered.

'You don't think I *did* anything, do you?' he burst out, in a creaking voice that wasn't his. 'I mean, tell me, Ralph, that you know the girl made up every bloody word.'

His friend's candid gaze met his. 'I know you did not intend any harm, Lucas. But I also know that not one of us can – at least not any more – discount how our words and actions make other people feel. How each of us behaves has consequences which have to stand up to rigorous analysis. I'm not preaching, it's just the world we inhabit. A good – probably a better – world. Look here...' He patted Lucas's arm. 'Put it behind you. Enjoy what's ahead – the many good things. Heidi will be back soon', he reminded him, with mounting desperation, it sounded like.

'Yes.' Lucas swallowed. Every time he thought of having to tell Heidi of the Moira verdict he felt ill. He could picture how her face would fall as the disappointment sank in; the way the light would drain from her beautiful, once adoring eyes.

'This will all blow over,' Ralph blundered on. 'It will take time, but it will. Trust me. And we'll meet up again soon, okay?' He gave Lucas's shoulder another squeeze before retreating into his house.

Lucas pedalled gingerly back towards town. Three o' clock and the bell towers were chiming. The city lived and was moving inexorably on. Only he felt dead and left behind.

29

Early on Tuesday evening, Esther was mildly astonished to find herself setting off for Cambridge without any of the usual last-minute flurries. A feeble attempt at postponement by Lily that morning had made her all the keener not to back down, especially when it became clear that Matteo would be out.

'I'll bring food,' Esther had said firmly, 'something veggie and delicious.'

'Don't worry, Mum, I've got loads of stuff and can rustle up something,' Lily had insisted, so plaintively that it had taken all of Esther's willpower not to start quizzing her on the spot. 'If you could be here by seven, that would be great, so long as that's not going to make you too late for getting back...' Esther had assured her seven was fine, and rushed out as soon as her morning work stint was done to buy some flowers and a brick-sized bar of chocolate. Both were on the car seat beside her, the flowers bunched inside dampened kitchen paper and silver foil to stay moist, and lying on top of her blue winter coat, thrown in as a precaution against the increasing autumn cold.

Working the pedals as she drove, Esther was aware of her new, wide-legged, black trousers – a reckless catalogue purchase that had fitted perfectly for once, as well as arriving in the promised twenty-four hours – sliding smoothly over her legs. She had picked out a smart, white, collared shirt to go with them, and her favourite, fuchsia-coloured jacket, and then stood for a few moments looking at herself in the mirror. It had felt good to dress well for Lily, and there was some natural colour in her cheeks. She looked poised and strong. She *felt* poised and strong. Buoyant, even. Bullish. Another, sustaining, photo-postcard of some South American waterfalls had arrived, along with the treat of a *love you mum,* and though Lily was clearly in some sort of dip, Esther was almost relishing her own determination to yank her daughter out of it, no matter what it took. As she had performed a final mirror-twirl, the somewhat glib words with which she had inadvertently impressed Marcus over the weekend had floated back to mind. Yes, parenthood certainly did keep evolving, terrifyingly; but for the first time in a very long while, she was feeling more than up for it.

What Esther was also aware of, however, was that all this new can-do certainty, while connected to her children, had rather more to do with the unexpected events of Saturday night. Who knew that several hours of torrid yet tender sex with a handsome, kind, younger (by ten years almost to the day, they had gleefully worked out) semi-stranger could produce such miracles of empowerment? That the encounter was just a one-off, as both she and Marcus had, mutually and not at all sheepishly, agreed afterwards, made it all the better. It meant there was no follow-up to worry about, no potential embarrassment or awkwardness; nothing, indeed, beyond the friendly hug and a cheery wave on the doorstep with which they had said their farewells at six o'clock the following morning, Marcus hurdling over the fence to pack up for his shoot in Amsterdam. Esther had closed the door and trotted back upstairs in search of more sleep, which hadn't arrived.

The next day, sleep-deprivation had done nothing to crush her energy levels. On the contrary, she had been a dervish of efficiency, spinning through chores and work, jotting a clear to-do list in Viv's journal and ticking each item off with a thick black marker. A young man called Ed, fresh out of a garden design course and putting cards in people's letterboxes, had agreed to return with a nifty machine for munching cuttings and an estimate for digging over and planting grass seed. By Monday night, five thousand words of lively, appealing, jargon-free copy for the *Women's Wellbeing* launch magazine had been re-edited and despatched. Finding a little time on her hands, Esther had even found herself sitting down at the kitchen table and blowing the dust off the bits of the broken pot, left for so long on the window sill, and doing her best with superglue. She and Lucas were broken, but that didn't mean the little vase didn't deserve the chance of a longer life. A somewhat lumpen, jagged jigsaw of an object emerged, but useful nonetheless for things like paper clips and stray buttons, Esther reasoned, setting it on the dresser.

* * *

'Shona?'

'Esther, oh my God, I am the lousiest friend, how the hell are you?'

'Not too bad. I'm in the car – plugged in – on the way to see Lily. How are things?'

'Oh, they're insanely hectic – for Carole too – ridiculous case-loads... sorry we couldn't say yes to your Halloween thing...'

'It wasn't a *thing*, just...'

'Esther, I feel so *bad* I haven't been in touch. How are you *really*? Hang on, let me close my door and clear the decks a little.'

'Actually, I am good...' Esther stopped as Shona did some noisy moving around, taking a moment to consider the default readiness to offer sympathy. Even with their recent on-off communications, that was how it had always been: Shona, positive and enamoured of Carole, and her, full of self-put-down and negativity, usually about Lucas. To the point where Esther had wondered sometimes how much simpler and better life might be if she, too, could find it in herself to settle with a lovely female partner instead of a selfish, buttoned-up male.

'So, tell me, dearest Esther, how you are managing. I've got to jump on a call, but not for at least ten minutes...'

'I'm fine, Shone, truly. It's just been such an age and I wanted to touch base. Fix up a time we could meet. Just you and me?' Esther could hear the beat of a pause as Shona hesitated. She and Carole 'moved as a team', was what she always liked to say, and Esther, in the past, had done her best to respect that; but, with her new, clear head, it seemed suddenly just as reasonable that members of teams should be allowed some time away from each other, especially if it was to enable a long overdue catch-up with an erstwhile close friend.

'Can I get back to you on that? I mean, it would be lovely. But otherwise... how *are* you, Esther?'

The readiness to pity was there again, and it made Esther defiant. 'I am seriously happy, thanks, on all fronts. Dylan and Lily have been going through various ups and downs, but nothing that can't be sorted. Work is in a good, busy phase and... well... you might be interested to know that you are speaking to a woman who has recently enjoyed a night of unbridled passion with a hot young actor...'

Shona yelped. 'Who? How? When? Is it serious?'

Esther laughed. 'No, it's not serious, and that's the best thing about it. But you get to your call now and I'll tell you all about it another time. Just let me know some dates that work, even if it is months away, and we'll make it happen.'

Esther drove for a few more miles before ringing Viv. Since the chances of a call being taken were slim, she wanted her voice message clear in her head. No rambling, no hint of self-pity. She would make it about wanting to see Viv, for *Viv*. The Marcus adventure would get a mention, and feeling on top of life, but not a lot else. She would suggest the cinema, Esther decided, pleased at the idea, some soppy romcom for just the two of them. She would say she missed their closeness and wanted it back. She would say that she bloody loved her.

* * *

'Why did you *drive* anyway?' Lily said, clutching the chocolate and putting her nose in the carnations after they had said their hellos.

'Because I actually like driving and didn't fancy a dark and dingy train-ride back tonight,' Esther replied mildly, inwardly flinching at how much more washed-out her daughter looked since the weekend; her normally shiny hair tucked, thin and flat, behind her small ears, and her lovely milky skin broken by faint red patches round her chin and mouth. 'Something smells good.'

'It's just onions and beef for a Bolognese. Matteo hates to break the no-meat rule, but as he's not here I thought I'd be wicked,' she said, speaking in the colourless voice of one taking no joy in her crime. 'And you like it, right?' She opened the door wider so that Esther could step from the outside staircase entrance into the little kitchen.

'I love it,' Esther cried, finding it hard not to overcompensate for Lily's lacklustre mood, 'and to be cooked for is *such* a treat. I am one spoilt mum.' She kicked off her heels and removed her bright jacket, draping it on the overladen peg behind the kitchen door, pursuing a deep protective instinct to dial down her appearance to something more in line with her daughter's; though, in truth, that would have been hard, given that Lily was in her oldest, baggy-kneed, tracksuit bottoms and a shapeless, long-sleeved T-shirt, grey from wrong washing cycles. Her small, pale feet were bare and, like her fingers, sporting now broken flecks of red nail varnish from their treatments at the weekend. 'Right then.' Esther rubbed her hands together. 'Set me to work.'

'There's nothing to do. Just relax. Thanks for these.' Lily dropped the bunch of carnations – in their wrapping – into an empty coffee jar that barely reached half way up the stems and added a splash of water, before picking up a wooden spoon and prodding at the chunks of pink mince and glistening onion sizzling in a small blackened frying pan on the hob. 'Maybe the mushrooms, then?' she said as Esther hovered. She nodded at a box of large muddied field mushrooms sitting on the little table squeezed up against the wall, next to a recycling crate over-flowing with cardboard and paper.

'There's a chopping board, and a decent knife somewhere, in the sink, I think.' Lily gestured vaguely with her spoon.

Esther wiped the board, which was dirty, and rolled up her sleeve to fish inside the washing-up bowl, packed with several meals' worth of crockery. She managed to pluck out a thick-handled, serrated knife and ran it under the tap before returning to her task.

The mushrooms peeled beautifully, the skin coming off in long thick sheets. 'So, is Matteo rehearsing or—?'

'Why are you doing that?' Lily was standing over her with the spoon.

'What?'

'Peeling them. The skin is the best bit.' The spoon dripped a couple of blobs of mince on the floor as she swung back to the hob.

'Sorry, darling. No more peeling. Guide's honour.' Esther cast round for something with which to wipe down the mushrooms instead, eventually settling on a grubby tea towel. 'All those auditions must have been quite a pain for you,' she pressed on. 'Has Matteo found a good new lead singer?' She shuffled the tea towel to find a clean corner.

'Actually, Matteo's in New York.' Lily rammed some spaghetti into a big saucepan and carried on chivvying the meat in the pan, turning it and chopping at it. 'A last-minute grand gathering of the clan. They were going to wait till Thanksgiving, but a bunch of rellies – there are so many of them – couldn't make it.'

'Oh, well, that's nice,' Esther said cautiously. 'So, he'll be seeing his dad.'

'Amongst all the others. Hey, do you want a drink? We've got some white, I think.'

'Juice, water – anything is fine. Whatever you're having... but, darling, I expect you wish you were in New York too, don't you?'

Lily snorted. 'No way. I could have gone, but I've got a load of work, and it's nice for Matt to do that stuff alone.' She had opened the fridge door and was staring inside, gripping the handle, with white knuckles.

Esther hesitated, torn between pushing too hard and not asking enough, understanding only too well the reluctance to spill one's problems on demand. Her daughter's back was rigid, and Esther's conviction that there was a serious problem with Matteo deepened. All the auditions with girls, some of them from Matteo's and Lily's school days. Maybe something had happened. Lily and Matteo had been together for so long after all; a point of make-or-break was bound to be reached. 'I don't mean to pry, and I know I've asked before, but are you sure everything really is okay between you two? I would love you to feel you can tell me anything, Lily darling.'

'We're totally okay. I mean, he drives me nuts, but yeah... totally.' She snatched a half-empty bottle of white wine out of the fridge and kicked the door shut with the back of her foot. 'It's nothing special, sorry.' Lily landed the bottle on the table with a thump, and swung back to the hob, her slim shoulders performing a steep rise and fall in what looked like a concerted effort to summon calm.

For a few moments neither of them said anything and the silence felt oddly awkward.

'By the way, Mum. I've been wanting to ask.' Lily had taken the chopping board and begun beating the mushrooms into the meat – to a pulp, by the look of it – between adding generous squirts of ketchup. 'About Dad and Grandad. I mean, Matteo's family have been shitty to each other, but somehow, they still muddle along. But Dad not seeing him, it's because of Granny, right?'

'Yes, that certainly brought things to a head,' Esther said, her caution intensifying. She had never known Lily like this, so spiky, so *angry*.

'But how bad was Grandad, anyway?' Lily blurted, spinning round and folding her arms, sticking her chin out in her determined way. 'Was there physical abuse – to Granny? Or Dad?'

Esther shook her head. 'Oh no, nothing like that, at least not that I'm aware... in fact, I am sure not.' Esther hesitated, maddened that, even now, she had to be the conduit for information that belonged to Lucas, not her. 'No, the awfulness then was more about the general misery when Dad was growing up, the mood-swings – you know, from Grandad's drinking – and all of it compounded by him being pretty lonely, I think. When Grandad got struck off, I know there was some bad bullying – children can be so cruel—'

'Shit, I was going to make garlic bread,' Lily cried, bringing the interrogation to an abrupt end, '*and* there's no Parmesan. Will you be okay with normal cheese?' She became a whirlwind, draining the spaghetti, dishing out the Bolognese, and grating a nugget of Cheddar into a cereal bowl, before setting two heaped plates of pasta on the table and dropping into the seat opposite Esther.

Through it all, Esther sat, a model of serenity, on the stool that was too high for the table and always gave her a backache, feeling like someone waiting for a storm to pass. Behind Lily's head she noticed a photo stuck on the fridge door among several others, of Dylan, looking goofy with a pint of beer. She bit her lip.

'So, how's your garden?' Lily asked, as if making a polite effort at conversation with a stranger at a formal dinner.

'My garden is fine, thank you for asking,' Esther replied evenly. 'This is delicious, darling. Garlic bread would have been too much.' She eyed Lily, busily turning the contents of her own plate into a goulash instead of actually eating it. 'Not hungry?' Despite not wanting it, she took a small sip of the wine, which was tart.

Lily raised a few threads of spaghetti to her mouth with her fork and then set them down again. 'Mum. There's something I've got to tell you.'

Esther's pulse quickened. Here they were, then. At long last. She looked properly at Lily's pinched face, wishing only that she possessed a magic wand with which to wipe away the wretchedness. 'I guessed there probably was...' she ventured, keeping her expression steady, as a new thought flowered inside. An obvious thought. Her own skin had gone to pot at similar times. It wasn't ideal. It would be tricky. But it would be fine. Lily was shaking her head, tightening her folded arms and chewing at her beautiful lips.

'It's Dad.'

'Dad?' Esther's Zen state collapsed in sheer surprise, shattering the comforting chat about accidental pregnancy for which she had been preparing. 'What about Dad?'

Lily was folding her entire mouth inwards, in a bid not to cry,

Esther realised, reaching past their plates and catching hold of a hand, which was immediately pulled away. 'He has... has...'

'What, sweetheart, what has he done? Take a deep breath, Lily. It will all be all right. Whatever it is—'

'No, Mum, it won't – it *can't* – be all right,' she wailed. 'There was this rumour, from one of the singers, she didn't know Dad was my... but I didn't believe it...'

'What rumour, Lily?'

'That Dad had been... involved... with a *student*, Mum.' She spoke through sobs, dabbing roughly at her running eyes and nose with her long sleeves. 'But now it's in the papers. The girl called him out. *Inappropriate* behaviour. It says the college have been trying to hush it up and that Dad has been suspended. Until the girl has finished her degree. See for yourself.' She reached into the recycling box and slapped a folded newspaper between their plates. 'Not pressing charges, it says, but that's obviously because they have reached some kind of *settlement*. I've tried to call Dad...' her voice thick with disgust '...but his phone's off. And I was actually glad, because I wouldn't know what the fuck to say anyway. And I am also glad that Matteo is away, because I can't face telling him either. It is *so* gross... and I've got so much going on, and now this... from *Dad*.' She buried her face in her hands.

Esther had already picked up the paper. It was the local *Evening News*, from the day before, folded open at the relevant page. She studied the small paragraph of text, under the headline *Professor in Alleged Sexual Harassment Case*. There was a tiny smudgy photograph of Lucas beside it, in full peacock regalia at some ceremony or other. Esther read the sentences quickly, and then a second time, more slowly. The identity of the student wasn't disclosed, beyond the fact of her being a first year. Only Lucas's name and position were outlined in all their glory. It had to be some sort of leak, Esther speculated, since colleges were big on protecting their public images. 'But he wouldn't do such a thing...' she murmured, scanning the piece again.

She looked up to see Lily staring across the table, no longer crying, her eyes huge and aghast. 'How can you even say that, Mum? How can you even *know*?'

'I just do. I know your father. He wouldn't.' Esther spoke very quietly, surprising herself at her own certainty. 'It was probably just one of those things—'

'One of those *things*...?'

'I mean, a hideous misunderstanding.' Esther looked again at the article, her mind leaping to how Lucas would be taking what had happened: his precious job, his precious popularity, gone, the sledge-hammer to his pride. Her ex-husband was maddeningly cocky, maddeningly charming, every student's mentor as well as best friend; he revelled in adulation; he knew how to flirt, but he was not a man to make stupid and ill-advised advances to a barely formed adult. Besides, he had Heidi. It didn't make sense. She reached into her handbag and pulled out a pack of tissues, handing one to Lily.

'Have faith in your father, Lily. He's going to need it.'

'Mum, why the hell are you *protecting* him?'

'I'm not. I'm just saying what I think,' Esther countered quickly. 'How's Heidi about it all, anyway?'

'Heidi? I've no idea, Mum. She was in Germany last I heard.'

For a moment Esther tried to feel glad, but it was all too ugly. She concentrated on Lily instead, getting up to put her arms round her, having to bend awkwardly because of her being on the lower stool and there not being much space. 'Thank you for telling me, darling. I had a feeling something big was wrong.' She cupped the back of Lily's head, feeling her soften as she stroked her hair. 'No charges being brought is good. Being suspended will be very hard for your father, but he is pretty resilient, as we know, right? And he will talk to you, *soon*, I am sure, once he has got his head round it all himself. Okay?' She pulled back, holding Lily's gaze until she had managed a nod. 'In the mean-time, I have reason to believe you are in possession of a quantity of chocolate, and if there was some tea to go with it, we could perhaps take both and settle in front of the telly for a bit.'

The suggestion was leapt on, and they were soon wedged snugly on the sofa, watching an episode of a Netflix drama that Lily was deeply into, about separated siblings finding each other as adults. They dunked their chocolate chunks in the tea, as they always used to, demolishing the entire bar, Lily saying it would make her skin even crappier than it currently was, and Esther lamenting the obstinate mound of her belly. Hugging out their goodbyes an hour later, Esther dared to believe that, for all the circling problems, they had at last found their way back to some of what had been in danger of getting lost. 'I want more regular chats from now on, okay?' she commanded from halfway down the steps.

'Yes, Mum,' Lily replied, blowing her a kiss. 'You're the best.'

* * *

Driving down Lucas's street was not Esther's original intention. She had been on the third roundabout heading out of town when the car, almost of its own accord, it felt like, completed the circle instead of going straight on. It was ten o'clock and several lights still blazed in uncurtained windows dotted across the block, a handsome sandy-bricked Georgian conversion with a big white portico of an entrance. Esther double-parked, letting the engine run as she stared up at Lucas's lounge, evidently lit up too, behind firmly lowered blinds. She had been there a couple of times in the early days, dropping off and picking up various bits, but it felt odd, still, to imagine him in there, living his separate life. Especially now, alone, processing the body blow that Lily had shared.

Esther looked across at her phone, silent on the passenger seat. There was no 'duty of care' any more, she reminded herself. There was nothing. Except knowing him. Better than he wanted to be known. Yes, he had grown to hate that. Being seen through, and criticised. But then she hadn't liked it either. A good marriage took fortitude as well as kindness, she reflected sadly, and maybe, among all their other obvious problems, neither of them had possessed enough of either. Inhaling slowly, she picked up the phone, quickly pressing Lucas's number and then ending the call when it cut straight to a recorded message.

A little further down the street, there was a large space, easy for pulling into. Gritting her teeth, muttering to herself, Esther drove on and swung into it, getting out and slamming the car door in one swift motion. Having reached the entrance porch, she sent a text.

Am downstairs. Just had dinner with Lily.

She gave it a minute and then pressed the buzzer to the flat once, long and hard. When there was no reply to that either, she gave it a second go before striding back to the car.

She had reached out. Reaching out only worked if the other party reached back. Maybe Lucas imagined she wanted to crow over his disgrace. Maybe he didn't even know she knew. Esther let out a small screech, slamming her palm against the steering wheel. It didn't matter. It was none of her business. She turned the engine on, but then snatched her mobile again, texting.

Hope u ok. Remember it will be fish and chips soon. Please talk to Lily.

30

Lucas stood with his back to the wall beside his front window. Edging a couple of fingers under the blind, he lifted it an inch or two and peered through the crack. Newly alert to the dangers of unwanted attention, he had heard a car pulling up outside, and the hum of the engine as it idled. The vehicle was half out of view, and in the late evening darkness it was hard to make out anything except that it was small and silver. By the time the door buzzer sounded, he had retreated to the sofa, his bunker for most of the day. He sat up with a moan and reached for the cushion that had been under his bad leg. Hugging it with both arms, he rocked slowly, through the next ring and the silence that followed, willing whichever bloodhound it was to give up.

It had begun that morning. When he'd ventured out for milk, there had been a woman with angry red lips and big kohl-rimmed eyes, who had stepped into his path, waving a press ID card.

'Professor Shaw, would you like to comment on...?'

No, he wouldn't. Lucas had spun on his heel and gone back inside, making a mess of getting the door open, so the woman had had the chance to finish her sentence and then repeat it, again, and again. 'No comment,' Lucas had mumbled, and then shouted, hating the note of panic in his voice, aware of the journo snapping pictures with her phone and the impression he was creating of being someone with something to hide. Not long afterwards, there had been a couple of phone calls, one from a woman who could have been the doorstepper, the other from a smooth-voiced man who said he was from a local radio station. Lucas had switched his phone to silent after that, vowing only to answer numbers he recognised. Ralph had called, with kind words, and then the Master, both agreeing with his grim guesswork that the leak to the papers had come from Charlie Giddings and advising silence to ride it out. By then a new wave of Twitter notifications had started, queuing up on screen, and though Lucas kept telling himself that he didn't need to read them, it turned out that some self-sabotaging part of him did.

The vitriol, posted by strangers, made him quiver. These people, who knew nothing of him, and nothing about the truth of his exchanges with a student seeking help, were ready to brand him a liar, an abuser, a misogynist, a rapist, deploying every hashtag Lucas had heard of supporting such themes, and many he hadn't. A statement, asserting his innocence and apologising for any harm inadvertently caused, had served only to pour oil on the fire. They were baying for his blood; and though Lucas knew they were just a faceless rabble, unaccountable except to their own consciences, unlikely ever to cross anything but his virtual path, the effect was like a detonation of his hopes, of his very being. Once proud of his two thousand or so followers – not bad for a literary dinosaur, he liked to joke – he now closed the account, then turned off his phone altogether.

It was gone ten o' clock, but Lucas knew there was no question of sleep. Every creak in the flat, every rattle of a windowpane, made him jump. Barely having eaten since the lunch at Ralph and Catherine's the day before, he still had no appetite. Forcing himself to consider the contents of his fridge anyway – an open pack of ham, some wilting broccoli, a piece of crusty cheese, two eggs – he dug the least spongy apple from the bottom drawer and slumped back on the sofa to watch the late news. A suicide bomber in Kabul; a minor earthquake somewhere in China; shortage of international aid in Yemen. Lucas gnawed mindlessly through the soft fruit, thinking that at least his woes were too paltry to make national headlines. Or were they? With a sudden sickening dread of what might follow, he turned the television off too.

Music, then. Fumbling, Lucas found the console for his speaker system and scrolled through his playlist to the preludes and fugues. But for once there was no solace to be had there either. Even Bach had let him down.

Lucas knew what he would do next. He had been aware of it all along as the only course of action, waiting in the wings of his mind, requiring only that he turn his head and acknowledge it. First, he had to email Heidi, in order to rule out the possibility of her deciding to try and communicate with him. Not due back from the off-grid excursion to the Black Forest until the following night, it was unlikely, but he couldn't take the risk. If she messaged or rang and he didn't respond, there would be ructions. Heidi would smell a rat, bombard him with notifications, try harder, get upset. She would almost certainly conclude that the verdict he had assured her was 'still pending' – part of a confidently fake, holding email sent after Ralph's the day before – had come through, with some grisly resolution.

I do get the fact that how I behaved made Moira feel uncomfortable, you know…

Lucas had grasped at Ralph's words because, while not believing them, it was dawning on him the degree to which he was going to have to pretend – to Heidi and everyone else – that he did.

…that I got things wrong. That she has a right to her own reactions. I'm not a callous idiot. I do understand. The verdict, when it comes, may well mean some time out for me…

he had warned, in a bid to prepare the ground,

…but the mediation seemed to go well, so we shall see. Time out would at

least be good for my paper of course! The most important thing to say,
however, is that I am longing to see you, darling. Let me know your flight
details as soon as you get back to Bonn and I shall be at the airport next
Saturday. I can't wait, Liebchen. I am thinking of you all the time.

Now, under the heading 'Further News', Lucas wrote quickly.

And now I have food poisoning! Must have picked up something at Ralph's.
Going to turn my phone off and try to ride it out. Will call as soon as I am
better. See how all bits of me are falling off and falling apart without you. Lx.

Lucas read and reread the final sentence, wondering whether to
lighten it with an exclamation mark. It sounded dramatic. It was
dramatic. It was also, he realised bleakly, the truest thing he had told
his fiancée in a very long while. Apart from the fact of loving her,
which he hastily added as a postscript.

After he'd pressed send and closed down all his tabs, some of the
sickening urgency receded. He had all night, after all, Lucas reflected
grimly. And all the next day if he wanted. He went to the bathroom,
drinking from the tap after he had washed his hands and then
splashing water on his face. He paused to glare at himself in the basin
mirror, his dark eyebrows dripping, his eyes wild, but swung hastily
away as he glimpsed a reflection of his father.

At the kitchen cupboard that served as a drinks cabinet, Lucas
hesitated again, while knowing the cause was lost. A lifetime of eager
but careful consumption meant he knew exactly what it contained.
Three student years of binge-drinking had taught him the necessity of
such watchfulness, along with the ghoulish adage that the sins of the
father could be passed on to the son. Genetics or psychology, it made
no difference – when he drank, he wanted more. He wanted, quite
simply, not to have to stop. Learning *how* to stop had been like
mastering the art of walking a tightrope. Gradually, the lapsing binges
had lessened and collegiate life – and Esther – had filled the gap. The
period after Esther left had been hard, but he had managed. And then

Heidi had stepped into his life, removing the desire and the danger completely.

Lucas yanked open the cupboard. In recent days, its contents had drastically diminished. A half bottle of gin, the slugs of brandy, a couple of bottles of red, one of white, along with some unpleasantly sweet sherry, had all been consumed, Lucas reasoning that to run down *existing* stocks was both 'allowed' and, in the current stressful circumstances, entirely reasonable. Just two bottles remained, both tucked at the back behind some cartons of long-life juice, which had been bought for and ignored by Dylan: a bottle of Chateau Marjosse, secured thanks to a college sale of bin-ends the previous Christmas, and an unopened Glenfiddich, gifted by a grateful postgrad in the spring. The best till last, and how fitting, Lucas mused darkly, carrying both bottles through to the sitting room and then going back for a bottle opener, the largest of his wine glasses, and a lead-crystal tumbler. The tumbler, sole survivor of a wedding set from Esther's parents, had acquired a small chip on its rim, he observed as he set it down, sadness welling up from nowhere.

It made sense to start with the wine. A little excited now – here was something to *do* after all, something that would make him feel better – Lucas fetched his biscuit tin, glad to see it contained two old digestives and some broken crackers. He shovelled them into his mouth as he started to drink, trying to keep to sips and failing. Swig after swig, it was as easy on the throat as Ribena. The alcohol hit his bloodstream with a rush. Once the bottle was empty, he lowered himself to the floor and lay spreadeagled on his back. The ceiling, painted white during his refurb, was starting to crack, he saw, hairline fractures, visible only because of his worsening – lengthening – eyesight.

Lucas was aware of the tumbler on the table watching him. Waiting for him. Viewed from the floor, the flat struck him as unbelievably small suddenly; a soulless white cube; a prison. Keeping him safe, but keeping the world out. A memory stirred, not of a particular incident, but of an old feeling. Distress, that was it. Aged eleven and lying under the cold white tent he had made of his sheets, palms pressed against his ears, not managing to block out the slurred shouting of his father coming from downstairs.

Lucas sat up fast and opened the whisky. As he filled the tumbler, three fat fingers' worth, he saw that he had somehow spilt several drops of wine across the newspaper he had retrieved so idly from the doorstep on his return from Ralph's the previous afternoon. The drops had landed on the seedy little paragraph about his *alleged* crime. They could have been blood. His blood, Lucas thought bleakly, seizing the paper and making a roaring noise from the back of his throat as he hurled it across the room.

Drink was his only ally now. He pressed the tumbler against his forehead, trying to stop himself from downing it in one go. He ached for the oblivion that would follow. The demons of regret, of fear, crouching round the corner; he needed to dodge them. He would do this now, and then he wouldn't do it again, Lucas vowed. Ever. He just needed to do it now. So he could sleep. So he could forget. For a little while.

He put the tumbler to his lips with fresh purpose. *Come on*, he told it, *take me away*. On he drank, doggedly, rhythmically, forgetting the chip in the glass and finding the metallic taste of blood entering the punch of each swallow. But no forgetting arrived. No sleepiness. Instead, shame began to fill him, as steadily as sand through an hourglass. The very same shame that had choked him during the endless endurance test of each school day; the sniggers, jibes and kicks; for being the son of the alkie doctor, who was gossiped about and despised by all, not just for the tell-tale tremors in his hands and pungent breath, but for his closeness to Iris, the practice nurse. Life went on, said Lucas's mother, who didn't have to go to school after the whistle-blowers had done their blowing; who had instead set her mouth and held her head high, taking on more houses to clean and longer shifts in the post office. Life went on. Until, eventually, it turned out that it didn't.

Lucas rolled onto his side to sit up. The heating had gone off and his feet, just in their socks, were stiff with cold. His eyes, casting round the room for purchase, fell on Dylan's postcard. His body started to shake. He had thought he could be better. He had thought that if he tried hard enough, for long enough, he could leave all that was bad behind.

* * *

There were no parking spaces outside the house. There rarely were late at night. Esther had to drive on for another fifty yards before she found a suitable slot. Walking back to her front door, she was glad of her blue woollen coat, which she pulled up around her ears. Not yet half way through September, and the night felt like a plunge into winter. Esther slid her fingers deep into her pockets and tipped her head down against a sudden gust of icy drizzle that almost blew her off her feet. Dylan-worry hovered, as it always did, but it was Lily who sat, still, in the centre of her mind, a little happier at least, her burden shared, though only Lucas could really give her the reassurance she needed. Lucas, who was not *her* problem, Esther reminded herself, as she had been doing throughout the drive home, her mobile silent on the passenger seat.

Preoccupied, eyes down, she was only dimly aware of a person walking towards her. The pavement was wide, and she had already reached the lamp post aligned with Sue and Dimitri's front door. Esther steered a little more towards it, wanting to allow more space for the person to pass, registering only someone who was tall, dark-coated, and wearing a flat cap. When the figure promptly stepped into her path, putting hefty arms around her, she uttered a cry of sheer surprise. 'What the...? Chris?' His face, half hidden under the peak of his hat, was jubilant. She tried to push him away, but his arms were clamped.

'Esther. At last.' He rocked her from side to side, as if they were slow dancing. 'I've been waiting. Worrying, actually... was the traffic bad? From Cambridge? And how is Lily?'

'Chris, what are you doing here?' Esther asked dumbly. He had suddenly released her, and she was tempted to run. The decision not to flashed out from a clear lucid corner of her brain, processing options with the fury of a computer: Dimitri and Sue's house, behind his head, was as dark as hers, and Carmela's for that matter. The street was dank and empty. Her front door, a mere twenty-second sprint away, would need her two keys, floating somewhere on a small brass ring in the mess of her handbag; impossible to weaponize, let alone be grabbed and smoothly applied to double-unlocking – not without giving her interlocutor ample time to take actions of his own. Whatever they might be.

'Why am I here?' He was laughing and shaking his head. 'I hardly need to tell you that, now, sweetheart, do I? To see you, of course.'

'Chris, just go home.' Esther slowly edged nearer her little gate.

'But this was our night, Esther, we agreed...' He was moving alongside her. The gusty drizzle had stopped as suddenly as it had arrived, and he had taken off his cap and was squeezing it in his hands. 'You are so beautiful, Esther, you do know that, don't you? Just as you know the effect you have on me. Right from the start.' He reached out to stroke her head, gripping her arm when Esther tried to duck away.

'Let go of me. Now, Chris. Let go. Or I will scream.'

'Look, all I want is to talk, okay?' There was no relenting in the grip on her elbow. 'Two minutes of your time, then, Esther. Is that so much to ask?'

Her front door was nearer now, just behind him, the gate hanging open in its usual derelict way. But still, in any tussle – with her phone, or her door – she would lose.

'*One* minute. If you let go of my arm.'

He released her elbow at once, shaking his head disconsolately. 'We had something, Esther, something good...'

'No, Chris, we did not. And we never...' His mouth flew at her face, finding her cheek. Esther jerked free, not quickly enough to avoid a brief repulsive stroke of his tongue in her ear. She charged towards her door. Time slowed. She was aware of Chris, lumbering rather than sprinting, behind her, but also, quite suddenly, of the flashing electric blue dots in the new installations fixed at different angles above Dimitri and Sue's front door.

'Go away, or I shall call the police,' she shouted, spinning round and finding her house keys in one easy hand-dive into her bag. 'Go away, and never contact or come near me again.' She spoke loudly, disgustedly and in a tone of command she did not recognise. 'We are on camera, Chris, so I shall report you anyway. For trespass and harassment. With proof.' She gestured in the direction of the protruding cameras, while taking care to keep her eyes fixed on him.

He had started shuffling backwards, scrunching his hat up more tightly. In the beam of the street light, she could see his eyes blinking behind the lenses of his glasses, wide with alarm. 'But I haven't...'

'Yes, you have, Chris. Finding out where I lived, bombarding me with messages and gifts after I had asked you not to. I bet you even followed me to the bloody garden centre. It stops, do you understand? It wouldn't exactly help things with Kelly, would it,' Esther hissed, with a venom she had no idea she possessed, as he continued to shrivel before her eyes, 'for the police to know her father is a stalker?'

The fear in his face turned to terror. 'You fucking bitch. You wouldn't... I am not a...' The sentence was lost as he took off down the street, breaking into a clumsy run.

'Yes, I would,' Esther yelled after him, so loudly that she did not register Dimitri's cab arriving from the opposite direction, until it pulled up alongside the house.

'Only managed to leave my phone at home, didn't I?' he called cheerfully as he hopped out, leaving the engine running and the hazards on. 'All right there, Esther?' He paused to squint down the street where the figure of Chris Mews had already merged into the darkness.

'Yes, I... all good, thanks, Dimmy. Just seeing off an unwanted visitor.'

'Really?' Dimitri, halfway down his path, stopped and looked at her properly. 'Anything you need help with, Esther, you have only to say the word.'

'No, honestly. All good. But thanks for asking and thanks for installing those.' She pointed at the new cameras as she turned to go into the house. 'They make me feel a lot safer.'

'Pleased to hear it. Mind you...' Dimitri threw the devices a disparaging look '... we'll all feel safer still when the bloody things start working properly. The lights should be red, not blue. They've promised to come back next week. Laters, Esther. Take care, now.' He waved before bolting inside.

Esther leant back against her door as soon as she had closed it, aware of her heart rate settling. To her surprise, she really did feel fine. She would report the incident to be on the safe side, but it was close to inconceivable that Chris Mews would be stupid enough to return. And not being cowed by what *could* have happened was something she was getting better at. Coping *in* the moment, trusting her own instincts – she was almost proud of herself. She bent down to stroke Chico, who had staggered sleepily into the hall, before shaking the rain off her coat and hanging it up. Then she texted Lily – and Dylan's dead phone for good measure – telling each child that she loved them and always would, no matter what the world threw in their paths.

CRACKS

31

'It all sounds frightening and horrible. Well done, for managing. Golly, what a hectic time you've been having, what with the Lucas business, and Dylan to worry about too. You poor thing, Esther. I hope you did report the man to the police in the end?'

'Yes. Or at least, I gave details to one of the people manning the 101 switchboard.'

Esther had been deliberately matter-of-fact about everything, wanting Viv to understand that it wasn't sympathy she was after, but still couldn't believe how cursory – how skin-deep and pointless – their conversation already felt. As if Viv was going through the motions. She scanned her friend's face, dimly searching for some evidence of the woman who, not that long ago, had been eager and ready to discuss everything under the sun, the various travails in their respective lives included. They were sitting in the cinema foyer, with ten minutes until the start of their film. Over three weeks of virtual silence, and Viv had even dodged this chance for a proper talk over a meal, citing drop-offs and pick-ups of the two younger children as the reason. The holiday in August, which had ended so badly, felt a world away, as Viv's pale face testified, the dusty freckles back to near invisibility and with her hair already a little darker and longer, not curving quite so neatly round her chin. Her eyes were as sharp as ever, but not quite meeting hers, Esther was increasingly certain, as well as sporting the cloudy violet under-patches that were always a sure sign Viv was short on sleep. 'There is no "poor thing" about any of it, Vivvie,' she said quietly, 'or at least, I didn't intend there to be.'

'No, I wasn't trying to...' She smiled briskly, giving a business-like slap to her thighs. 'Anyway, hadn't we better think about going in? I might powder my nose first.'

'Powder your nose?' Esther repeated, unable to contain herself. Viv never used euphemisms. Viv hated euphemisms. And her black trouser suit, a stalwart Esther knew well, was hanging off her. 'Viv, are you sure you are all right?'

'Of course, I am all right, I just need a pee before the film. What about you?'

'No, you go ahead, I'm fine, thanks.' Esther watched her walk away, despair deepening at the continuing glacial manner, and at her own naivety in imagining that Viv agreeing to this longed-for girls' night out would see a grand resolution of everything.

Oh God, she really *was* thinner, Esther saw, as the door to the Ladies swung open at last and Viv strode out, orange coat over one arm, her black trouser suit flapping loosely round her frame. She patted the sofa space next to her, but Viv merely pointed in the direction of the sign for their screen and set off up the stairs.

'You are ill or still angry,' Esther declared, desperation and hurt getting the better of her as they settled into their seats, in the middle of an auditorium that was still virtually empty because not even the trailers had started.

'I assure you I am neither,' Viv replied smoothly, 'and I am *very* much looking forward to the film. So just relax, Esther, can't you?'

Esther sank deeper into her chair as an advert for gym membership began, marvelling that prising open her locked box of a daughter and seeing off six-foot-tall stalkerish admirers could feel less of a challenge than spending time with her closest friend. The film, a story about a broken engagement that got fixed, turned out to be good though, and spending almost two hours laughing side by side with Viv, between shedding a few tears – always at the same moments – still felt like something to be treasured.

'I feel like I've become a loose thread,' she ventured, wanting to hang onto the closeness as they emerged back into the foyer. 'It's like, now I am on my own I don't quite fit anywhere any more. No one knows what to do with me. Family. Suitors. Exes. Friends...' Viv was already pulling her coat back on. 'I mean,' Esther pressed on, 'that is clearly how it feels for you. And Shona, come to that,' she added quickly, when Viv didn't take the bait; 'blowing me off now more times than I can count. Not to mention the Amersham crew. Do you know, Dad sent me an email the other day – wildly early as usual, about his annual, pre-Christmas "surprise party" for Mum's birthday – and honestly, apart from the "love Dad" it could have been written to one of his golfing pals.'

Viv chuckled and Esther's hopes soared.

'You are the opposite of a loose thread, Esther,' she declared, briskly doing up the big white buttons on her coat. 'Shona is wrapped round Carole's finger, and always has been. Your father is always weirdly formal, and that is part of his charm. And for the record...' she paused, pulling a white pompom hat out of her coat pocket '...seeing off creepy dates and having one-night stands with young nephews of neighbours clearly suits you – I mean, you look amazing, Esther. Unless it is some powerful vitamins or a new foundation cream...' She faltered.

It was as if she was trying to be her old self and for a moment it was almost worse than anything. They had reached the exit and both put their arms out to push the door at the same time. It granted the first close-up eye-contact of the evening.

'What's up, Vivvie? You look so sad. Or still furious. Please tell me which. And if it is because I have leaned on you too much, then I am *sorry*. I just don't know how to *be* with you any more, or what I have done *wrong*, apart from saying those vicious, untrue things in your lovely holiday house when I was drunk and stressed out of my mind. I miss you, Viv. I miss *us*. I *need* you, Vivvie—'

'No, you don't, and just shut the fuck up for one blessed moment, can't you?'

Esther snapped her mouth closed. They were out in the street, the biting air wrapping itself around their legs and Viv already striding on, throwing glares at Esther as she continued to address her. 'You do *not* need me. And, apart from dear Dylan – who is at least in touch and who *will* come home, when he is ready – you've got it all under control. Masterfully. As usual.' Her eyes glittered for a moment. 'Even Lucas, I have no doubt.'

Esther could only gawp, while her brain scrambled to the texted x that had arrived from Lucas that morning, a delayed response to the consoling message she had sent after trying his doorbell. 'Lucas is good at looking after Lucas,' she said steadily, 'as I think we can all agree.'

'We can,' Viv replied, speeding up. 'Now I have to get back. My car is down here.'

'Mine too,' Esther lied, having to trot to keep pace, her coat and hair flapping, while Viv was as neat as a parcel, coat fastened up to her neck, bag strapped across her chest.

'Viv.'

'What?'

'I thought your work was about communication. So, *communicate* with me.'

Viv halted and turned on her. 'You just don't bloody give up, do you?' She dug into her pocket as she spoke, pulling out a packet of cigarettes and a lighter.

Esther let out a small cry. 'Viv, you don't smoke. At least not for fifteen years.' She watched, astounded, as Viv plucked a cigarette out of the packet with her mouth, snapping the lighter into action and inhaling greedily.

'What the fuck, Viv? You're actually scaring me.'

'Brian and I have been going through... a thing.' She paused, to inhale again, turning away to release the smoke in a slow cloud that promptly drifted back into their faces.

'Oh no, Viv, I am so—'

'Shut up, Esther.' She took another drag and then dropped the cigarette on the ground, grinding the hot tip under the sole of her boot. 'I have sworn to Brian that I would not do this. I am breaking my promise to Brian. I knew I would if I saw you. I knew.'

'Your *promise*? What promise?'

Viv let out a low moan. They were by an empty bus shelter and she had reached out a hand to steady herself against the side.

'Vivvie, just tell me. Nothing can change how much—'

'Oh yes, it can. It has. We cannot be friends, Esther.'

Esther belted her arms across her chest. She was in her warm blue coat, but suddenly very cold. 'You are mad.'

'Brian likes you,' Viv snapped.

'Me?' Esther started a hoot of a laugh and quickly swallowed it away. 'I like Brian,' she said levelly.

'Oh God, Esther, you are so bloody naïve sometimes.' Viv had the cigarettes out again and was lighting another one.

'Am I?' Esther gasped, as bewildered as she had ever been in her life.

'My husband likes you. *My* husband. Likes you. A lot. I'd always sort of half known, but left it alone. Then in France – when yes, you really, *really* pissed me off, and he grabbed the chance for that tête-à-tête with you afterwards – I saw the two of you from the window. It was obvious how he was loving every minute...' she took a sharp breath, batting away Esther's hand as it attempted to hold one of hers '...so much so that he steps in, Mr Gallant, to drive you to the bloody airport *despite* my having *said* I would shift my client to do it... so...' she paused to breathe again, and Esther found herself too transfixed, too appalled, to interrupt '...so I got him to admit it...the extent of it. I used my skills.' She flashed a look at Esther that was as much about triumph as pain.

'You idiot.'

'Really? Well, thank you, Esther.'

'I would never do anything with Brian,' she said in a flat voice.

'Fine. And he has said the same. But that doesn't stop it being *there*.'

'Viv, this is utter nonsense.'

'You cannot undo *words*, Esther, or *feelings*. He doesn't want you to know, and he doesn't want to see you. It's a mess. The worst we have ever known. My God, if he knew I'd even told you he would be furious, and rightly so, because I have broken my word... my *word*. You're just so bloody good-looking, Esther, and *nice*, and yet never quite seem to grasp it, or enjoy it, going on about things like not being the weight you want, totally failing to notice that men trip over themselves because of staring so hard as you walk by. Not to mention women, but I'm not even going to go there.'

'Good, because every word is insane.'

Viv was close to tears and Esther again tried to touch her, only to be shaken off.

'It is not insane, it is true. And I blame Lucas, frankly, for somehow keeping your self-esteem so under wraps – so caught up in his massive ego – that you've not a clue about your own worth... until now... yes...' she nodded '...maybe now you are starting to get it. But I cannot have you near my husband,' she went on softly, brushing away a stray tear. 'He doesn't want it, and I don't either.'

'Well, you are *both* idiots. Especially *you*. With your expertise.' Esther flapped her arms around, not knowing how to find the words for the implosion taking place inside her. 'Picking at something that was fine, and making it *not* fine.' She slapped her palm against the Perspex wall of the bus shelter. 'I thought you lot were supposed to know better. I thought you *professionals* didn't pull things apart without knowing how to put them back together. Really, Viv... this is beyond *stupid*, and you can tell Brian so from me.'

'I am telling him nothing,' she whispered with a defeated feebleness Esther had never seen before. 'We have got ourselves in a hole, and I am sorry but I cannot, right at this minute, see a way out. I can't just step away from it, Esther, from how it makes me – us – feel. But thank you for at least... trying. I know that is what your anger is about.

Like I say, you don't give up on people, Esther Shaw, and it is one of the many remarkable things about you, as well as the most self-destructive. Like staying with Lucas all those years...'

'You are not diverting me with Lucas,' Esther retorted. 'What about physician heal thyself, eh? Put that in your pipe instead, because this is total shit.'

'I've really got to go now.'

'Me too. And I do not want a hug.' Esther sidestepped her, flapping her own arms again, this time in a shooing motion. 'You don't deserve one. I do not fancy your husband,' she yelled as Viv walked away. 'I never have and I never shall,' she hollered, even louder, widening her eyes defiantly at a strolling couple giving her curious looks. She was too exasperated even to cry, while Viv did not so much as twitch, let alone break stride.

32

It wasn't until Heidi joined the dispiritingly long queue for passport control that she realised she had managed to leave her earphones on the plane. They were new and top quality, but even so, she had to plumb all her inner resolve to muster the energy to go back. Worse than the annoyance was the recognition that the oversight was part of an uncharacteristically distracted state of mind. The decision to put Wolfgang out of his misery that morning, not to mention having to return to the UK – to Lucas – with the ring still buried somewhere under mud and leaves on the Drachenfels, were part of it, but Heidi knew full well that the causes reached beyond that, beyond even the outcome of the mediation, which had apparently come through at last, and which Lucas had promised to tell her about that evening. In fact, she was a nervous wreck, Heidi realised, her heart racing even more, as she headed back into all the crowds she had so successfully left in her wake, hastily texting Lucas to warn him of the further delay to what had already been a late flight.

Trying to progress back through the on-flow of passengers was like swimming against a mighty tide. Like her life now, Heidi couldn't help thinking. A few months ago, there had been a clear, straight, bright path to follow, and now, everywhere she looked, it was foggy with uncertainties. Heidi didn't do negativity. She excelled at being sunny and positive and always had. From babyhood she had lit up a room with her energy and vibrancy. She was a dynamo. Everybody said so. Nothing was beyond her grasp if she put her mind to it – Heidi had grown up to the tune of such mantras, and had never once doubted them. Doors opened if you pushed hard enough and willed them into giving way. Enjoyment and success in life were about an attitude of mind.

Such beliefs had been among the many themes discussed during the course of her five wonderful days in the Schwarzwald. Her friends – all in their early thirties – were high-fliers like her, hard workers with big dreams and big ambitions. They had walked and talked until their muscles ached and their throats were raw, and then talked some more, round campfires, and later, stargazing from their sleeping bags, united in the thrill of being youthful, fit, and in command of their destinies.

And now she couldn't even keep track of a set of earphones, Heidi reflected morosely, reaching the plane's open door at last and explaining her quest to a cleaner already poised to start work. When, two minutes later, she found the little plastic box exactly where she had left it, tucked between the magazine and the safety instructions card in the back of the seat in front, she felt a little better. She strode back towards passport control, remembering again her father's wise words from their many Lucas discussions, it having proved impossible to keep shtum about the Moira crisis as Lucas had specifically requested.

'Do you trust him?' her father had asked simply; and when Heidi, holding his kind, steady gaze, had said that yes, she did, he had reached for her mother's hand, saying, 'Then that is all that matters. Trust. It is everything.'

'But we are here for you,' her mother had put in hastily, being always the one to worry more. 'If ever things go wrong, dearest, remember you can turn to us.'

Heidi spotted Lucas the moment she emerged into the arrivals concourse, standing a little back from the line of waiting friends and relatives, staring into the middle distance. He looked deeply tired, she observed at once, thinking it again even when she was in his arms, and his beautiful green eyes were lit up with the pleasure of having her there.

'I have missed you.' He kissed her as if he might take bites out of her, speaking in breathless staccato bursts. 'So very, *very* much. Are you okay? Really irritating about the earphones, thank God they hadn't been taken. Awful about Wolfgang. But at least you were there, right? Your grandparents must be heartbroken. And your parents, are they all right? And Stefan? Did you eat on the plane? I've got in a few bits and left them ready at yours, but didn't go mad.'

'How kind to meet me, but such a boring way to spend your Saturday night,' she teased, reassured by the rush of her own delight at seeing him again, but slightly puzzled by his quickfire talking – almost as if he, too, was nervous, which was a little disconcerting. Lucas excelled at being sure of himself; and, though it could be annoying, it was a trait she found very attractive.

'There is nowhere I would rather be than here. With you. It's all I want. For ever.' He squeezed her to him again, so hard it grew almost uncomfortable. For one unforgivable moment it cast Heidi back to the contrasting goodbye with Elias, the banker, before she'd boarded her train for the journey home, his arms cradling her as if she were a precious object, saying as much as his mouth brushed her ear. He had phoned her when she reached Bonn too, to remind her, he'd said, that the second post-doctoral thesis that would lead to her professorship could be conducted at any university in Europe. Including the Goethe University in Frankfurt, where he happened to be employed by Deutsche Bank. His tone had been joking. They had both laughed. Like all her friends, he knew she was engaged to a Cambridge academic; though Heidi had kept the inappropriate behaviour allegation out of the fireside chats, loath to dent the impression of her enviable life.

'Which is why I have brought you this,' Lucas went on, releasing her and whipping out a tall single rose from a slim tote bag hanging over his shoulder. 'For you, Heidi, love of my life. There are more at your flat, but I didn't want them all to have to weather the car journey.'

'Oh, Lucas...' Heidi took the rose and put her nose to it, her eyes pricking with tears for the second time that day, which felt half nice, while also being a reminder that her emotions were unnervingly near the surface, that she wasn't quite herself. 'The ring, Lucas,' she blurted, 'I feel so terrible—'

'Feeling terrible about that is forbidden,' he said jauntily, picking up her case and looping his arm through hers for the walk towards the car park. 'Rings are just objects and these things happen. We shall simply buy another...'

'So, it was definitely insured?'

'Oh yes. Very insured.'

'You are limping, Lucas, with your bad muscle, so please let me...' She tried to take over the suitcase but he fought her off.

'It is much better. You must look after your rose.'

'Well, at least pull out the handle, then,' she murmured, doing it for him.

'And now, Lucas, what has the college said... the mediation? I am on edge...'

'Let's save that, shall we?' He threw her a smile that managed such a combination of determination and pleading that it felt impossible to argue. 'It's not too awful. A mix of good and not so good. I'll tell you all about it when we get to yours. What I really want to hear about is *you*...'

'But I can't believe how long the decision-making took,' she interjected. 'I imagined – I am sure you said – it would all be settled on the day.'

'Yes, that is what I thought too, but there you go. It is done with now.'

She tugged on his arm, kissing his shoulder. 'Well, that is good to hear, and I shall be patient. But you don't look so well, Lucas. Are you properly better from the sickness? After Ralph's lunch?' she prompted when he did not immediately reply.

'Oh, I see, yes. Absolutely. It dragged on a bit, as these things do. I'm only sorry it meant I've not been up to proper communications. Though I didn't want to keep bombarding you either, not with your walking trip and then just trying to chill with your family... ah, there's the car, and now I must find a machine to pay. Then I want to hear all *your* news, darling, especially the trekking – the Black Forest is a place I'd love to go. Do you think you could bear to return there one day, with me in tow? That's all I want, Heidi, you and me exploring the world together...' He let go of the case and swept her hair off her face to kiss her again, hungrily. 'Thank you, darling, for loving me, for believing in me, for everything.'

* * *

Later, in her bed, Lucas's love-making had the same urgent ardour, but then he couldn't finish.

'Sorry. That's never...'

'It doesn't matter,' Heidi put in quickly, too kind to say that it sort of did matter.

'I'll make it up to you, I promise. In the morning.'

'Lucas, it is fine. I am tired too. Let us go to sleep.' Minutes later, his breathing settled into an audible rhythm. Lying awake, her body humming, Heidi reached out and trailed the backs of her fingers across the dark hairs on the forearm he had draped over her stomach. His head was turned towards her, his mouth slightly open, displaying the tips of his strong even teeth. Without her he *fell apart*. Heidi rolled the words around her mind. Lucas had written them to her and then reiterated the phrase that evening as they picked at the awful oily, over-salted supermarket snacks that had constituted her homecoming dinner, the immaculate, blood-red roses parked between them, in two vases because there had been so many.

Bombay mix, cheese and onion crisps, tubs of coleslaw, rubbery prawns drowning in a sickly, sweet sauce, and hunks of a supermarket baguette. Heidi had begun eating only to be kind, and then found herself glad to have something to swallow as Lucas at last announced the stark details of the long-awaited outcome of the managed talks with Moira. There had been a little bit of press attention too, he added quickly, while she was still wide-eyed, processing both the drastic verdict and his extraordinary composure in describing it. He had closed his Twitter account as a precaution, he explained in the same almost serene manner, but it had all died down now and wasn't anything to worry about.

'But... two years, Lucas. *Two years.*'

'Yup. Not ideal, I know. But it draws a line under the whole sorry business, with no question of pressing charges, and of course I shall be on full pay. It means I can work like a fiend and devote more time to you.'

He was smiling in the new, determined, defensive way that felt so difficult to counter. *Be positive*, Heidi reminded herself, it was what was required and what she supposedly excelled at. 'But this press attention, tell me...'

'Oh, it was just a local flurry. A small article. Leaked by Moira's father, is our guess.'

'Moira's father? Why do you think he would do that?' Lucas's expression seemed to freeze for a moment. 'I mean, wouldn't any father want to protect his child from the spotlight in such a situation?' Heidi persisted, frowning as she thought of her own, close family. 'If it is true, it is horrible, Lucas.'

'I couldn't agree more, but who knows what anyone's true motives are for anything?' Lucas spoke energetically, reaching for the champagne that had formed a part of the welcome feast, in order to refill his empty glass, for the third time, by Heidi's calculation.

'Anyway, it's over and doesn't matter,' he went on, still with the cheery eagerness that felt almost too much, 'and perhaps Moira, maybe safely ensconced in college as we speak, without the threat of my "terrifying presence"—' he painted inverted commas in the air with his forefingers '—might even be starting to wonder if what she did was justified. Now, that would give me satisfaction.' He laughed darkly, shaking his head to himself.

'I have been thinking about Moira, Lucas.'

'Have you? Yes, so have I, far more than I would like. Mostly, I try to work out what the bloody girl thought she was *doing*. Coming to me that day, all doe-eyed, and then... well, we both know the "and then", only too well.' He took another swig of his drink, swilling it in his mouth for a couple of seconds before swallowing.

'I need to talk to you about her.'

'Okay, my love. Talk away.' He pushed the tubs of food to one side and took hold of her hands, gently rubbing her lower wrists with the pads of his thumbs in a way that felt more like a nervous tic than a caress.

'She is such a very young girl, Lucas, uncertain of herself; and you are a powerful man. How you use that power is important. The smallest thing to you could feel very big and frightening to her, or anyone like her...'

'Yes, sweetheart, I think I have gleaned – and said – that much myself, many times. Though thank you for going over it again. Much appreciated.'

'No, you have not said that. Not exactly.'

'Ah. Not *exactly*. My mistake. Maybe you do not think I am clear enough in how I express my thoughts. Maybe you even, secretly, enter-tain *doubts* about me in other aspects of this dire and demeaning situa-tion.' He had let go of her wrists and was leaning back in his chair, looking at her down the length of his nose, his irises glinting under the hoods of his eyelids.

'No doubts,' Heidi said firmly, resolving to ignore the iciness in his tone. Her father's voice was in her head again. 'I trust you, Lucas,' she said solemnly. 'In everything.'

'Well, there's a matter for rejoicing.' He picked up his glass again, draining it. 'Hallelujah.'

A disbelieving laugh escaped her. 'Lucas, I am trying to make things better. I have said something important. How dare you be angry with me?'

'I am not angry, Heidi,' he countered, his voice so harsh she felt her stomach turn over. 'I fully understand that, albeit unwittingly, I allowed Moira to feel threatened and overwhelmed by my educated male privilege, that she felt *invaded* instead of *helped*, as I intended. More than anything, however, I am just so utterly fed up with the whole subject of Moira Giddings, and the way she has been allowed, on the basis of *virtually nothing*, to throw a giant, fucking spanner into my – *our* – entire life.' He reached again for the bottle, freezing in momentarily comical astonishment when Heidi swiped it off the table first.

'I hate you drinking. It changes you.' She clutched the bottle to her chest.

'No, it doesn't. It's just a fun thing to do from time to time. And sometimes, yes, when the world is throwing crap at you, it can help. A crutch, of sorts, if you will.'

'And would your father have said the same thing?'

Lucas emitted an incredulous whoop. 'That's what I love about you, Heidi, darling, you just don't hold back. You shoot from the hip. Pow – pow – pow.' He got to his feet as he spoke, firing an imaginary pistol round the room with such abandon that his chair toppled backwards, landing with a crash on the wooden floor. 'Yes, oh sweet one, my father was a stinking, unfaithful, vile alcoholic, who, for a couple of decades or so, succeeded in ruining the lives of many people: mine, his mistress's, and my poor mother's included. As I believe I confided in you during our courting days, I have had to build something of a fortress over the years in order to keep him out... a fortress that some have found hard to cope with... but not you. To you, I have opened myself utterly. And so, to attack me for a measly celebratory glass of fizz or two when we have been apart so long...' He stopped, tracking Heidi, who had been backing away from him, edging round the table, carefully stepping over the chair and going into her kitchenette, visible from the table via a hatch in the wall. Keeping her eyes on his, she tipped the bottle over the sink.

His face went rigid and then collapsed. 'It was decent stuff, and wouldn't keep, that's why...'

'I do not like you when you drink, Lucas.'

'But I love you,' he croaked, deflated suddenly, his eyes shiny with emotion.

Heidi shook the empty bottle for the last few drops – there had only been a glassful left anyway. 'I do not want any more food. I was not hungry actually.' She spoke in a monotone. 'I only ate not to hurt your feelings. Now I am going to make myself a peppermint tea, and think maybe you should leave—'

'No,' he groaned, already staggering round into the kitchen. 'Please, no. Forgive me, forgive me, I'm an arse. I do not deserve you. But I *shall*. I promise I shall. Just give me the chance, darling Heidi...' He fell to his knees at her feet, sobbing like a child as he clasped her legs. 'I'll do anything you ask, anything. *Ich liebe dich... ich liebe dich...*'

Heidi held herself stiffly. 'Have you lied to me, Lucas, ever? About anything?'

'No, no, no. Never.'

'Now is your chance, Lucas. If you have anything to tell me, it is now.'

'I have nothing to tell you, except that I love you, and always shall.'

Heidi had looked down at his hair, sprouting from the crown in its neat thick boyish spirals. For several seconds she had looked rather than touched, fighting down the overpowering, frightening sense of meeting him for the first time. Of *seeing* him. A broken version of the person she had fallen in love with.

* * *

Three o' clock, her phone said. Heidi checked for messages and returned it to her bedside table. Nothing from Elias, which was just as well. She held her left hand up above her face, flexing her pale, empty fingers. The ring would have shone in the dark, a blue planet circled by its diamond moons; but it had always felt heavy. It had caught on things. It had impeded how she gripped bike handles, carried shopping bags, and the way she lathered shampoo into her hair. Marrying, she saw suddenly, was taking on the weight of another person. It was an additional burden to carry. Theoretically for ever. Lucas would no doubt say he was doing the same for her, but it seemed to Heidi that there was no equivalence. She was happy Heidi, with a deeply connected and high-functioning family. There were no demons other than a cheeky younger brother and the shared sadness at her father's much older parents no longer being around. She hadn't erected a fortress to live behind. Her only buried secret was the very recent swoosh of arousal at the graze of Elias's five-day beard against her neck, the warmth of his breath in her ear.

She sighed heavily, rolling away from Lucas. The fog in her head was back, worse than ever. He was breathing more noisily, and it was distracting. She tried aligning their breaths but it didn't work. They weren't in sync. She had a go at lying on her stomach instead, burrowing her head under the pillow. To send him home, to *not* touch him as he wept, had proved beyond her. But something deep inside had shifted, something big, and it made her fearful.

NOVEMBER

33

Esther's eyes travelled on round the room, taking in the familiar furnishings, the gimmicky guitar clock that hung above the bed, a fifteenth-birthday gift from her and Lucas, the shelves and desk, chaotic with Dylan's bits and bobs. All of it looking dejected, as if the whole place – like her – were still holding its breath for his return. Apart from an occasional hoover, she hadn't been able to bring herself to do anything, not even change the sheets. But Dylan was still alive – as the intermittent trickle of postcards kept testifying – and it was time to summon her courage and give the place a proper clean.

Esther stripped off the bottom sheet and then sat on the bed, holding a pillow to her face in the hope of finding some scent of Dylan, but getting nothing more than stale linen. For a moment she let all the usual longing and the worry fill her. She had brought Viv's journal upstairs with her and picked it up now, wanting to write something about her feelings, as the thing was designed for, but then made a note of something to tell Viv instead, in the emails she had taken to sending whenever the mood took her, deciding not to care that the new impossible situation meant getting nothing in return. She then jotted a couple of work thoughts down too, galvanised by alarm at a recent suggestion by the CEO of her healthcare client that the launch magazine should become a broader-ranging, monthly publication with her in charge. Everyone was supposedly thinking about how to make it work, Esther most of all.

Starting on the duvet buttons, she almost lost heart. It might be high time, but it also felt like a new stage, close to giving up. To spur herself on, she took a photo of the room and sent it to Lily, saying:

Braving a tidy-up! Eeek. Wish me luck!

It being a Sunday, Esther had high hopes of hearing back straight away. She stayed online, giving the two ticks a couple more minutes, but they didn't turn blue. Any excuse to contact Lily and she had been grabbing it, letting her know she was there. Matteo, long since back from his trip and up to speed on everything had helped enormously, but Lucas, as Lily kept reporting despairingly, was still keeping his distance, making the continuing gossip about his suspension even harder to bear. Esther messaged Lucas now, on a fresh surge of frustration.

Talk properly to Lily. She needs your help in coping. It isn't just you going through this. E.

Scooping up the bed linen, Esther ferried it onto the landing and hurled it down the steep little staircase, aware as she did so of her head throbbing from the previous evening's Halloween dinner. Not at her place, in the end, but Dimitri and Sue's, a result of their pleading when Esther had tried to cry off a few days before. A kitchen supper, just the three of them, Sue had said cosily, but insisting it had to be in fancy dress. Esther at the last minute had swathed herself in a double sheet, using quantities of safety pins, only to feel somewhat feeble when she had been greeted by Dimitri in a diaphanous witch outfit – channelling a hint of Widow Twanky – and Sue, resplendent in a scarlet onesie with a forked tail, a horned headband perched in her wild carrot-red hair.

'Ah, good, he's popping in,' cried Sue, when the bell rang, just as they were settled with drinks. She returned a minute later, followed by Marcus and a waif-like, fuzzy-haired child in a tutu and an anorak, tugging on her father's arm in a manner that suggested she would have preferred to stay in the street. The anorak, black and flecked with pink glitter, was hanging off her tiny shoulders like a half-shed skin and the ballet pumps on her feet, also pink, were toe-capped with dry mud.

'Hey, everyone, this is Lola. We're on a flying visit,' Marcus announced genially, smiling at them all.

'I am a fairy, but not with wings, so I *can't* fly,' Lola pointed out, rolling her eyes at her father's dimness, and performing a half-hearted waggle with the small wand clutched in her free hand.

Sue clucked. 'Hello, Lola, you are gorgeous, that's for sure. Let's get that coat off and I'll fix you a juice.'

'Loads of fairies don't bother with wings,' Esther said, while Sue poured out an orange juice that was met with a violent headshake, as was an attempt to remove the anorak.

'Sorry. She's tired, and buzzing with sugar,' Marcus apologised, scooping her onto his hip. 'We just came to say hi, really, didn't we?' He gave her a nuzzle, saying something in her ear that made her giggle.

'You are a ghost,' she cried, swivelling to look at Esther and smiling broadly enough to reveal a gaping hole that had recently played host to a front tooth.

'I am indeed.' Esther swung out her arms to display the full glory of the bedsheet.

'Well, I have a magic wand, so watch out.'

'Yeah, watch out, you.' Marcus laughed. 'Apologies for my own lack of razzle-dazzle, by the way.' He tweaked the weather-beaten sheepskin jacket he was wearing, and threw a regretful look at his jeans, which had frayed hems sitting on trainers far dirtier than his daughter's shoes. 'Forty-eight-hour whistle-stop visits round Europe and something has to give. But I promise I've *not* forgotten the cat,' he added hastily, pulling a guilty face at Esther. 'Turns out eleven-year-old male tabbies are not in hot demand, but the re-homing centre keep on assuring me it *will* happen.'

'It doesn't matter. No rush. I'll hand him on to Dimmy and Sue when I've had enough,' Esther joked, earning an unreadable glance from Sue. A flurry of exchanged looks between her and Dimmy then produced the joint, shy announcement that they were eight months off expecting a baby, and had been told – because of Sue's history – to be wary of many things, including cats.

'Apparently they can carry this thing called toxoplasmosis,' Sue explained meekly, once Marcus's and Esther's exclamations of delight had died down. 'It can make you miscarry or do terrible things early on to the baby. Sorry.'

'Don't say sorry – you are banned from my house, forthwith.' Esther laughed as Marcus accepted a beer from Dimmy, and Sue herded them all into the sitting room. She promptly disappeared back into the kitchen, while Dimmy beckoned Lola over to the television to help him scroll through the Disney channel.

'So everything got sorted with the arrangements for your aunt, then,' Esther ventured, twiddling the stem of her wine glass and wondering if Marcus was remembering the last occasion they had been in a sitting room together, back in September. 'Those nightmare logistics.' She kept her expression impassive, glad he could not see the images sky-rocketing in her head.

'Yep, all done and dusted.' His tone was business-like. 'Hordes of family and friends. The weather was great. Not a single hitch. Enough ceremony to please a pope. Just the house to sell now, and then I'm done. Dropping Lola back with her mum tonight and then it's Holland again tomorrow. A fun shoot though, I have to admit. Great crew. Great city.' He smiled in his easy way, and Esther decided to be proud of the straightforwardness of what had happened between them. It felt so simple, so *grown up*. Sex wasn't everything. It was just part of something, if you wanted it to be.

Ten minutes later, after Marcus had bolted a few mouthfuls of Sue's delicious lamb tagine, and Lola had been persuaded to eat a banana, they were gone. Esther had stayed for a couple more hours, unwisely helping Dimitri finish a bottle of wine over a conversation that had rarely wavered from the subject of pregnancy, before gathering up the folds of her sheet and scooting home.

It would be hard to think of two people more deserving of a baby, Esther reflected now, wistfulness threatening, as she set to the task of creating a measure of order out of the mess on Dylan's desk. She picked a random podcast on her phone and worked methodically, dropping obvious rubbish into the black sack she had brought up from the kitchen for the purpose. Spraying copious amounts of aerosol as she dusted, she began to arrange and stack all the stuff she dared not throw away. The tidying was about hope and love, Esther told herself, the wistfulness increasing as she registered that the two people doing the podcast, a celebrity comedian and an athlete, were walking and talking – about emotional well-being – in Shropshire. Near Ludlow. Near Lucas's family home.

How was he? Really? According to Lily, he was still barely leaving his flat – 'lying a bit low', as he apparently put it in one of the breezy texts that their daughter was now supposed to accept as sufficient communication. And how was Heidi being? Did the woman understand the extent of the shame, the visceral pain that Lucas would be going through… to have his entire reputation, built up over decades, trashed? His hubris had certainly deserved a comeuppance, but not that.

The athlete had been in a car crash and had needed to learn how to walk again. The big wild sky and beauty of the Shropshire hills had helped her come to terms with the loss of her career, she explained, by showing her new perspective, new hope, new meaning. Esther listened intently, finding herself cast back to the very first parental visit with Lucas, shouting through her open passenger window – her hair flapping and streaming around her ears and mouth – at the outrageous magnificence of an area of which she'd had no previous knowledge, with its winding, broad, lush valleys, skirted by the high lowering ridges, shifting that day between black and purple and green as the sun had nudged its way through the banks of cloud. Landscape derived meaning only from its human associations, Lucas had countered bitterly. Turning in her seat, Esther had seen the contained suffering in his rigid profile, the concrete set of his jaw. She had placed her hand over his as it worked the gearstick, squeezing gently, willing some of the hurt to enter her.

Esther realised she was gripping the aerosol. She and Lucas had found something, and then lost it. She had been jealous, of Cambridge, of Lucas's passion and growing status. She had felt swamped by motherhood, got fed up, become distant. She had, sometimes, turned her back on him. She had begun to lose faith.

Esther put down the spray can and switched off the podcast. She lowered herself into Dylan's little desk chair, a dizzying loneliness rolling through her. Into the third year now of a reacquired single life and on the battling went, but she was managing better. Bloodied but unbowed, as some poet had said. But oh God, what was the point of a life lived so alone? Esther clasped the edge of the table.

She seized Viv's journal, wanting to write the word *LONELY*, in caps, underlined, but then couldn't find the little pencil – because it was in the heap of bedding probably. There had to be one on the desk. As she rummaged, the flap of a beige folder flopped open and a photo slid out: a selfie of Dylan and Mei Lin, lying on some grass, heads close, puckering their lips at the camera. Esther's heart lurched. Dylan – a piece of him she hadn't seen. Tears pricked her eyes as she drank it in. He looked so heartbreakingly young. As did Mei Lin. Esther stared harder, it gradually dawning that this wasn't a picture from the summer just gone, but from the one before.

She shook the folder, and more slid out. Picture after picture, some of Mei Lin on her own, most of them together. Sitting at tables, on benches, on buses, outside shops, balancing against stone walls, or statues, on bridges, by fountains, and on a windy, pebbled beach somewhere, the pair of them peeking out from under a huge, bright, stripey towel. There were pencil sketches too, extraordinarily accomplished ones, some of the photos, and some of Dylan, in profile, sleeping,

AMANDA BROOKFIELD

eating, sticking his tongue out. Esther riffled through them all again and again, absorbing the fact that the precociously self-assured girl she had met just once, over three months before, on the morning of her birthday, had been a friend to her son on a scale beyond her wildest imaginings. Not known about, even to Lily.

34

'What about that one? The sapphire. You said you liked it a minute ago.' Lucas pointed to the ring at the back of the cluster of options now laid out on the blue velvet mat in front of them. It sat between an emerald and a solitaire diamond – both already dismissed. He had long since stopped thinking about the price-tags. He was too focussed on wanting to see Heidi's face light up the way it had when he went down on one knee and opened the ring box on his impromptu visit to her flat back in August, a quarter of a year and a lifetime before. They always seemed to be on eggshells now. It had taken weeks of gentle coaxing just to get her into the shop. 'Late nineteenth century, didn't you say?' Lucas glanced at the man behind the counter, a hint of begging in his eyes.

'Oh yes, indeed, sir. An exquisite piece.' The jeweller obligingly picked up the sapphire ring in his deft, white-gloved fingers, giving it another unnecessary buffing with his small cloth before handing it to Heidi for re-examination. 'Circa 1880. Reputedly made for the coming of age of the eldest daughter of one, long-forgotten, Lord Hastings. He had seven greedy daughters, the poor man, which may in large part have contributed to his seeing out his years in a debtors' prison.' As he tittered, Heidi carefully set the ring down. Her eyes roamed around the rest of the dazzling selection, while both men watched her avidly. Every gem in every combination anyone could wish for was there, surely, Lucas reflected grimly, except of course the one she had originally accepted, back when life was simple and the summer sun bright. Heidi had repeatedly insisted she didn't want a replica made – it wouldn't feel right she said – but now it seemed she didn't want a new one either.

'Lucas... I am sorry... can we go?' she murmured, stepping back from the counter, and pulling him with her in a bid not to be overheard.

'Of course, darling.' Lucas spoke brightly, wary of the salesman hovering, and cheering himself up with the fact that Heidi had, just that morning, after some much-needed, mutually satisfying love-making, agreed not only to the visit to the jeweller's, but to a date for the wedding. Mid-June. The summer solstice. He had already written to Claire Moore venturing to ask if the chapel might be available.

The door gave its little chime as it released them back into the street. 'There is no urgency, darling. We have eight months, remember?'

'Assuming the college says yes and that there's no danger of Moira being around.' She spoke sullenly, concentrating on her hands as she fed them into her thick leather gloves.

'Term will be over, and Moira will be long gone.' Lucas slid his arm across her back as she zipped up her thick coat, trying to provide a comfort that he could not himself feel.

'Okay. Now I must go.'

'To do your Flaubert turn. Bringing Goethe in where you can.' He smiled at her fondly.

'That is my hope for the lecture, yes.'

Lucas could sense she was eager to head off, even though it was still only four-thirty and the lecture hall just a five-minute stroll away. 'Then, tonight you—'

'Tonight, like I told you already, I have my spin, then I'm dining in college, and after that I must do more planning for my supervisions next week, and tomorrow morning I have a faculty meeting, then I shall do my own work in the afternoon.'

'You could always work at mine?'

She patted his arm. 'I know that, Lucas, and thank you, but I am never so productive there for some reason...' She smiled and he saw a glimmer of what he yearned for. Then her phone rang in her pocket and she pulled a regretful face, signalling that she had to take the call as she walked away.

Lucas watched until she was swallowed up by the busy street, his pulse pumping, wondering who she was talking to. Every moment she was away from him now, he was haunted by such things. Time sat so heavily on him, that was the trouble, while Heidi, as she lamented daily, did not have enough of the stuff.

Around him, the university was in full flow, halfway through term already and sweeping on, not needing him. The sole upcoming appointments in his diary were the optician, to tighten the too-loose frames of his first ever pair of glasses, and a session with the physio, because the calf muscle, though healed, seemed to have transferred some of its troubles to his Achilles tendon.

A formal hall dinner would be nice, Lucas mused wryly, casting a longing look up at the high walls of his college, poking above the line of houses on his left. He didn't use the street itself any more, if he could help it. The college, wanting to protect its skin rather than his, he was sure, had closed ranks, issuing no response to the newspaper article, to which – so far and thank God – there had been no follow-up. The remaining eye of the storm was his alone. Acquaintances he bumped into – even Ralph – asked only about his paper, or Heidi, or Lily, or Dylan, the situation on that front now being known. One colleague had even claimed to be envious of such a long teaching break, a misguided attempt at lightness that had made Lucas want to land a knee in his groin.

Walking on, away from the familiar, tall walls, Lucas experienced a wrenching pain, deep in his innards. He had belonged inside those walls once, felt trusted and secure, but now, suddenly, the business of being shut out seemed complete. He couldn't face Lily. He wasn't sure of Heidi. He wasn't sure of anything. The old, bleak rootlessness was sucking at him again. Esther had understood that, the extent of it. Her message when the story broke, 'one day it will be fish and chips', even the recent telling-off about how he was avoiding Lily, suggested that on some level she still understood, or was at least fully engaged with what was at stake and trying to offer ways through, even if they were naïve and wrong.

His phone buzzed, but it was Lily and Lucas knew that if he heard his daughter's voice, he would weep. He waited, hoping she would leave a message, so he could hear it anyway. But she rang off, leaving nothing. Lucas trudged on towards his flat. A night alone, and already there was only one way he could think of getting through it.

35

Esther stared up at the imposing, wrought-iron gates. There were gold tips on the spikes, which matched the rim on the letterbox and the shiny plaque advertising the house number. When she approached the intercom system, a light came on from some high vantage point on the house, picking her out like an actor on a stage, accentuating the darkness of the November evening. Somewhere nearby a church clock struck six. She had parked a couple of blocks away. It had given her the opportunity to take in the luxury of the area: the elegant driveways, the huge detached houses peeking over the tops of high privet hedges, the glimpses of grand front steps. The street itself, a stone's throw from Richmond Park, was lined with four-wheel-drive vehicles and robust trees, whose drifts of wet, dead leaves had blown against her shins and clung to the soles of her ankle boots as she walked.

Leaving the pictures strewn across the rest of the clutter on Dylan's desk, Esther had made it to the garden centre just before closing. She had spotted Darren almost at once, fielding stray trolleys from the car park. On recognising her, he had looked a little afraid, perhaps reading the purpose in her stride.

'How's it going, Mrs Shaw?'

'It's going very well, thank you, Darren, but I need your help. About

Mei Lin. Dylan's girlfriend... ex-girlfriend.'

He had kept on clanking his trollies. 'Like I said, Mrs S, I didn't really—'

'I need to know how to contact her, Darren. She's not in any sort of trouble,' Esther had reassured him quickly, 'nor are you for that matter, and nor is Dylan. I also completely understand that you might not know off the top of your head, but surely there is someone you could ask? If not her phone number, then maybe where she lives?' She'd positioned herself under one of the floodlights, blocking his route back towards the entrance. 'I would be so grateful.'

He'd given a little shrug, tugging at the rings in his earlobes and sighing heavily as he'd pulled out his phone. 'If you give me your number, I'll see what I can find out.'

Standing in the glare of Mei Lin's home security lights twenty-four hours later, half wondering if she was already being scrutinised, Esther took a moment to compose herself. The opulence of the house was breathtaking, and cast her back to all those first impressions of Dylan's unannounced guest round the breakfast table on her birthday morning: the hint of entitlement in the girl's demeanour, the slightly hard-to-take confidence, the cool assertion of her very grown-up vocation. However, it was the possibility that Mei Lin was travelling with Dylan that had arrived as she'd galloped down the stairs and out of the house to the garden centre, along with the thought that maybe the whole reckless adventure was being funded by a fat allowance. In which case it was parents she would be dealing with and not the girl, Esther realised, taking a deep breath before pressing the buzzer.

Another spotlight immediately came on, more like a torch in the face it was so blinding and near.

'Hello?' It was a man's voice, gruff with the readiness to turn her away.

'I am here about Mei Lin.' Esther aimed for a tone of quiet command rather than desperation. 'I'm the mother of a friend of hers, Dylan Shaw.' There was no reply, only a pause, followed by a faint squeak as the gates started to swing apart.

Waiting for her in the open door at the top of the broad stone steps was a slim, heavy-haired Asian man, in his late forties, she guessed. He was wearing crisp, dark suit trousers, a close-fitting, blue and white, floral shirt, and expensive-looking, hybrid trainer-loafers. 'I am Mei Lin's father. How can I help, Mrs Shaw?' He spoke in the same polished British accent as his daughter and with a tone containing a distinct hint of unwelcome.

'I am so sorry to turn up like this, with no warning. It's about my son, Dylan, who—'

'We always enjoyed having Dylan here.'

'Did you? Oh my... that's... I... I enjoyed meeting Mei Lin too, although it was only the once. Look, Mr...'

'Chen. Jo Chen.'

They shook hands, with an awkwardness that felt mutual. 'My son – Dylan – took off without warning nearly three months ago,' Esther blurted, her cool command deserting her, 'to go travelling... and seeing as he and Mei Lin were... I just wondered if...'

'Ah.' His face softened, and he beckoned her inside, under a dazzling chandelier spraying arrows of light across the ceiling and up a broad set of stairs further along the hall. 'Mei Lin,' he shouted up the staircase. 'Come down and talk to Dylan's mother.'

Esther blinked, clutching her handbag, fighting disappointment.

'Can I offer you a refreshment of any kind?' he asked, gesturing for her to go through a doorway into a room on her right.

'No, thanks, I am fine. How kind of you to call her down. I really would appreciate a quick word,' Esther muttered, noting a tan, pull-along, executive suitcase parked by the door and walking half on tiptoes to reduce the clack of her boot heels on the marble floor, which was white and veined with blue, like expensive cheese.

'I'll fetch her,' he said, after they had waited a few moments. 'Sorry to be in disarray,' he added, a somewhat baffling remark given the pristine, museum-like grandeur of the room, 'but I've just returned from a trip. Twenty years, and I've yet to get the hang of jet lag. Make yourself at home.'

Esther was not brave enough to do any such thing. Two blue silk sofas, the size of boats, were set at opposite ends of the vast, oblong space, each decorated with identical lines of overlapping gold scatter cushions that looked as if they had never once in their lives been disturbed. Between them, set in angled pairs, were hefty armchairs with chunky, carved legs and seats so deep and huge she was sure her legs would swing free of the floor if she dared to sit on one. She lurked by the door instead, listening to the thud of Jo Chen's footsteps receding up the staircase, and then the faint muffled sounds of what sounded like disagreement. After several more long minutes, hearing a slammed door and lighter footsteps, she dodged deeper into the room just before Mei Lin appeared.

'Hello, Mrs Shaw. How are you?' The question was pitched as a polite statement rather than an actual enquiry. Her pale angular face, half hidden by the geometric lines of her long fringe and side curtains of hair, appeared composed and inscrutable, but she remained in the half-open door, as if ready to bolt should the need arise.

'Mei Lin, please forgive me, barging in on you like this...' The girl was daunting; the expressionless set of her face, the force of her inner resolve, coming off her in waves – such a contrast to the relaxed poses and sunny smiles in the photos with Dylan that Esther found it hard to get her words out. 'I just wanted to ask if, by any chance, you were in touch with Dylan... and could tell me exactly where he is, when he is planning on coming home... if he is really okay...'

The mask had broken into a surprised frown. 'Coming home? We broke up. After that time at yours. That afternoon actually. I haven't seen him since.' She shrugged. 'Sorry, not to be able to help.'

'No contact at all?' Esther exclaimed, making no secret of her incredulity. 'Really?'

'Look, Mrs Shaw, I ended it and he took it bad, okay? Like, he wouldn't give up. Ultimately, I had to block him.' She rolled her eyes, sighing. 'So, I'm sorry, but I really can't help you. We had our time. Then it stopped. I mean, all is fair in love and war, right?'

'Yes, I suppose it is,' Esther murmured, her thoughts flying to

Dylan, going through a heartbreak none of them had known about. It struck her too that this girl, though fabulous in her way, would also have been a mighty tornado arriving in the life of a softie sixteen-or-seventeen-year-old boy, still in the thick of the aftermath of his parents' divorce. Dylan would have fallen hard. A first love. It would have made him believe nothing else in the world mattered. That was what love did. Until it fell off a cliff or was snatched away. Her poor, poor boy. 'Thank you, Mei Lin, for telling me, for being so straight.'

The girl had relaxed, rubbing her arms and contorting her pretty features into a proper show of sympathy. 'I hope he is okay.'

'So he used to come round a lot, did he?' Esther ventured.

'Yeah, we used to hang out here. He was cool. He hated that college.'

'Yes, I sort of knew that, but maybe not the extent of it,' Esther admitted. 'Just like I didn't know the extent of... you and him...'

'He didn't want you to know.'

'No, I see. Okay.' Except, she didn't see, and it wasn't okay, Esther realised grimly, because the not-knowing had meant no safety net was held out, no understanding to cushion his fall. She had been too wrapped in herself to notice anything that mattered. 'If he ever does get in touch with you again, would you let me know, do you think?'

'Sure, no problem.'

Esther wasn't sure whether to believe her, but knew it was time to go.

Back in the cavernous hall, she noticed the executive case and jacket had gone. 'Please say thank you to your father.'

'Sure.' She opened the door and then punched some numbers into a small panel on the wall, bringing the gates to life. 'I really do hope he is all right. He wanted us to stay friends but then just couldn't handle it. I've been channelling some of my own feelings into my work. Like, where would artists be without break-ups, right?'

'Right,' Esther muttered, hurrying down the steps, afraid that the formidable, swinging iron jaws would start to close before she got through them.

ART & CRAFT

36

'Can you trust a self-portrait, that's the big question?'

'But it looks so in-your-face honest. They all do.' Esther gestured at the paintings ranged round the big airy room, their heavy gold frames gleaming under the natural light pouring in through the raised roof of the museum. 'And this one is like he's staring straight at the camera. A selfie. It's so unflinching, so warts and all. Literally. I mean, look at his ugly bobbly nose, and the rheumy old-man eyes, all glinting with despair, don't you think? Or maybe with that sadness that comes with being very old and very wise, when you've seen it all, good and bad.'

'But Rembrandt's in control of the image,' Marcus countered. 'He can make us feel what he wants us to feel.' He reached out and pushed a strand of Esther's hair back over her shoulder.

'Manipulating us, you mean, like, say, good actors?' Esther quipped, standing very still, until the tingling in her neck had stopped. 'Oh, but look at this one.' She skipped on to the next portrait, aware a moment later of Marcus arriving behind her. It was so nice to have some viewing space. In the Van Gogh Museum the previous afternoon, extra busy no doubt because of it being a Saturday, they had had to fight for every peek. 'I'd put this one in my sitting room. Above the piano.'

'Along with the two you picked out yesterday? We'll have to organise a lorry in that case.'

'Good idea. That Van Gogh will go in the kitchen, and I'll have his wheatfield in my bedroom, right opposite the bed, so I wake up to it every day. And as for this one...' Esther checked her free leaflet. 'It's called *The Jewish Bride*, but no one knows who the couple really are.'

Marcus peered more closely at the portrait. 'I like how gently protective he is. Do you see, with one arm round her back and the other touching her heart?'

'And she looks sort of thrilled but shy, don't you think? Like she can't quite believe her luck.'

'To me, it's love,' he declared stoutly. 'In action. Physical. Spiritual. The whole shebang. Does it say that in your little book?'

'No.' Esther laughed, putting the leaflet away and checking her watch.

'We're all right for time. I've got it all under control. One more room here. Then we pick up your bag from the downstairs lockers and head off for coffee and torte in the little café I told you about. Unless you've lost the locker key, of course?' He sounded almost hopeful.

'Key safe.' Esther patted her coat pocket.

'Right. Good. In that case, I shall be able to keep my promise of posting you back onto the Eurostar in time for your late afternoon tea with Sheena.'

'Shona.'

'Shona...' he tapped his temple with his index finger, in a show of one working hard to retrieve information '...the busy lawyer friend from your uni days with the enviably loving, super-successful, equally busy partner, Carole.'

'Impressive. And there I was thinking you've only been pretending to listen to all the chatter about my mundane whirlwind of a life.' Esther shot him a grin, before trotting across the room to check out a series of younger self-portraits, which, like every treasure in the Rijksmuseum, they were having to enjoy at top speed thanks to the spectacular failure of their pledge to make an early start.

'Sweet Esther...' Marcus had growled sleepily from behind her, sliding all four of his limbs over hers as she'd attempted to get out of bed when her phone alarm had gone off '... "it is not yet near day. It was the nightingale and not the lark that pierced the fearful hollow of thine ear..." or, as Romeo was trying to say, can we pretend it's still the middle of the night?'

'No, we can't. And spouting lines from a play will get you nowhere. We have showers to get under, art to enjoy, and I have a train to catch...' She had spoken firmly, while her body, softening against his, had already been communicating a rather different message.

Standing alone in front of the paintings, Esther swayed a little as she remembered what had followed and the intimacies that had punctuated the night. At some point she would be tired – they had slept so little – but for now she was wildly awake, hyper-tuned to everything beautiful. A weekend in Amsterdam had been nowhere in her November plans. The previous Sunday she had merely messaged to ask if she could keep the cat, a text composed upon her return from Mei Lin's, when, huddled heavy-hearted on her sofa, she had felt the animal arriving on her lap, stepping cautiously as if the space might prove to be unstable. Chico had never attempted such close proximity before. Even so, he was just a cat, Esther had told herself, tentatively stroking the thick fur, wary of the talons, but enjoying the animal's weight and warmth. He was a comfort, and she was lonely. And they were making something like progress, it had occurred to her suddenly, so who would want to put a halt to that?

Come and visit next weekend. I need someone to be a tourist with

That was how Marcus had pitched the invitation, which had arrived along with effusive exclamations of gratitude at being relieved of the burden of his aunt's pet. Esther had replied with a thanks-but-no-thanks, keeping it jolly, by way of a mask for the fact that she was still too preoccupied with her new discoveries about Dylan to feel jolly about anything. She wanted Viv, as usual, but couldn't yet muster the wherewithal even to compose one of her emails, or 'status reports', as she had taken to calling them in the subject box. Marcus had tried again later in the evening, by which time Esther had been greatly cheered by an email from Shona, saying she had a window of time to herself the following Sunday, and what about a restaurant lunch?

So no can do

Esther had told Marcus, surprised when he had merely pushed back harder.

Why not ask your friend to make it tea at the St Pancras Hotel instead? Then you can have the best of all worlds. No accommodation costs this end and tickets at bargain prices.

He had sent a couple of links, to the hotel's impressive tea menu and viable train departure and arrival times, signing it,

Whistle-stop Expert. (And it would be nice to see you).

Who knew adopting a cat could generate such fringe benefits?!

Esther had countered, after Shona, delighted by the reason, had agreed to the rejigging, instructing her to have a reckless and carefree time.

* * *

'Well, I must say, I like this not-seeing-each-other-much.' They were out of the gallery and seated in the café Marcus had been raving about, sipping lattes and plunging forks into a shared fat wedge of apple torte oozing molten fruit.

'Me too.' Marcus playfully tapped her fork with his as it edged across the middle of the plate. 'Boundaries. That is what we are good at. Well, some of us, anyway.'

'Yeah, right.' Esther laughed, relishing how nothing felt at stake, because nothing *was* at stake. For all her physical exhaustion, this hare-brained, unlooked-for time-out was having exactly the restorative effect she had hoped for. The world, with its worries – Dylan, Lucas, Lily – could wait for once. It wasn't going anywhere, and neither was she. In the meantime, the trick was to enjoy the moment, to be *present*, as Marcus had explained in a bit of a soapbox moment during the course of their first meal out on Friday.

Defeated by the cake, Esther sat back, eyeing her companion. Marcus was not a worrier. He excelled at being in the moment, perhaps because he was an actor, she mused, or perhaps because he was genuinely comfortable in his own skin. And an extremely handsome skin at that, as she could now truly testify. After their love-making that morning, she hadn't been able to resist saying as much, offering teasing praise at his popping muscles. It was just leftovers from the Visigoth training, he had assured her in his jokey way, promising that the sloth-ful, pot-bellied, bent copper assisting the Dutch police would soon emerge triumphant.

'You know how they say the real passion in a relationship only lasts for six months?'

'Do they? Right.' He threw her a quizzical look. 'Do you mind if I eat all this?'

'Not at all. Be my guest.'

'But please, do go on.'

'So, all I was thinking is, if that is true, then not meeting someone very often might help spread the time span out a bit.'

'Good logic. I like it.' He licked his fork, assuming a comical frown of concentration. 'We barely see each other. We like it when we do. A lot. Six months becomes seven. Maybe even *eight*.' Under the small wooden café table, his legs found hers and gave a quick sandwiching squeeze of her knees between his.

'Exactly. And, Marcos...'

'Aha... Marcos, is it? Now I *am* on my guard.' He laughed, pushing aside the empty plate and signalling for the bill.

'That just slipped out... what I just wanted to say was... well... to thank you – genuinely – for such a fun weekend and for not minding my venting... about Dylan and so on. Not in the spirit of our agreement, I know, but Lily is still wobbly and it's sort of easier to talk to a disinterested party and—'

'Esther, stop it. There is nothing to thank me for.' His dark eyes were serious for once. 'You have listened to me too, right? Boring on about Lola and her bloody mother... it sounds like you have been through the proverbial mill and, for the record, if any loser of a man ever dares to break Lola's heart, I shall not be accountable for my actions. In fact, I may need locking up.'

'Good. I mean, not about you being locked up. But about understanding. Thank you.' When the bill arrived, Esther tried and failed to hijack it, but there was no time to argue. Marcus quickly took charge of her bag, a small old sports holdall of Dylan's, which they had successfully retrieved from the museum locker, and they headed back out into the thrum of the city centre.

Esther suggested the metro, but Marcus insisted on taking her to a nearby taxi rank, a couple of times having to yank her back out of the path of cyclists, belting in herds along the city's impressive grid of bicycle highways, as lethal as speeding cars. As they crossed a particularly picturesque canal bridge, with a backdrop of tall, quaint shoulder-to-shoulder houses, she asked him to pose for a photo. He agreed, but with reluctance and immediately putting on his sunglasses – a timely and salutary reminder that they were not a 'proper' couple but a part-time one.

'No, I can manage from here,' she assured him, when he then tried to get into the cab and started waving euro notes. 'It's been lovely, and I'll see you when I see you.'

'Rock-solid boundaries.'

'Granite through and through.'

'Excellent.' He kissed her lightly and then pulled her against him, whispering, 'I've been meaning to mention – when you were in that chic ghost costume the other day, it was all I could do not to rip all those bloody safety pins off. With my teeth. Just so you know.' He released her, grinning.

'How depraved,' Esther murmured, sliding into the taxi, glad they had found a way back to their easy teasing. 'Maybe you'll need locking up after all.'

37

Heidi sat in the hush of the chapel, letting her gaze travel round the faded blue velvet kneelers, the grains in the ancient wooden pews, the gold-corniced ceiling, before arriving at the blazing brightness of the cross embedded in the high alcove behind the altar. It was wrong to feel more holy in an especially beautiful holy place, she told herself, but she always had, right from Sunday mornings in the Lutheran church of her childhood. Over the years, the fervour had subsided, but never died, sitting inside her like a pilot light.

It hadn't been Heidi's intention to visit the chapel, confirmed in an email from the Chaplain to Lucas that morning as being at their disposal on Midsummer's Day the following year. She had been about to set off on a run that would end at Lucas's flat, when he'd rung with the good news, asking, as he had taken to doing, if she would mind looping past the college to check his pigeonhole for post. It being a Sunday, the college had been quiet. She had taken the couple of papers and envelopes from Lucas's slot, zipping them into her little backpack, and then stepped out of the lodge just as the choirmaster and a group of students were emerging from the chapel on the far side of the court-yard. A rehearsal for a service, Heidi had guessed, or maybe one of the many Christmas concerts now being advertised all over town.

Uncertain if it was allowed, she had waited for the cohort to disappear and then tried the chapel door herself. She'd half expected it to be locked, but it had eased open at once, with a small creak. Inside, her trainers squeaking faintly on the heavy stone-slabbed floor, Heidi had found herself slipping into one of the back pews.

Eyes closed, she willed the little flame inside her to grow. She wanted peace, she wanted answers. When neither arrived, she opened her eyes and concentrated instead on the Old Testament scenes in the stained-glass windows, exuberant colours on fire thanks to a sudden burst of sunshine outside. She liked Jonah the best, Heidi decided, stuck half in and half out of the jaws of the whale and looking as astonished as he was terrified. It reminded her of how she had felt in the street outside the jeweller's, taking the call from Elias instead of having a proper goodbye talk with Lucas. The mounting realisation that she did not *want* another engagement ring had been too huge to put into words. She had lost the one she'd loved, along with the uprush of joyous certainty as she held out her finger for Lucas to slide it into place.

That Lucas had been trying so very hard didn't help. Ever since the upsetting showdown after the airport, he had a new, intense way of asking how she was and what she was up to. If she said she wanted a couple of days to herself, he acquiesced with a look of desperate acceptance that made her feel guilty. Was he going to drink? she would ask, like some gaoler, and the greyness would enter his face and he would say no, and she never knew whether to believe him. He would read her doubt and get angry, adjusting the new spectacles he hated and raising his voice to say that he had made a promise and was sticking to it; that all he wanted was *her*, to get properly fit again, and to work. His dining-room table had become his new workstation, with his computer, books, document piles and pen pots laid out with the precision of a draughtsman. He was making 'real' progress, he claimed, and though Heidi rejoiced at this, there was something about the rigidity of the lines on the work table that unnerved her. As if he was penning himself in. When she stayed over now, this new, preciously guarded set-up also meant having to eat their meals on their laps instead of facing each other more easily across the table. Sometimes, Lucas even flicked the television on as they ate – finding an interesting documentary or news programme, almost as if, like her, he was increasingly afraid of where too much talking might lead. Work was at least a safe subject. If she asked about Dylan, or Lily, he snapped. They were grown-ups, he said, and making their own way.

Heidi looked again at the altar, trying to picture herself and Lucas getting married, being blessed. He wasn't a believer, but wanted the full service – the full monty, he had called it, having then to explain the phrase – because *she* wanted it; an act of love, he called it.

Heidi did not become aware of the Chaplain until she drew level with the pew. She stiffened, but Claire Moore merely paused to nod and smile before proceeding towards the altar, where she crossed herself before settling onto her knees for some communing of her own.

Claire Moore was single, Heidi knew that from Lucas, with no sign of a partner of any gender. Had surrendering to God meant surrendering her femininity? Heidi wondered now. Or did the Chaplain have a secretly wild and vibrant private life? The thought catapulted Elias into her head: the brush of his unshaven face on her bare skin, the pleading in the phone call outside the ring shop. Heidi shivered. There had been no further communications, at her insistence, nothing to stoke the fire; but the image of their farewell had somehow remained fixed in her brain, popping up, an involuntary erotic reflex, when she least wanted it.

'Hello, Heidi, how lovely to see you. Such good news about your wedding date.' The Chaplain had floated back to her pew. 'It took a little juggling, but we got there... and tell me, my dear, are you well?'

There was a sudden tenderness in her voice that caught Heidi off guard. 'Oh, yes, most well, thank you,' she stammered, 'and I hope it was acceptable to come in here without an invitation.' She stood up, a little too swiftly, as it turned out, and for a moment had to grip the smooth wooden pommel by the end of her pew while the stained-glass windows whirled.

'Of course... I say, are you quite okay there?'

Heidi was still gripping the pommel, watching her thin white fingers and thinking how many thousands of worshippers over the centuries had clasped the same soft worn wood in their hands.

'How about a cup of tea?' The Chaplain spoke gently, placing a hand round Heidi's elbow and steering her out into the aisle and towards the door.

Claire Moore's rooms, tucked on the top floor of the staircase next to the chapel, were like a burrow, every wall lined with full bookcases, and every possible surface laden with objects. There were two levels, linked by a step that looked slightly crooked, as if the walls had shifted position over the years, which they probably had, Heidi reflected, given the famous antiquity of the place.

'Do take a seat,' the Chaplain urged companionably, indicating the larger of two armchairs on either side of a small fireplace. She then set about filling a small plastic kettle from a corner basin, keeping her back to Heidi as she dropped teabags into two large mugs, both blazing the message 'Keep Calm and Carry On'. 'Milk?'

'Just a little, thank you,' Heidi murmured, half an eye on the mantelpiece beside her, where several official invitations fought for space among ornaments and a silver-framed photograph of a younger version of the Chaplain with her arms round a couple who, Heidi guessed, had to be her parents. Next to that was a box of tissues.

'I love Sunday afternoons,' the Chaplain chattered as she filled the mugs. 'Between services and meals. An in-between time. Tolstoy talked about in-between moments, didn't he? How, for all our grand plans, all the most important things happen in the lulls, when our backs are half turned. Sugar?'

'No, thank you.'

'Ooh, I wish I could give the stuff up, but I can't.' She stirred one mug vigorously and then handed the other to Heidi, dropping into the second armchair.

'Those are your parents?' Heidi glanced up at the photograph.

'Bless them, yes. And me when I was a slim brunette.' She let out a hearty laugh, leaping from the chair to fetch a tin of assorted biscuits, which she placed on the little table between them before sitting back down. 'Tuck in, won't you?' she said, taking one herself. 'Lucas mentioned that you had a lovely visit to your parents before the start of term...' She paused to brush a few stray crumbs off her chest. 'That must have been nice.'

'Oh, yes,' Heidi said quietly. 'I am very lucky to have a wonderful family...' She took a swig of the hot tea, shocked to hear the melancholy in her own voice.

'It can't have been easy for either of you, these last few months.'

'No.' Heidi found herself examining the bourbon biscuit that she had selected and did not wish to eat.

'Though resolution, thank the Lord, was found,' the reverend continued evenly. 'No one thinks Lucas did anything wrong, as such. It was a lack of understanding more than anything, a miscommunication—'

'But it has broken him,' Heidi cried, the words erupting out of her before she could stop them. 'He is not... the same. I don't know if I can fix him... if I... am enough... if we *have* enough...' She threw herself back in her chair and closed her eyes.

The Chaplain sighed heavily. 'The truth is, no one can fix anyone, and in my humble experience it is invariably a mistake to try.'

'But Lucas is so changed,' Heidi confessed miserably, putting her mug and untouched biscuit down on the hearth. 'He is not the man I thought I knew...' She shook her head, unable to go on, and taking a tissue from the box the Chaplain was holding out to her.

'I cannot – would not presume to – offer you advice, my dear.' The Chaplain sank back into her own chair. 'I would say only this. That getting to know someone takes a long time. A lifetime. And at some stage in any close relationship – not always at the same moment – a point is reached where each person stares into the other's soul... perhaps not always liking what they see...' Her voice had grown slightly distant, as if she was remembering something from her own past, Heidi decided, finding that it made her listen more intently. 'But then, as I say, the other person may do the same. And I have no doubt that God would say that love is about being able to accept what you find, forgiving it, being loyal to it... oh, look, you've got me going now...' She leant across to pull a tissue from the box, and spent several seconds trumpeting into it.

'One of those in-between moments.' She gasped, balling up the tissue in her hands. 'I think we've just had one. Well, I have anyway. Life pouncing. Follow your instincts, my dear, that is all I can say. Don't tell your heart off for not feeling as you want it to. Just let it speak. Then you'll know. And now...' She clapped her hands and stood up. 'Having imparted my deepest thoughts, I am afraid I have to boot you out so I can think what on earth I am going to say to my Evensong congregation. And remember, God loves us, whichever way we jump.'

Outside, it was almost dark. Heidi did her fleece up to her chin and adjusted the straps on her backpack as she made her way back across the courtyard. Stepping into the street, she took a deep breath and then set off at a sprint. She would let her heart decide. She would be brave.

38

As the train slowed for the final, ugly hinterland approach to St Pancras station, Esther woke from a doze in a sudden panic that she might need her passport again. Not finding it in her handbag, she rummaged in the holdall, groping round her clothes and washbag, and the novel she hadn't opened.

Tiredness was catching up with her, Esther realised, desperation mounting, as she plunged her hands deeper into the holdall. This time she dived so deep that her fingers found the edge of the flap covering the base of the bag, which was loose – an ideal black hole for things to disappear into. And there it was. Esther let out a small gasp of triumph as she plucked the passport free. It was half open at the mugshot page, the least favourite photo of her ever taken, by a kind chemist on a frazzled day when a family camping holiday in Brittany had loomed alongside the realisation that the expiry date had passed.

Except that it wasn't her face, but Dylan's that stared out from the page. Esther rubbed her eyes. She blinked. She closed the passport and turned it over. Then she opened it again, checking the date. That she had unearthed this possession from the gritty bottom of a bag used by her son was clearly not possible. Because Dylan was in Argentina. And it definitely was his current one, the photo taken in Cambridge three years before, Esther standing impatiently outside the booth while he crafted his hair into the spikes deemed mystifyingly necessary before pressing the start button. Esther held the picture nearer, recalling in the same instant, clear as a sunbeam, that her own passport was in the outside pocket of her handbag.

* * *

'Anything is possible with technology these days.'

'Fake *postcards*?'

'Fake anything,' said Carole airily. 'There will be websites. You should see some of the cases I've prosecuted – the deceptions and intricacies that are now run-of-the-mill. Trust me, this is low level. And they're not fake anyway, by the sound of it, just computer-generated, to look as if they have come from somewhere they haven't.'

Esther fell silent, feeling faintly snubbed rather than comforted. Shona had excused herself to find the Ladies and without her – as always – it seemed to Esther that she and Carole were struggling. That Shona should have brought Carole along after all, without warning, had done nothing to ease her already heightened state of anxiety. To not know all over again where Dylan really was – how he was – had capsized her fragile equilibrium. On all sides, everything she had been managing – from seeing off Chris Mews to coping with Viv's banishment – felt unmanageable. By the time she'd staggered into the hotel tea lounge, having run all the way from the station because she was late, the chance of the date with Shona had felt like a godsend. Someone to pour her heart out to. Someone who cut to the chase, and picked out what mattered. Spotting Carole, sitting in her stiff way alongside Shona at a corner table, Esther had been tempted to turn and run. She could have claimed transport delays. It would have been easy. But then Shona had seen her and stood up to wave, revealing in the process the smart black panels of what was clearly a maternity dress.

'Cooeee,' she cried, getting up and weaving her way, with difficulty, through the tea tables, to greet Esther properly. 'Sorry, I wanted to surprise you on my own,' she murmured as they hugged, 'but I had a dizzy turn, and Carole put her foot down. Problems with blood pressure – it's been dodgy – which is why we haven't breathed a word. Just in case... you know.'

'But this is tremendous... both of you... how exciting...' Esther managed, operating mostly on autopilot as they arrived at the table, where Carole offered up her cheek in the cool way that never failed to feel disdaining.

'We are thrilled,' Carole declared, helping Shona settle into her chair, and then shaking out one of the table napkins for her onto her lap. 'But there is a way to go yet, and we cannot be too careful.'

'I'm only six months,' Shona explained, casting a helpless look down at her swollen stomach, 'and like I said, there have been a few swerves in the road.'

'Perhaps best not to go into those now,' Carole interjected smoothly. 'We want to hear all about Amsterdam,' she said as a waiter arrived with a trolley of tea things, including two multi-tiered silver servers, laden with cakes and sandwiches, which he transferred to the table. 'As you were late, we had already ordered,' she said, lifting the teapot lid and giving the contents a vigorous stir.

'We hoped you wouldn't mind,' Shona chipped in.

She was the very opposite of minding, Esther assured them, inwardly marvelling that she could ever have imagined the closeness of the duo was something to envy. It had definitely got worse in the long gap since they had last met. In fact, it creeped her out. If she were Shona, she would be tearing her hair out and screaming *let me do my own bloody napkin*. When pressed again, by both of them, about her weekend, she had skated over Marcus and talked obligingly about how fine the art galleries were, before blurting out the baffling discovery of Dylan's passport.

'I need the Ladies,' Esther said now, getting to her feet, 'and I can see where Shona's got to,' she added, scooting off before Carole could say anything.

Shona was at the basins, running a comb through her hair, which had been reduced to flat curls by a recent chopping. 'It's gone sort of weird.' She jabbed at the limp, floppy waves with the comb. 'But Carole likes it.'

'Wait for me, won't you?' said Esther, disappearing into a cubicle.

'So, Dylan's in the UK – that has to be good, doesn't it?' Shona said, the moment Esther reappeared. She had transferred her attentions from her hair to her face, dabbing concealer over the high colour in her cheeks between further disconsolate pokes at her hair.

'I suppose. Except it could still be Ulan Bator for all the difference it makes.'

'*Someone* must know where he is, Esther. I mean, no one just goes off-grid these days, least of all the young. They need the grid, for heaven's sake, it's their lifeblood – much to their detriment half the time, but there you go. What about Lily? They were always close, weren't they?'

Esther shook her head miserably.

'Oh, come here.' Shona put her arms round her even though she was washing her hands. 'He'll be fine. That boy of yours was always one to plough his own furrow – or at least to *try* and plough his own furrow, despite your and Lucas's best efforts. Sounds like he didn't want to retake those exams, that's for sure.'

'There was also a girl, who broke his heart,' Esther murmured, 'another thing I've only just found out and Lily didn't know about.'

'Well, there you go,' said Shona stoutly, 'he's a typical teenager. Like we were, once upon a time. Telling our families anything – are you kidding? He's licking his wounds. Till he gets fed up and appears on the doorstep.'

'Thanks, Shone.' Esther tugged a couple of paper towels out of the dispenser and dabbed at her hands. 'And you're all right, are you?'

'Oh, yes...' She circled her belly with her arms.

'No, at least, I mean, between you and Carole. Is all well? I mean... I am always *here* if...'

'If what?' said Carole, poking her head round the half-open door.

'I think Esther's making a pitch for godmother, darling,' Shona answered quickly, 'but she'll have to join the queue, won't she?'

'I'm just glad the pair of you hadn't been kidnapped,' Carole said dryly. 'I've settled up. My treat, Esther.' Her face flexed in and out of a smile. 'All set, Shona?'

* * *

At home an hour later, Esther's distraction was temporarily broken by a surge of guilt at the sight of her new pet, his stomach more of a barrel than usual thanks to the quantities of food she had left down to cover for her absence. He was probably ready to return to the freedoms of coming and going through a cat-flap, but the chance of losing something else now felt even more unconscionable.

'Soon, puss, soon,' she muttered, dumping the bag at the bottom of the stairs, before taking Dylan's passport out of her handbag and placing it, photo page open, on the kitchen table.

She poured and drank a tumbler of water, and then a second. Her fatigue had entered a new phase; her head pulsed, hyper-alert, but empty. Dylan. She tried to find him with her mind, to think him into being, but all that arrived was more shame at her selfish blindness, for two years so ensnared by her own challenges that she hadn't looked hard enough at her son's. Her son. And Lucas's. Esther studied the little photo seeing as never before that, for all the differences in eye and hair colour, the likeness between the two of them was uncanny; the shape and set of Dylan's eyes, the broad forehead, the contours of the cheeks and jaw – he was the spit of Lucas. And both so handsome. Lucas. Longing flooded into the emptiness inside her head. A timeless longing, for the father of their beautiful offspring, for what they once had, all of it now shattered.

Carefully, Esther found herself crossing the kitchen and reaching up to the top shelf of the dresser for the mended pot. Such an early gift from Lucas, presented with all the early courtship worry as to whether she would like it or not. She ran her fingertips over the hardened baubles of glue now holding it together. Life, for precious objects, for people, was so fragile, so cobbled together. From mess-ups like Chris Mews, to marvels like Viv, no one had an easy ride. All that mattered in the end was kindness. To see this so clearly felt not just new to Esther, but vital; something to be shared. With Lucas most of all. She needed to speak to him anyway. He didn't yet know about Mei Lin, let alone the passport.

She picked up her mobile and hesitated. To want – so badly – to talk to Lucas was odd. She didn't quite trust it. She began to key in the number, manually, so as to give herself time to think, and then stopped as a new notification arrived.

Thx for the great visit. M

Esther tapped back quickly.

Yes, thx, it was fun. In other news: found D's passport so he can't be abroad and 'Sheena' is expecting. Babies everywhere. Happy filming. E

Esther returned to the phone's keypad, but the moment had passed. She turned off the lights and took her holdall upstairs instead, resolving to bring both Lucas and Lily up to speed the next day.

39

Lucas wondered how long he had been sitting on his sofa. He was still in his running gear: an old tracksuit top and the black Lycra leggings Heidi had given him the previous year, before their relationship was common knowledge. His feet were encased in new trainers, bought for a mind-blowing sum of money from a sports shop recommended by his physiotherapist. The shoes were exactly the sort of show-off gear he had vowed never to own, and so curiously light that, answering the door to Heidi that afternoon, he had found himself almost tripping over his own feet.

'You could have used your key,' he had said, the annoyance of the stumble still with him as she'd stepped inside.

'Hello to you too, Lucas.' Her face had been pink and moist from her own run, but instead of doing her usual thing of bouncing from foot to foot – the cool-down that only stopped after she had stretched out properly – she had closed the door and remained beside it, standing very still and straight. 'So now you are going out to exercise?'

'Later, I thought. Just decided to get ready. Did you get my post?'

Instead of answering, she tore the rucksack off her arms and thrust it at him. 'Yes, Lucas, I got your post. It is in there.'

'Heidi, darling, what on earth is the matter?'

She pushed past him, and marched to the far end of the sitting room, where she spun round, planting her legs and folding her arms in the manner of one preparing for combat. 'I went into the chapel.'

'Oh, good. I—'

'I spoke to the Chaplain.'

'Claire? Excellent. She—'

'So, do you not even believe in the *possibility* of a deity, Lucas?'

'What? I... no... I...' Lucas slowly put down the couple of envelopes and bits of paper he had extracted from the bag, doing his best not to look bemused. Their divergent views on the Almighty had never mattered before; but perhaps, he told himself, something had shifted with the date of the wedding now fixed. 'Heidi, sweetheart, I could say yes, but it would only be to appease you, and that would be wrong, surely. I don't believe in anything except the science of life,' he went on more gently, 'and humans doing their best to keep the planet safe and treat each other decently. You *know* that. I have never made any secret of it.'

'But, Lucas, don't you maybe even *wish* there were something more?'

There was real desperation in her voice. Lucas stared back helplessly, tempted, despite everything, to give a little ground. He wanted her happiness so badly, partly because of loving her, but mostly because it made her more loving towards him. 'I think everything about the existence of mankind is wondrous,' he ventured. 'I just do not believe there is a god of any kind behind it... which will in no way stop me being knocked sideways by the power of our wedding ceremony,' he rushed on, as her expression had tightened.

'Claire Moore and I had a very interesting conversation.'

'About me, no doubt,' Lucas said, bitterness creeping into his voice.

Heidi widened her eyes disparagingly. 'Among other things. Not everything is about you, you know, Lucas. She seems such a good person. In fact, I think you were very lucky that she was there for all the trouble with poor Moira.'

Lucas felt something like a small electric shock pass down his spine. 'Poor?' He kept his tone level.

'Yes. Moira is a victim.'

Lucas waited, his mouth drying. Heidi had retrieved her backpack from the chair where he had dropped it and was fiddling with its zip. 'Of me?' he prompted at last, in a deathly voice.

'Of a patriarchal society, of which you too are a product.'

He laughed softly. 'Oh, Lord, here we go.'

She had pulled the toggle out of her long hair and was refixing it, with quick angry fingers, back into a ponytail – a much tighter one that managed to pull yet more severity into her already savage expression.

'Well, my goodness...' Lucas laughed again, sharply this time. 'How good to hear what you have really been thinking all these weeks, darling. Perhaps it was you, not Moira's father, who spoke to the papers.'

'Stop it, Lucas. That is stupid. Of course, I would never do such a thing. You are misinterpreting.'

'Okay. Good. So, tell me, what *did* you mean, exactly?' He perched on the back of an armchair, digging deep for a tone of reasoned, amicable enquiry.

'I mean, Lucas, that you have tried to shut out the implications of what happened with Moira Giddings.'

'Nothing happened with Moira Giddings.' The words erupted as a roar – from somewhere deep in his gut – and her entire body recoiled. 'Sorry, Heidi, I...'

She used the bag as a shield, turning her back on him as she threaded the straps over her shoulders. 'The truth is, Lucas,' she said tightly, 'there are grey areas in the world, but you are not very good – not willing to acknowledge them.'

'Are we back to God, by any chance?' He put the question jauntily, as if they were having one of their early, lovely, big, free-ranging discussions.

'No, I am not talking about God.'

'Apologies. You will forgive me for having trouble following your line – or should I say lines – of thought.'

'Now you are being cruel.'

'*Me* cruel?'

'I think I had better go, Lucas. Give you some space...'

'Aha, yes,' he cried as she dodged round him, heading for the door. '*Space.* That elusive substance that used to be so straightforward. Now no one can get enough of it.'

'I cannot talk to you like this.' She gripped the door handle and he ran at her, flailing, in a bid to get hold of some bit of her to prevent her leaving.

'No, Lucas.' She fought him off, slapping the air and his arms. 'I am going. I need to be alone. To think. About us.'

'Heidi, wait...' He tried harder, attempting to block the doorway this time, but she pushed past onto the landing.

'In four weeks, term will have finished, Lucas. I shall return to my family for Christmas. Alone. I shall decide what to do.'

'What to do?'

'Whether to marry you.' She was almost at the lip of the main staircase, and tossed the words back at him, so softly that for a nanosecond he thought – hoped – he might have misheard.

'But I love you,' he began, only for the words to be drowned out by the receding patter of her footsteps.

Still in the doorway, Lucas fumbled his phone out of his tracksuit pocket and called her. When she didn't pick up, he left an apologetic pleading message for her to ring. When no call came, he sent a text, and then a WhatsApp. Retreating back inside, he sat on the sofa and tried the same sequence again, and again, and again. She would ring, eventually, if he tried hard enough, for long enough. Showed how much he cared. As the silence continued, he laboured over an email, crafting and recrafting the words of love, remorse and need. He was good with words. They would heal the rift, surely.

* * *

It was dark, but he could still go on a run, Lucas reasoned. He was dressed for it and exercise helped him think. Maybe he could do a route to Heidi's flat. He closed his eyes, trying to breathe, to keep the panic at bay. Somehow, sleep came, a thin restless state of half-waking. When he blinked the room back into focus, it was the corner shop rather than Heidi's flat that presented itself as an option. He had been resisting. For Heidi, the flat – his life – had become a drink-free zone, but what did that matter now?

One more call, Lucas decided. A final roll of the dice. He picked up his mobile, only to find the screen black from lack of power. Hope coursed through him. He loped into the bedroom for his charger and plugged the phone in with shaky fingers. During the moments of waiting he prayed to the God he had told Heidi did not exist. There were two new notifications, but only from Esther: one a missed call, the other asking for a group chat with Lily the following day.

The corner shop, then. Lucas thrust his overcoat on over his running clothes and put on the old grey beanie that Heidi hated, because it washed his skin out, she said, and smothered his beautiful hair. She had a thing for his hair, raking her fingers through it, tugging at it, when they made love. Lucas moved in slow motion, concussed, it felt like. So much so, that he almost forgot his house keys. Arriving at the top of the main stairs, he paused, looking down, wishing they were steeper, longer and made of concrete, not wood. There would have been a chance then, of doing a thorough job. A memory of his mother fluttered, a rag doll dangling from the apple tree. Iris had been the one to find her. An insult added to an injury so extreme that Lucas still found it the hardest thing of all to contemplate. The mistress finding the dead wife.

He was three stairs down when a faint clicking noise and a sudden uprush of icy air told him the main door had been opened. The sound of footsteps followed. Lucas's heart galloped. She had come back. He would say he believed in God. He would agree Moira was a victim. He would say any damn thing. But it was the top of a thick head of blonde hair that appeared round the curve in the stairwell. Dylan, he thought, trying and failing to say his son's name before the realisation that it was Lily.

'Heidi called me.' She spoke briskly, but fondly, skipping up the last few stairs. 'She said to visit, that she was worried about you. I brought some soup and a few other things.' She swung a bulging bag of groceries dangling from two fingers in one hand. 'You're on a break, she said. Sorry to hear that, Dad, but it's nice to see you all the same.' She looped her arm through his and led him back towards his flat door. Lucas let himself be steered, finding it hard to look at her, with her face so aglow from the cold air, so knowing.

'I thought I might stay over for a few days. If it's okay with you.'

He nodded, because he could not speak.

40

'He's not abroad?' Lucas said, for the third time, sounding as dazed as he looked. His face was bruised with tiredness, saggy under the eyes, the skin blotchy.

'And you went to Amsterdam with a friend,' Lily put in, also repeating what Esther had told them, but in a tone more reminiscent of a sceptical detective, 'using an old bag of Dyl's and finding his passport in the bottom of it. Last night. On your way back.'

Esther stared between the on-screen faces of her ex-husband and their daughter, side by side at Lucas's dining-room table, instead of dialling in separately as she had expected. Lily was radiating an energy that made her father's pallor even more marked; and they were sitting so closely, arms resting parallel and touching, that a pulse of the old ugly jealousy had stirred beneath her gladness that some sort of rapprochement had obviously been managed between them. Both had progressed from astonishment at the revelation of Dylan's faux communications, to resigned agreement that it was not such a hard trick to pull off, Lily citing a popular app that allowed photographs to be sent from anywhere in the world as postcards. Reinforcement of just how easy it was had been proven by another postcard landing on Esther's doormat that morning, of Mayan pyramids and bearing a *Love you Mum* that she had kissed with relief, while fighting down the confusing sense of him being both nearer and further away.

'And you knew nothing about this Mei Lin girl?' Lucas turned to address the question to Lily, his voice pained and flat.

'No,' she protested. 'I mean...' she made a visible effort to calm herself '...I already told Mum that ages ago.' She patted Lucas's arm and then threw a wan smile at Esther. 'Look, Dad... and Mum... the thing is, I *am* worried, obviously, but also, I have to say that I think Dylan is behaving like a total idiot, doing this to all of us. How is he going to get anything sorted if he just stays away?'

'Maybe we are the idiots,' Lucas said quietly. 'He's taken us for a complete ride, that's for sure.' For a moment he sounded almost impressed. 'Also,' he continued, sinking back into glumness, 'I can't help being marginally reassured that he is playing silly buggers from behind some screen in the UK, as opposed to snapping selfies from flat-topped pyramids or vertiginous waterfalls.'

'He's crap with heights anyway,' Lily muttered.

'No, he isn't,' Esther interjected, 'that's me.'

'He is, Mum. Quite crap, anyway. Remember the funfair when they stopped the ride?'

There was a silence as all three of them travelled back to Dylan, aged ten, being lifted down, hysterical to the point of vomiting, from the first open carriage of a giant wheel that had frozen because of some technical hitch. A day of planned family fun that had turned sour. 'So come on, let's make a concerted effort to find him,' Esther urged, noting again how defeated Lucas seemed. 'Lily, you know what social media sites he might be checking. Post a load of messages saying we know he's around and want him to get in touch and come home. He'll take it better from you.'

'Mum, he's not *been* on social media, and he must have a new phone... but of course I'll try,' she mumbled.

'And, Lucas, couldn't you Tweet or something?'

'No, I could not.' Lucas shook his head mournfully. 'It's not something I do any more. And anyway, frankly, the chances of such an approach doing anything to help are virtually non-existent. I could try and have a word with Jake though,' he went on, ignoring Esther's exclamations of encouragement and adding, his new grim face set hard, 'despite all the evidence strongly suggesting that Dylan has a very powerful desire *not* to be found.'

'Which doesn't mean he isn't badly in need of being persuaded otherwise,' Esther cried, anger flaring, both at her own helplessness and their collective ineptitude. 'I mean, there is hiding, and there is being *lost* – in yourself. Right? All I keep thinking,' she confessed bitterly, 'is why the hell any of us didn't talk to Dylan properly instead of going on and on about those bloody exams. Like exams really count for anything...' She could feel Lucas glowering, and had to clamp her teeth round the end of a biro to stop herself diverting the conversation further down a path she might regret, at least in front of Lily.

'He'll be back for Christmas, Mum, I bet you,' Lily assured her sweetly, her own clear eyes misting suddenly – a reminder, as if Esther needed it, that her elder child was a past master at putting on a front. 'He'll crack then for sure... I mean, Dyl may be a selfish douche, but he bloody loves Christmas.'

'Yes, he does,' Esther conceded, having to laugh, but also wishing, as Lily leant into Lucas and he put his arm round her, that she could be the one to offer comfort. 'It's nice that you two were able to do this together,' she said, finding something that felt not far off bravery herself. 'Are you with Dad for lunch today, then, darling?'

'No, just looking in...' The pair of them exchanged a glance. 'Catching up properly, aren't we, Dad?'

'That's nice,' Esther said, as Lucas nodded. 'And, Lucas, I do hope the whole business of the suspension—'

'Oh yes, that's all settling down, thank you. All good. Getting lots of work done. Looking ahead et cetera.'

'I am pleased for you,' Esther replied, aware she was being told to mind her own business, and reminding herself she had no right to expect otherwise.

'And I've got to jump off this call and get on with some stuff,' Lily pitched in quickly, back to full brightness. 'I'll do what I can, and let you both know, okay?'

She blew a kiss at the screen as she slipped off her seat and out of sight. Chico chose the same moment to hop up onto Esther's lap, trailing his tail unhelpfully across her face.

'You have a cat.' For an instant, astonishment drained every trace of dourness from Lucas's face.

'A rescue – he was my neighbour's, but she died.'

'But you don't like cats.'

'I like this one. And what's the point of life if you can't change your views?' Esther retorted, giving the cat a stroke that made him arch his back for more. 'Do you have any plans for Christmas?' she ploughed on, keen to divert the strong possibility of her comment sparking any unwelcome debate, Lucas rarely wavering from the opportunity to take offence. Instead, he picked up a pair of blue-framed glasses she hadn't seen before, and rubbed at the lenses with the edge of his jumper for a moment before setting them down again.

'Not as yet. Lots of moving parts, Christmas-wise.'

'Oh, okay. Because I was sort of hoping that Lily might come to Amersham?'

'Lily. Amersham. By all means.'

'At least for Mum's birthday, and then staying through for Christmas Day, but perhaps coming on to you and Heidi from Boxing Day?'

'Sounds fine. Whatever Lily wants. It's her call.'

They were both silent for a moment.

'Your mother's birthday bash, eh?' Lucas said, just as she was about to sign off. 'Twenty-third of December. Vol-au-vents and coronation chicken. Trifle and fresh custard. I remember it well.'

'You hated it. Every year. Without fail.'

'Yes, I did.' He gave a rueful chuckle.

'She still adores you,' Esther murmured wryly. 'Despite everything.'

'Ah. A woman of impeccable taste, your mother.' He gave her a thin smile, his eyes cloudy and sad as they momentarily held hers. 'Give her my best. And Patrick too.' A brief hand-wave and he was gone.

Outside, the street light across the road was flickering, even though it was still early afternoon. Esther crossed the room to peer out of the small front window beside the piano, pressing her legs against the radiator underneath it for warmth. A man in a flat cap ambled past, and she found her eyes darting to the now functioning red lights in the little camera above Dimitri and Sue's. The man could not have been less like Chris Mews. He was squat and bow-legged, comically similar in fact to the bulldog tugging him along by an extendable lead. A drear November day, but at least her sense of safety was settling, she realised. Except that without Dylan, it meant little. Only with him home, and safe too, would she feel whole.

BONFIRES

41

'Mum, where's Dad got to?' Esther had found Astrid at the bottom of the stairs, redoing her lipstick in the oval, brass-framed mirror that lived there for the purpose, beside a dire portrait she had commissioned from an amateur artist friend by way of a wifely gift many years before. The portrait was irredeemable in its awfulness – twee, and a poor representation of Astrid's formidable angular beauty – but Esther's father had nonetheless been typically, loyally vehement in its defence, choosing a hanging spot likely to garner the widest possible audience.

Beneath the mirror, on a shelf, lived a primary-school photo of Lily and Dylan sitting together, their childhood white-blond hair flattened and tidy, their grins self-conscious, but full of impish glee. Esther found now that she could only bear to look at it for a moment. The day before Christmas Eve, and all their efforts to eke Dylan out of hiding had failed. Only the postcards kept arriving, proof that he still had no idea that his duplicity had been rumbled. Receiving a card of the Inca ruins at Machu Picchu that week, sporting a cheery, festive '*Feliz Navidad madre! Dx*' on the back, Esther had even felt a twinge of annoyance in the depths of her anguish. From Argentina up to Mexico. Now supposedly whizzing back south to Peru. He really was beginning to treat them like idiots.

Astrid pressed her lips together, expertly spreading the colour as she eyed Esther through the mirror. 'Your father? Who knows? At the bottom of the garden probably, which is a bit much, given that Les and Virginia are still here. Fetch him in, darling, will you?' She waved her lipstick in the direction of the spacious drawing room, which was lined with black mock Tudor beams like the rest of the house, and where handsome sliding glass doors offered the easiest access to the lovingly tended half-acre of garden, long since swallowed up by the afternoon dark.

'Hang on, don't move.' Esther picked a tiny white feather off her mother's back, taking the opportunity to give her a half-hug, and feeling her skinniness through the smart purple dress. Despite her own much fuller shape, their features were still similar, she had to admit, far more so than Rick's anyway. He had, predictably, arrived late – in time for dessert – after which Esther had pinned him into helping her with the washing-up, so that they could have a proper chance to talk – though, as usual, her brother was the one with most of the chatter, occasionally remembering to ask her about her life, but always sticking to the facts rather than the emotions. Norwegian oilfields apparently conquered, he was in talks with a Chinese syndicate, he had reported excitedly, his dark eyes firing as he hinted at negotiations over big risks and big money. There was a woman in Oslo, but he brushed aside Esther's efforts to delve further. He had found Esther's account of Dylan and the postcards amusing, and when Lily had wandered in, Esther had gladly left them to it.

'So, have you enjoyed your annual surprise party, Mum?' Esther teased, touched to see that her birthday gift, a silk scarf of lilac and soft pinks, was still around her mother's neck four hours after its unwrapping, bringing out the intense light blue of her eyes, exactly as she had guessed it might.

'It's been lovely, of course,' Astrid replied in her dismissive way, 'especially having Rick – though your father is ridiculous, to make such a fuss every year, when I tell him not to. Getting me to make a trifle, because *he* loves it, and then commanding poor Janice and Ronnie to bring all that food. Lasagne is a bit heavy, I find, but there you go, it's the thought that counts.' She flashed her icy smile. 'And Judy doing the cake, poor woman, when she's still in pieces about Eric – I told you about that, didn't I? – in the clubhouse, of all places, though luckily the waitress had once been a nurse...'

'Yes, poor Eric, poor Judy,' Esther murmured, wondering what it must be like to reach an age where friends could suddenly drop dead of heart attacks after rounds of golf with fellow septuagenarians. Her mother was slightly tipsy, she realised fondly, and in danger of looking her age for once, with the meticulously neat blonde sweep of hair askew, and the blusher she had clearly just reapplied looking notice-ably overdone.

'I'll go and find Dad, then.'

'I'm worried about him, actually.' Astrid snapped the lipstick shut and dropped it into her handbag, which was parked beside her on a small woven-seated chair. 'He's always nodding off these days and sometimes goes all... *drifty...*'

'Mum, honestly...' Esther couldn't help laughing. 'I think naps are allowed at seventy-nine.'

'That's nothing. Personally, I'm hoping for thirty more years at least. *And* I'm worried about that son of yours,' she went on in the same quick-fire way. 'As is your father. It wasn't a subject for lunch, but *where* is the child, and *what* does he think he's playing at? That's what I want to know.'

'It's what we all want to know, Mum,' Esther murmured, lightly kissing the side of her head – unbothered by the usual flinch of surprise – and seizing her mother's smart green parka off the coat rack before heading out to the garden.

The darkness wasn't as thick as it looked from inside the house. Esther paused on the edge of the lawn, tipping her head to the sky and breathing in a big gulp of the cold air. The weather was clear for the first time in days, and the stars such big pinheads of light that even she could spot a couple of the constellations. The Plough. Orion's Belt. The same sky was glittering over Dylan, she comforted herself, hugging the coat more closely as she wandered on. Postcards, even computer-generated ones, at least meant he was alive, she told herself, doggedly, for the umpteenth time.

'Not a word to your mother,' her father grunted as she appeared round the corner of the hedge designed to shield this, less sightly, section of garden from the house. He was poking expertly at a small bonfire with a long sturdy stick, the stub of a cigar bobbing between his lips.

'I have a hunch she might be onto your smoking anyway, Dad,' Esther pointed out wryly, pondering all her parents' weird little asides and counter-briefings against each other. If managing such knots of misinformation and miscommunication was what a long marriage was really about, then she was sure she and Lucas would never have had the stamina for it anyway.

'I'm rubbish at gardening,' she volunteered cheerfully, picking up a stray leafy stick at her feet and lobbing it into the fire, where it hissed and spat, making the flames smoke. 'I've given in and got some help now. A landscape design graduate with the right equipment and big ideas for planting.'

'Not until spring, I hope.'

'Not until spring, no...' Esther faltered, not yet capable of bringing the new year into focus. 'You've spoiled Mum today. As usual.' She took his arm. 'She's so lucky to have you.'

He tossed the cigar stump into the bonfire. 'You're wrong there. I'm the lucky one.'

'Really?' Esther smiled to herself. 'Er... Dad, I think we can all agree you have a fair bit to put up with.'

'No, Esther.' He turned to look at her, his eyes blinking in a way that brought her mother's recent expressions of concern to mind. 'I'd be lost without her,' he said solemnly. He was getting more sentimental, Esther reflected affectionately, and it had been a long day – lots of food and wine, with no chance of a snooze.

'Shall we go back up, Dad? Les and Virginia are still here, and we could have a cup of tea—'

'She left me once. I had to beg her to come back.' He had turned his gaze on the fire.

Esther kept hold of his arm, her shock matched only by a deep reflex of reluctance to hear more. 'Dad, I am sorry, but please... you don't have to—'

'She did come back, and every day – every day, Esther – I have thanked God for it. I've held my tongue, but families stick together, love, that's the thing. You and Lucas – it's never too late, is what I am trying to say. Not with forgiveness.'

Esther let go of his arm. Inside she was shouting that he had no bloody right – to make her feel worse than she did already, let alone spill private details that she had no wish, or need, to hear; but he was old, and it was her mother's birthday, and Christmas just a breath away...

'And then Dylan would come home,' he went on, 'I'm sure of it. The poor lad, I've been so...' He broke off, choking. 'I miss him, love. I'm worried about him.'

'Me too, Dad,' she said heavily, at least understanding the source of his pain.

'I didn't mean to speak out of turn.' He pulled out a large handkerchief and blew his nose in two short blasts.

'I know you mean well, Dad.' Esther patted his back. Inside she felt turned upside down. Affronted as well as shocked. She had fought so hard not to feel that a failed marriage made her a failure. But maybe she was wrong. Maybe Dylan *would* be with them if she had stuck it out. 'We just have to hang onto the positives,' she muttered, grabbing at the platitude and then being rescued by one of Astrid's ear-splitting yodels – her mother's preferred method of urgent summons to anyone at the bottom of the garden. Her father came to life with almost comical speed, stamping out the fire and hallooing that he was on his way, between checking over his shoulder that Esther was hot on his heels. He was obedient to the core, and only now, aged forty-eight-and-a-half, did she have an inkling as to why.

Her mother was waiting for them just inside the sitting room, a cardigan draped over her shoulders, but still shivering pointedly. 'Shoes off. You missed Les and Virginia. And now Lily's being sick.'

'What sort of sick?' Esther murmured, carefully levering off her boots so as not to get mud on the carpet.

'What sort do you think? She's in the bathroom upstairs. Rick's dealing with it, bless him...' Esther was already on her way, stowing her footwear on the rack under the coats before taking the stairs two at a time. The bathroom door was wide open, revealing her brother, sleeves rolled up, manfully mopping with a big sponge and a bucket round the base of the toilet. Lily was sitting on the floor, propped limply against the towel rail.

'She didn't quite make it in time.' Rick pulled a face, emptying the bucket into the toilet and then refilling it under the bath taps. 'Too much bubbly, I think.'

'Really?' Esther dropped to her knees, brushing the sticky threads of hair off Lily's damp face and using a corner of the towel on the rail behind her to wipe away the specks round her mouth.

Lily moaned, shaking her head in resistance to these attentions before suddenly flinging herself at the toilet, cradling the bowl as she retched. 'Barely drank... the prawns starter maybe...' She flopped her head down to be sick again, before slumping back against the radiator, tears starting to mingle with the mess on her face. 'Sorry... yuck... sorry... so gross...'

'I've had it worse,' Rick assured her cheerily. 'Food poisoning is hell, especially shellfish. I think it's related to botulism, which is basically the worst...' He dried up, as Esther gave him a beady look.

'In Italy I got sick,' Lily gasped, through half-sobs, 'after some... clams... maybe it's returned.' She made another lunge for the toilet, but then sat back up as the spasm failed to materialise.

'I think some more detergent is called for,' Rick said tactfully, stepping over them and steering Astrid away from the doorway back towards the stairs.

'Lily, darling, there's no need to cry.' Esther slid to the floor beside her, doing her best to shift her into the crook of her arm. 'Rick is right. Food poisoning is awful, but it never lasts long.'

Lily remained stiff, refusing to nestle. 'It's not just that,' she said dully. 'It's Dylan, Mum.'

'I know, darling, I've just been talking to Grandad, we are all desperately—'

'No.' Lily shuffled more upright, sliding further along the wall away from Esther. She let her head drop onto her chest and then raised it with a big intake of breath. 'He made me swear. A few weeks, he said. But now it's Christmas. It's Christmas and I'm done.' Her eyes remained fixed somewhere in the region of the shower attachment behind Esther's head.

Esther had stood up, finding that some part of her needed to be at a distance in order to bring the momentous thing Lily seemed to be saying into focus. 'Are you telling me that all this time...?'

'Yes,' Lily whispered, 'I am.' She tipped her head back against the wall, squeezing her eyes shut as tears streamed out of them. 'I'm sorry, Mum. I know where he is. I've always known.'

CHRISTMAS

42

Lucas stared through the windscreen wipers clearing and re-clearing the sleet that had been driving horizontally at the car since they'd traded the M40 for the M42 an hour before. The glimpse of the way ahead that kept being snatched away. It felt apt. As if he were lost in some hideous blizzard that had been secretly closing in for years, bringing him to this drawn-out and grisly reckoning. Beside him, Esther, at the wheel, was rigid with concentration. Lily lay in the foetal position on the back seat, supposedly asleep amid the folds of a duvet borrowed from Astrid's vast walk-in linen cupboard. Her exhaustion was understandable, not just from the food poisoning, but also because of the release of the burden she had been carrying since August. Four months. Honouring a misguided promise. But the foetal position was also about staying under the radar of the rear-view mirror, Lucas guessed, his daughter wary of catching his eye and triggering any more of the follow-up questions and imprecations that had been bursting out of him since he'd stumbled through the ticket barrier at High Wycombe station and into Esther's car that morning. Esther had had her turn, but he was still several paces behind.

Kidnapped was the word that kept flashing like a siren across his brain. Though it was not a term Esther had used in her frantic message about Lily's revelation the night before, it was perfectly clear to Lucas that it contained all the truth and terror of what had taken place. Two years of contact, Lily had confessed wretchedly, starting after his and Esther's split. Two years, then, of wooing, of *grooming*. Emails. Cheques, that were plain bribes for silence. Biding his time. Targeting Dylan. Naïve, impressionable, lovelorn Dylan. Easy prey. A son for a son.

* * *

'We should stop at these services.'

'The next.'

'What, the M5?'

'Or Droitwich.'

'That's too far, surely... Lily...' Lucas spun round to confront the back seat as a terrible new thought occurred to him. 'If you have seen fit to tell *either* of them that we're coming then my wrath will know no bounds.'

'I haven't, Dad, and I wouldn't,' she croaked. Anyway, the signal is crap,' she muttered, her voice half muffled by the bedding.

'Despite which, the pair of you have been managing to chatter away all these weeks, have you?'

'No. Just a few messages. I told you, I tried to get him to leave, but he wouldn't.' Only Lily's nose upwards was visible over the bedding now, sharpening Lucas's determination to prise her out.

'And claiming not to know about Mei Lin – was that all fabricated too?'

There was a long pause. 'Dear God, Lily...'

'No...' she cried, and then faltered. 'At least, I knew they were friends – they came to Cambridge a couple of times, okay?'

'To Cambridge?'

'When Dylan bunked off...'

'Are you listening to this?' Lucas looked at Esther, also shaking her head in despair.

'But I never knew they were, like, *together*,' Lily wailed. 'It was only twice, and ages ago...'

'Do you know, Lily, I am not sure I will ever believe another word you say? Not a single bloody one, about anything...'

'Lucas,' Esther hissed.

'I thought I could trust you, Lily,' Lucas ploughed on bitterly. 'You, of all people, I thought—'

'Lucas, enough.' Esther raised her voice this time. 'Do *not* get me started on the subject of trust, okay?' She took her eyes off the road to glare, boring into his soul, it felt like. 'Without Lily, there would have been a total blackout. She was the one who insisted he stay in touch. She deserves credit for that.'

'Great. Yes. The bloody postcards. We thank you, Lily, for that small mercy.' Lucas swung his gaze back to the wipers. The sleet was thickening now, becoming more like snow. 'Sorry.' He reached out and put his hand over Esther's as it lay lightly on the gear stick, letting his palm rest over her knuckles. She made no acknowledgement of its presence. Indeed, the expression on her face, staring straight ahead – the focus, the contained strength and pain – reminded him suddenly of how she had been in the throes of childbirth, her strong jaw set in defiance of physical agony. Never had he been more in awe of Esther's power, her courage and her faith in herself.

And now the very progeny of that courage and endurance had turned on her as well as himself, formed a gang with the worst, most forbidding person they could have chosen. His grip over Esther's hand tightened.

'I'm sorry, but I really need to pee,' said Lily miserably, sitting up and peering out at the whiteness streaking past the car windows.

'It had better be these services, then, unless it is too late.' Lucas released his hold on Esther in order to point out the sign, only just legible under its flecked screen of snow, and then tensed his entire body as she promptly threaded her way across three slushy lanes of heavy traffic.

They made use of the facilities, bought sandwiches, cereal bars, fruit, and bottles of water, and then stood a little apart as they took to their phones. There was a message from Heidi, one of the new curt ones.

I am sorry for your news and wish you luck today. H.

Lucas read it and reread it, trying to suck meaning from the gaps. She was thinking about him. She was sorry. But still no kisses. A few feet away, he was aware of Lily delivering a hushed status report to Matteo, and of Esther, sending lots of texts by the look of things, but making no calls. They had lives, it seemed to him, while he had nothing now but dread of what lay ahead, both that afternoon and ever after.

43

Dylan watched the old man eat his porridge, scraping the spoon in neat radial lines for each mouthful, from the outside of the bowl to the middle. He had stood guard over Dylan as usual for the cooking, his breath full of the wheeze that was worse in the mornings, checking everything was done as he had coached.

'Remember the chestnuts need doing,' he said now, taking his porridge bowl to the sink and washing it up. 'Nutmeg, butter, bread-crumbs, pepper and salt.'

'I did that already, Gramps, remember?' Dylan received a nod, surly because of the *Gramps*, and then forced himself to wait, patiently, while the old man reached for the egg box on top of the fridge, its contents still warm, Dylan having rootled them out of the hen-house straw that morning. Noting the flinch of discomfort as the old man stretched, worse than usual, it looked like, Dylan sprang up from his chair.

'Would you like me to...?' Another pointed glare sent him hastily through the washing ritual of his own bowl instead. There were rules. It didn't do to break them, but it meant you knew where you were.

'We agreed on poached,' his grandfather growled, gently lifting the lid of the egg box with the slowness and awe of one expecting to find treasure. 'Not your forte.'

'But I can so do them now,' Dylan cried, 'just how you like them.' He stood close until his grandfather relented, pushing the eggs towards him before sitting back down, rubbing his big gnarled hands over his chest where the pain that was never mentioned began. It was heartburn, he had said, clutching the same spot when Dylan found him on the floor one morning, and then barking instructions to fetch a blister-pack of the tablets from the drawer beside his bed. The drawer was full of other pill boxes too, which Dylan had since worked out were delivered by the old lady called Iris who swung by in her blue van most Wednesdays, with a newspaper and fresh bread as well as the medicine.

Early on, Dylan and the old man had occasionally ventured the ten miles into town themselves, lumbering along in the twenty-year-old mud-encrusted Volvo that his grandfather called 'she' and talked to as if it were alive. But for a couple of months now, they had been eating solely out of the vegetable garden and the cavernous bench freezer in the outhouse, which was stuffed with fish, pheasant, sausages, steak, cuts of local lamb, as well as neatly labelled bags of vegetables, harvested from previous seasons. The only excursions in the car since November had been for putting Dylan through his paces in the bumpy field behind the cottage, the old man barking commands about using the mirrors, despite there being no other vehicles within sight.

Come December, his grandfather had stopped taking the lead in the vegetable garden too, instructing Dylan instead, between pointing out the bits of fencing that needed pinning down against the rabbits, and sifting through whatever produce got picked with his knowing fingers and hawkish eyes. Broccoli, Brussels sprouts, leeks, kale, parsnips – Dylan continued to be astonished at what grew in the damp and the cold, and how good vegetables he'd thought he hated could taste. There had been extra work that week, his grandfather predicting the bitter weather long before the forecasters, and commanding every single thing Dylan could lay his hands on to be dug, or gathered. Broad beans, runner beans, mangetout, cauliflower, it was like stockpiling for a siege, Dylan had grumbled to himself, his grandfather keeping vigil as Dylan followed orders for preparing the new pickings for the freezer, cutting, parboiling and letting everything cool before dividing and sealing it into bags.

The morning eggs were small, speckled, and flecked with bits of feather. Once the water was boiling, Dylan carefully tapped each one on the side of the pan – he had proved cack-handed at this in the past, their shells being so much thinner than supermarket ones – and then watched, amazed every time, at how the whites swirled and curled round themselves in the bubbling water.

His grandfather ate his methodically, like a task to be completed, before neatly putting his knife and fork together across his spotless plate. 'Bloody good. Thanks, boy.' He picked up the honey jar, which was almost empty, and the last from the shelf in the outhouse. Dylan knew he was thinking of the bees, which – he had been told – were originally acquired and tended by his grandmother; long-time residents of the two wooden hives under the big apple tree behind the outhouse, the entire swarm had disappeared overnight, back in October. Dylan hadn't minded unduly, the honey-collecting, dripping and scraping the stuff off the frames, had been the least favourite of his chores – worse even than scrubbing the shit from the hen house; but his grandfather remained downcast at the loss. Bees went for a reason – something had spooked them, he had declared, as doleful as Dylan had ever seen him. Even now, two months on, whenever he was outside, Dylan noticed him skirting the empty hives, throwing dark, hopeful looks at the sky through the bare branches of the apple tree, as if longing alone might bring the cloud swarming back.

'The broadband is down again,' he barked now. 'So, none of your games today.'

'It doesn't matter,' Dylan said, even though it did. The Internet was slow, but at least it mostly worked, which was more than could be said for the palm-sized pay-as-you-go phone – bought as a precaution against his mum checking his bills – that rarely managed to find a signal. Gaming felt like a major part of why Dylan had somehow ended up staying so long. He had made new friends through it, loads of them, including a girl called Zee, who lived in Perth, and to whom he had started chatting outside their online battling. Recently, they had had a joking exchange about meeting up for real, somewhere halfway like New York. *Though, I'd really like to visit London,* she had said. Dylan had been holding the sentence inside him, enjoying its possibilities, as well as the absence of pressure to do anything about them. Not yet anyway.

'And no studying required today. It being Christmas Eve.' The old man flashed a rare grin, revealing the strong white teeth that seemed at increasing odds with his skeletal frailty, and which Dylan found as unnerving a reminder of his father as the framed boyhood photograph of Lucas nailed to the wall beside the wood-burning stove – even through the age-speckled glass it didn't take a genius to spot the echo of his own features there. 'Though you shouldn't have stayed,' his grandfather added with the sudden gruffness that swept in from nowhere, especially after he had said something soft or kind. 'Iris knows I want her to put you on the train at Ludlow. Music needs facing, Dylan, and that's a fact.'

'Whatever.' Dylan stacked their plates and busied himself with the washing and drying ritual, giving the sink a scrub for good measure. He had never expected leaving to be so hard. Indeed, nothing about the visit had panned out as he had imagined. It was supposed to have been a stopgap, as well as a big fuck-you to his father for his total dick-headedness and the estrangement, so important supposedly, but not so that it ever got talked about. It was only because of their mum that he and Lily knew anything; but even then it was just snippets, to do with the drinking that cost him his doctor job, and the stressing-out of the granny they had never met to the point of her taking her own life. It was like some fascinating story about other people, and one that bore no resemblance whatsoever to the occasional short, friendly emails that had started arriving when his mum and dad had split up. The voice in the emails sounded like the total opposite of drunk, almost boringly so sometimes.

Tell Mum and Dad I'm in touch if you want to, but they'll probably insist I stop.

He and Lily had talked it through, and agreed it was their right to accept his emails if they chose. He was their grandfather, after all; and all he wanted, he said, many times, was the chance to know a little bit about their lives, and then only if they felt like it and had the time. Dylan rarely wrote more than a line or two, mostly complaining about school and work, but he never seemed to mind. The injections of cash were more exciting. Because the government would only get it otherwise, the old man explained in the no-bullshit way that Dylan had come to know so well, and which had rung through the response to his first tentative enquiry about the possibility of coming to see the Clun valley for himself.

Yes. Any time. Ludlow Station. Let me know date & eta.

Time out had been the plan, but very quickly it had felt to Dylan more like time travel: stepping into a world where all the things that tore him apart, that he had grown to hate, ceased to exist. Suffocating parents, exam humiliations, the Mei-Lin-shaped hole inside his heart, the mounting pressure – applied by every grown-up he came across – over what-to-*do* and what-to-*be*, all stopped. In its place was an old man who asked few questions, but who liked him to make his bed and pull his weight. Two hours of study a day was mandatory, but the subject matter could be anything. All that counted, his grandfather said, was the curiosity to explore and understand.

When Dylan got more into the gaming, the old man introduced a rule about computer time having to be earned. Catching Dylan out once – playing Sea of Thieves instead of reading up on the grisly atrocities of Stalin, as he had claimed – the old man, without a word, had unplugged every phone cable in the cottage. Dylan's screen had gone blank mid-game. He had thought about leaving then all right, but had stayed for one more day, which had become two, and then three, until he'd stopped counting. He had been a couple of weeks in at the time, with Lily's postcard plan under way, making him feel better, just as she'd said it would. When he'd told his grandfather about them, the old man had guffawed so heartily it had turned into one of those coughing fits where Dylan had to fetch water and pat him on the back.

* * *

Dylan was upstairs, lying on the bed in the room he knew had once been his father's, when he heard the faint rumble of an approaching vehicle. The cottage was so remote that he assumed it was Iris, or the nearest farmer, who sometimes came looking for escaped sheep.

He returned his attention to his laptop, holding out for a return of the broadband signal, so that he could send a response to Zee. He wanted to write to Lily too, whose pleas that he come back for Christmas had grown more and more desperate. He wanted to explain how it wouldn't have felt right to take off and leave the old man at such a time; although, a few hours into Christmas Eve now, with all the tasks Dylan could think of already done, including hanging a handful of ancient, chipped baubles on the smallest fir tree he had ever laid eyes on, it was starting to feel like being away from home over Christmas might be a bigger deal than he'd anticipated. It didn't help that his bedroom was even more arctic than usual, because the radiator was the one that collected all the air in the house, his grandfather had explained, when Dylan had finally dared to complain. He had been given a little key to 'bleed' the air out of it with, which he had lost.

Glancing up, Dylan saw that the wet flakes that had been flinging themselves at the windowpane all morning were hardening into proper snow, thick enough to screen out the usual view of the steep hillsides walling in their fold of the valley. A proper white Christmas, then, for once. And he felt good about his gifts for his grandfather: two books, sitting on top of the little chest of drawers behind the door, ready for wrapping when he got around to asking for Sellotape and paper. One was an American novel about a woman who kept bees, and the other a book about the battle to save Malta in the Second World War. The old man was keen on Churchill, and the war in general, having been born the year it started. 'The gripping story of an epic battle at sea...' the book blurb said, making it sound almost as good as one of his games. His grandfather's gift to him, Dylan already knew, was to be five hundred pounds. Lily was getting the same, and he was to be entrusted with both in the form of cheques – a pain, but he wasn't complaining.

The engine sound had drawn much closer. It had to be Iris, Dylan decided, aware of his spirits lifting. She was as no-nonsense as his grandfather, just as old, but more robust. Their Wednesday exchanges were always brief, but she had a way of radiating kindness and very early on had found a moment to press a piece of paper into Dylan's hand with her mobile and landline numbers written on it. 'Any time, you hear? *Any* time, and I will come.' She had been a lifesaver with his Amazon deliveries too, including the Christmas books, since defeated satnavs invariably meant everything ended up at the sorting office ten miles away.

When the engine stopped right outside the house, Dylan rolled off the bed and sauntered to the window. The snow was falling thicker than ever, and the Volvo, parked beside the outhouse, was starting to look like a sinking ship. Iris's van was as robust as its owner. But when Dylan glanced down, it turned out to be a much smaller vehicle parked under the lee of his windowsill. A silver Ford Fiesta, just like his mother's. It had left tracks on the lane that wound back up the valley, but which were fading rapidly under the falling blanket of snow.

As the occupants of the car spilled out of the doors, Dylan did not move. His heart beat wildly, with a happiness of sorts beside the dread. Everything was going to be terrible. But it was Christmas, and they had come.

It took the rapping of the cottage's heavy bronze front door knocker, to the accompaniment of what sounded like pounding fists, for Dylan to tear out of the room. At the top of the staircase, he took a deep breath, gripping the broad wooden banister rail, and beginning to descend very slowly, one step at a time. *Music must be faced.* His grandfather was in the sitting room, he knew, in the weathered leather armchair with the studs round its edges, immersed in a book on Isambard Kingdom Brunel, one of his many heroes. Beside him was the fire Dylan had laid, roaring in the grate, warming the thinning, still elegant frame, legs covered with a moth-eaten, tartan blanket.

There was another round of pounding and rapping and Dylan halted. *Music. Must. Be. Faced.* Oh, God. But his grandfather shuffled into view in the same moment, allowing him to remain where he was, hovering in a confusion of hope and fear and guilt, halfway down the stairs. From this vantage point he could see the full baldness of the old man's head, smooth as a bared skull beneath the white feathers of his hair. He was still reaching for the handle when the door flew open, presenting a person who at first glance looked too crazed to be his father – arms flung wide, snow coating his hair, eyebrows and the shoulders of his heavy black coat, his mouth wide and roaring. 'How dare you... my child... how dare you... how dare...?'

Dylan heard his grandfather say, 'Hello, Lucas,' but his dad's explosion into the hall continued, with shouting, swearing, and pushing his whole body into him. The old man put his arms up as if to defend himself, staggering backwards, losing his balance in the process. He began to topple, slowly, like a tree felled. Dylan hurled himself down the stairs, arriving just in time to cushion the fall as he landed.

'Dylan.' His father was aghast, breathing hard. 'Are you okay?' A flurry was going on around him, with his sister and mother pushing round the sides of the doorway and his mother winning the elbow-fight to get to him as he tried to help the old man to his feet.

'Dylan, darling...' There were tears in her eyes. 'John... are you both all right?' She tried to pull his grandfather by the arm, but he waved her away, leaning just on Dylan.

'Hey there, all of you...' Dylan grunted, not knowing how to sound, or what on earth to say. The old man, now upright, was gripping his arm so tightly that it hurt, and Dylan was holding him in return, as if, in the face of this invasion, they were each clinging to the other.

'We're here for Dylan,' his dad barked like an army sergeant, his eyes boring into the old man as if he were ready to draw a weapon if he so much as moved.

'John, we need to take Dylan home,' said his mum, much more gently.

'Hello, Esther. I had gathered that this wasn't a social call. Hello, Lily.' His face softened at Lily, who was hanging back, her face the colour of paper, her eyes stricken and darting between them all, like a crazy person.

'Hey, Boo.' Dylan found his sister's eyes, holding his with such a combination of apology, support and an oh-God-what-a-shit-storm that without the old man hanging on him, he would have thrown his arms round her.

'Hey, Dyl. Sorry, I had to.'

Behind her, the door blew shut on a gust of snowy wind, trapping them all in the little hall. His grandfather let go of him in the same instant, clutching the banister post instead.

'Dylan, pack your things,' his father commanded, his voice flat and cold. 'Mum and Lily will help you. John and I are going to talk.'

'I'm not going to pack.' Dylan's heart was skipping again, but for his grandfather now, still hanging onto the stair post, his head bowed. They couldn't just leave. They couldn't. But his mother pitched in, telling him to do as he was told, dropping her gaze to her snow-crusted boots instead of his pleading eyes. 'But, Mum...'

'It's all right, lad,' his grandfather growled. 'Do as they say. Make yourselves some tea though, Esther, before you go. And there's cake. In the tin by the kettle.'

'We don't want *tea*,' thundered his father. 'In here, with me. Now.' He flattened the sitting-room door as wide open as it would go, slamming it shut the moment the old man had shuffled inside.

44

'You need to start it in second.'

'I know. I have been.' Esther had stuck her head out of the car window and snowflakes were blowing against her teeth and landing on her tongue. Lucas, leaving Dylan and Lily still ranged behind the bumper, approached like some Arctic explorer back from a foray, the hood of his coat pulled over his beanie, his eyebrows and upper lip crusted with snow.

'Lucas, this is hopeless.' The cottage was some twenty yards behind them, the spiral of smoke from its chimney a drifting pencil line against the heaving white sky.

'No, it isn't.'

'I've been in second, and the wheels are still spinning.'

'Try again.' He stomped back to the children and a few moments later thumped the roof by way of an instruction to restart the car. The engine burst into life and lurched forwards as the three of them pushed harder than ever before, allowing the car to find such a promising rhythm that Esther knew she had to keep going. As she pulled away, she could see the children and Lucas in the rear-view mirror, blurry figures receding in the blizzard. Beneath her, the tyres squeaked and crunched over the freshly fallen, deepening snow, gathering purchase.

Esther dared not look too far ahead, at the snaking hill that needed to be climbed in order to reach the upper road, which had a chance of having been gritted, Lucas had declared just before they'd left, though, from the closed expression on John's face, Esther doubted it somehow. She had said nothing then, just as she had made no enquiry about the repeated crescendo of exchanges emanating from the sitting room. Dylan's safety was one thing, but the rest of it was Lucas's war. The extent of this had only truly dawned as they'd journeyed that morning, when Lucas had begun coiling into himself, wide-eyed at the unfolding familiar landscape, a man seeing ghosts.

At Lucas's stormy entry into the house, Esther had shuddered, reaching for Lily's hand. Her own fearful anger was darker, quieter. At the sight of her gaunt-faced ex-father-in-law stumbling into the hall, his pole-thin drinker's frame even more painfully in evidence than two decades before, a visceral wave of sheer revulsion had coursed through her. And half-cut already, she had observed grimly, frantically looking for Dylan as John had tripped and staggered. At the sight of her son – a new, thicker-set, taller version of him – hurtling down the stairs, she had uttered a cry, dropping Lily's hand to reach him, only to hesitate at the realisation that he was coming to the aid of the old man. The maelstrom around her had shrunk to white noise. Only Dylan had been in focus, staring about wildly as he'd propped up his grandfather. While Lucas had continued to shout, and then to bark orders, she had edged nearer Dylan, waiting until John had been hustled into the sitting room before lunging to hold him properly. She had hugged as much of him as she could get her arms around, telling him over and over how forgiven he was, how loved, before letting Lily have her turn.

After the two of them had raced upstairs to get on with packing, as she had urged, Esther had stood in the hall while her heart slowed, closing out the warring voices through the door beside her, breathing freely for what felt like the first time in years. The good sense of seeking out the toilet finally made her move. It was still set at the back of the house, just as she remembered, but now accessed through an orderly cloakroom. Several coats, appropriate for assorted weather, hung side by side on pegs, among them a black padded anorak, which she recognised with a start as Dylan's. Two huge pairs of muddied wellingtons, one green, one black, stood side by side underneath, parked on fresh squares of newspaper. The room gleamed, from its terracotta-tiled floor, to the white handbasin in the corner, and the plump, fresh towel hanging from its brass rail. Behind the door, a large, green brolly, glistening from recent use, flopped out of a wooden umbrella stand, beside an eagle-headed walking stick that Esther remembered from before, its features now worn smooth from use.

Fixing tea made no sense, she knew. The plan – their sole, agreed aim – was to scoop up Dylan and get the hell out, heading back to Esther's for a full family debrief, before she and the children returned to their Amersham Christmas, and Lucas to his Cambridge one, with Heidi, Esther assumed. They had even bought food supplies for the return journey.

All the same, Esther found herself going straight from the cloakroom into the kitchen, where she filled the blackened old kettle and set it on the hob. Out of mild curiosity, she then eased the lid off the checked green, slightly dented cake tin sitting next to a poinsettia in the middle of the old oblong oak table. Expecting something shop-bought and half stale, she was surprised to find herself looking at what was clearly a home-made Christmas cake. It smelt rich and sweet, and was decorated with two worse-for-wear plastic reindeer, wedged up to their stomachs in thick choppy icing, and a disproportionately large blue wooden angel, who had pitched forwards onto her face, smudging an otherwise immaculately composed scarlet and lime *Merry Christmas!!!* headline. Esther gently set the figure upright, ramming it deeper into the icing ocean for safety, before putting the lid back on. The exclamation marks stayed with her. Whoever had put them there must have been feeling exuberant. Or ironic.

She turned to the fridge in search of milk. There was time for a quick cuppa, she reasoned, since who knew how long Lucas would be?

Fifty years was a lot to get off a chest. As she moved around, faint strains of laughter floated down through the low rafters overhead, filling her with a fresh wave of grateful wonderment. Dylan was all right, and the bond between her children nothing short of extraordinary. He had needed to get away and saw it as a chance to meet their grandfather properly, Lily had mumbled in the car, with the manifest reluctance of one still despising her own disloyalty. They had each other's backs, she had added simply, with the new hint of defiance that Esther was starting to recognise. And who wouldn't want that? Splitting parents bringing children closer, it was a good thing, surely.

The fridge was roomy with a handle as big as an iron. It gave a neat click as Esther tugged it open, revealing an astonishing array of contents: a half side of cooked salmon sprinkled with herbs and lemon slices, a bowl of home-made potato salad, a dish of diced sprouts, a turkey in a tinfoil nest, heavily draped with bacon, and a crystal glass bowl full to the brim with stiff-peaked, glistening brandy butter. Esther was still taking it all in, when a burst of footsteps into the hall was followed by Lucas bellowing that it was time to go. In one swift move-ment, she pushed the fridge door too, whisked the kettle off its ring just before it whistled, and rushed along the passageway. Arriving in time to see Lucas's legs disappearing onto the landing, she gingerly put her head round the open sitting-room door. John was motionless, parked in a hearthside leather chair facing away from her, a tartan blanket draped over his legs, flames licking and snapping round what looked like a fat new log in the grate beside him.

He turned his head slowly, as if sensing rather than seeing her. 'You look well, Esther.'

'John, I just want to say that what you have done... going behind our backs... it is unspeakable.'

He shrugged, plucking at his blanket with his big knotty fingers. 'He asked to come, Esther. He knew that you and Lucas would have forbidden it. All I did was say yes.' He put a hand to his mouth as a phlegmy cough erupted, swallowing it down so noisily she had to look away in disgust. 'Lucas certainly did not mince his words.' He started a grim, throaty chuckle that became another cough. 'Safe journey, anyway,' he growled, once this too had been swallowed. 'I won't see you off out in the cold, if you don't mind.'

'Of course, we don't want seeing off,' Esther replied stiffly. He was slurring his words, but part of it had to be fatigue. Lily's insistence in the car that he no longer touched alcohol had prompted snarls of derision from Lucas, along with a terse, biting reference to the scores of broken promises that had peppered his upbringing and then continued to destroy his mother.

'We'll be on our way, then, John...' she started, halting as Dylan bolted past her, reaching the armchair in three strides.

'Gramps. I don't want to go. They're making me.' He had dropped to his knees, and was patting the old man's arms between trying to seize his hands. 'You've been amazing. You've been... I can't really...'

'Off you go, now.' John jerked his fingers free, burying them in the folds of his lap rug.

Esther had gone rigid. She had prepared herself for many things, but not this. The power the old man seemed to wield. Dylan being so in his thrall, it was as strange as it was unsettling.

'Will Iris come by, do you think?' Dylan's voice was pleading now.

'Probably.'

'I'll call her, shall I?'

'No, you shall not. Get on with you, now. Do as your mum and dad say.'

'But I've got presents for you, Gramps. I've left them on the bed because they're not wrapped yet. Just a couple of books I thought you'd like. I was going to put them under the tree.' Dylan threw a desolate glance at a small, sparsely decorated potted fir in the corner of the room.

Esther hovered at a distance, finding that she felt too like an interloper even to speak. Lucas called it grooming, but the way Dylan was talking did not sound like that. The icing exclamation marks shimmered at the back of her mind. The entire situation remained unacceptable, but now unhelpful tremors of pity were surfacing too.

Because of starting to see John through Dylan's eyes, Esther realised; her darling son, with his pure, open heart; and because, for all the ugly facts of John's life, as a man who had caused so much damage to the people he was supposed to love and protect, her ex-father-in-law was still pitifully frail and elderly. And – as Dylan seemed more aware than any of them – it *was* Christmas.

'Go on, all of you,' John barked with such ferocity that she jumped, the pity evaporating. Dylan meekly clambered to his feet, casting sad eyes at her. 'Before the weather closes in,' John continued testily. 'You're on borrowed time as it is, I would say.'

Lucas had appeared in the doorway in the same moment, clutching bags and looking business-like, saying that the upper road would be gritted and they were leaving now. John had turned, but only to fix a wry, maudlin gaze on the small latticed window beside the hearth, an empty noughts and crosses grid against the sheet-white outside.

* * *

Lucas squinted at the car tracking up the hillside, willing it on. Wind was picking up the snow now, blowing it off the ground into his, Dylan's and Lily's faces, adding to the onslaught already tumbling out of the sky. Pushing the car, a team of three, with him in the middle and the children on either side, had felt good. When the wheels, after lots of slithering, had managed at last to get a proper grip, they had all cheered, slapping their frozen hands together as they had started to jog in its wake. The direness of the situation had so far called for action, not conversation, and Lucas was glad of that, too. He wasn't sure he could have managed proper talking yet, not with all the words that had passed between him and his father, still lodged in his throat like stones.

Pushing the car, he had been dogged by flashbacks, his body prick-ling all over again at the feel of the thin, hard cage of bones beneath the old darned jumper as he had steered his father into the sitting room. A dark part of Lucas had wanted to shove then all right – with as much force as he had exerted on Esther's spluttering Ford; to make the lanky frame sprawl and tremble, not just for the obvious crimes – kidnapping Dylan, driving his mother to her grave – but so that the bastard might feel as crushed as Lucas once had, a little boy, powerless and ashamed, crouching in corners.

'You don't fool me,' he had hissed, releasing his hold once the door was closed, trying not to be riled by the self-pitying hang of his father's head, the exaggerated rubbing of his arms where he had been gripped, the meal he was making of his tottering, just as he had in the hall, getting everyone running to his aid. Dylan in particular. Soon, there would be crowing about that. Sneering. Lucas knew his own parent. 'And if you have fooled Dylan, it is because he is a good kid.'

'I did no fooling...' His father had shuffled round to face him, his hawk-eyes fixed, and blinking slowly, sizing up their prey, it felt like.

'You *stole* my child.'

'I did no such thing, Lucas. I reached out, as I believe they say these days. And when Dylan reached back... it was... I couldn't... I don't have much time left...'

'Bullshit. You *bought* him. And Lily. You disgust me.'

The eyelids fluttered, and he took a few steps back, gripping the edge of the leather armchair. 'Dylan was sad, Lucas. About a girl. And hating his new school. And because of you and Esther—'

'Me and Esther? How dare you?'

'Yes, you keep saying that. But I *dare*, Lucas,' he rasped, the anger stirring, as Lucas knew it would.

'How the hell did you know, anyway? About me and Esther?'

He blinked properly, for a moment looking almost sheepish. 'Patrick drops me a line. From time to time. Grandfathers united... look, I was sorry to hear it...'

'Patrick had no right. And you have no business being *sorry*. I do not care what you feel, about anything, do you hear? About me. Or Esther. Or the world. And for the record, you don't fool me about the booze either. Whatever sob stories you've spun to the children, or anyone else. I know you. I *know* you. Which is why I have kept away, and will continue to do so. As will my children. *My* children. So, if you ever try to make contact with Dylan or Lily again—'

'You'll what, Lucas? They're adults. And I shall contact whomsoever I choose. Tired now,' he mumbled suddenly, starting to edge round to the front of the armchair, using both hands for support. He lowered himself into the seat with a heavy sigh. 'Lucas.' He paused to breathe again. 'I am sorry I wasn't a better father, but there were pressures. Your mother...'

'Don't you dare...' Lucas let the sentence hang, aware how often he had used the phrase, and in danger suddenly of feeling feeble. He focussed on swallowing instead, trying to disperse an extraordinary and unexpected lump suddenly clogging the back of his throat.

'She was a depressive, Lucas.' He had covered his face with his hands and was speaking through his fingers, his voice thin and weary. 'She threatened countless times to take her life. I kept it from you. She wouldn't stick with her medication. Sometimes, it felt as though she wanted to punish me with her misery.'

'Punish *you*?' Lucas managed a scornful laugh. In spite of himself, his mother was in his head, not the usual unbearable imagined scene, but a close-up of her face, her smile, with its sad, haunted eyes.

'It was bad. *I* was bad. It was hard. I lost my nerve... at work... at life... found pleasure elsewhere, wherever the hell I could... behaved so terribly...' He turned in his seat, ensnaring Lucas with his piercing eyes. 'But these are things I have dared to imagine you might know a little about yourself now...'

'Stop. Shut up. Not another word. I am nothing like you. *Nothing*.' The monstrous shameful throat lump had given way, making it necessary to shout his way through the words.

'Then I met someone,' his father went on doggedly, 'fell properly in love, but there was no question of leaving. Your mother couldn't have borne it. I was trapped, and it made me cruel. I am sorry, okay, boy? *Sorry*.' He had been speaking with mounting vehemence, leaning further and further out of the chair, twisting to keep Lucas's full attention. 'But I lost everything, can you see that? Everything.' He fell back into the chair, as if exhausted. 'I paid the price.'

'No, Dad, *I* paid the price,' Lucas had whispered, already at the door, his fingers round the handle. He would not say the word 'goodbye'. Good riddance would have been closer to the mark.

* * *

When the car started to slide backwards, it was Dylan who hollered the loudest, breaking into a cumbersome, skidding run up the hill. Within moments, it spun sideways and backwards, ending up at an angle, its rear wheels buried in a roadside ditch, rendered invisible by snow.

'We'll call the farmer – get a tow from a tractor,' Lucas cried, having overtaken Dylan and reaching Esther first. She was fine, she said, ignoring his outstretched arm as she clambered out. Lucas backed away, catching a glimpse of his face in the side mirror in the same instant, streaming with sweat and melting snowflakes, his eyebrows frosty crags. He looked a hundred years old. Like his father. Like father, like son. The same path, the same fate. Life was just about getting stuck on a carousel after all – you thought you'd got off when you hadn't. He would end alone and bitter, with coat-hanger shoulders in old darned sweaters, and a secret stash of whisky to numb the pain... a pain that included the new, deeper knowledge of his mother, sick as well as sad, too fragile to brave the world on her own.

Lucas put a hand to his mouth to stifle a sob. There was Heidi, he reminded himself. The thought of her lit up his mind like a flare. He was still capable of love. During the course of the final services stop that morning, he had sent another desperate text to Germany, begging to be taken back. There had been no reply. Not even a brusque one. But there was hope. Being able to rescue Dylan proved it. There was always hope.

'No, Lucas. We are not going to call a farmer, or anyone else,' Esther was telling him, raising her voice against the swirling snow, already pinging open the boot and reaching in for the bags. 'We'll carry what we need to the house.'

'Esther... we can't. I can't.' Lucas stood, blinking and helpless. Somewhere, in the corner of his eye, he was aware of Dylan moulding snowballs and lobbing them at Lily, making her squeal.

Esther kept talking, handing him bags, saying the children could sleep in the small room with the bunk bed, that she would take the sofa, and he could have Dylan's – his – room. She broke off to yell at the children to stop playing and come and help.

'No,' Lucas croaked. 'I can't.'

'Yes, you can. You will.'

'To let him think that suddenly it's all okay...'

'He doesn't think that. He knows nothing is okay. Come on, Lucas. We've got no choice.'

'I'll take the sofa.'

'Fine. Now get the children loaded up, while I fish my handbag out from behind the front seat.'

The wind dropped quite suddenly as they plodded back towards the cottage, enveloping them in a silence that felt hard to break. Only Esther spoke, saying that necessity was the mother of invention and all would be well.

'There's loads of food, actually,' Dylan ventured, when they reached the shelter of the porch and were kicking off their sodden footwear, Lucas's shoes having fared the worst. Lily and Esther both had leather boots on, while Dylan was protected best of all, in the green wellingtons Esther had seen in the cloakroom. 'And there are chickens, Boo – I'll show you later...'

'We are staying because we have no option,' Lucas interjected coldly. 'We shall not look at chickens. We shall eat our own food.' He gestured at the bag of sandwiches and crisps dangling from Esther's frozen fingers. 'And just as soon as this bloody snow starts to ease, we shall leave, in the middle of the night if necessary.'

'Well, I won't.' Dylan had put down his bag and planted a hand on each hip. 'Tomorrow is Christmas Day, and Gramps and I are roasting a turkey. Tonight, there's salmon and stuff. And how you can hold a *grudge* anyway, like *for ever,* I just don't get it...'

'No, Dylan, you do not get it,' Lucas said through a clamped jaw, 'because your own upbringing has been so bloody—'

'Brilliant? Has it, Dad? Really?'

'Dyl, shut up,' Lily hissed.

'Can we go inside?' Esther pleaded, sharing a despairing look with Lily, who was looking equally stricken. 'And, Dylan, you don't know what you are saying,' she added sternly. 'Dad went through so much...'

'Did he, Mum? Right. Well, I want to hear it from Dad. How are Lily and I expected to understand if he never explains?'

Father and son had squared up in front of each other, eyes inches apart in the confines of the little entrance. Dylan was the broader as well as the taller one now, by several inches, Esther observed, finding a moment to be amazed. 'Lucas. Please. Let's get inside.' She had put an arm round Lily, who was looking faintly blue-lipped and chalky-faced. 'Hot baths. Tea and cake. Bed-making...'

'In a moment, Esther.' Lucas held up a hand, not moving his head.

'Yeah, come on, Dad,' Dylan urged, insolent now, and baiting, 'let's have it. Gramps was like this total drunk, who lost his job and made your life hell. Which is why you left, and Granny... did what she did...' He faltered, adding in a much smaller voice, 'Is that it?'

'Dylan, that's enough...' Esther cried, but Lucas held up his hand again.

He had flinched at Dylan's onslaught, but then tightened his face into a mask. 'You have the gist of it exactly, Dylan. And maybe, at a more appropriate moment, I shall be able to explain the effects of love-lessness and fear, of adult dysfunction and *sadness*, day in, day out, on an only child.' He fired the words like bullets, his eyes greener than Esther had ever seen them, and more desperate. 'But in the meantime, forgive me if there were aspects of my upbringing with which I have not wanted to burden my own children. And now your mother is right, we should get this over with and go inside.'

'Okay...' Dylan was caving visibly, his shoulders dropping, his burst of defiance past. 'But, so you know,' he muttered, picking up his bag, 'he, like, really *doesn't* drink now, and also it's obvious he misses Granny loads. Her ashes are under that tree, by the hives.' They all looked, in the spell of the moment still, as he threw an arm in the direction of two barely visible white humps and a tree in the snowscape to the right of the cottage. 'She did the bees, and when they swarmed off recently, you'd think he'd lost her all over again. And also, sorry, Dad,' he blurted, 'but when someone ends their life, it's like *they* are doing it, right? Not anyone else.'

In the stunned silence that followed, John opened the door. 'If you're coming in, then get on with it,' he grunted. 'I've put the kettle on.'

45

Once known, a person could not become unknown, that was the problem. Esther had given up on sleep and rolled onto her back, letting the thought take her over, as it had been clamouring to do. The days of worrying about Lucas should have been well behind her, but in the twenty-four hours since they had braved entry into the cottage, it was the incessant, involuntary monitoring of her ex-husband's state of mind that had been getting her down the most. No aspect of the situation was easy for any of them; but for Lucas, she knew, it was like his worst nightmare. Even being aware of that was a burden. Having to witness the undercurrents of emotion raging beneath his rigid show of compliance, finding it so painful sometimes that she simply had to look the other way.

The only reason any of it – Christmas Eve and Christmas Day now, too – had been remotely bearable was thanks to the children. Lily, understandably, remained a little off colour with regard to food, but from the moment they'd trooped back into the house, past the inscrutable expression of their grandfather, she and Dylan had become buoyant, like the reunited siblings they were. In cahoots. Bickering over nonsense, joshing who should get the top bunk in their tiny room, their laughter ringing round the cottage like a jolly soundtrack mismatched to a dark script.

John, to his credit, had helped too, by promptly retreating to his room. Lucas, in something of a trance, had refused tea and taken himself off to the sofa that he insisted would serve as his bed, not hers. Determined to get on top of things, Esther had embarked on a quest for bedding. Meeting with little success, she had gone to consult Dylan, finding him curled up with his sister on the bottom bunk, sharing a set of earphones to listen to something on Lily's iPad. To her surprise, he had sprung into action at once, clearly eager to show off his familiarity with the house as he'd led the way to various cupboards and a large tea chest, from which he'd plucked out stiff towels and blankets, as well as several impressively creaseless pillowcases and sheets. He'd then helped make up all the beds without being asked, confessing cheerily during the course of it that he liked ironing.

Esther's amazement had deepened when he'd taken the lead with supper preparations too, bragging about how to make the perfect hollandaise, and why potato salad was best jazzed up with chilli and leeks, between bossing Lily about where to find the plates, glasses, and cutlery for the table. Water glasses only, Esther had remarked wryly when giving a status report to Lucas, whom she'd found still ensconced on the sofa, padded out with a pillow and blanket she had delivered earlier, and staring dejectedly at his phone.

'Where is he?' he had asked at once.

Esther flopped into the leather armchair with a heavy sigh. 'Still in his room. Hiding, I suppose.'

'Good.'

'This isn't easy for him either, Lucas.'

'I don't care. I hope he stays there.'

'When you talked, what did he say exactly?'

'Exactly what you would expect,' he muttered. 'Dylan had come of his own accord. None of it was his fault. Blaming everything – everyone – but himself. I can't get a bloody signal.' He shook his mobile. 'And the Wi-Fi code Dylan gave us doesn't work. What about you?'

'Nope. Not a sausage.' Esther had long given up on hoping for connectivity. Every attempt to update her parents, and Viv, had triggered nothing but clock icons or red exclamation marks.

'It's nice to see him, though, isn't it? Dylan, I mean.'

'Yes. Yes, it is.'

'And he seems—'

'I had a faint signal just now.' Lucas was moving his phone around like a compass, tipping it at different angles. 'This bloody place.'

Esther left the chair to close the curtains, summoning patience. 'Dylan says the connection is always dodgy, even without blizzard conditions. Remember, Lily told us? Apparently, you can always get through from the top of the hill, although that's not really an option now.' It was Heidi Lucas wanted to speak to, of course. His fervour at the services the day before had been plain, eyes boring at the little screen, thumbs flying. Hats off to Heidi, Esther reflected dryly, for clearly being confident enough to keep him on his toes. More confident than she had ever managed, anyway. She paused at the window, the edges of which were so caked in snow that the darkness outside resembled a black porthole.

'It's just one day, Lucas,' she murmured. 'And Dylan has clearly... thrived.' She chose the word carefully, bracing herself. It hadn't been what she had expected either. When Lucas remained silent, she picked up the hearth poker, her thoughts flicking to her own father as she prodded the molten embers. Everything, everywhere seemed to have turned upside down; almost as if the truth was being shaken out of them all. It was terrible, but also – somehow – good. 'Boxing Day at the latest, and we'll be gone,' she told Lucas, because he had abandoned his mobile at last and was looking so wretched, 'with the help of ten farmers if necessary.'

'Twenty.'

With John upstairs, getting through the evening hadn't proved so bad. He was giving them time together, Dylan had reported proudly, after returning with a rejected plate of salmon and various salads, all of it so delicious that Esther had to rein in the urge to remark on the fact after every mouthful. That his grandfather was almost certainly seeking sustenance of another kind crossed her mind, and Lucas's too, she knew, grateful that even in his distracted state he recognised it wasn't the moment to say so. There was a way to go yet. They had to pace themselves, keep the peace.

'We'll go tomorrow if the weather clears,' Lucas announced during the course of a somewhat awkward parting at the bottom of the stairs, he and Esther dodging each other in order to embrace the children. They each murmured their final goodnights, without her, or either child, contradicting him.

But the weather hadn't cleared. It had proved a Christmas Day as cold as any Esther could remember, the sky a low ceiling of cloud, the fallen snow compacted beneath it to unassailable solidity. Icicles hung off the ends of the gutter and the tap by the front door. Lucas, going out to see if he could climb the hill, had slipped over on a patch of ice and returned crestfallen and swearing. Esther had busied herself in the kitchen with Dylan and Lily, proud of her two children's determined energy, doing her best to feed off it herself. Once again, John had made it easier for them all, staying holed up in his lair, allowing Dylan to take gleeful charge of the Christmas meal, wielding utensils and pans like a bandmaster, chopping, basting, stirring, and blithely announcing, during the course of sharpening a knife the size of a cutlass, his intention to do a catering course in Manchester. He had already been checking out colleges, he'd declared, throwing a defiant look at his father's raised eyebrows, while Esther and Lily had whooped with enthusiasm.

'Lucas, say you are pleased,' Esther scolded, eliciting the closest thing to a smile Lucas had managed in two days, followed by the astonishing reward of seeing him leave his chair to put his arms round Dylan, and slap him heartily on the back.

'That is good, Dylan,' he said gruffly. 'Well done. I am pleased. I am proud. And what you did, coming here, was very wrong, but how you've coped... it is... a wonder.'

'Actually, there's a bottle of champagne,' Dylan cried, looking so lit up from the praise that Esther could have wept. 'I had a word with Gramps just now, and he said we could have it with the meal if we wanted.'

Esther was aware of Lucas slowing down his movements, of the pause before he answered, the effort to keep his tone free of edge. 'And why, may I ask, is there champagne if he is teetotal?'

'To show he doesn't need it,' Dylan replied crisply. 'He explained it to me. Like proof of willpower, sort of thing. It's there, but you don't care.' As if on cue, a faint coughing drifted down from upstairs. 'Dad? Mum? It's in the cellar. Shall I fetch it?'

'Not for me, but you all go ahead', Lucas murmured, not catching Esther's eye.

'Oh, and I nearly forgot,' Dylan added breathlessly, having started to leave the room and then bouncing back in, 'when I gave Gramps his presents this morning, he said this was for you, Dad.' He tugged a small blue box out of the baggy back pocket of his jeans and handed it to Lucas. Stuck on the lid with Sellotape was a large tag, on which was written

LUCAS LOVE DAD

in large, wavering capitals.

'Lucas, shouldn't we get him down here with us?' Esther murmured. 'I mean, to at least eat the Christmas meal? It is, after all, his food, his home, and—'

'Oh, I already asked,' Dylan cut in breezily. 'He keeps saying he is happy where he is. But that he's also glad we're here... just so you know...' He tailed off, clearly losing confidence at the expressions on their faces.

The wary dread in the way Lucas removed the lid from the box made Esther's own heart gallop. Inside was a silver napkin ring, which he examined for a moment, holding it up under the kitchen light before slowly returning it to the box. 'My mother's,' he announced hoarsely, immediately excusing himself to go to the toilet. By the time he returned, hollow-eyed, Dylan was carving the turkey, and explaining how he had made the cranberry sauce.

* * *

Esther squinted at her wristwatch. Two o' clock. She had slept a little, and it was rain that had woken her, she realised, a downpour, thwacking on the roof, thudding on the snow. If it carried on, they'd be able to pack up and go in just a few hours. She closed her eyes and then blinked them open at the sound of a gentle knock on the door.

'Yes?'

It opened slowly with a series of creaks, and Lucas slid through the gap. 'Hi. Sorry.'

'Hi. It's okay.' Esther shifted upright, holding the sheets against her T-shirt.

'I just can't... sleep.' He walked to the window, running his hands through his hair in his trademark expression of stress, and then parted the curtains to peer at the silvery deluge outside. He was wearing socks, Esther noticed, as well as tracksuit bottoms and a thick woollen jumper, which even in the dark she recognised as one she had bought for him herself.

'I know. It's been hard... a lot to... take in. I like Dylan's new career plan though... lovely to see him so passionate.' She bent her legs up, shuffling further out of the way as Lucas sat down on the end of the bed, dropping his head into his hands.

'That fucking present.'

'Yes... unexpected. But also... sort of... touching?'

'The children are getting money,' he groaned, ignoring her questioning tone. 'Dylan told me. He talks straight, that boy, I'll give him that. Five hundred pounds. I mean, that shouldn't be allowed, should it? *Buying* grandchildren because you've made a fuck-up of raising your own.'

'No, it shouldn't, but...' Esther studied Lucas's hunched back. 'Maybe he isn't buying them. Maybe he wants a relationship with them. Maybe he wants to do better in the few years he might have left.'

'But *why* should I allow it?' Lucas hissed. 'After what he did, after how he was... to *me*. It's not fair...' He broke off, perhaps hearing the petulance in his voice, as Esther certainly did.

'You've not been a total fuck-up, anyway, have you? I mean, apart from a recent... glitch – which *will* pass, by the way – I think most would agree that you have managed a pretty stellar career.' Esther paused, marvelling at her urge to bolster his spirits, at her capacity to care, how it could not be switched off, wondering if it was a sign of weakness or of strength. 'And there's Heidi,' she pressed on.

'No, actually. There isn't. At least, we're on a break. Called for by her.' He delivered the news sullenly, keeping his back to her. 'The trouble that girl's allegations caused, it managed to come between us...'

'Lucas, I am so sorry.'

'And I sort of went off the rails a bit over it... some drowning of the sorrows... which didn't help matters. Though I've stopped that now. For good.'

'Drinking?'

He nodded.

'Wow.' Esther released the word quietly, trying not to sound too astonished, understanding better the refusal of the Christmas champagne, which in the end none of them had had the heart for anyway. 'I mean, seriously?' she added, before she could stop herself. This was Lucas, after all, whose passion for wine was his favourite hobby, who could read a book about grapes and vineyards with the absorption most people reserved for a bestseller.

'Not managing to stay fully in control, I'd be no better than him, would I?' His voice was so thin and bitter she could hardly hear it. The shoulders shrugged, once, twice, and again, until it dawned on her that he was weeping.

'Lucas...'

'I'll be fine.' He shook off the tentative hand she had dared to place on his back and wiped savagely at his face with the hem of the jumper. 'I can't just *forgive and forget*,' he growled, 'like he wants. Like Dylan and Lily want. When we talked, he broke the big news that Mum was a depressive like that makes everything okay. When it doesn't. It just meant she needed *more* care, *more* love. Instead, he went and...'

Esther waited. Instead, John went and slept with other women. She knew this was what Lucas had intended to say. That the words had not emerged felt somehow significant. 'I do not think forgiving means forgetting,' she said carefully. 'In fact, I don't think it should. But it takes time, and has to be when *you* are ready. Though, the thing about not forgiving...' She hesitated, wary of the tension in him, and thinking suddenly of her own difficulty in processing their failure as a couple, holding onto all the easy blame and resentment instead of trying properly to understand. 'The thing about not forgiving,' she repeated, 'is that it can be terrible for the person doing it. Because it weighs them down, stops them from moving on and enjoying life...' She let the sentence hang.

'Esther, would you mind if I lay down for a bit?' Lucas mumbled, already turning to crawl onto the bed. 'Just to close my eyes. I feel so worn down. That sofa... I haven't slept. I just want some... calm.'

'Okay. Hang on.' Esther shifted closer to the wall to make more room, propping herself up against the headboard with the pillow, while he stretched out on his back beside her. The bed was not designed for two people. Like the one in her shared flat, all those years ago. Esther let the memory form, staring it down: the first date, the courtship that had led up to it, the wooing, the kissing. The loving.

'Thanks. Sorry, Es.'

'It's all right.' Esther spread the duvet over them both, careful not to touch him.

'I peed in this bed,' he said quietly, after a few moments. 'Every night. Until I was fourteen. My mother stopped even mentioning it. She put a plastic cover on the mattress. Stripped the sheets every morning, like it was normal. The plastic used to rustle, every time I moved. God, I hated the rustle. When I finally stopped, they bought a new mattress. Dad burnt the old one, saying how much it stank.'

'Lucas—'

'I think he might be dying, Esther. He's so bloody thin, and the coughing, and when we talked, he said he didn't have long... which of course he doesn't because he's almost eighty... and he bloody would say that, wouldn't he, the bastard? Wanting to guilt me.'

He had turned away from her, bringing his knees up to his chest and hugging himself like a child. Esther gently shifted herself into the same position, putting an arm round him, the rest of her body bracketing his, but not touching. 'Like I say, give it time. All that matters now – all that has ever mattered – is the children. Our children. To get them home and back into the tracks of their lives.'

His breathing sounded heavier, more settled. She inhaled deeply, readying herself to try for more sleep. For a few seconds their breaths were the only sound, one then the other, taking it in turns.

'Thank you, Esther.' He shifted his body, turning his head, and suddenly his mouth was seeking hers. The familiarity was a shock: how he tasted, the smell of his skin. His cheeks were wet with tears and slid against hers as they kissed, with a hunger that cast Esther back into the intensity of their earliest days, the need to merge, as if half consuming each other were the only way of being fully alive.

'No. Lucas. No.' She pushed him away, gulping for air.

'Do you have someone else? I have wondered. Many times.' He had raised himself onto his elbow and pulled back to look at her, his face ghostly in the dark. Outside, the rain beat like a million drums and Esther's pounding heart felt part of it, lost inside it. The question caused the image of Marcus to form in a technicolour she usually resisted because it defied the spirit of their deal. 'No... at least... not really. But it's not that, it's because...'

'Esther, please... just... oh, please...' He lowered his face towards hers. 'It's not as if we're strangers. We were once so close. We could be again. Please, darling.'

46

Lucas strode up the lane towards the car, humming to himself, Esther's car keys jangling in his coat pocket. He had woken at seven, refreshed from a short but deep sleep in his unforgiving makeshift bed, with the full glare of a sunbeam on his face, cutting through the gap in the sitting-room curtains like a laser. His shoes were stained and still faintly damp, but his feet were full of bounce. The day sparkled, laundered by the cycle of snow, rain and the new full-throttle sun, blazing out of a sky of deep denim blue. The road streamed and gleamed with melting water. On the verges, snow sat in shrinking clumps. Up across the valley sides, the white fields sported vast scars of shining brown and green. The car, still askew with its rear wheels over the ditch rather than in it, looked more of a mishap than a calamity.

Lucas's mobile pinged into life just as he reached it and he knew, instantly, that it was a message from Heidi; that he, quite literally, held his life in his hands. The path it would now take. He had to crouch down to look, shielding the screen from the sun's glare with his trembling free hand. It was a long message. Lots of sentences and capital letters and exclamation marks. No endearments. The words danced. There was RING and STEFAN and FOUND and MIRACLE and ANSWERED PRAYER and GOD.

Lucas staggered to his feet, using a hand to support himself against the side of the car, pinpricks of light bursting in his peripheral vision. He was dizzy. Not from standing up too fast. Not from an empty stomach – Dylan's full monty fry-up breakfast had been sensational. Not from happiness either, or even relief. Gratitude was what was gushing through him. He threw his mobile high up into the air, arching backwards, throat bared at the sky, to catch it. 'Thank you,' he shouted, to whichever Master of the Universe had chosen to grant him a reprieve. 'Bloody thank you.'

The messaged had contained endearments, but only at the very end.

So you see, dearest Lucas, it is what I prayed for. It is a sign. We have been tested, but we were meant to be together. If you will still have me, I am yours. Heidi xxx

Lucas turned to look back the way he had come, at the valley coming to life before his eyes. The thaw after the freeze, like in a fairy tale. Magic, the world was brimming with it. A lost son, a lost ring, lost love, all found – a wand had been waved, and he didn't care why or how.

Fired up with adrenalin, and noting that the Ford was more or less horizontal, at right angles to the slope, Lucas decided to take the risk of releasing the hand brake and giving the car a shove. He used his back for the task, hooking his hands under the bumper. It shunted forwards with unexpected ease, and then started first time when he tried the ignition. A cautious four-point turn completed, and he was cruising back down the valley, allowing himself, for what felt like the first time in his entire life, to acknowledge the beauty of the little stone house in which he had been raised. Halfway down, he turned the engine off and let the car coast, winding his window open. The cool air ruffled his hair. Birds warbled.

The hall was stacked with packed bags, Dylan's rucksack – Lucas was relieved to see – dominating the pile. Both children and Esther were in the kitchen, clearing up, organising leftovers in the fridge.

'I managed to retrieve the car.'

'Yes, we saw. Well done.' Esther didn't quite look at him. She was starting to butter two pieces of toast and had a pot of Marmite open. 'This is for your father. I thought you might take it up to him.'

'He's still in his room?'

'He came down and did the hens, and then went back upstairs,' Dylan answered, frowning. 'He told me that he'd eaten much earlier – porridge and honey, he said – but we don't have any honey left and I couldn't see the pan. When we get to the top of the hill, I'm defo calling Iris.'

'Iris?' Lucas went to the sink, where a saucepan from their breakfast was soaking.

'Here.' Esther handed him a cloth she had been using to wipe surfaces.

'Iris, oh, she's, like, this old lady who calls by every week,' Dylan explained airily. 'A nurse from way back, apparently. She's cool actually, always saying I can phone if I want... it just feels so mean *leaving* him, Mum,' he burst out.

Lucas worked the cloth hard, and to little effect, over the layer of cooked egg coating the bottom of the pan. Dylan, he knew, was addressing Esther, not daring to make the same plea to his father.

'Darling, it's not mean,' Esther assured him coolly, handing Lucas a scouring pad he hadn't spotted, sitting in a saucer by the sink. 'By all means call Iris.' She paused, no doubt recognising the name, as Lucas had. 'But your grandfather, as you know very well, is independent, not to mention proud of the fact. Besides...' she threw Lucas a glance '... you could be seeing a lot more of him yourself soon, couldn't you, if you do end up going to college in Manchester?'

'And Matteo and I will totally visit,' Lily piped up, full of brightness and bustle as she returned knives and forks to the cutlery drawer.

'He says he doesn't want big goodbyes,' Dylan went on mournfully. 'That we are to just go.'

Lucas balanced the saucepan upside down in the drainer. 'And are you looking forward to getting back to London, Dylan? Catching up with your old friends?'

Dylan exchanged looks with his sister and mother. 'Actually, I'm kind of hoping to meet up with a new friend soon. I've been telling Mum and...'

'Dylan has met someone,' Lily chipped in gleefully, but also sounding impressed. 'Gaming. Some crazy Australian girl who thinks he's nice – what are the chances of that?'

Dylan gave a bashful shake of his head. 'But first, Dad...' he took a moment to cast an affectionate glare at his sister '...I thought I might hang out in Cambridge for a bit, with you... and Lil, of course... and then head back to London in the new year?'

'And this catering course, where is that going to fit in?' Lucas asked, trying not to mind that a fair amount of planning had clearly gone on in his absence. He looked down at the plate Esther had placed in his hands. Two pieces of toast covered with drifts of butter and marmite, cut into triangular quarters and arranged in a neat, enticing circle.

'I need to get a Level Two in cooking or technical first, which I'm not sure yet whether to do in Cambridge or London. They also want four minimum grade 4 GCSEs, including English and Maths, but obviously I've already got those.' He grinned in triumph, and Lucas did not need Esther firing eye-bolts to know not to say anything downbeat.

Inwardly, the old despair flickered. Dylan had nine GCSEs, even if they were mostly middling grades; and could have got four A stars at A level if he had only... what? Lucas threw a look of despairing fondness at his son as he sprang round the table, in a baggy T-shirt splattered with something and his unlaced, beaten-up trainers that somehow never tripped him up, grabbing the saucepan out of the drainer and drying it with a jokey flourish, between flicking the tea towel at his sister. Life had got on top of him – something Lucas could relate to only too well, if he allowed himself to; and yet here the child was, half a year shy of nineteen and obstinately ploughing his own furrow, as sunny-faced and confident as Lucas had ever seen him, under *this* roof of all rooves. It was like another thaw, an internal one. More magic. Things stuck fast for years, working loose.

'So, it's going to be Michelin stars, is it?' he quipped. 'I can't wait, and Mum too, I'm sure.' He and Esther smiled at each other properly, for the first time since the night before, and the promise of the day felt complete.

* * *

'We're just about off now. Dylan said you didn't want goodbyes, but I've brought you toast. Esther made it. She asked me to say farewell and thank you.'

Having rapped firmly, Lucas started talking the moment he opened the door, a part of him steeling himself for the first sight of his parents' bedroom in thirty years. Decorated in blue and white stripes instead of the yellow he remembered, and with the bed against the wall on the left instead of the right, it didn't give him the jolt he had feared. His father was sitting in a straight-backed chair by the window, a book flat, spine-up, on his lap, a glass of water perched on the sill, his old-fashioned, half-moon glasses on the tip of his long nose. As Lucas crossed the room, he started coughing, a horrible bubbling sound that kept surfacing despite his visible efforts to swallow it out of existence. Lucas arrived at the chair and then stood by feeling like a dumb waiter, holding the plate of toast, waiting for the fit to end. Even then, his father did not pay him any attention, reaching instead, a slight tremble visible in his fingers, for the water glass. He had deteriorated, Lucas realised, even in the two days of their visit.

'Put it over there, could you?' He gestured at the bedside table. 'I might have it later.' He picked up the book. 'You'd better be gone now. The sun won't last.'

Lucas cleared his throat, not moving. 'So, Iris comes by.'

'Yes, she does. Now and then.' He put his finger to the text on the page, moving it down, line by line, as he started to read. Just as he always had, Lucas remembered, even when it was a bedtime story. He had done the voices too: squawking parrots, roaring bears, croaking frogs, spouting whales. He had been good at the voices.

'Thank you for the napkin ring.'

He nodded.

'And Dylan, he seems okay.' Lucas's nails whitened as he gripped the plate. He balled his free hand into a fist. His father never made anything easy, for himself or anyone else, and maybe there was something to respect in that, even if there had been no hope of seeing it as a child. 'You are right, Dylan and Lily are both old enough to choose whom they see, and I won't stand in the way of that.'

His father turned the page of his book, his eyes making a show of travelling, but the tracking finger had fallen still.

'Thank you for what you told me. About Mum.' Lucas had to wrench each word from his throat. Esther's verdict on forgiveness had been insightful and impossible to disagree with, but that didn't make it easy. There were some places no magic wand could reach. 'Look, I said some harsh things, Dad. I didn't trust you. But I shall try to, all right? From now on.' He crossed the room and set the plate on the little table next to the bed. 'There. That's what I wanted to say. And also, eat the damned toast. For Christ's sake, Dad, you're a bag of bones.'

He went back and placed a hand on the bony shoulder, lightly, feeling no revulsion, only pity, and then hurried from the room.

Downstairs only Esther remained in the hall.

'All set, then?' she asked blithely, fiddling with the buckle on her handbag, though it didn't look as if it needed fiddling with.

'Esther, come here. Please?' Lucas held out his hands. 'It's okay,' he said, seeing the reluctance and suspicion flood her face. 'Just a hug. And a thank you. You were right,' he murmured, as their arms, firm and kind, encircled each other. 'Last night. It would have been wrong.'

'Yes. It would.'

'You always were the wiser one,' he said softly as they stepped apart. 'Please forgive me for not being better at appreciating that.'

'Okay, thanks. No violins necessary. But thanks. The kids are good to go.' She led the way out of the house, to where Lily and Dylan were already settled on the back seat of the car, with both the front doors open and waiting. 'Lucas?' she called, as he hung back. 'What is it?'

'I'm not going, Esther. Believe me, I want to...' Lucas gulped, hardly able to believe himself what he was saying. 'There is nothing I want more, in fact, but I couldn't live with myself if...' He groaned. 'Yes, he's managing, and obstinate, but it's clear he's seriously unwell and some extra help needs to be put in place.'

'Oh, Lucas.' Her eyes were glassy, but she was smiling.

'I'll speak to Iris. But, Esther, there's another thing...' Lucas hesitated, uncertain until this moment that he was ready to tell her. 'It looks as if Heidi and I are back on, which is another reason to thank you... because...'

'I know the because, Lucas. I am pleased for you, truly.'

While Esther settled herself behind the wheel, Lucas put his head inside the car to explain his decision to Lily and Dylan, kissing them both and promising he would see them in a few days. After recovering his bag from the boot, he stood and watched the car climb steadily out of the valley, giving it a last wave as it reached the crest before heading back into the house.

HOMECOMING

47

Esther managed not to cry until she was in her own hallway. She lunged at Chico for comfort, promptly causing the animal to scuttle back into the kitchen. Dropping her bags, she lowered herself onto the hall floor, surrendering to the tears that had been building ever since the children had scrambled out of the car while she'd hovered in the station taxi rank, shouting their love-yous and goodbyes as they tore off into the early afternoon dark.

It had been so much fun in the car with the pair of them, in high spirits, chattering to each other, and to Esther's parents, put on speaker for a group call by Lily. Christmas gifts awaited them all, Astrid had cried, applying pressure for them to head to Amersham there and then, while Esther had insisted – to the background of grateful face-pulling by her offspring – that they were exhausted and maybe some-thing could be arranged for New Year's Eve. On her own, no doubt, Esther suspected, her spirits dipping even as she made the offer, since there had already been chat about a Cambridge fireworks party, to which Dylan might get an invite, Lily had teased, if Matteo agreed and he played his cards right.

'I like having the both of you,' she had told them, as the countdown to the drop-off had drawn near. 'Can we do more of it, do you think? From time to time?'

'Sure,' they chorused, with a heartfelt intent that Esther knew was no guarantee of making it happen. They had so much going on in their lives, and that was how it should be.

'With Dad?' Lily ventured.

'I hope so. Sometimes. Dad and I are good,' she added quickly, aware Dylan had tensed, and it suddenly crossing her mind that Lucas's night-time visit to his old bedroom might not have gone unnoticed. 'We had a big talk last night. Cleared a lot of air. About your grandfather, among other things. It's great that he decided to stay on – not easy for either of them. Brave, actually. You should both be proud of him. And, Dylan, you can be proud of yourself too – if we temporarily set aside the unforgivable fact of you running out on us for four months, dragging your sister into the deceit, spinning lies...'

'Yeah, yeah.' Dylan groaned. 'Get to the proud bit.'

Esther reached out and ruffled his hair, laughing at the evident irritation it caused. The first part of the journey had seen some serious talking about what had happened, both children offering apologies, and Dylan fiercely defending his reasons as well as his grandfather. He had even answered a question or two about Mei Lin, saying he didn't miss her, with enough vehemence for Esther to suspect that he did.

'The proud bit is because I suppose you have ended up being a bit of... a... bridge... a way for your father and John to...'

'A bridge,' Dylan squawked. 'I'm a bridge, Boo. Are you jealous?'

Lily pulled a face. 'You are an annoying bridge, that's for sure...' She broke off as her phone pinged, and then announced, an edge of cautious reluctance in her voice, that Lucas and Heidi had settled on Midsummer's Day for their wedding and wanted her to be a bridesmaid. 'They were on a break, but I guess that's over.'

'Bridesmaid beats bridge,' said Dylan philosophically, scrunching up an empty crisp packet and lobbing it at the back seat.

'How lovely for you, Lily. Dad told me it had been a bit on-off lately, so that is brilliant news.' Esther was aware of sounding rather too jolly. She could feel the children's antennae waggling, and was eager for them to know there was nothing to pick up on; or at least nothing significant. Her congratulations to Lucas that morning had been sincere. Their kissing in the early hours wasn't something she would easily forget: so startling, so intense, so unquestionably seductive. As Lucas had whispered, his lips brushing her ear, they weren't strangers. There had been a deeper temptation too – the allure of imagining that love-making might close their broken circle, lay down some sort of marker for the start of the new-found, hard-fought tenderness and respect that navigating the traumas of the last few months had wrought. But Lucas was Lucas, and Esther had hung onto that. Wrung out, vulnerable, and wanting her, yes, but mostly, she was sure, seeking the comfort of sex with a woman, even the one who happened to be his ex-wife. To succumb to sex would have been a lurch backwards and Esther knew she would have regretted it bitterly.

'So, come on, then, Mum,' Lily urged, clearly emboldened. 'I know you've had a date or two...'

Dylan emitted the high-pitched moaning sound of a man close to the breaking point of his tolerance.

'I did try a bit of online dating,' Esther admitted, managing a rueful smile even as her stomach tightened at the memory of Chris Mews. 'There was a three-month free-trial thing, but it's run out now, and at the moment I don't feel much inclination to sign back on. Never say never, though, right?' She had shot Lily a grin in the rear-view mirror, laughing inside at the difficulty of a mother explaining to her offspring, even adult ones, that she had found a no-strings, hot-yet-tender sex arrangement with a handsome, half-Portuguese actor, which suited her needs perfectly.

Except when it didn't, Esther reflected glumly, slumped still among her travel bags, the weeping having receded to self-pitying sniffles. Because, in the end, life alone could be a lonely business, especially returning to a chilly, empty house after an extraordinary roller-coaster Christmas, while your ex was loved up with a new life-partner, and the two people whom you cared about most in the world had – rightly –

abandoned you to pursue their own fun. When not even your cat wanted to be near you. Yes, the take-it-or-leave-it hook-up sure had its limitations then.

Esther unzipped her overnight bag for the handy pack of tissues she knew was inside. Seeing Viv's journal, she took that out too, balancing it on her lap as she blew her nose. Behind her back, the hall radiator was clicking into life, warming her spine, easing out the stiffness from the long drive. Chico had reappeared, but was keeping his distance with gymnastics along the bottom stair, throwing out his best look-at-me glances through his paws.

Write your life! Esther shook her head at the familiar, impossible command as she eased out the many times lost-and-found little pencil that lived in the notebook's spine. Riffling through the pages, she chuckled ruefully at the very first, scathing 'happy bloody birthday to me' entry, and all the haphazard jottings that followed: grocery lists, to-pack lists, to-do lists, work thoughts, the torn-out pages to write to Viv in France, and to message the squatter who had never returned; gauche efforts to describe the genius of Dutch masters along with the occasional stab at actually pinning down her own feelings – the little book had indeed become a biographic chronicle of sorts. A messy mishmash, just like her life. Just like any life. Esther sighed, pressing open a clean page. It was too soon to even begin to try to find words for all that had just happened. The past, at least, had started to feel more understood. And the present, for that matter. It was the future that now required attention.

NEW YEAR RESOLUTIONS
Not to mind being alone. (Be serene! Self-reliant!)
Get Viv back.
Push for full contract (4 days a week)
Phase out piano lessons – except Billy!
See Shona more
Have parents to Sunday lunches REGULARLY because one day they will DIE

Devise conversion of house & garden into oasis of beauty
Find D's thrill-seeker voucher and book a date!
Start jogging. Once a week min. (NB: option to abandon after one month)

The list grew as the afternoon wore into the evening, Esther adding to it between emptying the cat litter, fixing herself tea, eating many biscuits, filling the washing machine, sifting through her post, and then running herself a deep, hot, foamy bath. Before lowering herself beneath the suds, she set her phone to a new 'Chill' playlist, and lit a scented candle that had been gathering dust since Lily gave it to her the Christmas before.

When her mobile rang, cutting through the music, she forced herself not to move. She was half asleep, bath foam up to her chin, wisps from her makeshift bun trailing in the water lapping over her shoulders. Deliciously tired, when she eventually clambered out, she slipped straight into her favourite, old, pink pyjamas as soon as she was towelled dry and then browsed for a new book to take to bed, only then checking who had tried to ring. It was Marcus and he had left a voice message.

'Esther, can you call? Need a word. When you have a moment.' He sounded irritated.

Esther yawned, and opened her book. She was serene. She was self-reliant. She was not at anyone's beck and call, and certainly not in the mood to be summoned to a bed in Amsterdam – or Timbuktu, or wherever the hell he was this time. She was also too knackered even to read, she realised, putting the book down and turning the light out. Even so, sleep took a while to arrive, interrupted by ripples of wonderment at the turn-arounds of the last few days and at the notion that the trickiest things could work out, if you stuck to what you knew was right, and gave them time.

48

When the children were small, Esther had loved the period between Christmas and New Year. With the manic build-up and absurd pressure of the Big Day past, it had been the loveliest of limbos, with leftovers to snack on and no work or school or college timetables to rush around for. Lucas would hole up in his study, while Dylan and Lily were allowed to lounge for half the day in pyjamas, playing with their new presents, requiring barely any parenting beyond being shooed into the garden for air and some refereeing over the occasional fall-out. A deserved pause, it had always felt, before the start of the whirligig after the turn of the year.

Waking up to the London drizzle, however, groggy from her too brief, too deep a sleep, Esther immediately sensed the danger of feeling nothing but the limbo and none of the relaxation. She wrote a letter to Viv, to stave it off – a proper letter, on proper paper – starting many times, with attempts at flourishing prose and convoluted arguments, before letting the words pour out exactly as they wanted.

> *Dearest Vivvie,*
> *Point one: "Breaking up" with a friend is not actually allowed, under international law.*

Point two: I bet Brian is feeling as crap and fed up about it all as me (and you).

Point three: No offence to your professional skills, but surely sometimes digging out innermost thoughts can turn no-biggy deals into huge issues.

#Just Saying. #ImissyouandImissUS.

NB: Please add CALLING ESTHER to your New Year Resolutions List, which you will obviously be working on, and which I know will start with packing in those ciggies. Mine, you will be impressed to hear, is already very long, and includes GETTING AS FIT AS VIV, which I'm going to start right now by jogging to a post box.

PS. I also know you are bursting to hear all the deets about finding Dylan

PPS. Lucas came on to me and I said NO! (after a snog)

PPPS. Did I mention I bloody miss you?

Having sealed the letter, folded many times because she only had a too-small envelope, Esther found a stamp and then decided she had better keep her word about the run, despite it being – by some way – the least appealing item on her entire list. Attacking the challenge five days earlier than strictly necessary was already an achievement, she told herself, rummaging for her old trainers and a combination of clothes to keep her warm and relatively dry, before zipping the envelope into an inner pocket.

She turned left out of the house, ducking low as she ran past Sue and Dimitri's so as to minimise the chances of being spotted. Seconds later, the rain intensified and the street morphed into a wind tunnel, blasting her flimsy cagoule hood back off her head even with the chin toggle at its tightest. Every dent in the pavement became a puddle and by the time she turned into the high street, having to slow to a walk because of all the shoppers braving the sales, she was drenched from head to foot.

Was there anything more dejected than Christmas decorations after Christmas? she wondered, pausing under a café canopy, and worrying for the chains of angels strung across the street, tossed into mad dancing by the onslaught. The café looked cosy and inviting, though. She peered through the window, lined with tables and diners, only to pull back at the sight of Marcus, sitting alone with a mug of something topped with whipped cream. Escape was her first thought, but he had already glanced her way, puzzlement creasing his face before recognition fully dawned. Because she looked like a shipwreck survivor, Esther guessed, as he proceeded to beckon with elaborate hand-signals at the empty chair opposite him. She shook her head, indicating her sodden state, but he promptly left his table to stick his head outside the café door.

'It's warm and dry in here.'

'I'm on a run.'

'Really?'

'Well... I've... done a bit of one.'

'Great. Haven't you earned a break, in that case? I wanted to talk to you. I left a message,' he added in a slightly accusing tone.

'Yes. I know. Sorry. I didn't know you were around. I only got back yesterday afternoon and it's been... busy.'

'Yes. Sorry. Me too. Look...' He stepped out of the way of two new arrivals, talking at her over their heads as they shook out umbrellas. 'I'd appreciate a word. It won't take long.'

'Right. Okay. Just for a minute, then – though I might seek out the Ladies first,' Esther muttered, 'given the state of me.'

'Great. I'll order you something. Coffee? Chocolate? Tea?'

'Cappuccino. Thanks.'

Arriving at the table a few minutes later, her puce face and dripping hair having proved beyond salvaging, Esther draped her sodden cagoule on the back of the chair opposite him and sat down.

'Your coffee is on its way. Good Christmas? At your parents, wasn't it?'

'Yes... that is... it got a bit... complicated.' Esther grimaced, aware suddenly how drained she was, and in no mood to go into everything. She noticed that there was an air of exhaustion about him too, with shadows under his dark, handsome eyes, and a tense, tugged-down look to the corners of his normally smiley mouth. 'Dylan is home though, which is good.'

'Hey, that's great news. I am so pleased for you.' He clapped his hands, turning a few heads.

'Thanks,' Esther murmured, touched in spite of herself at his display of enthusiasm. 'It is pretty wonderful, yes. Turned out all this time he had been with his grandfather – Lucas's dad, the one he doesn't speak to. We had to go on a family rescue mission... long story. But what about you? Was the Portugal Christmas fun? I thought you were heading straight from there to Holland?'

'Slight change of plan. We wrapped ahead of schedule, so I thought I'd grab the chance of some more time with Lola, except it turns out they made a last-minute decision to go to the Caribbean. St Lucia. As you do.' He scowled. 'And now my agent has lined me up auditions for two projects in London – both live theatre, Chekhov in January, filling in for a late pull-out, and Gloucester in King Lear for a summer run, which is rather more hairy – not that I'm complaining.'

'He's the duke that gets his eyes pulled out, right?'

'That's the one.'

'Well, all that sounds jolly, and also action-packed,' Esther muttered, distracted both by the puddle her cagoule was making on the floor, and by the rising conviction that she didn't want to be slotted into a hectic timetable.

'What is it?'

He was looking at her with some concern. She swiped at a rogue drip that had somehow found its way onto the tip of her nose, aware suddenly that, for all the resolve and good intentions, she wasn't just exhausted but also feeling somewhat fragile. For three days she had been in the thick of seismic change, tectonic family plates shifting; to suddenly flip into small talk was beyond her. 'We're all closer to falling apart – to falling off the grid – than we like to think,' she blurted. 'Dylan, Lucas, Lily, my friends – me...'

The arrival of her coffee broke her flow, and Esther was acutely grateful. For a moment it had felt as if she were unravelling and might never stop, forgetting all their boundaries. 'Thank you very much for this. Much needed.' She picked up the coffee, housed in a cup the size of a soup bowl, cradling it in her palms. 'Sorry for not being better company. Post-Christmas fatigue, or something.'

'Did you want the chocolate on top?' he asked, in a bid to change the subject, Esther guessed, and not blaming him.

'I *always* love chocolate, Marcus,' she assured him dryly, taking a sip of the coffee and then another, feeling a lot calmer. 'So, what was this word you wanted?'

'Yes.' He straightened into a stiff, weirdly awkward upright position, knotting his hands together on the tabletop. 'Look, Esther, this is hard. I am sorry if this is a bad time for you, and you know I respect you and totally accept that so far everything between us has been going pretty well, and just as we agreed... but...'

Esther glazed her eyes, while her tummy performed a slow, painful contortion. Not wanting to be squeezed into a busy schedule did not mean wanting to get the boot. She was half tempted to put a hand over his mouth. She knew what was coming. She could have written him a better script. Instead, he was already losing his nerve and veering off on a tangent about deciding to live for a while in his aunt's house. Esther could only nod, inwardly marvelling at the unfair, nonsensical business of feeling hurt by an arrangement designed, specifically, to prevent such an eventuality.

'You probably noticed the for sale sign has gone. That's because we've decided to put Carmela's house into a family trust and I shall pay rent.'

'I hadn't. Fantastic. Good for you.'

'So, here's the thing.'

God, she hated that phrase. She sat back in her chair, pushing her empty mug away and folding her arms. Defensive, she could hear Viv say, raising them even higher across her chest, not caring.

'You are such a strong woman, Esther, one of the most remarkable I have met, and I am totally aware that you never wanted anything heavy or long-term or...'

The need to speed him up became too much. If only to stop him saying *totally* again. How could he not know that the fall of an axe was best delivered quickly? 'It's all right, Marcus, I *totally* get it. It was only ever a stopgap, and of course you want someone who...' She dried up at the dawning realisation that he almost certainly *had* found someone. Women walked out for all sorts of reasons, but men left only when they had the next partner lined up. Where had she read that?

'Someone who?'

'Who wants to settle and maybe have a family...'

'A family?' He seemed angry. 'I've got Lola. Us a *stopgap*?'

Esther's gaze unfroze. 'Yes... at least... I thought you were saying...'

'I am saying, Esther, that keeping it casual no longer works for me. And that actually, it hasn't for a while.' He slapped both palms on the table, making her teaspoon rattle in its saucer. 'I know it's a risk, but I had to tell you. I've been wanting more. Of us. I want more,' he repeated sternly, blinking several times, perhaps disconcerted by the way she was gawping. 'I love *being* with you, you see.' He shrugged helplessly. 'Every time you go, all I want is for you to come back again. I've tried hinting, but you've always brushed it aside.'

'Have I?'

'I've even wondered sometimes whether you are still in love with Lucas.'

'Have you?' Esther examined the hand that had been stretched across the table and placed over hers. 'But I don't love Lucas.' The certainty of the words felt good. A certainty that had, in truth, taken a while to arrive, she realised.

'Okay.' He started a nervous laugh, and reined it in. 'Well, that's good. Because... well, I know I found it difficult to let go of Izzie. More so than I've let on. I mean, for a while I sort of hoped she'd come back, for Lola's sake if nothing else...'

'Lola will be all right.' Esther put her other hand over his, as her thoughts flew to Lily and Dylan. That family bonds could never just dissolve was one of the new insights that had settled inside her, even if, like Lucas, you had spent thirty years trying to pretend otherwise.

Marcus was staring at her, looking faintly exasperated. 'And now I just have no idea what you are thinking. About my... proposition.'

The waitress came, said something neither of them heard, put the bill down, and left again.

'I am thinking that...' Esther tried and failed to stop herself smiling, savouring both the instant evaporation of all the hurt, and the power of life to wrong-foot her, again, this time so pleasingly. 'I am touched by your proposition, and I promise to think about it.'

'Think about it? Oh, God. For how long, do you think?'

'For how long do I think I'll think?'

'Oh, I get it.' He shook his head, grinning and rueful. 'So now I am a figure of fun.'

'*Totally.*' The way colour and relief were flooding his face made her like him more. 'Prepare for months of merciless mockery.'

'Months, eh? Well, that's a promising start, at least.' He picked up the bill.

'I'm afraid I haven't any money.'

'We could always try doing a runner. I mean, you're certainly dressed for the challenge.' He chortled to himself, whisking out a ten-pound note and putting it under the condiments stand, before rushing round to help her back into her wet coat.

Out in the street, the cloud had broken up, and it had stopped raining.

'Could I walk you home, ma'am, or would you prefer to continue your run?'

Esther pretended to give the matter serious consideration. 'On balance, I think a walk holds more appeal. Also, I need a post box,' she remembered suddenly, pulling the fat little envelope out of her inner pocket, where it had stayed miraculously dry.

'Excellent. I believe there's a post box if we cut down second left.'

'I believe there is,' Esther quipped as they fell into step, between dodging oncoming pedestrians.

'Would you consider taking my arm? Or better still, holding my hand?'

'My goodness, the man is a fast-mover. But I am a bold, as well as a strong woman – many thanks for that compliment, by the way – so... all right, then.' They both laughed, enjoying the silliness; but as they interlaced fingers, the intimacy of the contact sent a wave of heat up Esther's arm, so intense she almost gasped out loud. Lucas, to her disappointment, had never been a big one for public shows of affection. Indeed, the only serious hand-holding she had done in decades was with the children, wriggly and resistant, in need of guidance crossing roads.

'Nothing like a real letter,' he said as she popped the envelope through the slot, not asking anything about it, which she liked.

'Do you think we could take things step by step?' she ventured, holding his hand more tightly as they headed on towards their street, half felled by a sudden hammer-blow of apprehension as to what she was getting into; the balance of joy, disappointment and fresh heartache that might lie in store.

'Yes, we could, Esther. We already are. Look. Side by side. One step in front of the other. Easy-peasy.' He laughed, nodding down at their feet, her soggy trainers and his scuffed boots, moving forwards in one smooth rhythm along the wet pavement.

THE GIFT

49

'You don't have to go through with it, you know.' Viv picked a grape off the bunch in the fruit bowl.

'I know I don't. I want to. Well, I don't *want* to, but I *will*.'

'You've nothing to prove, at least not to any of us who care about you.' Viv popped another grape in her mouth, idly reaching for the journal gift she clearly didn't recognise, as battered as a well-thumbed bestseller, and open that morning at a page listing all the things Esther had to remember to take with her. 'Have you got this lot, then?' She brushed away a few cat hairs.

'Read it out and I'll tell you.'

'Calming drops. Hah. Sensible woman.'

'That was your recommendation, the homeopathic stuff.'

'So it was. What next? Hat... well, that is less sensible. I mean, it's April and how is it going to stay on?'

'It might be freezing up there,' Esther countered, folding tinfoil round the sandwiches she had made, and checking that the lid on the thermos was tight. 'I'm taking one anyway.'

'Fine. Whatever makes you feel comfortable.'

'Yeah, like that's an option.'

'Picnic.'

'Check. Which you will be in charge of.' Esther waved the tinfoil bundles before dropping them into a recyclable shopping bag.

'Phone.'

'Check.'

'Are the kids coming?'

'Yup. Meeting us there.'

'And Marcus?'

'He said he'd rather gouge out his own eyeballs,' Esther replied dryly.

'Can't wait to see his play.'

'Me too. If I'm still alive.'

Viv chuckled. 'I'm not a betting woman, but I would say the odds of that, happily, are in your favour. By the way, is Lucas showing up?'

'Lucas? God, no. It was Dylan's present, and nothing to do with Lucas. Besides, he's busy with his work, as per, not to mention the increasingly grand wedding plans – which I know he will be hating, by the way...' Esther started to laugh and checked herself, too distracted even to enjoy sniping. 'And he has his hands full with John, of course, who's apparently holding on remarkably. The kids say that, like them, he's been visiting a fair bit, which is amazing. As is the fact of it no longer being my business, though Marcus and I are going to pop down over Easter.' She set the packed bag on the table. 'Good to go, and, Viv, I cannot thank you enough for offering to do this.' She went round the table to give her a hug. 'I couldn't cope with eating breakfast, let alone driving a car.'

'I shan't watch,' Viv declared archly, some ten minutes later, when they were on their way. 'And, for the record, I still think you're mad.'

'Yes, so do the children, which is sort of marvellous...' Esther managed a wry smile. 'To be the one alarming them for once, instead of the other way round.'

It felt less marvellous, the closer they got to the M4. 'Tell me stuff,' she begged, with Viv having fallen silent too. 'I need not to think. How are the kids and Brian getting on with their bicycles in Italy?'

'Apparently, they're not missing me at all, and ditto. The house to myself for an entire week. God, I love it. I get so much more done. I eat at stupid times. I binge on box sets. It's the perfect holiday.'

'But only because it *is* a holiday,' Esther pointed out with feeling, the memory of her own aloneness still vivid. 'You know they're coming back, which is precisely why you can enjoy them being away.'

'True, O wise one.' Viv threw her a look. 'You truly are wise, Esther. In fact, you'd have made a much better psychotherapist than me...'

'No bollocks this morning, please, Viv, I'm not up to it.'

'It is not bollocks, it's the truth. The way you kept on at me, pointing out my idiocy, not letting me go, your lovely status reports, I shall never forget it... helping me towards sense. The couples therapy has been astonishing. I mean, we've reached the point where I can even *tease* Brian about you now...'

'Oh, God, poor man. Not too much, I hope.'

'No, not too much,' she said softly. 'Hey, and maybe go steady on that stuff,' she added, glancing at the passenger seat as Esther squirted more homeopathic drops onto her tongue. 'I think it's supposed to be three every six hours...'

'Well, I've had loads more than that, and actually, please, can we not talk any more? Because I think I need to just look out of the window or I might be sick.'

'Such fun times,' Viv murmured, 'driving my best friend towards her worst nightmare.'

'Blame Dylan,' Esther said grimly, staring through the car window up at the sky, the first convulsions of real terror starting to twist her insides.

When the crane initially came into view only a couple of minutes after they had turned off the motorway, Esther's first, grateful, thought was that it didn't look *that* high. The nearer they got, however, the more it grew. By the time they reached the reception area and car park and the milling clusters of spectators near its base, it had become an Eiffel Tower. Every time her eyes flew skywards, a wave of nausea gushed through her. Someone who had clearly jumped just before Viv parked was now dangling like a pin on a string. Even spotting Lily and Dylan heading their way as they walked across the car park – it was all she could do to smile. Lily arrived first, with Matteo trailing behind, the pregnancy they insisted had been genuinely not realized, rather than lied about, now visible as a distinct bump under her blue hoodie. Behind them, Dylan was hanging on tightly to the girl called Zee, visiting from Australia and supposedly travelling on through Europe, though there had been no sign of it yet. Her son, white-faced and almost mute, looked rather as she felt, Esther was touched to note, when it got to his turn for a hello. In the same instant, Marcus sprang out from behind a van parked alongside the hut of a registration office, clutching a lavish bunch of flowers, which he immediately shoved behind his back, saying they were for afterwards – if she survived.

'Hey, I thought we agreed you would talk her out of it,' he scolded Viv, putting his arm around Esther. 'I know you'll do fine,' he whispered, pulling her close, 'and of course I couldn't not come.'

'I'm glad you're here,' she admitted in a small voice.

'We've seen a few now,' he went on with a cheerfulness that Esther knew was all about boosting her, 'and, you know, it really doesn't look too bad, and is all over in, literally, *seconds*. But get this, the best news of all is that we can do it as a pair. I've asked and they say it would be fine. They strap you together. I'm totally happy to pay and it could be fun. What do you say?' He waggled his eyebrows. 'We leap *à deux, ma chère*.'

Esther smiled. That Marcus was such a thorough romantic was a continuing source of surprise and pleasure. As was the protectiveness that lay behind this last-minute suggestion. 'I say that you are transparent, and very kind, and no, thank you. I have come here to jump alone.'

Over his shoulder she could see the next person riding upwards in the metal lift that led to the jumping platform. The lift could bring her down again if she wanted, Esther told herself. No one could *make* her jump. No one would love her less. Maybe they would even love her more.

A man in a high-viz jacket with a clipboard came up, checking off her name and asking her to follow him to be fitted for a harness. Esther waved farewell to her little crew of supporters, managing a rictus smile.

The harness straps went under and between her legs, as well as across her chest and back. The man with the clipboard asked her to get on some scales. Her weight dictated the correct rope-length for the jump, he explained cheerily: too long, and she wouldn't bounce back up.

Esther took her place in the row of plastic seats provided for waiting jumpers. She knew her friends and family were all looking at her, but she couldn't look at them. She was deep inside herself now, mining for a courage that was not there. She was a vertigo sufferer and she was going to jump off a crane. There were four people to go before her. They each swung like stick-men off a towering, distant gallows. They all screamed, even the men.

At the last moment, Dylan came bounding over.

'Mum, just to say good luck, and you are the best, and actually a total Wonder Woman and I never, like, meant for you to actually pick the bungee jump. It was just a joke, and Matteo says to tell you he did it in the US and you don't actually feel a jerk or anything, it's more, like, gentle, and also you go up and down quite a few times and the landing isn't so bad...' He was steered away by Zee, still talking.

Travelling up in the lift, Esther did not look at anything except the face of the young man riding with her. No older than Lily, he had a springy afro, warm brown eyes, and a rolling, easy manner. 'Your first time? You'll be just fine, Esther,' he said when she nodded bleakly. 'Max up there will give you a countdown to go,' he continued, checking her harness. 'You're the twentieth today, and everybody has had a great time. You are strapped in just fine. You're going to do great. I'll hand you right over to Max, and he'll take care of you. A fine view from here, wouldn't you say?'

Esther gripped the metal railings. Vertigo was connected to the fear of throwing yourself off a height. To do this was, she realised now, simply impossible. Looking down was not possible either. She looked out instead, half seeing the shimmer of the Thames, and the grey swarm of Slough, and the creamy April sky. The fear was visceral now. She could not move, let alone jump.

Somehow, she was standing with the man called Max. The rope

had been clipped to her harness. The wind blew at their faces, gusting her hair across her eyes. 'I can't,' she tried to shout, but no words came out.

'I am going to count you down, Esther.' He stood close. He wasn't touching her, but she wished he would. She wished he would just pick her up and throw her out and be done with it. 'You've got this, okay?' His accent was Australian, his eyes a piercing green; greener even than Lucas's. They held hers. 'Okay, Esther, here we go... three... two... one...'

She plunged, flailing in a cold rushing nothingness, her stomach in her mouth, her skin stretched and flapping from her bones, the wind punching down into her lungs through her open mouth, fighting with the scream she released but couldn't hear. The stretchy rope would break her fall. She couldn't feel it yet. But she knew she would.

ACKNOWLEDGMENTS

I cannot overstate my gratitude to the impeccable editing and story-instincts of Sarah Ritherdon, my magician of an editor, and to Boldwood Books, for their continuing faith in my work. Thanks too, must go to the rigorous copy-editing of Sue Smith, whose forensic eye for dropped stitches is as brilliant as it is unnerving.

'The Split' is my second 'lockdown' novel, the first draft emerging during the course of 2021. My tolerance to isolation was wearing thin, and I want to thank my wonderful sons, their partners, and all the close friends whose unfailing support helped me through. Special mention must go to the weekly lockdown Zoom group of old university friends, who kept asking, dutifully, how 'the writing' was going, and then listened patiently to my convoluted responses, between throwing out often wild – but always very welcome – ideas of their own.

Last, but the opposite of least, I want to express my thanks and love to the David to whom this book is dedicated. Guardian angel as well 'proof reader' extraordinaire, he helped me keep belief in myself and in the telling of this story, until it was the best that it could be.

August 2022
Amanda Brookfield

BOOK CLUB QUESTIONS

1. Did Esther still love Lucas after they divorced?
2. Is Lucas a monster?
3. Do Lily and Dylan, the children, hold the most important power in the family?
4. Was Moira's accusation about Lucas an over-reaction?
5. Does Viv matter more to Esther than her relationships with men?
6. Is trust as much an issue when you are dating online as when you are relying on old-fashioned chance encounters?
7. Can a once healthy marriage always be repaired with forgiveness and hard work?
8. Do you think Lucas & Heidi and Esther & Marcus will live happily ever after?

MORE FROM AMANDA BROOKFIELD

We hope you enjoyed reading *The Split*. If you did, please leave a review.

If you'd like to gift a copy, this book is also available as an ebook, digital audio download and audiobook CD.

Sign up to Amanda Brookfield's mailing list for news, competitions and updates on future books.

http://bit.ly/AmandaBrookfieldNewsletter

If you'd like to read more from Amanda Brookfield, *Good Girls* and *The Other Woman* are available now.

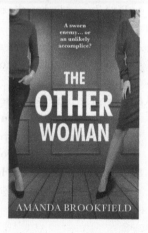

ABOUT THE AUTHOR

Amanda Brookfield is the bestselling author of 15 novels including *Good Girls* and *Before I Knew You*, and a memoir, *For the Love of a Dog* starring her Golden Doodle Mabel. She lives in London.

Visit Amanda's website: https://www.amandabrookfield.co.uk/

Follow Amanda on social media:

- facebook.com/amandabrookfield100
- twitter.com/ABrookfield1
- instagram.com/amanda_and_mabel_brookfield
- bookbub.com/authors/amanda-brookfield

Boldwood

Boldwood Books is an award-winning fiction publishing company seeking out the best stories from around the world.

Find out more at www.boldwoodbooks.com

Join our reader community for brilliant books, competitions and offers!

Follow us
@BoldwoodBooks
@BookandTonic

Sign up to our weekly deals newsletter

https://bit.ly/BoldwoodBNewsletter